sky blue

sky blue

A NOVEL

TRAVIS THRASHER

MOODY PUBLISHERS
CHICAGO

Cover Design: John Hamilton | johnhamiltondesign.com
Cover Image: Paul Mason | Photonica
Interior Design: Smart Guys design
Editor: LB Norton

Library of Congress Cataloging-in-Publication Data

Thrasher, Travis, 1971-
Sky blue : a novel / by Travis Thrasher.
p. cm.
ISBN-13: 978-0-8024-8668-4
ISBN-10: 0-8024-8668-1
1. Literary agents—Fiction. 2. Psychological fiction. I. Title.

PS3570.H6925S56 2007
813'.54—dc22

2007010563

We hope you enjoy this book from Moody Publishers. Our goal is to provide high-quality, thought-provoking books and products that connect truth to your real needs and challenges. For more information on other books and products written and produced from a biblical perspective, go to www.moodypublishers.com or write to:

Moody Publishers
820 N. LaSalle Boulevard
Chicago, IL 60610

1 3 5 7 9 10 8 6 4 2

Printed in the United States of America

For Kylie Shea Thrasher

Here come the blue skies here comes springtime.
When the rivers run high & the tears run dry.
When everything that dies.
Shall rise.

"Love Is Stronger Than Death" by the The

everything in its right place

THE HEART OF THE MATTER

In my dream I hold my child. She is precious, beautiful with her mother's blue eyes. They pierce me with their control, looking at me, loving me, needing me. I'm a new man with new feelings. It's the way I always imagined fatherhood would be.

I've had this dream three times in the past month. It's not the kind you wake up in the middle of with a gasp, sweat dotting the forehead, a grip of desperation running throughout. It's the kind you roll out of and wonder if it's true, then are disappointed to find it's not. It's the kind a man might have after a couple years of trying. The kind a man might have when that dream is almost out of reach.

I think of this as I sit on the couch, waiting for Jen. I can no longer read the manuscript in my hands with any real sense of judgment. I'm too nervous. The three gin and tonics haven't really helped. The soft music in the background doesn't either.

When Jen finally walks through the door, it only takes ten minutes before she puts words to the thoughts I've known she's held for a while.

"This is the last time."

I'm careful with my response, careful about the ground we're both on. "We can hope so."

"I'm not going through this again."

"You have to be positive."

Her eyes meet mine. "I've been positive. Maybe that's my problem."

"Jen—"

"Positive isn't going to make a baby come faster."

"Why don't you sit down?"

"It's not going to change anything. And I'm not going to lie, and I'm not going to keep trying."

My wife stands on the wood floor at the edge of our family room. I watch as she takes off her heels and sweeps a hand nervously through her hair.

"Look, just don't—"

"Don't what?"

"Jen."

"Don't give me that." Her eyes don't back down.

"You're already talking like you know what the answer will be."

"Do you know something I don't?"

I can only shake my head.

"I know my body. I already know the answer. I don't have to take one of these stupid tests to give you an answer."

"That's unfair."

"Life's unfair, but that doesn't change anything."

"Just don't make any edicts."

"Edicts? Edicts?"

"Don't laugh."

"This is not an edict. It's a fact. You're the one who wanted to try one more time, and I'm the one who said okay. You always get what you want, don't you? Colin Scott, the master persuader."

"Jen, you know you still want to try."

"I did this for you."

"And maybe it will work."

I stay on the couch, knowing that if I go to her she'll just turn her back and move away.

"This is the last time," Jen finally says. "This is the last time I'm opening up one of these things. This is the last time I'm trying. This is the last time, I swear. . . ."

She starts to cry, and I stand up. "Jen, don't—"

"No—just—I'm fine. Really."

"Why won't you let me hold you?"

"Because I'm fine."

She shakes her head, wiping her tears.

"What is it?"

"I feel like we're cursed. That I'm cursed. That God doesn't want us to have a baby. That he knows better."

I give a sharp, bitter laugh. "There is no God. He would have answered prayers if there was."

"And you've prayed?"

"No. But I know you have."

She disappears into the bathroom. I'm left alone, in the quiet, to sit and wait.

Once, five months ago, Jen was convinced she was pregnant. Those daily temperatures were doing something different. We had already opted for the insemination route and this was our third month of trying. Something about this month was different. Jen's outlook and feelings and body were all telling her it was real.

Even the pregnancy test gave us hope. It didn't say she was pregnant, but it didn't quite rule it out either.

This was our life up to that point. Ovulation tests that always seemed to be curiously hard to read. Temperature charts that looked like bad connect-the-dot pages. Ways to improve my sperm count. Intimacy on demand.

But Jen felt it, believed it, knew it. It had finally, *finally*, happened.

I remember kissing her belly, holding her tight, trying to celebrate the way I thought I should. I remember feeling convinced along with her, a feeling of joy leaking over, being unusually exuberant for a controlled man like myself.

All the right things couldn't create a child. On the day she would find out in the doctor's office that she wasn't pregnant, both of us would feel burned, our skin too sensitive to touch.

Something changed then, something small that I knew now was monumental. Hope is an amazing thing, and the lack thereof brings amazing pain.

The last time I hugged Jen, truly hugged Jen, was the day she told me with full faith that she was pregnant. It wasn't the last time she needed a hug, but the last time she so readily accepted it. Maybe because she thought she deserved it. I don't know.

There's a lot I don't know these days.

I wait for her. And when she finally comes out of the bathroom, her face tells me everything.

For a moment she just stands facing me, the look of sadness and despair and anger compressed into something deeper, something different.

I'm the first to look away. It's not right, but then again, none of this is right.

She walks into the kitchen.

"Jen . . ."

"Just a minute."

And that's it. It's over with.

Sleep doesn't come. Why would it? Why should it cooperate?

She is a room away from me, thirty or forty steps down the hall through the doorway and under covers. Where I should be.

But I need space. So does Jen.

We could be holding one another for dear life, two of us against the world, survivors of the apocalypse hunkering down and keeping each other warm. Instead I sit out here, a dreary manuscript on my lap, the ice cubes in my drink almost melted. I stare at the wall behind a table of photographs.

It's the morning after.

The morning after. What a line. Nothing much good comes after a line like that. *The morning after*. Hangovers. Regrets. Shame. Second thoughts.

Jen doesn't spare any time. I love her honesty. Always have.

"I need some time."

"Some time for what?"

"To be on my own."

"Jen."

"Stop saying my name over and over."

"Why are you doing this?"

"Because this isn't working and you know it. What do you want me to say? Do you want me to fake it?"

"You're frustrated."

"Yes, and I'm tired, but that's not what this is about. This isn't working. Do you want this? Do you really want this?"

"Maybe we can think about other options."

"It's not about a baby. That's not the issue."

"We don't have to make any decisions."

"I've already decided. I need some time away."

"From me?" I ask.

"From us."

"Don't do this. Now. Before my trip."

"There's always a trip."

"It can change."

"It's not going to change, and you and I both know it. Sometimes it's easier being away. Look—I get it. I know. And right now I'm too tired to fake it and too tired to lie."

"I don't want you to lie. I just—don't make any decisions."

"I need some time away from you to think about things."

"What things? What do you have to think about?"

"Whether we still belong with each other."

I hear her footsteps down the hallway, the door closing. She's not angry, she's exhausted. I don't blame her. Nothing I can do will change this. Not a hug, not a word of hope, not a promise. Nothing.

She is the love of my life that I discovered one Chicago night under the stars. But that night seems so long ago, seven years after the fact, both of us so different, our lives so busy and so disconnected, our hopes so out of reach.

The scariest thing about finding the love of your life is the possibility you might lose her. But that doesn't stop anyone; it certainly didn't stop me.

On the Road

"And Ashton is just starting to get into soccer, and he's already better than the rest of the first graders."

Lisa Beck has been talking about her family for the last half hour. I listen attentively, looking interested in the photos she shows me, never once trying to shift gears to business. An author's well-being *is* my business, and if she wants to share how her daughter fell off her bike and had to get five stitches on her elbow, that's fine.

She wouldn't be able to remember Jen's name if someone put a gun to her head. That's okay. I don't particularly want her knowing anything about Jen.

"—they all came to my last book signing carrying signs and acting like fans and everybody wanted to take their pictures—"

It's late morning, and the author across from me drones on about her amazing life and amazing family and her amazing abilities. Lisa Beck has made gushing about herself into an art form. She seems truly convinced that the entire world doesn't revolve around the sun, but around her and her silly little stories.

"I saw a display of your books in O'Hare this morning," I tell her.

"I just don't understand why more airports don't carry all of my books," she says in this weird sugary-sweet way. "Maybe it's just because O'Hare is a bigger airport and . . ."

She continues on, but it doesn't really matter what's coming out of her mouth. It's the same theme, the same point.

Lisa and I sit in the plush lobby of the four-star hotel in Phoenix where they're holding a writers conference. Someone high on crack decided to make me the keynote speaker at this event. They're paying me, too. I've done quite a few of these.

But knowing Lisa would be here gave me another reason to come. Lisa is one of thirty-four authors that I agent. And she is at the top of that list in terms of income earned and potential.

"So—how's the next book proposal coming along?" I finally manage to squeeze in.

For a brief second, I see something on Lisa's face I don't like.

"That's one thing I wanted to talk about."

Lisa Beck might be attractive somewhere under her large physique and her caked-on makeup. The photo she uses on her books, all paperback so far, shows a trim blonde ten years younger. I've never said anything about the photo. But sometimes I see the surprise on fans' faces when they greet her for the first time at a book signing. They're nearly all women in their forties or fifties who devour Lisa's romances like delicious, fat-free cupcakes.

"This is hard, so I don't know where to begin." She tightens her lips and gives me one of those double blinks, the sort a cheerleader might do in high school when wanting to get her way.

oh no

"What's wrong?"

"Colin—you know that I think the world of you. That I owe so much to you. And it just . . . it breaks my heart to do this. . . ."

And now, accepting the Academy Award for best actress in a starring role—

I'm sure whatever look is on my face right now, it's not a good one.

"To do what?"

"You know that things have been so busy for you, and I think that's good. I think it's great."

And I think you couldn't care less about my workload.

"It's just—I've been a little worried—"

"A little worried about what?" I ask, my tone still stable, comforting, calm.

"I know about Vivian Brown and the new book she's working on."

Here we go again.

"Vivian is not my client, Lisa."

"But she's your firm's client. And I understand—there can only be one Vivian. The time and attention should go to her. Anybody like that—she deserves it."

"Mr. Roth represents her," I remind her.

Bernard Roth is my boss, the guy the agency is named after. I'm sort of second-in-command, if such a thing exists.

"You've told me yourself how much time and energy you put into her."

"Sure, but that doesn't affect how I work with other authors."

"You're her primary editor, aren't you?"

I shake my head, even though yes, I am. And I'm still hoping, waiting, dreaming of the day when Roth might hand me the reins *and* some of the royalties attached to Vivian Brown.

"I know that takes up a lot of your time, as it should," Lisa says, dripping with sincerity and heartfelt compassion.

The love is just flowing.

"Lisa—I'm always honest with you. You know that. If I thought I couldn't devote enough time to you, I'd drop some of my other authors. I've always told you—you're my number one priority."

"I hate to have to do this, Colin."

Underneath the smile and the eyes that believe flirting still works, underneath the earnest expressions and sincere platitudes, I know the shrewd businesswoman who exists. I've seen it manifested in a hundred different ways, from refusing to hand in a manuscript to a publisher due to her concern over marketing efforts to getting an editor fired simply because he tried to make her writing better. Lisa is the embodiment of passive aggressiveness. I just never thought it would rear its ugly head at me.

I remain silent, waiting to hear what she's going to do. We were getting ready to send out a proposal for her new series. She told me I would have it three weeks ago. I should have been more proactive.

"I've been talking with some other agencies—"

here it comes

"—and after much thought and prayer I decided to go with Stuart Koep for my next big deal."

For a moment I can't feel my body and I don't breathe and I think of Stuart's little frame and feel like finding him out and strangling him. But it's not his fault. He's just doing his job.

I breathe in. Outwardly I'm still in control, showing no sign of stress or concern.

"I don't understand," I say to her. "Is there something I did?"

"No, of course not," she says, so consoling, so sweet. "You know it tears me up to do something like this. It's just—I'm thinking of my family. I need to do what's best for them."

Jumping ship a hundred feet from shore?

"But is Stuart—yeah, he's a great agent, sure, but why—?"

"He wants to move me over in hardcover. He thinks it's a good idea."

What a self-centered snake. And no, I'm not talking about Stuart.

"We've had this discussion before, Lisa. Haven't you told me—several times—that you were fine not making that transition?"

"Please don't get upset."

I breathe in again. *Calm stay calm just relax it's okay.* "I'm not upset. I just want to understand your thought process. We discussed the timing."

"I know. But I just—well, Stuart thinks the timing is ideal. And you know—I've been hoping to have it happen. There's more opportunity to bond with my readers and gain more exposure if I go the hardcover route."

Let's be honest. There's more cash to be made.

"Lisa—I'm afraid of pushing that button too soon. You know that."

"I know. I just—like I said, this breaks me up inside."

Lisa Beck strives to be the next Danielle Steel. And that's fine. Dream big and shoot for the stars. But those little housewives who gobble up her $7.99 books are going to have a rude awakening when the price triples, even though the quality is still oh so much the same.

I take a sip of coffee and suddenly wish I were away from here, away from this fraud of a human being in front of me, away from the masses all clamoring to be exactly like her, away from an industry that encourages this travesty.

"May I ask you one thing? And I want you to be honest."

She nods and still looks as though her smile and bright, flickering eyes are all making it okay. Maybe if she were a young Audrey Hepburn look-alike, I'd swoon and say, "Whatever you want." But she's not, and I'm not swooning.

"If we didn't represent Vivian Brown—would that have changed anything?"

Lisa glances down and thinks for a minute. "Well, it's not about that."

But I remember the news several months ago about Stuart losing one of his big names. Publishing is just like professional sports. A big name swaps teams or agents. It's the way the whole world works. Lisa Beck was my top author, but she could never be the Roth Agency's top author.

She'll be the top author now. All she had to do was destroy all credibility with the champion who helped get her there in the first place.

Later that afternoon, I'm floating down the lazy river at the hotel pool, staring at the sky and thinking of my father. He's the reason I'm here at this writers conference, lounging on this inner tube. It's not often a man can pinpoint the beginning of a lifelong passion or a lifelong profession. But I can, and it was on our L-shaped gray sofa, listening to my father read.

All of my most vivid memories of my father revolve around books. He was an English teacher, and spent long hours in a dimly lit room known as The Study, where he hovered over high school papers on Faulkner and Hemingway. But every evening, before he slipped off to his nightly tasks, he spent at least half an hour reading to me. He read me the Chronicles of Narnia and the Hardy Boy mysteries and, when I was older, *The Lord of the Rings.*

Kate, my younger sister, could never sit still for very long and usually wandered off or fell asleep. But I loved these adventures. They taught me about friendship and courage and love. Like my father, I became a fan of happily-ever-afters.

I've often wondered what other common traits we shared. There wasn't enough time to find out. My father died when I was twelve, yet the magic and the dreams stayed with me. Those were his gifts to me before he passed away.

It would take another nearly twenty-five years before the dreams and the magic inside of me would eventually die too.

"Hemingway once said, 'I can write it like Tolstoy and make the book seem larger, wiser, and all the rest of it. But then I remember that was what I always skipped in Tolstoy.'"

The smug face pauses for a moment behind the podium. For dramatic effect. Everything with Ted Varrick is done for effect.

"Write the book of your heart. And always, *always*, remember the reader whose heart you can move . . . and break."

The big guy sits down in the seat next to me as applause from four hundred pairs of hands showers over us. He nailed it. Of course. Now I'm doing clean-up duty.

So much for being the keynote speaker.

I stand and go to the podium. My notes remain untouched behind me.

In the front row, I see the grin coming from Lisa Beck. I haven't spoken with her since our earlier meeting and don't particularly plan to. I can't help thinking of the knife wedged in my back, the blood dripping on this stage. It's going to get slung out to the crowd in just a few moments.

The mass of attendees at the Phoenix writers conference look my way with hope and inspiration on their faces. Ted Varrick has filled them with this, this inflated hot air. It will eventually leak out, and they'll have to realize the cold, hard brutality of the craft and industry they're choosing to enter.

And the bitter business side that nobody—nobody—ever bothers mentioning at events such as these.

Somebody has to paint a more honest picture.

"Good evening," I start, looking directly at the faces below me. "My colleague is smarter than I am, and far more articulate about the craft of writing. But since I'm better looking, I get to go last."

They laugh, which is good. They won't be after a few minutes.

"Isn't this resort incredible? I was wading around in the pool this afternoon and think I might have burnt my ankles. But as I was sitting there, I decided I should be as honest and open with all of you as possible. So—let me try to share a decade's worth of experience spent as a literary agent. And I'll try to be Hemingwayesque—short and to the point.

"As you know, Ted and I work for the Roth Agency, which represents over a hundred authors. Some you've never heard of—some are unpublished as of today—and others include, yes, Vivian Brown."

I wait for the applause to die down. As I do I glance at Lisa and let my eyes just stay on hers for a moment. I'd mention her, but—well, she no longer works for us.

"As Ted mentioned, publishing is a noble profession. Writing can be a sacred vocation.

"But the thing is this. . . . There will be a hundred thousand books published this year. A hundred thousand, this year alone. Most will be lucky to sell ten thousand copies. The average book sells around seventy-five hundred copies in its lifetime. That's it. The percentage of books that sells over a hundred thousand? Less than 5 percent. The percentage that sells over a million? You don't want to know.

"Everybody has a story to tell. Nobody wants to *write* that story, however. They want to *be* writers. Because in their minds, writing is noble. Or dare I say, sacred?"

I pause. For my own dramatic effect.

"We've heard quotes from Hemingway, from Thomas Wolfe, from Steinbeck. But writers like that are gone. They've been replaced with pop stars and politicians and television personalities. Most who don't even write—they only get their names front and center in large type on the cover while ghostwriters are paid a small sum for their services.

"A publishing slot that should go to some bright, talented, shining novelist is given in a heartbeat to a celebrity telling all about her ridiculous life. And even those who do write their own books, those who are talented enough to develop a following, get dumbed down. Everything's a genre these days. Have one success, and they'll brand you. *The Firm. The Chamber. The Testament. The insert-noun-here,* and you too can name the next Grisham book.

"It has to be a simple, consumable product for the masses. It has to be easily identifiable for the little old lady buying books in her local Wal-Mart in Nebraska. Pick up a twelve-pack of toilet paper and get the latest Vivian Brown novel.

"Talent, my friends, is highly overrated in today's publishing world. It's not about talent. It's about the almighty dollar. And when those start to multiply, publishers take note. Authors take note. They're no longer awed by amazing prose. They're moved by money. And you can write the book of your heart, the story of your dreams, and it might simply not matter. Because some hack of a writer is telling the same story for the tenth time and getting paid ten times more than you'd ever *dream* of making."

The expressions that face me no longer look inspired. But they don't look away. Not one face looks bored.

"All of you here are writers, hoping to get that first big publishing break, hoping to be represented by agents like Ted and me. But let me ask you this. You're writers, but do you have anything unique to say? And if you do, will you work for hours on end, sometimes deep in the pit of night, sometimes early in the morning, even though the work you do might never be rewarded?

"Will you develop thick skin in order to persevere? Will you develop good listening skills to hear the input you need? Will you be able to open your heart on the page, only to have it trampled upon? Can you bare your soul in story form, and yet remain a professional when trying to sell it?"

I pause, even though there's no need for dramatic effect. Not anymore.

"Can you keep trying, page after page, book after book? Because if you can, then—and only then—you have a chance. But even then, the odds, my friends, are against you."

I brush back my hair and think for a second. The words are all there below, in a big pot of chunky stew. Normally I carefully pick and choose, but tonight I'm just scooping them up in my hands and dropping them, letting them splatter everywhere.

"The thing you have to realize, that you have to tell yourself, is that it doesn't matter. Nobody really cares about you and your words. They're just words. I see so much schlock on my desk it's ridiculous. It makes me want to give up my job and go into the cement business. And I'm not just talking about wannabe authors, either. I'm talking about the big names, the big books that you see in your local Target. These stories have lost something. These authors have managed to be content with mediocrity. It's insulting to readers, to writers before them, and to people like yourself."

The faces look at me. Sad faces. Confused faces. I could keep going for hours.

"And no matter how hard you work, and how talented you are, sometimes it's out of your hands. Sometimes it's so completely and totally out of your hands that you want to take those hands and strangle someone. But you can't. All you can do is try and then, if you're lucky, if you're very lucky, you'll get that break. Prayer isn't going to help. Talent isn't going to help. It's a hard, brutal profession, and it's one that will bring you face-to-face with fear and rejection on a daily basis.

"Sound like fun? How many want to sign up now?"

Someone coughs in the room, and it sounds so awkward, so loud. A woman in the back stands up and leaves.

"My colleague ended with an inspirational quote from Hemingway. Here's another quote that I'd like to leave with all of you. It's from the great contemporary novelist John Updike, and it's one that is quite fitting for today.

"You all dream of fame and fortune. And I say dream away. But remember Updike's words."

I produce the slip of paper with the quote written on it.

"'I think what's most disturbing about success is that it's very hazardous to your health, as well as to your daily routine. Not only are there intrusions on your time, but there is a kind of corrosion of your own humility and sense of necessary workmanship. You get the idea that anything you do is in some way marvelous.'"

Again I look down at Lisa. They say it's always good to picture the person in the audience you're speaking to. And I'm doing exactly that.

I look back at the crowd before wrapping it up.

"Dream big. Dream of success. But realize that it's going to take a lot of work—and I mean *a lot* of work—to get there. And you're going to have times—you're going to have days—that make you question what you're doing here in the first place. Days that make you want to vomit because you feel so bad, because you feel so lonely and desperate, because things are so utterly out of your control.

"Publishers want you to believe that they're in control. But they're not. Nobody's in control. And all you can do is hope that maybe—just maybe—you'll get lucky."

Beloved

My office is my sanctuary.

It's on the seventh floor of a brick building on Michigan Avenue. Roth has worked in this structure for forty years, first in a tiny nook at a former paper company, then in a crowded office when he opened his literary agency. Since then, he's bought the space around it and now owns a quarter of this floor, including the office where I sit staring out the window at the morning sky. I'm the first in the office, as usual. On this mid-May morning, the silence almost hurts.

The phone rests in its cradle, missing the glow of a voice mail alert. My cell phone rests on top of a manuscript in a similar situation. Already twenty minutes into accessing my e-mails, I wait for some sort of word from Jen. There was no message when I got in late last night from Phoenix, and all I got was her voice mail when I called.

Her job as a costume designer for movies takes her away, and keeps her away, just like mine. But I wonder how serious she is with this time apart, how far she's going to go, how soon she's going to give me some sort of word.

We communicate via technology. Phone, e-mail, text messaging.

This is not a life bound together. It's a postcard, with a beautiful color photo on the front and a little space for words on the back.

Hey Jen I start to type on the twenty-inch flat screen in front of me.

I've tried calling a few times and have missed you. I know you're busy on the set, but give me a call. Something happened with Lisa Beck that I want to tell you about. And I'd rather do it live and not via voice mail or e-mail.

There are a lot of things I've been thinking about lately, lots of things to say.

I think about that last sentence and then delete it.

I'm going to be around the next few days. I have Book Expo coming up in LA where we have the release party for Kurt Dobbs's new novel. That better go well. Please call or e-mail, okay?

I miss you.

I think of that last line. What's wrong with me when I'm reconsidering telling my wife that I miss her?

I keep it in. And simply add Colin before pressing Send.

I look out the window, just beyond my computer screen. The sky above Lake Michigan is growing lighter, and this is one of the things that makes me happy. I used to get energized simply by opening up a great book and sitting down to read it. Now all that does is remind me of my work, of the contracts and the authors and the deals and the figures. But the sky and its natural beauty and its never-ending variety in light and color and mood always keep a small fire lit inside me. A wick of hope.

Staring back at the unchanging computer screen, I wonder how long that wick has left to burn.

It's all in his eyes. And in the thick dark brows above them.

That's how Bernard Roth commands and controls. I know this through experience. I know this as I walk to his office.

The Europeans, they love this guy. They're the ones who lord over the publishers in New York. For some reason, they like Roth and his style. It's one of his legendary claims to fame.

No matter how long I'm around him, Mr. Roth still intimidates me. This was his company when I first sat down with him for an interview ten years ago, and it's still his company. Regardless of what I bring to the table and how influential and beneficial I am to the agency, he owns it and controls it. And he does it with those eyes that stare me down as I walk into his office.

"Just got your e-mail," I tell him as I stand by the doorway wondering if now is the time to talk.

"Thought you'd be at home," Roth says to me, unblinking.

"Yeah, well, I needed to come in. Get prepared for Book Expo."

"You should take some time off. Sounds like you need it."

I nod, knowing he has already heard details from the conference. I'm sure Ted sent him an e-mail giving him a nice, juicy summary.

"Why don't you have a seat, Colin."

Thirty-five years old and I still have to go to the principal's office.

Roth's office is not much bigger than mine, but seems to reflect the sixty-seven-year-old man who still works just as hard as the guys half his age who work around him. There are plaques and awards tucked in between overflowing bookshelves, and photos on his desk and on the shelves of him with his family and his "family of authors," as he likes to call them.

Roth is on his third marriage, to a woman younger than I am, and last I knew he owned four houses. While I was having a meltdown in Phoenix he was vacationing in one of those houses in Naples.

He starts off with a bemused curse. "What happened in Phoenix?"

I sit in a leather armchair that's stuck next to a bookcase and across from his desk. There's no space between me and the desk.

"I was a little moody and painted an accurate picture of publishing."

Mr. Roth chuckles. He has a thinly cut beard, probably trimmed once a week. Maybe it's the mild accent from growing up in London, but Mr. Roth reminds me of Sean Connery. Balding, but making it look remarkably good. He wears a sports coat, one of many, a tailored dress shirt, and uncreased slacks. His wrinkled skin is tanned.

"I don't care about your speech," he says. "Maybe that will keep some of the dreck away. I'm talking about Lisa. What happened with her?"

"Lisa doesn't like being number two at our agency."

"She said that?"

"Of course not. She can poison you and make it sound like she's ministering to the poor."

"Is it a done deal?"

"Yes."

Mr. Roth looks at me with a stare that doesn't waver. He doesn't look angry. He doesn't have to.

"I thought you had her handled."

"I did too."

"What was the status of the next contract?"

"She wanted to hold off on negotiations. Now I know why."

For the first time his glance shifts off me. Roth is calculating, trying to set a strategy.

"I've invested more time in Lisa this last year than in any author over the last ten," I start to tell Roth. "There was nothing we could have done—she wants to be Vivian Brown, and she's just jealous."

Roth raises his hand to say okay, no big deal, let me keep thinking. He understands the value of a pause, of silence in a group, of making people wait.

"This doesn't exactly surprise me," he finally says.

"Yeah, me neither. But all along, what could I do except go along with her? She made us a lot of money."

He nods. "She's never going to be a fraction of what Vivian Brown is. I think Lisa is a smart gal—she knows the part you play in Vivian's work, Colin. But I thought she was smarter. Because her only chance of becoming anything remotely in the ballpark of a Vivian Brown was to stay working with you. Whoever she gets to represent her will only be after one thing."

"It's Stuart Koep."

Roth laughs, the wrinkles around his eyes curling up. "That ends another promising talent. Amazing."

"I was thinking I could spell out some benefits of staying with our agency and—"

"It's done," Roth says. "She's done. Let her go."

This is Roth's style. He makes decisions like the flick of a switch. When he decides on something, that's it. It can be an agreement or a manuscript or a wife or an employee. When he is finished with something, that's it, and he never looks back.

"Tell me something," he says. "When was the last time you went on vacation?"

I actually don't know. "I was in Colorado a few months ago."

"Somewhere not involving work."

This time I chuckle. "You know me."

He nods. "Yes, I do. Tell you what. I'm going to have you come to Laguna Beach with me next month."

"Okay."

He lights up again and laughs. "It won't be a vacation, if that's what you're wondering. Chelsey will keep me busy enough down there. I've persuaded Vivian to meet me there. The good news is, she'll be handing in her manuscript."

We knew it was coming, the entire industry and world knew it was coming, but still this is surprising. Part of me wondered if Vivian would actually finish it.

"You know how obsessed she is about leaks," Roth says. "And I don't blame her. But I'm going to ask for two manuscripts, one for each of us. She trusts you. Probably more than me. So it'll be for work, but maybe you'll have some time to breathe in the ocean air. It does wonders for the soul."

"I would love to."

"And bring your pretty wife with you."

"Yeah, sure. That'd be great."

I get so much junk e-mail it's an abomination. And when Ted Varrick arrives at my doorway in the late afternoon, I can't help but think that he's part of the spam of my life I'd like to permanently delete.

"Didn't expect to see you here," he says.

"I'm not really in the mood," I say right off.

"Here's the best quote from Phoenix: 'Prayer isn't going to help. Talent isn't going to help. It's a brutal profession.' I mean, why didn't you just tell everybody to go kill themselves?"

"How many of those listening are actually going to make it?"

"Didn't you once tell me our job is about giving people a chance?"

"Yeah, and I remember you laughing at that." I'm looking back at my screen, not worried about Ted and his antics.

"You never know if the next Vivian Brown is sitting in that audience."

I look up at him and shake my head. "You don't have a clue, do you?"

He's waiting for something else, but it doesn't come.

He doesn't realize that *Sliding into Forever* came into these offices flawed and full of literary flab. Roth knows this too well, but it's something not discussed much. Not anymore. After you sell twelve million copies of a first novel, people don't talk about those things anymore. The publisher, the author, the audience, and especially not the agent.

Varrick doesn't realize that no matter how many Vivian Browns might be out there, to negotiate for and reap the rewards for, there has to be someone smart and talented enough to make it work. Make the words matter. Make the literary work last.

I used to believe that I could.

Now I'm wondering if anything lasts.

On the Chicago sidewalk on my walk home this evening, the sun already gone and the city lights already on, a nagging thought scratches at me.

I think somebody is following me.

I'm serious. For the last four or five months, I've had a nagging feeling that someone's watching me, tracing my steps and tracking my moves.

I haven't told anyone, not even Jen. The relationship I have with Jen is not one where I come baring my soul or insecurities. She knows them, of course. But I still don't display them on a platter for her to examine and mull over. Ours isn't that type of relationship. She would tell me to suck it up and get over it. Or, in the case of being spied on, she'd tell me to stop reading so much.

It's crazy, of course. It's from the busyness of the last year, the constant tiredness that has started to evolve into insomnia. I think the less sleep you get and the more tired you become, the harder it is to have sound sleep. The kind where you're seven layers into, deep into, with no disturbances and nothing but sweet baby sleep.

I know what it's from. One of the things keeping me awake, both literally and psychologically, has been Lisa Beck. And now—

I walk the city street and get that feeling. Someone watching me.

Ever see a face two or three times too many?

Ever stare at someone and see him look away, caught in the act?

I would tell Jen, but what could I say?

Get some sleep she would say *stop reading so much fiction* she would joke *have another drink* she would say *it's just a season* she would say.

So I say nothing.

But the images keep chasing after me.

The face keeps following me.

I breathe in. I'm in my apartment, in another office, in front of another computer monitor, waiting for another answer. I'm usually patient, but not with this.

A framed print on the wall next to me shows the back of the album cover for *Abbey Road*. I love the image of the words set in brick. Something nobody can ever erase. The Beatles putting out yet another masterpiece and etching their name on stone, as if to say, "We're not going anywhere, and this will be here for the rest of time."

Still no word from Jen. I'm worried. I debate about e-mailing or calling. Nothing I'm doing is getting any response.

I decide to call her cell. It goes into voice mail.

"Jen, come on. What's going on? We need to talk. Please. Call me. I'm at home. Anytime. I need to—we need to talk. Please."

It's not poetic, but it's honest. I don't push, because I know pushing sometimes works against me. Normally I give Jen her space. But this isn't just an argument. This is a life we're dealing with, a decision about whether to move on.

My bedroom feels deserted, my bed far too spacious. The last time I looked at the alarm clock it read 2:43 A.M. Sleep is a stranger tonight.

Just like my wife.

I wonder what it would be like to be able to tell her everything. To say anything. That's what intimacy is, what love brings. And I know that I love Jen, but it's just different for us. She doesn't need to know the day-to-day stuff, the details that I want to leave behind when I walk out of the office. She says I carry it with me, and that's okay, I don't need to unpack it in front of her. She has her life, her movies and her art and her costumes, and I get that. We never have enough time to fully share, to fully unload.

So we skip over details.

I wonder.

Don't details matter?

I can still picture the way she looked the first time I saw her, standing on the edge of a crowded ballroom at a movie premiere afterparty. She wore a lime-green dress that clung delicately to her tall and slender figure and made her raven, shoulder-length hair stand out. Creamy white, flawless skin struck me at first, but then I saw her eyes. And they conquered me in an instant.

Eyes the color of the sky, haunting and alluring even as they spotted mine and greeted them in a friendly and disarming way.

These are the details, the small parts that add up to a life and a love.

In my bed in the middle of a night, I'm scared there aren't enough details.

I'm scared that they're too vague, too undefined, too fill-in-the-blank.

Is it too late to start filling?

On my morning commute to work, taking the L, I experience déjà vu. A glance in the crowd. A freaky glance. Someone that looks twisted and sick, someone staring me down. Then gone.

Over lunch, entering the restaurant for the business meeting, someone brushes up against me, and I turn to look and see a tall figure leaving.

On a city street corner, I see the face again. Haunting eyes, almost lifeless, yet they blink. Deep brown eyes. White skin. And a high forehead with slicked-back hair. It's a face I've seen for a while, a face that seems to watch me.

It's gone amidst the work crowd.

I'm exhausted. The workload and the lack of sleep are getting to me.

The place I work out is a ten-minute walk from our apartment. This evening, after a long day at work, I came to work out some of my anger and stress.

I see him again while I'm on an elliptical machine; he's downstairs, with the strength training machines. He's tall, several inches taller than my six-feet-one. He's in sweatpants and a sweatshirt, but he doesn't look sweaty. He stops and looks at me, then he smiles. Not a kind, friendly smile, but the sort of smile a child molester might give an approaching youngster.

I wonder who he is.

I stop and get off the machine and head downstairs to find him.

Of course, he's gone. I wonder if I really saw the man, and if he was really looking at me.

You're losing it Colin get some sleep get something get some help.

I've already been here an hour and have worked out enough animosity for one day. In the locker room, I undo the lock and open the door. Something falls out, a piece of paper that someone had slipped through the top of the locker.

It's a 5-by-7 sheet of printed paper, mostly black with spots of red splattered on it that look like blood. Something else, too. Something that looks like a piece of skin, a body part, bloody and dripping.

There is one word at the top. *DISMEMBER.*

Then, at the bottom, also in red, are the words *By Donald Hardbein.*

Donald Hardbein. The name is familiar.

Now I get it.

I look around the locker room to see if he's there. The tall guy must be Donald.

This is the book he's been trying to get me to represent. I've rejected him several times and recently asked him to stop calling.

Guess Donald doesn't take no for an answer.

The cover looks pitifully amateurish, something done on a computer. But the title has changed from the original one. And the look and feel . . .

I crinkle up the mock book cover and toss it aside.

It's easy to forget about the nut-job author wannabe named Donald Hardbein when I get home and check my e-mails and find there's one waiting from Jen.

Colin:

What I need you to do is let me handle things here. I don't want to hurt your feelings or make you frustrated. I just want to be left alone for right now. I need to work this out on my own. It's how I handle things best. Please try and understand.

Jen

I read it again and again, the words not sufficient, the meaning somehow hidden from me. I try to make sense of the statement, the paragraph, this situation, our life. I'm too tired. I want to hear her voice, but it's so far away. I want to touch her soft skin, but it's somewhere else, under cover, hidden from view.

The screen glows in the darkness, and for a long time I just stare straight ahead, waiting for something else, for something more.

The Call of the Wild

Publishers are idiots.

This is all I can think when one of them, Jack Ward, is sitting across from me, eating breakfast like a famished man in between telling me they're dropping Kelly Moyet from their house.

Day one of the Book Expo show in Los Angeles is starting off with a bang.

"You can't fault her for being a few weeks late," I say.

"She's a few months late, and that's not the problem," says the bald-headed, stocky guy, without looking at me. "It's her sales."

"Her book has barely been out over a year."

"And it's gone nowhere," he says, finally glancing my way. "We don't feel right putting out a second book we already have doubts on."

"She's got a lot of eyes watching her."

"Yeah, but she's doesn't have a lot people buying her. You would have thought some of those reviews would have mattered."

"They do matter."

Jack looks surprised by my comment, then continues working on his omelet.

"I've seen some of the new novel, Jack. It's good."

"Second novels usually aren't."

"Her first hasn't even gone into mass."

"And it might not."

"Meaning?"

He's finishing up a piece of bacon. I've watched him eat this meal with a strange, removed fascination. I think I took four bites of my oatmeal. I never eat much at these conventions.

"We're not asking her to give back any portion of the advance. And you can relax—you don't have to either."

"What's she supposed to do with this novel she's spent the last year and a half working on?"

"Get some of those 'eyes' to put some money where their mouths are."

"Jack, this just isn't right."

"Oh, it's not, huh?" He squints his thick eyebrows and looks at me without blinking. "We tried and we worked with her hard to get a decent book. We got a great book, if you ask me. But nobody was interested. We've had a lot of returns. And we've been told to downsize, to clean house and make fewer slots with bigger names."

"Those big names were once small," I remind him.

"An author can't just write a beautiful little story nowadays and expect to build an audience."

"They do it every year."

"The media wanted some beautiful, hip twenty-eight-year-old."

"Well, Kelly's twenty-eight," I say.

"Yeah, and she's a hermit who lives in Nebraska and writes about Manhattan. She's got a great voice, but frankly that's all she has. Her look doesn't fit her chick-lit tone."

"Since when do looks factor into the equation?"

"When you're investing half a million on an author who's competing with young, hip novelists. She said it herself. She hates doing media."

"You've gotta be kidding me."

He takes a sip of coffee. "We signed her for a three-book deal, and the first book tanked. I'm sorry, Colin. These things happen. She'll publish again."

"Jack—"

"I know the timing could probably be better."

This is the first thing he's said that's truly taken me off guard.

"What do you mean?"

"I heard that you and Lisa Beck parted ways."

"Really? Funny, I don't recall *PW* printing that anywhere."

"Stuart mentioned it."

"Boy, he works fast."

"I'm sorry, Colin. I'm not a big fan of Stuart, just so you know. You made Lisa who she is, and everybody knows it."

"It's just business," I say.

He nods, his face lighting up. "*Exactly*. It's just business. These authors don't understand that, but that's what it comes down to. It'd be so much easier if they could just understand that and take off their diapers."

As I said, publishers are idiots.

"So," Jack says, feeling we've covered Kelly Moyet long enough. "How's Vivian Brown's novel coming along?"

I walk the floor of the Book Expo, passing ten thousand new books waiting to be shared with the world. Each one coming from someone's heart and passion and energy and life.

Yet, it's just business.

That's what everything surrounding me boils down to.

Business.

I can't help thinking about my own personal stake in it. How, in a span of a week, my business has lost the revenue of two of its biggest clients.

I'm already trying to think what I'm going to tell Bernard, when I hear a voice call out, "Mr. Scott." The voice is animated, breathless, as a young man rushes toward me.

"Hello, Ian." I wonder if I have the emotional energy to talk with him.

The man standing in front of me on the convention floor beams in excitement and brushes back light brown hair that needs a serious cut. He's carrying a briefcase with who knows what inside (though I have a good feeling what's inside and would wager money on it) and wears a badge that shows a name of a publisher I don't recognize. Anybody can start a publishing company these days and publish a book. There used to be a mystique about our industry. Now there's just mediocrity.

"I wondered if I'd see you," he says.

I know Ian Pollock fairly well. He and I are both a long way from home.

"So you flew out here just for the show?" I ask him, looking around to see if anybody else I know happens to be walking by.

"Yeah. I'm staying with a college buddy. I've set up some appointments."

"With who?"

He lists a few names I've never heard of, but that probably bodes well for Ian. He doesn't have an agent yet, but has been after me for a couple years now. The fact that he lives forty minutes away from our offices in Chicago doesn't help. He's visited our offices half a dozen times, maybe more.

"I'm still trying to sell *Passover Lane.*"

"Good for you," I tell him.

Time is ticking. Well, it would be anyway, even if I had an hour to spare. But I really have to go.

"Ian, I've got to run to another meeting."

"Yeah, okay, that's fine. You mind if I walk with you?"

I nod my head. We begin to move again.

"I've rewritten *Passover Lane* again."

"You take some of my suggestions?"

"Sure. Some, I mean. I didn't take all."

"Did you lighten it up?"

Ian smiles. That means a big, fat nope.

"Writing comedy's hard," Ian says.

"Yeah. But remember. Nobody wants to read five hundred pages of a young man's angst."

"What about Albert Camus?"

"What does that have to do with anything?"

"People study him. He's renowned. He never had to write comedy."

"Yeah, but you're trying to be published. Remember that."

"Is there a chance—"

the moment of truth

"that you would take a look at it? Again?"

Hence the briefcase.

"Ian—"

"No, Mr. Scott, listen. I've done my homework and know what it takes. I mean, I know that this book might not be it, but I don't want to give up. The other books I've written—most are bad and aren't going anywhere. But this one—I think it's got some potential."

John Gardner once said that the essential ingredient for any novelist was drivenness. And Ian—well, I have to give him credit. The guy is remarkably driven. With thick skin, too.

Ian has written around seven or eight "other" books. Novels, maybe a short story collection in there. I think he's sent the Roth Agency every one of them. I've read perhaps four. I did read some of *Passover Lane.* I wouldn't say Ian has an abundance of talent. But I'd give him a contract just on his persistence.

Besides—talent can only take you so far in this business.

"You can always send it to us—"

"I know, but that's the thing," Ian says, his eager young face burning with sincerity. "I don't want it stuck in some pile. I know you don't want the whole thing. Maybe just take the first twenty pages and look at it? Please?"

I nod. He clumsily opens up his briefcase, a faux leather one, and gives me a folder that has black magic marker with the bold declaration of *Passover Street.*

"Shouldn't this be *Passover Lane*?" I ask him in curiosity.

He looks at the cover page, then blushes and lets out a curse.

"Ah, man, I did that really quickly—"

"No big deal," I tell him.

"Maybe you'll have time to read it. Sometime."

"Maybe," I say. "It was good to see you."

We shake hands. Before he walks away, I say something I know I might regret.

"Don't give up."

"No way," Ian says with a grin I can't help but admire.

The Ians of the publishing world still give me glimmers of hope.

The huge discrepancy between the Lisa Becks and the Ian Pollocks doesn't come down to talent. In some ways, I see more talent in Ian than I do in Lisa.

What it comes down to is money. Money earned. And the only way a publisher makes money is based on a name, and the only way an author gets a name is to have some lucky breaks and make a mark in the glutted world of books.

The unfortunate reality is, like the publishers and booksellers, I make my living off the Lisa Becks, not the Ian Pollocks.

I'm having an out-of-body experience. I'm hovering over this small table and these uncomfortable chairs on the edge of the carpeted convention floor tucked in a corner of a booth. It's one of the big publishers and they love to have their big meetings on the big floor where big people can see them. But me, I'm small and I'm invisible and I'm floating over Darren Burford (big publisher man from the Big Apple) and Ellen Richardson (big fantasy novelist from big city in Oregon) and Colin Scott (one-time big agent man who's doesn't give a rat's behind about sitting in this meeting). Darren wears a suit and a tie and talks about wanting to raise Ellen to the next level, and I don't care a teeny, tiny bit. I see my lips smile and my head nod and I hear myself utter a few words, things like "great idea" and "keep me in the loop on that" and "that's critical for Ellen's career," but I don't even remember the idea two seconds after I suggest it and I don't want to be kept in the loop on anything and I am really not especially interested in Ellen. I am hardened plaster between two pieces of wood.

My existence is crucial to this meeting. Without me, these two people would never have connected. But Darren's hollow promises and amazed interest combined with Ellen's excited but sole focus on her writing suddenly bores me to a glazed donut status. Each sentence takes a bite out of my focus. My concentration and my grin suddenly begin fading, and I am thankful to have only been scheduled to meet with the publisher for an hour.

After the meeting ends with gushing pleasantries, Ellen follows me like a baby duck waddling after her momma. She continues to talk to me about her book ideas and her desires and her excitement about her new contract as I nod and feign interest and look for the nearest vendor so I can get some coffee to keep me awake.

". . . and everything about when I met Thomas, it was just inspired, it was almost divine in some ways. Do you ever get that feeling that something is almost heaven-sent? Thomas was, so much so. He just shared everything he could about the whole world of computers and the Internet, and when he explained what he did—"

This isn't her husband she is talking about with such fervor. It's a guy who helped her do research on her historical novel.

Heaven-sent? Get over yourself.

We walk on the red carpet, and I find my coffee and order a cup and listen. I listen. I am paid 15 percent to listen. Does Ellen ever once step back and shut up and ask how *my* life is going? Of course not. She doesn't need to. If she were to do such a thing, and some authors might, I would be brief because I know they would begin to glaze over as well if I talked too much about myself. This isn't about me. It's never been about me. It's about them.

I think that at some level, every author has to be a self-centered person. Fiction or nonfiction, it doesn't matter. What else would drive somebody to an empty page or a blank computer screen with the notion he or she had something unique to share? Everything worth saying has been uttered in some form or another. Every story has been told. The so-called experts aren't really experts; they're just taking material from the past masters. They just add their own voice and style and their naïve belief that what they are doing is so important that it is worthy of crowds stopping everything to pick up their book, their literary masterpiece, and enjoy it.

Writing is a leap of faith. A crazy leap of faith only the brave and the batty attempt.

"Do you think that's possible?" Ellen asks.

She is talking about marketing, the oh-so-important subject to an author. So many authors don't understand book marketing and never will, and yet they always bring up the subject. Deep down, Ellen wants Darren and his publishing house to say, "We love your book so incredibly much, we're not holding back. We'll be doing Super Bowl commercials and four-color ads in *USA Today.* Nothing will stop us because your book is an American treasure just like you are."

Authors never admit it, but deep down, in layers like an onion, that's what they want. They look at the big names and want what they have. Stephen King and Tom Clancy and Danielle Steel and especially our very own Vivian Brown. They want that, but the reality is they will never get it. They can talk all they want about marketing and the next level, the glorious, ridiculous "next level," but it still doesn't matter.

"Anything is possible," I tell her, and yes, this is true.

Anything *is* possible. But Ellen's work is not going on Oprah, is not hitting the *New York Times* bestseller list, and is not going to get the A-level book treatment. She wrote a nice love story set in the eighteenth century, and her audience will enjoy it, and if all things go right, she might sell close to a hundred thousand copies. That of course is only mass paperback sales, but still nothing to shrug at.

We chat for a few more minutes, and I look at my watch and tell Ellen I need to go. She hugs me.

"Thank you for being such an advocate for me."

I smile and feel like a fraud.

John Steinbeck once said, "If there is a magic in story writing, and I am convinced that there is, no one has ever been able to reduce it to a recipe that can be passed from one person to another."

There's no magic in what I do. What publishers do. We trade recipes. That's all. And someone else makes them up.

I'm trying to get off the floor when a hand grips my shoulder a little too strongly. I turn around to see a familiar face. It's a tight face and smile that just reek of plastic surgery or Botox or something like that. The hand is a bit too slender and soft for my liking.

"The famous Colin Scott," Stuart Koep says, with not just a hint of disdain. "Every author's champion and best friend."

"Staying busy?" I ask.

"Always," he says with a well-practiced smile.

"Spent much time with Lisa?"

The comment doesn't faze him a bit. "I understand she told you the news."

"Are things that tight, Stu?"

"I hear your speech at the writers conference has been making the Internet chat rooms."

"I gotta say, that's a little tacky even for you, Stu."

"First off, it's Stuart. And all I'm doing is the best for an author whose career is taking off."

I laugh.

You have no idea what you're getting yourself into.

"I think Lisa has finally found an agent who really embodies her spirit," I say. "And her soul."

It is 11:30 P.M. I can't sleep. The mahi-mahi I ate a few hours ago still swims around in my stomach. I've already gone through one whole showing of ESPN and nothing else interests me. My brain is too fried to read but too keyed up to sleep. Still no word on the Jen front. So I check e-mails and then decide to send one.

Hi, Vivian.

I stop for a minute and think. I don't e-mail Vivian much. I don't send random notes to her or call her up on the phone to chat. She's a bit reclusive in her northern California residence, especially since her works have sold millions and she's become a celebrity. She's also a true artist, someone who sees writing as very personal and almost sacred and who doesn't want to be bothered. Roth pays me to keep nuisances away from Vivian, along with making her writing soar.

For a second I think about deleting the e-mail, but I'm exhausted and simply want to communicate to an author I admire and like.

Sending this e-mail from Book Expo in good ole LA. You should be here. Everyone's asking about you and the "next book." I want to wear a T-shirt that gives the following answers: "No, she hasn't finished it," "Yes, she's almost finished," "Yes, we're very excited about it," and "Yes, it'll be as big as or even bigger than the Marover Trilogy."

Yeah, I'm sure you'd love all this attention, huh? Sometimes these things even get tiring for me—can you believe that? My big question: exactly how much starch can one man really consume in a five-day period?

I've got some business matters that I'll be running by you when I get back to the office. A few details to keep you in the loop regarding

Sliding into Forever. It looks like the movie's really going to happen. No—don't roll your eyes yet. I'm serious. I told you this producer was good for his word. We've got to set up a date for the two of you to meet. I think you'll like him.

Just wanted to say hi and that I hope you're doing well. Should I say I can't wait for *In Your Memory*? Oh, wait, I've already told you that. Like a thousand times. You probably get sick of your agent calling and asking about the next baby. But what a next baby this will be. I'm excited. I really am. So is Mr. Roth. Of course the negotiating and bidding war will be fun. But—I'm being honest, this isn't just the agent talking here—I can't wait to read it. It's been awhile since I read something that—well, I should be polite and say it's been awhile since I've been overwhelmed by a manuscript. And coincidentally, it's been awhile since I read a Vivian Brown novel.

Take care. Colin.

I send the e-mail into cyberspace and know that Vivian will probably read it tonight. She keeps crazy hours, working late into the night and then sleeping in the mornings.

I reread the e-mail and know it's far too trivial, far too chummy. It doesn't sound like me. The guy deep down, the one that only a few people really know. Yet this is the Colin she knows. The guy with a smile, the encourager, the motivator, the friend.

Sometimes, when I'm irked and in an irritable mood, I want to take credit for those millions of copies of the Marover Trilogy that have sold. Readers often say that book one, *Sliding into Forever*, is still the best, a classic along the lines of Narnia and Harry Potter. The second and third are great and wonderful, but the first is what broke her out, "put her on the map." And the first was the one where I, going through Roth, gave the most input, the one where Vivian took the most guidance.

Why does literary success pave the way toward mediocrity?

I would never say this to Vivian, of course. Some might argue that books two and three were deeper, more ambitious, more bold and thematic. It doesn't matter. Vivian was just another author when she sent her manuscript to us years ago. Without a name and with barely a chance. Something I found in the slush pile.

That's the beauty of publishing. You never know what you might find on a page, inside a spine, on a shelf.

Would I like more credit? Of course. Thirty-five years old, I deserve a little.

This is a trial run for the Vivian Brown contract. I know it. Mr. Roth knows it. The publishers bidding know it. Because everybody is at Book Expo, it happens that we can meet with the publishers personally, along with the author. Most of the time we do this without an author at hand.

This is how it works. One of our top authors is ready to negotiate a new contract. In most cases this happens before they start writing the book. We get the money up front so they can be satisfied and secure in the publishing deal, and then and only then they will begin to start writing. That is, if they even know how to write. But that's another story.

The Roth Agency sends out packages to all the major players, the big publishers who will be interested and able to handle a megadeal with our author. We announce that we will be taking meetings to talk about the aforementioned author and proposal. Publishers and editors will meet with us to ask questions, throw out reasons why their publishing house is the place to go to, and so on. This only happens for big deals. Huge deals. And even then, not all publishers bite.

The author in the spotlight this afternoon is Dr. Fritz Nissen. Nissen is not an author, he's a celebrity. He earned his own talk show after making the rounds on all the others a few years ago. His first book became a runaway bestseller: *It's Not about Me, Try You.* He's an in-your-face counselor with a great sense of humor and tons of stories to tell. He can't legitimately write a paragraph, much less a book, but that's okay. That's what co-authors and ghostwriters are for. Dr. Nissen carries the name and the message.

Put into perspective, most Grisham novels sell three million copies the year they come out; so far *It's Not about Me, Try You* has sold close to eight million. It appeals not only to a husband and wife trying to work out their differences, but to a marketing manager trying to cope with his peer at the office. It is fresh and full of wisdom and humor. It is a colossal success.

Dr. Nissen wrote—or should I say concocted—a follow-up book, but that had already been in the works before we knew how big *It's Not about Me, Try You* would become. We want not only to brand Dr. Nissen, but to sign a deal for close to a dozen products. This might sound insane, but the publishers are lining up and foaming at the mouth. With the success of his talk show and the public platform he has, Nissen's next book could topple his first.

So the dream goes.

We set up shop at the Westin Hotel in downtown LA, not too far away from the convention floor. We have eleven meetings scheduled, most half an hour in length. Three of the "big guns," as Roth calls them, are scheduled to meet for an hour. Representatives from each publisher arrive at our hotel suite, meet Dr. Nissen, Mr. Roth, and me, then proceed to talk about the proposal we sent out weeks ago. After their meeting time expires, we remind them that the following Wednesday morning is when the bidding will take place.

That will happen back at our office in Chicago, over the phone. Even though I help out, like Ted and the rest of the office staff, Bernard ultimately handles those calls. Just as he will with Vivian. I handle lower-level calls, but not big ones like this. Some conversations will be pointless, and he'll tell them so. "You're in a ballpark, but it certainly isn't ours," is a Rothism he likes to use. He knows what to expect from the names and the publishers on line. Most are New York houses, but a few others like to dip their toes into the water, but they quickly get back out. They can never get the nerve to hold their breath long enough to take a dive and go for the treasure at the bottom of the publishing ocean.

I arrive at the suite an hour before our first meeting. Breakfast foods are set up by the kitchen area, along with several carafes of coffee and juice. I still carry the Starbucks cup I purchased fifteen minutes ago. Speaking of oceans, I've got one filled with java just above my belt.

My briefcase holds forty gray folders with *Dr. Fritz Nissen Publishing Plan* printed in a nice, fancy font. Each publisher will get a folder, two or three depending on the people they bring, reminding them of what Nissen and the Roth Agency are proposing. We don't talk figures on a day like today. But even though we say that to them, some publishers will come right out and suggest an amount. That can be referred to as a preemptive bid. In some cases, that's a good thing. But with the scope of the Nissen deal and how big it might be, we will tell them that we won't be entertaining any offers or bids today. We will wait to have them fight over one another.

This isn't cereal or soap or toothpaste I'm selling. It's the American Dream wrapped up in a dust jacket with your smiling mug on the back and a bio the size of Texas in the flap copy. All for a glorious hardcover price of $29.99.

It's the movie *Groundhog Day*, except instead of the same day repeating itself over and over, it's the same half-hour meeting replayed time and time again. The handshakes and smiles, the invitation to coffee and muffins or later in the day soda and snacks, the sitting down and introductions, the short small talk and the grand pooh-bah speech by Mr. Roth about the desire and commitment to Dr. Nissen and the success of his first book and the need to capitalize on this moment now in Nissen's publishing career.

Some of the publishing people ask questions, but mostly they talk about their interest and excitement about the proposal. We know most of these people and the publishers they work for. Some rattle off bestsellers they've published to try and impress Nissen, but Roth and I already know and don't really care. Even when the publisher of Nissen's first book comes with their interest and their reasoning that *they* made Nissen into who he is today, saying it in a nice and gentle matter, Roth and I know it's coming. After a while in this business you've heard everything, and it's like watching a trailer for a movie that you've already seen. You want to fast-forward and get to the end.

I keep quiet for the most part, with Mr. Roth leading and Dr. Nissen acting like a prom queen being pursued by a gymful of boys. Nissen is perfect for this, because if dollar figures are mentioned or the conversation begins heading down the serious funnel cloud discussion, he'll crack a joke, even at his own expense sometimes, and make the mood lighter. He *should* crack jokes and feel light-headed and hearted. He is expecting to sign an eight-figure advance for publishing more books than he'll know what to do with. Yes, that's right. No typo there.

An eight-figure advance. And the Roth Agency gets—you got it. Fifteen percent of that.

What's the name of that old Pink Floyd song?

Money. Lots and lots of money.

But even knowing this, I hear the demons of doubt begin to whisper. In the seventh meeting, as Ramona Baker talks with Roth about her publishing house's interest in Nissen, I begin to zone out. I pay enough attention, in case they need something important, like a can of Diet Coke or a question about book eight in the multi-book deal. I can do it all. I am the one who came up with the list of titles. Me and the office attorney, Darcy. But I begin to zone out, knowing that this guy sitting across the table from me will be signing a deal for over ten million dollars, perhaps far higher, and he will be doing pretty much zero percent of the writing himself.

Normally I don't care, it's no cause for concern, because I work at the agency that takes 15 percent of the take, writer or no writer. It doesn't matter. But I wonder if it should indeed matter. If this meeting is hypocritical. I think of all the authors all over the country working into the wee hours of the night trying to perfect something that will never get published, never see the light of day. All while Dr. Nissen readies his hand to pen a deal with book concepts he didn't develop for books he won't write or publish or market or sell. Books with his name crowding the cover, with embossed edges and bold letters. Books that will land his name on the bestseller lists and fill his bank account with many more figures and help his talk show in the ratings.

Understand why it doesn't necessarily feel right?

I wonder what would happen if I suddenly screamed at the top of my lungs about what a crock all of this seemed to be. If I just stood up and shouted "Open your eyes" and "Get a life" and "This is a joke."

I keep my mouth shut, except when opening it to answer a question. The day ticks off, and the muscles in my smile are straining near the very end. I listen and learn. This is how it is done, and how we will do it for Vivian Brown's book. This is just an appetizer to the bigger meal.

Near the end of the day, Roth directs his sharp eyes onto me and lets them linger for a few seconds. I try to appear alert and focused. He gives me a quick grin and winks, a sign a father might give to his son as they sit on a boat waiting to reel in the big fish.

Then, almost on cue, the phone on my side vibrates. I slip it off my belt and see the name in the small window. *Jen Cell.*

I'm not sure how many days it's been since we've talked. I haven't tried connecting since her last e-mail.

I excuse myself, knowing they won't miss me as one of the publishers continues to talk about needing to go golfing with Nissen. Please. I go into the hallway and answer the phone.

Jen is crying.

"What's wrong?" I ask.

"Everything."

"What happened?"

"What happened?" she asks. "What do you mean, what happened?"

"Did something happen at work?"

She gives me an incredulous laugh. "Of course not. Work's fine. Everything is fine." She curses.

"Jen?"

"How do you think I feel about everything?"

"I have no idea. That's why I've been wanting to talk."

"This isn't something to e-mail about, Colin. Or something to dialogue while you're in LA and I'm in Massachusetts."

"I know that."

"It's just—this is the way it goes, I guess."

"The way what goes?"

"How it ends."

"Nothing is ending."

"We can't have a child."

"You don't know that."

"Oh, I know. The writing is on the wall. It's clear. God is saying nope, give it up, why bother."

"There are other—"

"Just stop," she says. "When would we find time to be parents? We can barely be husband and wife."

"We can adjust."

"And how's that? Who's going to adjust, Colin? Who?"

"Jen, please—" I sigh. "Look, I can't—right now, this isn't the best time."

"Of course it's not. Timing is just something we can never get right."

"Let me give you a call a little later, okay?"

But she's already left.

I want to go find her and make things right. But I can do neither.

She was vulnerable, and I couldn't reciprocate.

Timing is everything.

It's an hour before the book release party.

I sit on the edge of the hotel bed and reflect that I've spent a lot of nights in beds I haven't made. I sit and see the reflection in the mirror and instantly think *clichéd scene.* The angst-filled character looking at himself in the mirror is supposed to convey a soul-searching moment the moment of decision the moment at hand such drama so gripping so utterly trite.

What am I doing? When did I stop caring? I used to love authors and was their advocate and their "best friend," and there was a reason I earned that label. Something changed. I changed. And I know this didn't happen today, or on this trip. The novelty wore off sometime not too long ago. The gnawing fact that most authors carry inflated egos and bruised psyches and never-ending crises of personal trauma, a fact that I overlooked for years, is no longer in my rearview mirror but in the path in front of me, a barricade to the road I'm driving down. Either I'm going to drive right through it or go off-roading and wander down some other path.

Either way I think I'm in trouble.

I lie back on my bed. The semi-darkness of the room and its silence feel good. I am not a difficult man, a mean man, but I suddenly hate not only what I stand for, but what I do. I'm tired. And I want somebody not to talk, but to listen to me. They always do what an agent wants them to, but they never listen.

Agents are soulless, heartless, gutless, right? That's what the true legendary ones have been. I am the one who has helped his authors while negotiating with strong teeth. I have been their champion. I have been their best friend.

But being a champion and a friend only goes so far.

I don't want this anymore.

Maybe I'll take all the money I've saved and put it into a new house in the suburbs. Oh, wait. I've already done that.

Maybe Jen and I can move there. Start over.

We can get a couple dogs. I can walk them and pick up poop and mow the lawn and read the morning paper and live like a human.

Maybe, just maybe, Jennifer will come along with my idea, too. And if—*if* being a miraculous, mythical term used here—this actually occurs, and we can be together and the timing is right, maybe the forces of the universe will allow us to start a family.

Maybe.

We've been trying for so long.

It's 8:27 P.M.

It's twenty-seven minutes after the start of the party.

Twenty-seven minutes, and four people have shown up. I'm not including the author or the publishing people or the agents.

I'm in the lobby of the hotel, looking around and trying to see someone, anyone, who looks like they've arrived here for a party. They all look busy or bored, but nobody looks like they're searching for a book release party.

This is a complete and total disaster.

The room spins and the people twirl on the merry-go-round, and I try to figure out what to do.

Reality check #1: Kurt Dobbs signed on with a new publisher, and all of us, the author and the publisher and I, came up with this idea for the book release party.

Reality check #2: It's the second night of Book Expo, and we're competing with a lot of other functions and dinners and we knew that, but that's why we opted to have it in the Skye Bar at the top of the Westin.

Reality check #3: This has cost the publisher a lot of money, a lot if not most of the marketing money for Kurt's new novel.

Reality check #4: Kurt is insecure and needed encouragement to do this and relied on my judgment.

Reality check #5: I'm going to have to be the one to name the elephant in the room upstairs.

I can picture it now. Everybody playing this off, having drinks and laughing nervously and looking around and waiting for someone else to say something or do something. Four people have shown up. Four.

They're maybe worth a couple thousand per person.

I breathe in and out.

You can do this you can manage this don't think of anything else.

What is happening, why are the dominoes falling the way they are? What bad luck streak did I fall into? I take the elevator up and think of what I'm going to say and how I'm going to say it.

When I get to the top floor and exit and walk into the dimly lit blue hues of the swanky bar, it's exactly as I pictured it. A couple of marketing people from the big New York publisher are whispering by the door to the bar. They look like they've just witnessed a car crash. They look at me with disdain in their eyes.

It wasn't all my idea, I want to tell them, but I don't. I don't reveal anything.

I'm looking for Kurt.

He's sitting on a plush armchair next to a window overlooking LA. He's telling a story just like he always does—Kurt loves to entertain and make the masses, or the few in this case, laugh. He sips his drink.

I walk up to the small group. A VP from the publisher along with a couple of editorial people are sitting next to Kurt. The four people who came up here for the party have dwindled down to two; they stand near the bar talking and drinking. Free drinks, free view, cool. Who cares about an author and his ARC? What's an ARC? Who cares, it doesn't matter, we're getting free drinks and a free view, awesome!

I wait until Kurt is finished with his anecdote.

"You know, this is one of those nights that will become a great story to tell about the horrors of publishing," I say, trying to keep a smile going just like everybody else. "The reality is, nobody is coming. I think we might as well admit the obvious."

Kurt is a small man with beady eyes that can drill you down and a feisty spirit he keeps in check under a bookworm physique and a sarcastic persona. He forces a smile and looks at the others around him. "Not now, Colin."

"I just think that we need to—"

"Colin," he says, pointing a finger at me to hold it, as a teacher might do to a third grader who is babbling. "Excuse me for a second, everyone. Colin, can we talk outside?"

In the hallway, the door to the bar closed, soft music piping in the background, Kurt Dobbs unloads on me, first with a series of curses. I'm not sure if they're directed at me, at this situation, at the publisher, or at life in general.

"Okay, I get it, okay," I say.

"And how *dare* you bring it up in front of the others?"

"Kurt, I was just stating the obvious. You want to go the whole night without stating a word?"

"There were people who are here for the event. They heard what you said."

I want to say *No, they didn't, they didn't hear a word, stop freaking out.*

"What would you like me to do?" I ask, revealing my annoyance deep down.

"What would I like you—" He stops, apparently amazed that I asked. "What I would have liked was to have known this was going to be a train wreck before it happened. If you remember, *you* were the one who convinced me to do it."

"The publisher wanted something big. We all agreed."

"But I agreed with you. I trusted you, Colin."

"I'm sorry, Kurt. I really am."

He gives me a look that's beyond wounded. It's full of hate.

"I don't want your apology. I want you to do your job. I want you to get your head out of your behind and make a few decisions that will help my books, got that? I'm tired of marketing being the main reason why my books never sell. I'm tired of it, and I'm tired of stupid readers who don't get it, and I'm especially tired of you."

I hear a muffled cough and look behind us to see a man and a woman standing, looking at both of us with awkward surprise.

"Excuse us, we're here for the book release party," the woman says. "We're here to meet Kurt Dobbs."

You sit and stare down an empty sloping street lined with sidewalks and blinking stoplights. The car idles, and for a second you take your foot off the pedal and coast and wonder if you'll get sideswiped by some wandering street cleaner going fifty miles an hour, and you ask yourself if it'll make one bit of difference. You doubt it. But you blink and take a sip of your coffee and breathe in again.

Wonder what you're doing. Go ahead. Question it all. You don't have a clue, do you?

You're in the middle of Los Angeles at six-thirty on a Sunday morning, and Armageddon might as well have just occurred. That, or people just don't want to wake up around here.

The music plays loudly. Some cool rock station. One plus for LA. Cool rock stations that actually play good stuff. You can enjoy it for the moment. Now that you're alone.

Alone. There's a fine concept.

You went out to drive around and find a Dunkin' Donuts. They have Starbucks in the hotel, but you love Dunkin' Donuts coffee. And the way you felt when you woke up, you needed major help.

The SUV you're driving is not your own. Neither is this city nor this morning nor this schedule nor this life.

You're thirty-five. You spend your time sucking up to personalities and putting up with egos and stifling your own thoughts and emotions.

And in a couple hours, you'll be doing it all once more.

Drive, a voice says, and you want to floor the gas pedal and go. Get somewhere far away. An island where tanned, friendly faces greet Jennifer and you. Where they call you *amigo* or *chap* or *señor*.

You can live with those names.

You can't live with this.

You look at the time and notice that half an hour has evaporated. Your hours and days blur by. Blur and smudge like black ink on khaki pants. Merge and blend and corrode and you wake up and say I need something else.

Something more than the extra-large coffee at Dunkin' Donuts.

You're really in control, you tell yourself. Out loud or in your mind, it doesn't matter. You've got it all under control. That's what matters.

That's the lie.

The crisp blue dress shirt with the matching tie say control.

So do the shiny new shoes.

And the crisp shave.

And the cool cologne.

All a lousy cover-up.

You wonder if, deep down, they all might know. Can they see the redness of your eyes? Do your eyedrops really work?

You could use a drink. You had too many last night and you can still feel the aftertaste. But that's not your problem.

People are.

But you're in the people business.

And you're really starting to loathe them.

You drive on and search for your hotel and suck in air again and suck in warm coffee and try to regain control.

It's all about control, remember. Ownership. Authority. Control.

And you haven't had an ounce of any of those for a long, long time.

You smile and get ready.

It's about to begin all over again.

The Stranger

It's Monday after the trade show, and I leave a message for our office administrator, Darcy, letting her know I'm sick. She's surprised. It's been three, maybe even four years since I last called in sick. I don't name my illness. I'm frankly sick of Ted's cologne, sick of the condemnation I'm going to receive from Roth, sick of everything to do with publishing.

I decide to check in on the house in the suburbs.

On my way there I dial my younger sister, who lives in Miami. I rarely see or talk to Katie, but she left me an excited message to call her as soon as possible.

She answers her cell, and it sounds like she's driving her convertible.

"You okay?" I ask.

"Yeah. Got my message, huh?"

"Mom okay?"

"She's fine."

Mom lives with our stepfather, Gregory, in Fort Myers.

"You need to come down here. It's crazy. Okay, so hey—"

"Hey what?"

"I'm pregnant."

I go to say something and my mouth opens but nothing comes out.

"Colin?"

"Yeah."

"Can you believe it?"

"I guess—not really."

"Yeah, it's been a whirlwind sort of month."

"You're still with . . ." I forget her boyfriend's name.

"Michael, stupid."

"Oh, yeah."

I think they're living together, but I don't know for sure. I'm not sure if I've even heard Michael's name.

"It's sorta crazy—I mean, we were totally being careful. But nothing's a hundred percent safe, you know?"

My thirty-two-year-old sister laughs.

"I just found out, and I was like, well, I guess there are worse things that could happen."

I breathe in.

Just wait until Jen hears.

Maybe I won't tell Jen.

"And I think—well, after a lot of talk—we decided we're probably going to keep it."

I grip the steering wheel and feel sick. *After a lot of talk. Probably going to keep it.* Nice. Is she quoting that famous Madonna song?

"That's, uh, that's good. It's great," I say.

"What? Wait, hold on—"

I can't hear anything for a few moments. I keep my eyes on the road and wait to hear Katie. Her voice returns and she's laughing.

"What?" I ask.

"Oh, nothing. There were some people in front of my apartment screaming. You gotta come down here sometime."

"Just—make sure to take care of yourself," I tell Katie in a fatherly voice.

"I know. It's weird to keep thinking—I'll wake up and then think, whoa, I'm a mom. How bizarre, huh?"

"Completely."

"You guys gotta join us—then we can have little cousins playing with each other."

"Yeah, that'd be great," I tell her.

"And Mom—you should've heard her—"

"You told her?"

"Oh, yeah. She starts bawling and she's so excited and she says she'll be there right afterward, and then she—"

The reception goes bad again and I wait.

"—but then again, anything can happen," Katie finishes.

"Sure," I say, not knowing, not caring.

"Hey—I gotta go. Tell Jen and tell her hi."

I hang up the phone and glance ahead as I pass cars on their way to work.

Sometimes I just don't get life.

The property in west St. Charles is ten minutes from the downtown area. It's still surprising to suddenly come upon a few hills in the otherwise flat Illinoisian town, and to also be in the midst of a thick forest. There was a small ranch sitting on six wooded acres when Jen and I bought it. Now it's a lot with the remains of a torn-down house and an unkempt lawn.

I wind down the sloping driveway and pull my BMW next to the handful of trucks parked there. Pearce waits for me next to his truck. I get out of the car and offer him a cup of coffee.

"I can use that," he says, thanking me with a nod.

"How's it going?"

"Still doing cleanup."

"Last time I was here, there was a house right over there."

"Wait—did you wanna keep that?" Pearce laughs.

"I'm glad to see that ugly thing gone."

"Just wait till the new one starts going up."

"I've been tweaking," I tell him.

He shakes his head. "You gotta stop reading *Architectural Digest*."

"A guy gets to dream, huh?"

"You ever thought of becoming an architect?"

I sip my coffee and shake my head. "No sirree. Way too much time investment."

"How long have you been in publishing?"

"Twelve years. But just wait. I'm going to go out with a bang. Sell a major book and be able to do this sort of thing more often."

"My rates'll go up with each one."

"As they should."

"You know I'm kidding." Pearce is a stocky guy, with several days' beard evident in the morning sunlight and a friendly, world-wise smile that never seems to go away.

"I'm not," I tell him. "Hey—if I had time, and knew what I was doing, I'd be here helping you pound the nails."

"Pound the nails. Yeah, you *don't* know what I do."

This is the first side project of mine—buying a house, tearing it down, and replacing it with a new one. The 10,000-square-foot house is going to be monstrous and magnificent, and it's going to be an investment for Jen and me. I've always been a little wary of the stock market, and made this decision less than six months ago after pocketing a lot of change from a big deal at Roth.

I've already sunk thousands into it, and the real bills won't start coming until later this summer, when the building takes off. Lisa Beck packing her bags and going over to the Stuart Koep motel sure doesn't help my plan. Neither does the inevitable: Kurt Dobbs going somewhere else.

I'm looking down the road, as everybody does. Looking at the next contract for Vivian Brown that will land me a nice fat bonus, borrowing a little from the future.

"Too bad Jen can't see the house gone," Pearce says.

"Yeah. She wanted to take a sledgehammer to it herself."

"Where is she again?" he asks as we approach a heap of wood, drywall, and metal.

"Massachusetts."

"So she, like, what—does makeup and stuff for the actors?"

"She's a costume designer."

"Like for *Lord of the Rings* outfits and monsters?"

"She didn't work on those movies," I tell him, "though she did get a chance to drop by their sets in New Zealand."

"Cool."

"She's working on a contemporary movie. She gets to do what she does best: shop."

"Any big-name actors?"

"Actually, I don't know."

I'm not even sure when Jen's going to come back. *If* she's going to come back.

They have a lot of cleaning up to do before starting on the house. Pearce goes over the details—when the trucks will come, how easy it will be, where the materials will go to be disposed of. He shows me things like the approximate location for the front door or the back deck. It's exciting to visualize the house. I keep a folded-up drawing of the exterior with me most of the time. It was a design we tweaked and honed. There will be a massive stone turreted exterior with a cedar shake roof.

If I could, I'd work on this every day. Every Saturday morning for the last year, when I haven't been baby-sitting authors, I have spent conceptualizing and brainstorming and designing the mansion that we will soon start building. I've read books and taken some classes to help me understand the basics. And along with Pearce, I've talked to consultants who helped with the design and layout.

I recognize one of the workers and greet him. I've gotten to know a few of the guys on Pearce's crew. All good, rugged guys who are friendly and laid-back, straight shooters, just like him.

We found this property by accident. Jennifer and I had a party to go to—something connected to the Roth Agency, nothing too personal—and we were driving all around trying to find the house when we ran across this one. It had a For Sale sign on it, so we drove down the driveway. Illinois doesn't have lots of beautiful landscape and scenery, but this six-acre lot sure did. The house itself looked shabby and run-down. Jen hated going inside, but I constantly reminded her that if we bought it, the house would go bye-bye. She said we could never afford something like this, and I reminded her of my last big bonus.

"But with starting a family and everything, and the possibility—" she had started to say, but then stopped.

There was no reason we shouldn't invest in this house. The family question remained, and still remains, a mystery. A question mark. But this house . . . I finally persuaded Jen.

I also finally bought the property without getting her official okay.

It took us a few months to sign on the dotted line. Jen lets me handle our finances, and I knew that we would be a little stretched. That's why you get loans. The apartment in the high-rise tower off Lake Michigan—well, you can imagine how much that costs. Everybody knows renting is just throwing money away. This, I reasoned with Jen, was an investment. We could build a new house and then sell it and make a good deal of money. And then, maybe, *buy* a place for ourselves somewhere in the city.

Pearce hands me some papers with a dirty hand and we talk some more. He sips on his coffee, and I tell him I better get going.

"How was the conference?" he asks.

"Old."

"Really?"

"You got needy authors and greedy publishers," I tell him. "Same old story every time."

"Make any killer deals?"

"Not yet. But I'm visiting a big-name author this next week."

"Anybody I know?"

"Vivian Brown."

"The Marover books? My wife loves those."

"So do ten million others."

"What's she like?"

"She's reserved and proper. Very much a creative soul. I like her a lot. She's down-to-earth. Unlike a lot of authors out there."

"You sound a bit edgy today," Pearce says, his smile filling his face.

"Sometimes I wonder what it'd be like. Just to pound nails all day. Put up walls and create things."

"I like it."

"Yeah."

The walls don't talk back to you. The nails don't have feelings you have to cater to. You simply pound them on the head and go home and forget about them. And sooner or later, you get to see something you've helped create. Something you've created with your own two hands.

I come home to an empty apartment.

I suddenly think about that commercial where the guy comes home early in order to make dinner for his wife. He opens and chills the wine. Cuts the fish in careful slivers. Does a few things I don't even recognize, with fruit and fancy dishes. He prepares the food the way Emeril Lagasse might, taking a bite, smiling. Then his wife strides through the door, surprised, glowing, stunning in her beauty. She drops her bags—obviously she's been shopping or something important like that—and goes to meet the awaiting husband.

I hate that commercial.

There's an e-mail waiting for me from Donald Hardbein. I've been wondering when I'd hear from him again, especially after getting the cover slipped into my locker at the club.

> Mr. Colin:
>
> They say first impressions amount to much, so I hope mine served you well. We will soon meet, but permit me to introduce myself. I am the author of two published novels and have for some time been working on my third. After twenty-seven years, I finally finished it. Now I long to share it with you, and then, thus, the world. It is time for a new voice, a voice once muted and possibly muzzled, but now emancipated and monstrous in its confession of life and love and, ultimately, a longing for an afterlife and all that will ever and ever be.

My story? Just a nugget, that's all. You've seen the cover I had commissioned for it. The title sums up the drama: *Dismember*. Let's call it a cross between *Apocalypse Now* and *It's a Wonderful Life*. Ah, yes, I know, I can hear the unbridled curiosity. That, my friend, is the beauty. The terrific, glorious beauty of it all.

The reason I chose you is simple and yet utterly scientific: the *Publisher's Weekly* interview with you last year, where you remarked about working with Vivian Brown. I believe I could be another Vivian Brown for you. A male version, of course. I also chose you because I don't live far from Chicago. I hope to set up a meeting with you, and soon.

Farewell and fare thee well.

DH

There are parts of this e-mail I don't even understand. A cross between *Apocalypse Now* and *It's a Wonderful Life*? That took him twenty-seven years to complete?

Success breeds psychos. And ever since my name got linked to Vivian Brown's, I'm a magnet for them.

Five minutes after I arrive at the offices at 1030 South Michigan Avenue, Ted Varrick brings his Frankenstein-like stance to my doorway. I'm checking e-mails, deleting most, printing out a few, wishing an assistant could do this. It's a little too early for Ted's smug look.

"You keep going out there on the road, we might not have any clients left," he says.

"Should've joined me."

"Have fun in LA?"

"Always nice to be away from the office." I glance at him.

He smiles. "Had an interesting conversation with Kurt yesterday," Ted says. "He was calling for you."

"Amazing how you pick up more of my calls than your own."

"Darcy was out, and I was the only one here. Kurt's an unhappy camper."

"A short one, too," I say. "Roth here?"

"Today is your lucky day."

There are so many things I want to say, and I almost do. But I have to work with this guy. I have to see him pass me by a hundred times. Our office is not that big.

"Do you know if he booked the California trip?" I ask instead.

"What trip?"

"Oh, you didn't know about it?"

"About what?"

"Laguna Beach. Vivian Brown."

Ted's face turns a couple shades of red as he tries to figure this one out.

"Well, let me know when Roth gets in, okay? Thanks."

He nods and walks away, a big guy with the walk of a ten-year-old who's been thrown out of class.

I continue looking at the flat-screen monitor. An author we represent sends pictures of her new granddaughter. Thanks for sharing. I delete an e-mail from a name I've never heard, someone who has written a sequel to *The Catcher in the Rye.*

"I forgot to tell you," Ted says, coming by my door for another round, "Jon Berrin's people have been trying to get hold of you."

"Who'd you talk to?" I ask.

"I didn't talk to anybody," he says without any show of concern.

"You're really a team player."

"You know, Colin, I was reflecting on the 'team' while you were making a mess of things at Book Expo."

"That bored, huh?"

"And you know, I realized something."

"You should sell used cars?" I reply.

Ted is unfazed by my comment. "It's been quite awhile since you've scored big, hasn't it?"

"Helping with Vivian and Nissen is a full-time job."

"Yeah," he says. "Too bad you don't get commission off those. You need a hit."

"I don't work out of fear, Ted. You start doing that, you're screwed."

"Considering what happened with Lisa and Kurt, you might be too."

He gloats and then struts away.

I see an e-mail from Ian Pollock with the header *Just checking*. I wonder for a second what he's "just checking" on, then remember the twenty pages he gave me. They're in a folder somewhere, probably in my travel briefcase that's still at home.

I decide against opening the e-mail. There's too much to do. I'll get to it later.

People often walk into the Roth Agency offices on the twenty-second floor of the dated Chicago building and see Darcy sitting at her desk close to the door and figure her to be our receptionist or secretary. That's amusing, because Darcy Witt is the only certified lawyer we have working in our offices. She goes over contracts with a discerning eye and a meticulous personality. She's thirty-one, small and dainty and cute, with straight brown hair that could use more styling and a wardrobe that could benefit from a full day of shopping with my wife. Darcy's one stylish item is her small, hip glasses. She isn't quiet, nor shy, though most people think she's both. She is very intelligent, a reason Mr. Roth stole her from the corporate world, and she's incredibly thoughtful, a rare thing in our office full of thoughtless and outspoken men.

Our former office administrator, a leggy blonde who wanted to get into agenting, quit three months ago, and Roth has taken his time filling her place. We've had a revolving door of interns and temps. The current one is a guy in his senior year at the University of Illinois-Chicago. From my office I can hear my colleague Ted ordering the poor kid around.

Colleague sounds so nice and professional, doesn't it? Ted started at Roth a year ago. He came from a New York agency that he left after deciding to move to Chicago for a change of pace. Ted's a big guy, with a square face and thinning hair and lips that seem to move too much. He's articulate and smart and excellent in his job. The only thing Ted doesn't have is character. The only thing that drives him is his desire to earn more money and to sign as many contracts as possible.

I would never in a million years tell him this, but I envy his tenacity and his ruthlessness. The same way he envies my stature at Roth.

Ted and I went out for drinks one night after he'd been at Roth for only a week. In the course of having a few beers, Ted more or less told me that he was going to be taking over the reins of control at Roth within a few years.

"This is the way I see it. Roth is up there in age, and won't be around too much longer. He has two guys working at his place—two capable guys. He's thinking of handing the baton to someone else. To keep the name and legacy of Roth but to assign the responsibilities to someone else."

"You don't know Roth, do you?"

"I know him well enough. So he already has one guy who would be the natural candidate, right? So then why hire me? I'm not your assistant or anything like that. I think it's either because he wants to expand and grow Roth, which is likely enough, or it might be because he is dissatisfied and wants someone else who will eventually take the reins from him."

"You got this all figured out, don't you?"

"I think I do," he said with a cocky grin.

"And you don't mince words either."

"I don't have to. I long for the truth, like any writer."

"You're a writer, too?" I asked.

"Sure. I write. Have a few books in the works."

I laughed.

"What?"

"You know, for a second there I was actually just a tinge nervous. Not because of that Roth misconception. You obviously don't know him. But for a while I thought, wow, here's a guy who really knows what he's going for in the agency world."

"Yeah, and?"

"And you want to be a writer," I said.

"So?"

"That's a dangerous thing."

"I don't think it is."

"Sure you don't. More power to you." I hoisted my glass and toasted to Ted. "Cheers on your new job. And on your rise to power and glory at Roth."

A year later, and the baton still hasn't been given to Ted. But he keeps wagging his tail and waiting with his tongue out.

I get off the phone with Marjorie Hall. It's a little past seven, and the sun is heading down.

Ah, Marjorie Hall. God bless her and every one of her personalities.

She's a freak. A walking Sybil. One minute she's crying and telling me she loves me, in that motherly, sisterly, weird sort of way. The next she's cursing my name and threatening to deal with her publisher directly.

Today, she's crumbling. Her life and career and utter state of being are all in disarray, being held hostage by . . .

Zendrah's red outfit on the cover of *Zendrah's Cage*!

Zendrah is Marjorie's main character for the successful sci-fi series she writes under the pseudonym of James Kern. I try to think of what happened with the cover mix-up and if the publisher told us about the change and part of me whispers something in my ear.

It doesn't matter.

Zendrah. Does it really matter if Zendrah wears a red outfit or a blue?

For the love of Zendrah.

I tell Marjorie I'll call someone at her publisher tomorrow. Then she mentions a typo on the copyright page, and I want to say to her, "Marjorie, nobody reads the copyright page, nobody cares about that the same way nobody really cares if your name is Marjorie or James Kern or Herman Melville."

People read because they want to be entertained. They read Marjorie's books because they are good stories, thrilling yarns as they say, actually exciting sci-fi stories. If only the readers could know that the real and true James Kern that hid behind the curtain was more psychotic than any villain she could create.

So I finally get her to say the word of the day—good-bye—and I make it out the building for home when my cell phone rings.

I know better. But I open the receiver thinking, hoping it's Jen.

"Mr. Colin."

I want to curse.

I've never heard the voice, but I already know who it is.

"You're a difficult man to get hold of."

"Who is this?" I ask.

"It's your next Vivian Brown. Your next dream come true. Your next literary superstar."

"Look, I'm just heading out—"

"Hold on. Hold."

I wait for a moment.

"This is Donald Hardbein."

"How did you get my cell number?"

"The literary world is not that big, Mr. Colin."

"It's Colin."

"You would be surprised how easy it is to get your cell number simply by asking."

"By asking who?"

"That is certainly a question I cannot answer."

"I got your e-mail," I say. "Have you had a chance to see our writer's guidelines?"

"Yes, of course, but do we need such formalities?"

"I'm busy, and I really can't talk long."

"Yes. You can."

His tone startles me. The way he says his words sounds *creepy*.

"Excuse me?"

"I know you're a busy man, but you can talk."

"Look—I'm heading home right now and—"

"I see you."

He says this in a deep voice, almost whispering it. The crazy thing is that I believe him. He might have me in the scope of his high-powered rifle.

"How so?"

"Tall, lean figure? Handsome man, I'd say."

"Donald—"

"Please. Call me Hard."

"Yeah. Look, I really can't talk—"

"Do you believe in fate?"

"Yeah, sure," I say.

"A force determining events in advance? The inevitable?"

"Look, Donald—"

"Hard."

"Listen," I say, not about to call him Hard, "is this about a manuscript?"

"It's about life."

"Uh-huh."

"It's about destiny."

"That's nice."

"It's all about to change, Mr. Colin."

Yes, maybe he is the author of the next Harry Potter series. But I don't want to work with this head case. This is exactly why we have writer's guidelines. Because he might be calling from a little shack in the woods, where he's naked and holding a shotgun along with the novel that he wants someone to publish.

It's hard enough dealing with the talented authors.

"Don, really—"

And then the phone cuts off. And I'm left looking around, wondering if he can truly see me.

I wouldn't be surprised.

From the moment the limo picks me up and I greet Roth in the leather seat next to me to the time we get in our first-class seats and watch O'Hare slip away, I think of Jen.

The dark hair I want to caress. The eyes I want to be lost in. The long lithe body and the sensual voice and those lips and that love.

I miss her.

It's hard to concentrate on anything Roth is saying, but I do my best. This could be the biggest trip of my professional career, and all I can think about is my wife.

It's been several weeks since we last saw each other. At least five days since we spoke.

I couldn't care less about seeing Vivian Brown. *Vivian Vivian Vivian.* The name is beginning to annoy me. Just like Roth and his stories. Just like the terms *page count* and *royalty rate* and *ISBN* and *genre* and anything else about publishing.

I want to unlock a soul, and not be a soul unlocked daily, hourly.

I want to see a smile, not force my fake smile on everyone else.

It's Jen I want. And I want her now.

She is close to sixty, and it seems like she's gotten younger since the last time I saw her. Money and fame can do that to a person. Especially a fifty-something homemaker who spent time toying with a story idea that ended up selling millions. I greet Vivian with a handshake, not a hug, as Roth guides her into the spacious living room of his oceanside house.

"How was the trip?" Roth asks.

She's dressed like a woman half her age, in stylish jeans and a black collared shirt, untucked.

"I love to observe people, though I don't get a chance to do that much anymore. I still find it hard to believe that people recognize me."

Vivian has a soft voice, one of those you have to really pay attention to. I recall some business lunches where people could barely hear her talk over the din of the restaurant.

For a few moments we talk about fame and the irony that a novelist and housewife from northern California can be recognized and asked for autographs. That's what being in *People* magazine and on Oprah can do for you. That's what writing a three-part fantasy series that both children and adults love can do for you.

The comparisons with J. K. Rowling are always there, but Vivian's books were always written for adults and deal with far more adult themes. She has a remarkable originality in her novels and her outlook on life. She can take a ride on a bus and make it into some sort of otherworldly adventure. It's how she views the world around her.

"So, did you survive Book Expo?" Vivian asks me, referring to our last communication via e-mail.

Roth has a permanent good-ole-boy smile on his face. He glances at me, curious what I'll say. We haven't spoken about Book Expo, but that time will come. I'm sure it will.

"Everybody can't wait to hear about the next book."

"Sometimes I want to hear about the next book too," Vivian says with a warm smile that shows off the wrinkles around her eyes. "Sometimes I wish someone would tell me what the next book should be."

"Make sure you don't listen to them," Roth says.

There is a huge window that overlooks the hill below that flows into the beach and then the Pacific. The sun is setting and it's bright now, with blinds blocking some of the view. Roth gets a glass of wine for Vivian, and I pour one for myself.

I study her as she talks to Roth about the novel.

She wears small, fashionable glasses that probably cost a lot. Her hair is straight and cut to fall just below her shoulders. It's highlighted with light brown. She has more color than I remember, and her skin looks softer.

I remember the first time we met, at a small restaurant in San Francisco. It was after I read her first book and saw potential in it, when she first decided to sign on with the Roth Agency. She had thick, wavy hair that needed a cut, thick black glasses, and was about thirty pounds heavier than she is now. Yet her eyes looked the same. Bright-eyed and full of wonder—an expression often used for young kids, but that is how I would describe Vivian, then and now. That's how she looks when she talks about her writing.

I take a sip of the red wine and keep listening.

"Every two or three pages, I would stop and ask myself, what are readers going to think, what are they going to say?" Vivian says, very expressive with her face and her hands as she speaks in a soft tone. "Then I kept telling myself that I need to do exactly what I did for *Sliding into Forever.* Just go with my gut. Write the book and then let it sit. It's just . . . there are a thousand expectations out there now."

Roth states the obvious. "There are probably more than that."

"So do you have any perspective now that you've finished it?" I ask.

She tightens her lips and shakes her head. "No. All I know is that it's big. Very big."

"What's the word count?"

She looks at me and smiles. "It's big."

We sit in a seafood restaurant called Seaside at a table that overlooks the ocean. It's dark outside. We're into the main meal and on a third bottle of wine. Vivian is a lover of seafood, and is working on a yellow fin tuna the same way she writes: with meticulous precision. I notice she takes small bites, never talks whenever she's eating, and seems not to be affected by the wine.

So far there has been a surprising amount of small talk. Her time is valuable. She could be doing a hundred other things, so this meeting is important. Roth has already talked about our strategy for selling her next book, the publishers that he thinks will be the final bidders, the marketing emphasis that he wants to see. We talk about the title, *In Your Memory*, for a long time, but never get to any conclusion. I've noticed that it's harder pushing Vivian into a decision she doesn't want than it used to be. When the sales multiply, authors can be more obstinate. They have a lot more ground to stand on.

We're currently talking about the size of the novel. The conversation has been relaxed, informal, comfortable even.

"So how big is the novel?" I ask again.

For some strange reason, Vivian doesn't want to tell me. "Does it really matter?"

I look at Roth, because we both know it does. She might be one of the top novelists in the world, but the size of a novel still has an impact, especially in a world where everything is instant and short and concise.

"It doesn't matter, not for you," Roth says.

"The thing is, maybe there are two novels in this one. I don't know. I don't have a good perspective on it."

"We'll help you with that," Roth says.

"It's over five hundred thousand words," she says to me.

I nod and try not to appear bothered. And I'm not. I'm just thinking, how is it going to be packaged, should we do two books, how will the editing go.

"The Harry Potter books keep getting longer. Stephen King released *It* and *The Stand*, and those were mammoth."

"Don't worry about it," Roth says. "It'll be great."

I'm a little worried. I shouldn't be. I should be drinking it up and celebrating, but I can't help wondering what shape the manuscript is in. Vivian hasn't shown us anything. She's just given us a page synopsis, and that was brief.

Roth goes to the bathroom, and this leaves Vivian and me alone.

"You don't seem yourself," she tells me.

"I'm sorry. I just—I don't mean to be—"

"You're fine. Is everything okay?"

"Yeah, sure. I'm fine."

"You know, it's just a manuscript. That's all."

I smile and take a sip from my wine.

"You and I both know that if my first book had sold ten thousand copies, we wouldn't be dining oceanside with the famous Bernard Roth."

"Now *we're* dining with the famous Vivian Brown."

"Please." She laughs, and it's a very reassuring laugh. "I know Roth is complimentary and positive, and that's fine. But I want your honesty with this book. Okay?"

I nod. "Of course."

"No. I mean it. Things get different when you sell that many books. The writing—I need to tell you something, Colin."

"What's that?"

I look at her eyes and notice they're a little glassy. We've all had our share of wine. Vivian is a little more open and honest than I remember her to be.

"I've struggled with this story," she says. "It's been difficult. The weight of the world—the expectations out there—sometimes it's impossible to write. Sometimes it's hard because you look at the words and wonder if they're worth thirty-five million people reading them. You wonder if they're worth some huge hefty advance."

"They will be."

She puts a slender and warm hand on mine. "No, I don't want you to say that. Promise me. I don't want false praise. I want honesty. I need honesty."

I haven't been this surprised for a long time. For some crazy reason, I feel tears coming to my eyes.

"That's maybe the best thing an author has said to me in years."

"I don't want a sea of 'yes' people floating around me. I need some people to be honest. I tried so hard with this book. And I believe it's my best. But I—the reality is I just don't know."

"I will be honest, Vivian. I promise."

Roth stumbles onto the hard pavement of his driveway, and for a second I'm not sure what to do. I go to his side and get to one knee.

"You okay?" I ask.

I don't want to grab him and make him feel like a fool. He shakes his head and curses and laughs.

"These hills always get me."

"Let me help you up."

"I'm fine, really."

He takes a minute to get to his feet, then starts to sway toward the door. I keep a hand on his arm and lead him into the house. I search for a light, and he curses and laughs again.

We dropped Vivian off at her hotel ten minutes ago. I drove back from the restaurant, but didn't realize Roth was this inebriated.

"Can never find that thing. Get these houses confused. Sometimes I wake up and wonder where I am. How can a man not know where he is? But I wonder. Naples or Breckenridge or Laguna."

He wants to go into the kitchen but realizes his legs are a bit wobbly. He sits on the nearest seat. "You want a drink?"

"I'm good."

"Nah, come on."

"Really, thanks."

"Get me something," Roth tells me.

"What do you want?"

He laughs. "You're a good kid."

It's the sort of thing you say to your son, not to a thirty-five-year-old business associate.

That's fine. I feel like a kid to Roth.

"Get me something—a water or something so I won't have dry mouth tomorrow. We had a lot of wine, didn't we?"

I nod. "The bourbon didn't help."

"After-dinner drinks. So what do you think?"

I open a bottled water and give it to him. He takes a sip, and his eyes close shut for a brief second. Then he opens them and looks at me.

"The new book. What do you think?"

"I need to read it."

"Yeah, yeah I know. I got it."

His eyes close, and he drops the bottle of water on the floor. I scoop it up before it all drains out.

"I think it's time to get to bed," I tell him.

"All of this. Look around. What's the point, Colin? What's the point?"

His eyes look glazed, but they still have a lock on me.

"Chelsey doesn't care. She's somewhere, who knows where. What's the point? You know? Who cares? But you. You have someone who cares. Where is she?"

"You mean Jen?"

"Yes."

"She's on a business trip."

"So tell me," Mr. Roth asks, his speech now slightly slurring, "how'd you meet your lovely wife?"

"It's not a very interesting story."

"I would imagine anything to do with the beautiful Jennifer Scott is interesting."

"She wasn't Jennifer Scott at the time," I reply.

"Indulge me."

I take a sip from a bottled water. My body feels warm, my head swimming. I'm not a big drinker, but you do what you have to do. If Roth orders wine, I drink it. It's part of the dinner conversation. I realize now, sitting down, I've had a bit too much as well.

"Remember the premiere of that movie based on Max Towher's first book? *Circumstance*?"

"I recall you attending that for me. That was the undoing of our good friend Max, wasn't it?"

"I think it certainly helped," I say, remembering how the bright lights of Hollywood went to Max's head and unfortunately overshadowed his writing talents.

After the movie was released and bombed, it took Max forever to deliver a follow-up to *Circumstance*. And by then, it was too late.

"So you met Jennifer at the party?"

"She came up and offered to get me a drink."

I've told this story to Mr. Roth before, but he still barked out a laugh as though it was the first time he'd heard it.

"And that was it?"

"More or less," I reply, knowing it was far more, but how could I ever explain that to someone like Roth?

"Young fellas like you—always making it look so easy."

"I'm thirty-five," I say.

"Yes, but tell me again—when did you meet her?"

"Seven years ago. We've been married for five."

Mr. Roth nods, looking away at something in the living room. He releases a humorous curse, meant to express his contentment with the entire day. "I got some big news."

I look at him, unsure, almost afraid of what he might say.

"Your precious Jennifer is going to be very happy with today's meeting. This was a big day for you."

"Why is that?"

"I want you to be Vivian's agent. I want to give her to you."

I stare at him, knowing it's gotta be the wine talking.

"Mr. Roth, I—"

"Look at this. Look at me. You think I need more of this?" He curses again. "He who dies with the most toys doesn't win, Colin, and I know that. I'm just too much of a stick-in-the-mud to change my ways. You acquired Vivian years ago. You edited most of her first book. She's yours. I've been thinking about this for a while. And you've run into a bad streak lately. We all do."

I don't blink, don't move. I look at him, wondering if he's going to remember this conversation tomorrow.

"You're a good kid and a good agent, Colin. She's yours. You negotiate the next contract, you keep the monies, you get the recognition. She's all yours."

"I'm—Mr. Roth, I—"

"You can call me Bernard," he says. "Come on. Help this old man to his bed."

It's a strange thing to see my boss, this respected articulate man in his sixties, lying on his back on his bed. I'm about to go when he calls out my name.

"Tell me something," the slurred voice says.

"What?"

"Do you love your wife?"

"Sure I do."

"No, I mean, do you really love her? Do you wake up and take a breath and feel good because she's alive?"

"Yeah, of course."

"No no no no. Come on. I'm talking love. Devotion. I'm talking the real thing. I've never found it. I'm on my third. I mean, Chelsey, you've seen her. You think that's the love of my life? Colin, if you have it, if you have it—I tell you, Colin, don't let it go. All the Vivians in the world don't mean a thing." He curses and laughs. "Not a thing."

I nod and notice wrinkles around his face that make him look sad and lonely.

"Hold on to her," Roth says. "Don't let her go."

My hotel faces the ocean, just like Roth's house on the hill and just like the restaurant we ate at. Everything around here faces the ocean. It's hard not to. It's late, and I'm standing on the edge of a hill dropping down to the crashing waves of the Pacific. The west has an anger about it, a rugged edge to its blue skies. The moon lights up the water, and I stare at it, thinking of Jen, wishing she were near.

From the first time I met Jen, we both wondered if our relationship could actually work. She would fly in to Chicago, I would fly out to Seattle. We had racked up many miles dating like this. Hours on the phone. More spent typing e-mails. We talked about a future but didn't want to take the plunge into marriage haphazardly, as so many other couples did.

I guess that's why my proposal came as a surprise and a shock to her.

It was New Year's Eve. I can picture the giant ballroom floor with hundreds of beautiful couples. Men in tuxedos and women in evening dresses holding each other and swaying. I held on to Jennifer and looked into piercing eyes that would soon be leaving me to go home again.

Tonight it would stop. At least, I hoped it would.

I thought of all the reasons why I loved her.

"Ten!" the crowd shouted.

She was driven and focused.

"Nine!"

She was brilliant and knew exactly what she wanted to do and was doing just that.

"Eight!"

She laughed at my jokes and somehow found enough about me to interest her.

"Seven!"

That tender part in her that didn't seem to fit, the little girl who needed to be pampered and loved.

"Six!"

Silk raven hair I could run my hands through.

"Five!"

Her trim figure, lean and long and lithe. Not too athletic, not too delicate.

"Four!"

Her encouragement to me, and the way she could take my insecurities and evaluate them and shed light on them and help me get past them.

"Three!"

Her desire to start a family one day and have as many children as she could.

"Two!"

Those blue, teardrop-shaped eyes that could look exotic, sad, hypnotic, or sensual depending on the mood.

"One!"

And Jennifer and I kissed and embraced amidst a roomful of strangers. With golden confetti showering us and a sea of balloons engulfing us, I stepped back from her and took the box out of my pocket.

"Jen—"

I took out the ring.

Those eyes teared up, and she embraced me again.

"I love you," she said, which translated meant yes.

It's another empty bed in another unfamiliar room. I sit on the edge, unable to sleep, unable to dream.

I rub my tired eyes and wonder about the past day.

One deal after another. Vivian Brown. Bernard Roth.

IT'S SIX A.M. DO YOU KNOW WHERE YOU ARE?

The opening chapter heading for Jay McInerney's famous eighties novel, *Bright Lights, Big City,* pops into my head for some reason.

Some people end up in a profession and have no idea how they got there; it wasn't their original destination, and they're not sure what route they took to end up at this point. Not me. I know exactly how I got here. I have wanted to get here all along. And I can boil it down to one significant title.

To Kill a Mockingbird.

I was fifteen years old when I read it, not out of interest, but because it was assigned. And that did it. I wanted to meet Harper Lee, to meet other authors like her. I wanted to study the craft of writing, even wanted to write for a short amount of time. But literary fame and success did not fascinate me. I was interested in the concept behind a book, the nuts and bolts of a manuscript. I wanted to know how and why *To Kill a Mockingbird* worked, and why so many others didn't.

So I read more: Twain, Dostoevsky, Camus, Hemingway, Faulkner, Fitzgerald. Writers I was supposed to read, books the classes I took required me to read. And eventually I realized my gift came in analyzing the structures and the words and the concepts behind bestsellers.

And now I pawn off those words and concepts like cheap barter, haggling not over the quality but over the asking price. I home in on multi-book deals and royalty rates and six-figure advances and movie rights and everything that has nothing to do with the art I'm selling.

But I'm not selling art. I'm selling cheap paintings, unfinished drawings, doodlings that will be released in hardcover, front-of-the-store displays and end up on a curbside garage sale in its same original hardcover form, without wrinkled pages or highlighted passages and surely without a well-worn spine.

Instead of reading *The Stranger*, I've become a stranger. A stranger in a profession I am beginning to loathe.

The dim light in the hotel room depresses me, and I take out my phone to try and call Jen. I haven't seen her in a couple of weeks, and I need to hear her voice. I need a reality check. I need inspiration.

Maybe I'm just trying to shake off the fear that's quivering beneath the surface. A fear of being in this place. A fear of not being able to talk to Jen again, of not being able to see her, a fear of not being able to work things out.

A fear of one day having a house on the edge of the ocean and nobody there to share it with.

Catch-22

The manuscript rests in my tote bag, next to the computer. It's in the seat next to me, an unused first-class ticket. I keep staring at my bag. I think of the suitcase from *Pulp Fiction*; Quentin Tarantino never exactly revealed what was inside, but whatever it was got a lot of people killed or in trouble and it glowed and was obviously valuable. That's what this is. It glows and can get me in trouble, and I have no idea what it really is.

In the hotel room, and in the limo, and through the airport, between blurring images and motion and people and places and things gliding by, all I could think about was the consequences.

That's what I'm thinking about now.

I want honesty. I need honesty.

That's what Vivian wants, what she asked of me.

But Roth, and the rest of the publishing world, want the next book. Period.

This isn't working on a book from any old author.

This isn't like waiting for the next Harry Potter book. It's like waiting to see what J. K. Rowling is going to do next, after Harry is finished.

Success is often followed by failure. People love to see failure. And I'm right in the middle.

I open up my bag.

Just one page just read one go ahead.

I shouldn't. I'm tired. I know that this book means everything for my career. I still wonder if Roth meant what he said.

It's just a book. Just an early draft. It's not going to be perfect. There's no harm in reading it.

So I read the first page. No big deal.

Then I read a second.

And on page three, I realize that I'm utterly confused. Completely baffled.

Not by the tension or mystery but because I have no idea—no clue—what I'm reading.

Strange characters say strange things and do strange things. Actually, nothing happens, except a whole lot of back story.

I put the rest of the pages back in my case.

Uh-oh.

The first chance I get. My first big break. Not break, but *BIG* break. A chance to score the home run in the World Series.

Three pages . . . that doesn't mean anything. Right?

It's just three pages.

It's *only* three pages.

It will get better.

It's Vivian Brown, and the world is waiting for this book. They're waiting for her.

To fail.

And here I am. Stuck.

There are careers here. Her career. Roth's. Mine.

Especially mine.

I breathe in and look out the window. The clouds look light and fluffy, and I wonder what it would feel like to fall down through them.

The plane takes a dip, and I make sure the seat belt is buckled tight.

TENDER IS THE NIGHT

"Dad?"

I turn to see my daughter, dark-haired, beautiful, a woman of eighteen, a portrait of her mother.

"What is it?"

"What do you believe in?"

"What do you mean?"

"I mean, what do you believe?"

"That no matter what you dream for, it can become a reality. There's nothing you can't or won't do if you want to."

"That's what a father tells his daughter going off to college. I mean, what do you *really* believe?"

I take a breath and look at eyes of blue and am scared. I'm scared of this conversation because, unlike most times, I don't have an answer.

I take that back. I have an answer. But it's not good enough.

"I don't know," I find myself saying.

"You don't know what?"

"I don't know what I believe in. I don't know who I've become or what I'm meant for. I have no idea why one day is different from another.

I don't know why I'm here or why I'm doing what I'm doing. But I know this. I know this one thing."

She looks at me, and I say her name out loud. Saying it makes me feel good, wonderful, at peace.

"I know that I was meant to be your father."

"But . . . is there anything more? Is there anything to believe in besides ourselves?"

"I don't think so," is all I can say.

And I go to hug her, but she disappears.

And I wake up, on my own, in my bed in an apartment without toys or family photos or any evidence of a daughter.

Is there anything more?

I don't know.

How can I want to be a father—how can I feel the need to be a father—if I have no idea what I believe about anything? Including myself.

At the office, with Vivian's manuscript awaiting my thoughts and a meeting with a prospective author named Larry Gibbons scheduled, all I can do is think of my dream, and of Jen.

Are we really finished?

Part of me has held on to the belief that this is just a bump. She just needs some time. But time is growing.

So are my fears.

I call Jen and get her voice mail. I decide to send her a text message.

Please call. Need to talk. Where are you???

This tactic has never worked with Jen. But I want her at least to know that I miss her, that I'm frustrated with her, that I'm needing to see her.

I am afraid she doesn't need to see me.

Peter Benchley, the guy who penned *Jaws*, said this: "It took me fifteen years to discover that I have no talent for writing, but I couldn't give it up because by that time I was too famous."

Larry Gibbons could say that, too.

Do I really want to represent Larry?

The truth is, I think he's an abysmal novelist.

Bestselling, sure, but also really bad.

He's in town to discuss his next contract and to see if we're the agency for him. He just dumped his last one, a noted New York agent. That alone waves the red flag.

I think of the term "the next contract." Every single author wants to talk about *the next contract*. The next paycheck. The next affirmation of their talents. The next wheeling and dealing.

It's an hour before he's coming in, and I'm sitting in my office trying to read through his latest runaway bestseller, *An Unalterable Aftermath*. This is the sixth in his seven-book Chad Russell series. I call it the "Al" series. Every book starts with a similar word: *Terminal, Fatal, Final, Harmful, Irrefutable*. The seventh book in the series will be called—you guessed it—*Lethal Payback*.

As I'm reading, the only word that comes to mind is *awful*.

Sometimes you wonder who makes these decisions. Did somebody just sit down with a thesaurus? *Unalterable Aftermath*. Is there any way you *could* alter an aftermath? It doesn't make a whole lot of sense. *Lethal Payback*. Two bland words that have been used hundreds of times. *Fatal Fallout.* Ooh, gives me the shivers. *Final Consequence.* What else can a consequence be?

I know these books have sold in the millions. They've reached the *New York Times* bestseller list. They are for the John Grisham–Michael Crichton–Tom Clancy crowd. Men and women who like plot-driven novels with ruggedly handsome antiheroes and wretchedly awful bad guys. Those who don't mind dastardly adverbs and delectable adjectives. Lots of blood, violence, women who easily give themselves up to their studly protagonists, and outcomes with a neat little twist.

I can see why they've sold.

But the bigger an author gets, the more entitled he or she starts to feel.

Entitled. That's what it's all about.

Larry Gibbons started writing in his thirties and had a few literary novels published. They were ripped by critics because he was trying too many things and wasn't particularly good at any of them. "Ridiculous use of second-person perspective, for no reason" one of the critics stated, probably with a smile on his face. They died quick and quiet deaths. Larry could have easily stopped writing, his publishing dreams dying with those out-of-print tales.

But then he tried something different. He wrote a gritty pulp novel entitled *Puncture Wound.* Nobody had ever heard of Larry Gibbons, so it wasn't like he was switching genres in midstream. *Puncture Wound* didn't perform well at first, but it got good buzz and word of mouth. That wonderful, wistful phrase every author wishes for: word of mouth. And after another stand-alone book involving a different character sold moderately, the publisher came back to Larry asking for more "Carolina Cal" stories.

Larry brought the burned-out detective back for four more novels. And thus began his sales, his audience, and a string of ridiculously titled bestsellers: *Flesh Wound, Gaping Wound, Bloody Wound,* and my favorite, *Severed Wound.* It's like something from a Monty Python clip. But novels can basically be called anything as long as the reader will somehow remember it. *Oh, yeah, that "wound" series.* When they remember them, they buy them.

If you hit it big, your publisher doesn't want you to open the creative vault and begin to unearth story ideas you've lugged around for a whole lifetime. No. If something works, they want it to work again. And again. And again.

I'm curious to see what Larry thinks the Roth Agency can offer him. Especially since Roth himself can't be there to join us.

Our excuse is that he's meeting with Vivian.

Truth is, Roth is still in Laguna Beach.

I try to prepare myself. Not to critique or judge or conduct a personality profile. To sell.

First to sell Larry on us. Then to sell Larry to them.

This is what I'm good at.

And I keep reminding myself of that, over and over again.

The mouth moves and the voice verbalizes and there are words but you don't hear them get them really truly get them. You smile and you theorize but you're not here you're not really truly here. The man curses and jokes and pokes and you laugh it up with him but you're not really here.

You look around the room at everything. Everything in its right place.

The author and the agents and the talk and the words and everything in its right place.

His Southern drawl and Southern charm. Ted's smirk and stench.

The coffee mug hoisted up by the personal assistant. Darcy's hand taking notes.

You say something you don't mean.

You explain something you don't understand.

You suck it up and you sell and near the end of the three-hour meeting, Larry Gibbons is sold.

Yes, it's all okay.

Everything is good.

Every single thing is exactly in its right place.

Except you.

It's evening and I'm close to home when my cell phone rings. I stop on the street and feel a faint bit of hope grip me. It's been so long since I've heard from Jen. I just want a word, a sign, something, anything.

I pick up without looking at the caller ID. "Hello?"

"No voice mail this time?"

It's him again.

"Who is this?"

"Your next big ticket to fame and fortune."

I'm about to hang up, but realize I can't hear all that well. It might be Larry Gibbons.

I walk to get better reception, the evening sun leaking in between the buildings I stand next to.

"Who is this?" I ask again.

"Donald."

"Come on."

"Now now."

"Look—you gotta stop bothering me—"

"Hold on hold on hold on," he blurts out quickly. "Let me explain myself."

"Yeah."

"The e-mail I just sent you. Please disregard."

What is this guy talking about?

"I didn't—it's not quite there yet. And I don't want you going into this with a bias already."

"Okay," I say, wanting to get off the phone.

"I will be sending you the manuscript soon."

"Don—look—"

"Nonononono," he chimes in.

Maybe he's high on crack or something.

"I've got a winner, and you've gotta believe it."

"Sure."

"I know you'll feel the same. *I know it.*"

"How did you—"

But he hangs up before I can ask.

There are certain places in Chicago that remind me of Jen. For the first few years of our marriage, after her brave decision to move to Chicago from Seattle, I got reacquainted with the city I thought I knew. Jen has this amazing ability to discover new places and new things. A tiny family-run restaurant. A quaint Irish pub down a hidden alley. The Thai restaurant we love. An antique shop with amazing prices.

Jen finds new things because she's always looking for them. And in our magical honeymoon period, which for us lasted thirty-six months, the two of us were able not only to discover the person each had married but the city in which we decided to live.

I stop by a local pub to have a couple beers and a sandwich. It's nice to go to places and sit and listen to the crowd and not have to do anything. I leave around seven-thirty when the sun is setting. Walking the Chicago streets on summer evenings like this—not too humid, not too busy—reinvigorates me.

On my walk home I pass a tapas restaurant Jen found that had amazing food, drinks, and music. A great combination. We went there so often, the bartender would ask us what music we were in the mood for—upbeat or chill-out—each time we'd come in.

We haven't been there in a couple of years.

Both of us knew things would get busier. We hoped they would get busier. But I never really thought of those things, the ramifications of Jen having success in her work, the consequences of my life on the road. For a while I remember being blindly oblivious to the rest of the world. For a while it was just Jen and I, and there was so much to learn about this wonderful woman I'd married.

Does anybody ever really, truly know the person they love?

Even after all this time, surrounded by a city full of memories, I'm still not sure.

It's a little after eight by the time I open the door to the apartment, expecting to see darkness greet me.

Instead, I see a wall across from me shimmering in liquid light. Candles burn from various places: the dining room table, the kitchen counter, the living room. I count at least half a dozen as I close the door behind me and set down my leather briefcase. Instrumental music, light and ethereal sounding, comes from the bedroom down the hallway.

I can't help the smile on my lips. I slip off my suit coat and drape it over a dining room chair.

I walk across wood floors to the carpeted living room and toward the hallway leading to our bedroom.

The music grows louder.

For a moment I wonder if I'm in a dream.

"Jen?" I call out.

I pass the office and guest bedroom and get to the slightly open door to our bedroom. I nudge it open with a finger.

Faint light spills from candles on the dresser in our bedroom. It's a soft glow, a slight hue. A delicious scent reminds me of other nights like this.

"Am I dreaming?" I ask.

I hear footsteps coming toward me. Suddenly the weight of the world is gone, and I forget what the past week and month and year have been like. I forget the concrete encased around my heart and the metal siding plastered around my soul. I forget our last conversation.

I love this part of marriage, the eagerness for what is coming next, the expectation that never seems to die, the excitement of a late-night encounter with my beloved.

She steps out from the darkness.

I see the outline of Jen and try to find the words to tell her how beautiful she looks. She moves across the room and then stops, waiting, her eyes on me and the smile beaming on her full lips.

"What are you doing here?" I ask.

"Waiting for you. Now hush."

"Nobody's here. Why are you whispering?"

"Why are you talking?"

I let her embrace me. She looks up, and I can see the surprise on her face.

"What?"

"You're trembling," she says.

"I'm scared."

"Of what?"

"That this is somehow—the last—"

She stops me with a kiss, then nuzzles her mouth next to my ear. "I'm here, Colin, and I'm not going anywhere, and all I want is you next to me."

Her kiss is soft, and again I can feel my body trembling.

I don't say another word. Not for a very long time.

Before I awake, I hover in the glow of a memorable night. Blurred images, shapes moving in the dark, shadows and whispers and declarations. A glance at the dial revealing 1:28 and a sliver of light from a partially closed door and a sea of folds and silk. Of drifting off and then finally settling down and reliving it all until I awake to a "Colin."

The blinds in our bedroom are closed, and I can tell the day outside is overcast.

"You turned off the alarm," Jen says, sitting on the edge of the bed.

"I know."

"It's nine o'clock. Is that okay?"

"I'm taking the morning off. Or the day."

"Hungry?" she asks.

I laugh. "Very."

"I'm making breakfast."

"Do I have to get out?" I ask her with a grin.

She looks down at me, her hair swooping to one side of her matching black shimmering robe. What a way to wake up, I think.

"Not if you promise you'll make it worth my while."

Her kiss feels light and warm as I convince her to delay breakfast just a little.

"So when did you know you were coming back?" I ask her.

Jennifer sits with her back against the headboard, propped up by three pillows, wearing my Bears T-shirt. After breakfast we stayed in bed, watching television shows I didn't even know existed. There's a show on the cable channel Animal Planet that is all about baby animals. Jen watches it in fascination and adoration. They're showing a border collie giving birth to half a dozen puppies.

"Just a few days ago. And even then, I wasn't sure."

"You weren't sure about what?"

She shrugs. "A lot of things."

"Jen—"

"I don't want anything heavy right now. Please?"

I nod.

"How was your trip?"

"I wanted to tell you—it was big. Roth said that he's giving me Vivian."

"To represent?"

"To represent," I repeat. "Completely. Totally."

Her eyes widen, and she beams with surprise. "That is big."

"That's huge. It's exactly what I've been waiting for. Only I'm still not a hundred percent sure . . . Roth was a bit drunk when he said it. But I know he meant it."

"That's great, Colin."

"There's one catch."

"Being?"

"I started reading the new book."

"Bad?"

I nod. "The start, at least. But it's—it's really bad. It makes no sense. I'm not sure what I'll do if the whole novel is like that."

"You tell her."

"Easier said than done. Roth is expecting big things. He still gets a cut, of course. Regardless of what happens, he gets his cut."

Jen looks at me, her face absent of any makeup, her skin fair and virtually flawless. "It'll be fine."

I lean against her and feel relaxed, more relaxed than I have been in a long time.

"It's good to have you home," I say.

She glances at me. "It's nice to be home."

"It's nice not to be doing this for a reason, to just want to be together, you know?"

"Colin?"

"Yeah."

"Just . . ."

"Okay, yeah. No problem."

I'm getting ready to go into work, already a couple hours late. Jen sits on the edge of the bed and lets out a sigh.

"I'm so tired."

"Work?" I ask.

"Life."

I'm trying to keep things light, to not argue or bring up the obvious. So I don't say anything.

"You know how you've always talked about putting in your time? waiting for the payoff?" Jen finally asks.

"Only every day or so," I say.

"That's how I feel. But lately I've been on a roll. The people I've met—it's unbelievable. I sometimes wake up and realize I'm working with this huge name that I would have died just to be in the same vicinity of five years ago."

"It's all about perspective."

"I know. The scary thing is—if I do stop, for whatever reason, the movies will keep being made. They'll find another up-and-coming designer to work on their pictures."

I start to protest, but Jen stops me with a serious glance. "It's true. I'm just starting to build a name for myself. And if . . ."

"If what?"

"If I stop, what happens then?"

I open my mouth to ask about our future, our family, our plans, but I stop myself. It's been an incredible night and morning, and I don't want to talk about the B word.

"How much time do you have off?" I ask.

"I've actually got a flexible schedule for the next month."

"Really? Let's get away, Jen. Somewhere far away. Tropical. Hot. Away from—away from here."

"We can't go anywhere now. You're swamped."

"I have to read a manuscript."

"But you can't just decide to take off a chunk of time without asking."

"Sure I can. Roth doesn't care. I've been busy enough. Too busy."

"But I've been gone, and I need to be able to—"

"We need to get away," I say.

She looks at me, studies my face. Sometimes her beauty overwhelms me. Makeup off, just raw dynamic beauty.

"Jen—it would be good for us. It would feel like last night and this morning. A whole week of this."

"Sex can't cover reality."

"Yes, it can. Many times."

We both laugh. I move a hand to tickle her. She moves closer to me.

"Come on," I say. "Let's each write out half a dozen choices. Then we draw to see where we go."

"What about the house?"

"It'll keep on schedule. They'll be starting the framing just when we leave."

"And can you forget about work? At least part of the time?"

"Of course I can."

"You swear?"

"It'll just be about us, like old times. No distractions. I'll just be reading. No big deal."

"Okay. But whatever we draw, we go there, right?"

I nod. "Wherever."

She jumps out of bed and disappears. In a minute she's back with a sheet of notebook paper, which she folds and tears into a dozen pieces. She gives me a pen and six pieces of paper, and I write down places. Six warm, wonderful destinations. Frankly, I don't care where we go. If Gary, Indiana, comes up, I'll take her there.

Jen grabs a Cubs cap from the dresser, shuffles the slips of paper in it, and offers the cap to me.

"You choose," I tell her. "You're the lucky one."

She closes her eyes for a moment, then picks.

To Kill a Mockingbird

Rain falls. It's a gushing torrent that started three days before we arrived and appears to have no intention of stopping. They call it Tropical Storm Boris, which we first heard mentioned by a blonde meteorologist on a local news station.

The dark clouds and drenched surroundings that greet us in Cancun fit our mood. Jen hoped for the three essential S's of vacation: sun, sand, and surf. And none would be experienced today. After the bus takes us on a twenty-minute trip to the hotel strip, the narrow stretch of land consisting primarily of resorts, bars, and restaurants, we get out at the hotel underneath a massive canopy that shelters us from the monsoon. Jen looks out toward the street that resembles a poor, wet dog and then looks back at me.

Hotel Aquasoul lives up to our expectations, from the moment we set foot in the massive lobby with its ceiling that climbs twelve stories and lush greenery that falls over the walls of each floor. Soft, tranquil music that serves as a soundtrack for your dreams plays delicately in the background—loud enough to convey the mood but not enough to make out the song or the music. And even as we walk to the registration desk and look out the long, tall windows to see nothing but steady spigot-streams of water, the mood is still there.

"It's very pretty in here," Jen says.

I look down at her and smile.

"It's okay," she says, grabbing my hand.

It's nobody's fault. We'll try to make the most of it. The main thing is we're together. I look at those blue eyes and flowing dark hair and already picture myself in her arms.

So we'll have to spend more time inside.

I can think of many things to do.

From the king-sized bed in the center of the room, I can look out the sliding glass doors and see the ocean. We're on the eleventh floor of the hotel, the club level. Rain limits the view outside, the ocean beyond looking turbulent and lonely. I watch in hypnotic fashion as Jen gets ready. It's six-thirty, and we haven't stepped out of the room once since arriving. We're considering an early dinner. The question is whether to go out and brave the stormy conditions or eat in the hotel.

Sometimes I marvel, watching Jen get ready to go out. The dark locks and long, white body disappearing and coming back made up and dressed up, going from raw beauty to stunning magnificence.

I think of the last few moments. The last hour. I wish life could always be like this. It doesn't matter if the ocean rushes against the shore a couple hundred feet away from us. It doesn't matter if it's raining or snowing or hailing golf balls, or if it's a sunny, humid day. What matters is we're together, not worrying about schedules or trying to connect or leaving soon and saying good-bye. We're together.

"Are you going to get ready?" Jen asks.

Her hair is pulled to the side now, falling over one shoulder. Her makeup is already on. She wears a short, red silk robe I gave her a few years ago. This is definitely not the wear-around-the-condo robe. It only makes select appearances.

"You look stunning."

"Where do you want to go?" she says, ignoring my comment.

"How about we order room service?" I suggest with a smile.

"I didn't get ready to order room service."

She faces a mirror and continues playing with her hair. I can see her face in the mirror, her eyes that look straight ahead. They sneak a peek at me and see me admiring her.

"Stop," Jen says with a shy smile.

I know better to ask her *Stop what?* Guys are so transparent. I jump up and move behind her and give her a peck on the neck.

Her eyes sparkle and say, *There will be plenty more time for that.*

Everywhere I look, parenthood abounds. From the waiting families at O'Hare to the guy on the plane reading the birth-order bestseller. For once, I didn't think of the writer or the publisher. I felt a distaste that I wasn't reading it, that I didn't *deserve* to read it.

In the elevator going down, we see a mother and her two children. In the lobby, another family is gathered near the door. We pass a father and his daughter who look to be waiting on mommy. This is not the typical family vacation spot, like Disney or Universal Studios.

Maybe it's a conspiracy.

The mothers and fathers of the world have united. They've somehow slipped me drugs to nullify my sperm count and have given Jen egg-sleeping pills. They've bonded together to prevent us from entering their select but innumerable club.

There are enough parents in the world, they say. *And we care for our children in a special way you'll never live up to. We are part of a club that's better than Club Med and has many members but is really not for you so bye-bye.*

I look at the stunning woman at my side. I'm a successful, worldly-wise man with a beautiful wife, on vacation, and I'm thinking of sperm counts.

Everywhere I turn, there is a reminder of my failure. Perhaps that's too harsh. My ineptness, then. And even though I'm far away in a vacation spot with my wonderful Jen, there is not one thing I can do about it. The timing is not right. The moment is not right. Life is just not exactly right.

The planets aligned long enough to allow me to meet the woman of my dreams. Couldn't it happen for just one more moment to allow the two of us to answer another one?

Just one more dream answered. That's all I want.

Just one more.

There are a thousand things I want to say to the woman across from me, but "It's pretty loud in here" is not one of them. It's just a way to talk, to start a conversation.

Jen looks at me and says, "What?"

We sit in some Mexican restaurant the concierge recommended and gave us a coupon for. I've already learned Cancun is big on coupons. Everywhere you go somebody slips you a couple. Jen sips her drink and wrinkles her nose.

The mariachi band looks bored. They move around the large, crowded room, and I pray they don't come next to us.

I state the obvious. "I hope the weather's better tomorrow."

"It's getting worse," Jen says, looking out toward the open patio and the rain pouring over the cloth roof.

"It'll be fine."

"I wrote Hawaii down, you know? Aruba. I couldn't come up with six, so I wrote down—"

"I wrote Cancun down too," I tell her. "Maybe you picked mine."

"Yeah, but *I* picked it."

I reach over and grip her hand to let her know it's okay.

They bring us their version of chips and salsa. A few thick chips and this dry tomato-and-onion mix. It's fine, but it takes us four minutes to finish it. We talk about how much we miss our favorite Mexican restaurant and the chips and salsa there.

I order what I think is their version of fajitas. It's actually this jambalaya stew with strange chunks of cheese and mystery meat in it. Jen and I stare at the round pot and wonder what in the world I ordered.

"What made you leave?" I ask her.

"What do you mean?"

"I know you had your work. But this time, when you left, when you didn't call or e-mail, I didn't know—"

"Colin."

"We have to talk about it sometime."

She looks at me, and I can tell she is thinking. It's not that she won't discuss this, but it's timing. Jen needs to make up her mind on things, needs to understand how she feels about things before communicating.

"What do you want to talk about?"

"Everything. You and me, children, our future."

Jen finishes a bite and shakes her head. "I still have to figure that out."

"Three weeks wasn't enough time?"

"I was working, Colin."

"So was I."

"So what'd *you* figure out then?" she says, challenging.

"I just want to be with you. That's what I know."

"Sometimes that's not enough, Colin."

She says something else, but I can't hear. The rain is as loud as our dwindling conversation.

"Jen—"

"Colin, we just got here. Maybe if it was hot and sunny, I'd be in a better mood. I just don't want the heaviness. Not tonight. Okay?"

I nod. I look over at a large table with five couples. People our age, probably all vacationing with each other. I wonder what other couple—much less four other couples—we would get to go on a vacation with us. Most of the couples Jen and I used to pal around with have gone missing in our lives. Perhaps by accident. Perhaps on purpose. Most of them now have kids. The couples we used to hang out with are "couples" no more.

There is a long silence between us, and I can't help myself. "What are you thinking?" I ask.

"Nothing."

I'm not used to dinners with limited conversation. And I'm not used to quiet dinners with Jen. It feels like we're strangers who have just sat down to eat. Strangers who share this amazing physical connection, but who don't know what else to talk about or do.

"Want anything else to drink?"

She shakes her head. I can tell the dark mood has come over her.

"This afternoon was really nice," I say.

"What?" she asks, not hearing me.

I shake my head.

More should be said. I just don't know where to start.

Her hair is flat and clings to the back of her neck, and her eyeliner is smudged. We sit in the bus like kids coming back from a day at the beach, except we don't have towels and are wearing nice clothes. My new sandals got completely doused when we ran across the street to the bus stop and I stepped in a puddle two feet deep.

Ah, Cancun.

A young, portly woman steps on the bus wearing low-cut, tight jeans and what looks like a bikini-top ready to burst. She stands close to us, and I try to look past Jen outside the open window of the bus. Jen looks at her, then at me, and we both try to hold our laughter.

The young woman is pushing two hundred pounds, mind you. She's not *Sports Illustrated* swimsuit model material.

We've been on the bus for twenty minutes. There is flooding on the streets, flooding—I can't believe I'm even saying that word—and traffic on the narrow two lanes has bulged to a halt. Rain still falls. Of course it does. Why wouldn't it?

"Get me back," Jen says.

I wonder if she's referring to the hotel or to home.

After another ten minutes, the bus starts to pick up speed. The air blowing in is cold, but we can't close the window next to us. Both of us are freezing—I have a muddy arm wrapped around Jen's shivering shoulders.

We round a corner and the bus blows through a pool of rainwater on the street. It blasts into the bus and everybody on the right side gets soaked, just like they would in a ride at an amusement park.

Jen looks at me, dirty water dripping from her nose, and bursts out laughing. It's the first time she's laughed all night.

"This is horrible," I tell her.

The big woman next to us adjusts her top, which is doing a bad job holding in everything it needs to.

I'm feeling queasy.

"What else did you pick?" Jen says, a subject we've thoroughly destroyed.

"Don't," I say.

"I wrote down St. Lucia."

"Puerto Vallarta," I tell her. "Who knows—maybe it's raining there too."

"Maybe we're just unlucky."

"No we're not."

I give her a kiss on her moist cheek, but it doesn't lighten her mood.

"You gotta admit . . ." she says, a weary smile on her face.

"What?"

". . . we really do have bad timing."

I'm next to her, in her arms, and as connected as I feel to Jen, something is missing. We can't be any closer, yet there is a huge distance between us, a wall that I can't climb over or break through.

"Colin?" she asks in the darkness.

"Yes."

"I'm scared."

"Of what?" I pull her even closer.

"That this is all there is."

"What do you mean? You and me?"

"And our jobs, our apartment, our bank accounts, all of it."

"What are you talking about?"

"I'd give it all away. I'd give up everything just to be able to know, to be able to hold our child—" She starts to cry.

"It's going to be okay."

"Don't say that," Jen says. "It's not. I'm so confused, and I wake up and go to bed feeling so empty inside."

"It will pass."

"No, it won't. Every time I want to tell you how I'm feeling, how I'm really feeling, you tell me it'll pass, but don't you understand? It's not going to get better. I just feel so . . . so alone."

"But I'm right here."

"I know. And that's why I'm scared. That's why I'm confused. That's why I don't know what to do."

I see my feet dangling from high above the water. Clear, blue water that gently glides below me. My hands and arms are above me, and I'm drifting through the air. Occasionally moving up, then coasting down. It's warm and the sun is behind me and I can see the whole surrounding area and then I realize how high I am and I start to panic and not breathe. I try, but the breathing doesn't come. It's like I'm breathing in nothing. I'm choking. I can't move and my body is still flying and I'm gagging and then all of a sudden I jerk and feel a touch on my shoulder—

Colin.

It's dark, and I can hear her now.

Are you okay?

I breathe finally and find myself in the king-sized bed.

Colin?

"Sorry," I tell Jen.

I wipe sweat from my forehead and keep my eyes open. I feel light-headed, as though I just got off a roller coaster ride. Or an elevator ascending a hundred floors.

You sure?

"Yeah."

It takes me awhile to get back to sleep.

"Would you like another?"

I look at the petite, tanned woman with the pretty, flawless face and tell her "Sure."

She takes the empty glass away to get another.

Maybe I'm not sitting by the pool taking in rays, but I could get used to this.

It's somewhere between eleven and twelve. I don't have on my watch to know. Jen is getting ready in our room below, just a staircase away. It's still raining outside, still looking as gray and murky as the ocean water. I'm in the club lounge, a large open area on the twelfth floor with several rooms full of tables and chairs and sofas. I'm sitting on a leather love seat, looking out a wall encased in glass to the stretch of hotels and bars that is Cancun. The ocean is on my left. Nobody is in the water. Few people are in the streets either.

My drink comes, and I thank the woman. They serve breakfast and a few snacks up in the concierge level. Right now, I'm the only person in the lounge besides the attendant.

I'm on page 145 of *In Your Memory*. It's bad when you're counting the pages you're on like minutes in detention hall. Every page I finish fills me with bewilderment and stunned surprise. But mostly fear.

I can sell this, but what's it going to do to Vivian's career?

I want honesty. I need honesty.

I can see Vivian's sincerity as she says this to me.

Does she really want to know the truth? And it's only my perspective. What if I'm wrong?

I keep reading and know that I'm not wrong. Lit professors and fans of pop fiction would both agree that this story isn't strong. It's convoluted, and descriptive in places that shouldn't be, and it doesn't make sense.

I scribble notes in the margins. *What's this referring to? Where's this going?*

Confusing. Too much exposition.

On page 150, I write something else.

I'm not sure what's going on here. Am I supposed to be confused?

It's a scary thing, reading this. I'm not reading a typical novel. I didn't pay eight bucks for a paperback to read mindlessly on a plane ride. No. This is my future I'm reading. Vivian's future. Roth's future. A publishing company's future. Many people will be affected by these pages. These hundreds of thousands of words that may or may not move me and other readers.

So far I haven't been moved the least bit.

Every great artist has failures. Some have spectacular ones. Name a popular or critical author, and I can recount a book that missed its mark, that just didn't live up to the potential. This is the reason artists, whether they're musicians or photographers or painters or actors or writers, all walk a fine line. Because with every stroke of the brush or line uttered or written, they are setting themselves up to fail. Some don't worry about failure. Others cope via drugs or alcohol. This is why the greatest artists are sometimes those with the most messed-up lives.

It's just a story, I tell myself. *It's just a story and it can be made better. And that's what I'm here for. It's not the end of the world. It's just a story that's a little off track.*

But I know that it's more than "a little" off track.

"Colin?"

Jen walks over and sits on the leather chair next to the love seat.

"Hey."

"How is it?"

"Boring. And incomprehensible. But other than that, it's fabulous."

She laughs. "You going to stay up here awhile?"

I nod, and my eyes go back to the page. She says something else that I don't quite hear, and I tell her "Sure" and continue reading. She wanders off, and I figure she's going to get the magazines she brought with her.

And the rain keeps falling.

I slide the key in and out and open the hotel door.

"Jen?"

I find her sitting on the couch near the open sliding glass door. The rain continues to pour.

"You okay?"

"Yeah," she says quietly.

The television is on CNN. I sit down on the couch next to her.

"I thought you were coming back up."

"Last time I was there you didn't seem too interested."

"What do you mean?"

"You were buried in your book. I asked if you were going to come down to the room in a little while, and you said sure."

I look at her, but she's looking at the television.

"Jen, I'm sorry—I let the time slip away."

"I know."

"Hey, really. I'm sorry."

She looks at me and paints a sad smile on her face. "It's okay," she says.

We stare at each other for a few minutes. She's wearing a long, white silk robe. She's been waiting for me awhile.

"I'm sorry I didn't come down right away."

Jen continues to watch the television. I move over and kiss her neck. It's overcast in our room, just as it is outside.

She pulls away.

"Jen—"

She stands up, and her robe glides open. I see a glimpse of pearl white nylon adorning her long legs. She walks back into the bathroom and shuts the door.

I walk hand in hand with this beautiful woman, this stranger by my side. The masses move past, beckoning us to their club or their restaurant, promising free drinks and fun. The streets are still shimmering in their dampness, the reds and oranges and blues sparkling from buildings with loud, thumping basses and murky insides.

Jen wears her hair up, so I can see the back of her neck. A white shirt clings to her body, her khaki pants rising high above her ankles.

I suggest one of the clubs, but she shakes her head.

This place seems unreal. The people can be divided into starry-eyed tourists ready to party and jaded locals ready to sell. Smells vary from spicy foods to the sweet-and-sour smell of stale beer and liquor staining walls and sidewalks and doorways and souls. This is somewhere a guy goes for spring break, not for a getaway with his wife. This is a place you go to find fake love, not the place to embrace the real thing.

We walk hand in hand until we reach the Italian restaurant. Don't get the pizza, they warned us, but otherwise it's great food.

Two hours earlier, I could have been saying words of love and offering delicate and long kisses. I could have heard the rain falling and kissed her lips and brushed her disheveled hair and told her how much I loved her and how much this place and this weather and all of it didn't matter how all that mattered was the two of us forgetting the rest of the world.

Instead, I was reading a manuscript.

I hear the promise I made Jen.

It'll just be about us, like old times. No distractions.

But how could I know that the novel I'm reading would be atrocious? How could I know each page would be a pain to read instead of a joy?

I'm thinking about what to say to Bernard, what to say to Vivian, what to say to the publishers, the retailers, the market.

Meanwhile, I have no idea what to say to Jen.

"I need to tell you something," Jen says, as we're starting to eat our salads.

This restaurant is a lot quieter than the Mexican restaurant from the night before. The soft glow of a candle lights her face. I take a sip of my drink and wait for her to go on.

"There's an opportunity coming up."

"Another movie?"

She nods her head.

"How soon?"

"Right away. This fall maybe."

"What's it called?" I ask.

"*Immersion.* It's based on a bestselling novel."

"Oh yeah. Stephen Conroy."

"Have you read it?"

I shake my head. "I think I own a copy."

"It's a Gore Verbinski film. The director of *Pirates of the Caribbean. The Ring.* And guess who's probably going to be starring in it?"

"Robin Williams," I say, more as a joke than a reasonable guess.

"Come on. Who have I been talking about working with?"

"Brad Pitt."

"No," she says with a grin, "but close."

"Tom Cruise."

"It's a she. Verbinski directed a movie with Brad Pitt and this woman."

I'm totally lost.

"Think biggest star out there."

"Julia Roberts?"

Jen nods, not containing the smile on her face, not touching her salad. She takes a sip of her white wine.

"Can you believe it?"

"No. I mean, yes, of course I can. You're very good at what you do."

"You don't know what I do."

"I know as much about your job as you know about mine."

"You make publishers pay you big bucks for big manuscripts. Right?"

"That's like me saying all you do is pick out outfits they wear on the pictures."

"That is sorta what I do."

I take a bite of my salad. "I can't believe you didn't tell me before this."

"I wanted to surprise you."

"So where will it be filmed? I'm doubting it's in Chicago."

"North Carolina."

I'm actually a bit relieved. "Could be worse. It could be in Russia or somewhere."

"It'll be in the Smoky Mountains."

I take another sip of my wine. Background music pipes in a soft, swanky melody.

"Being in the Smokies with Julia Roberts. I could think of worse things."

"It'll probably be for a few months."

I nod. She's studying me to see a reaction, any reaction. I'm studying her to see what she's wanting from me. Affirmation. Celebration. Hesitation.

I can't help being disappointed. But I think of my string of recent work events—losing Lisa Beck and Kurt Dobbs and now reading a disaster of epic proportions—and ask the obvious.

"It's a big opportunity, right?"

She nods.

"Then what can I say?"

Jen brushes a piece of falling hair from her face. She looks down and picks at the salad. "Tell me what you're thinking."

"That it sounds like a big deal."

"No—tell me what you're *really* thinking."

I hesitate. I'm not as good at being brutally honest with Jen as she is with me. I can tell her good stuff all day long, but I don't want to put my emotional baggage in her lap.

"I'm just wondering where that leaves us."

"I know."

"I need to know where we are, Jen. Where we stand. I need to know—"

I need to know that there's one thing in my life that's right, one thing that's firm, one thing that is pure and good.

Jen looks at me with earnest, haunting eyes, waiting for me to finish. Finally she goes ahead. "Everything in my career is going right. I just keep thinking, one more picture. One more big picture. And that will be it. But every time, it opens another door."

"Then you should walk through that door."

"Do you really want me to?" she asks.

"It's not right to ask you not to."

"I just wonder."

"What?"

"Why is it—why do I *want* to walk through that door? I mean, sometimes I feel I want that more than wanting to start a family. And I know how selfish that sounds. But as each month passes, I keep questioning why some doors open and some remain closed."

I'm too surprised at her comments to answer.

"Is that fate or God telling us we're not ready to be parents? Maybe we're just not destined to have a family."

"How can you say that?"

"That's just how I feel."

"So you're saying that your work is suddenly more impor—"

"It's not *suddenly* more important than anything," Jen interrupts. "It's always been important. Sometimes I want to quit. Sometimes I want to get away. But when I start really thinking of the great opportunities I'm being given—it's hard."

"If we don't ever see each other, there's no way we'll be able to start a family," I say out of frustration.

"We need for me to take this job," Jen says.

That's a low blow.

"I told you—"

"You keep saying that the big day is going to come. And that's fine, Colin. But we don't know that for sure."

"I know it will," I say.

"You don't. You're having doubts about Vivian's manuscript."

"So you're doing this because of me? Taking this job because I'm not doing my share?"

"I didn't say that."

"More or less."

"I knew you'd get this way."

I shake my head and let out a bitter chuckle. "Don't give me that. I support you in *everything* you do. Everything."

"What's another six months?"

"You've already made up your mind," I say. "What's next? Deciding whether or not you want a marriage?"

She looks at me.

"Do you?" I ask.

"Remember our pact?" she asks.

Of course I do, I nod.

"This is what we do," Jen continues. "This is our life."

"Maybe it's pretty meaningless."

"The only meaning I'm trying to figure out is with you," Jen says. "There are things in your life that I can't control."

Ouch.

"What's that mean?"

"I'm sorry," Jen quickly says.

"Wanting to have a baby—and not being able to—that's not just out of my control, Jen."

"I know."

"You wanted this more than I did when we first started—"

"I know," she interrupts.

"Then what happened?"

"I'm good at my job. That's all I know. That's within my control. Everything else . . ."

"Yeah, I get it," I say.

"And I can't help it that I enjoy my work and you don't. You used to. What happened to you?"

I can't answer Jen. By the time our dinner arrives, I'm too frustrated to eat. I try to settle my emotions and let the wine calm my nerves.

"What do you want me to do?" Jen finally asks.

"I want you to do what you have to do. Okay?"

Jen looks at me, tightens her lips, and simply nods.

Ever seen the cover of Nirvana's most popular album, *Nevermind*? I'm immersed in it. And even though a part of me knows this is a dream, it's hypnotizing and haunting.

The floating baby in the water is my child.

He seems to be fine. He's not drowning or coughing, just gliding around.

This naked little baby boy.

And I'm trying to reach him, swimming furiously after him, trying to grab hold of his chubby little arm. I see little tiny fingers curled up just ready to be cupped by my own and tugged along to safety.

But a wave above shifts us.

I'm holding my breath and now I can't breathe again. But I stay underwater and make one last desperate lunge.

The hand almost touches his little arm. But I miss by inches.

And the undertow takes him away. I cough and suck in water, salty and cold and grimy.

Then I glide back up to the surface. Where I open my eyes and find myself in a king-sized bed next to a softly sleeping woman who I held in my arms as we drifted into layers of sleep.

I'm not usually a dreamer. But for some reason, they keep coming at me.

I wonder when was the last time I heard Kurt Cobain sing, and can't remember. It's not like I had a reason to imagine this.

I breathe in and find the air comforting.

At least this time I didn't wake Jen.

The clouds break. And behind the gray-and-white storm clouds, a picturesque, glorious painting appears.

I'm lounging poolside, and I've got fifty pages of *In Your Memory* left to read. Maybe a little less.

There's something in here. Some potential. A nugget of gold in the pan full of rock.

I'm already formulating ways the story can work. It will need major effort, but it can be done.

Vivian can do it.

It can go from mundane to miraculous.

I barely notice Jen, who comes and stands next to my lounge chair. I look up and all I see is blue, blue surrounding and encompassing us.

A sky-blue portrait stares down at me, and I can't help smiling.

"Colin, we need to talk."

"What about?"

She holds my hand. "Everything."

I nod, but my eyes go back down to the manuscript for a moment. Then I ask her, "Aren't you going to lay out?"

She's dressed in pants and a shirt. I remember her saying something about going shopping.

"Can you put that book down for just a minute?"

I nod, but stare at the page and know I can't stop, not now.

"—really have to go," she says, and I look up, knowing I missed something.

"You going to come back down a little later?" I ask.

"Colin?"

"Yeah?"

She looks sad for some reason. Her eyes match the sky above. She gives me a gentle kiss on the cheek.

"I didn't mean some of the things I said yesterday. About your work. I know how much—how passionate you are about books and publishing." Jen pauses for a moment and looks up, then glances back down at me. "But there are things you can't find in the pages of a book. Or in my arms. Sometimes you have to look somewhere else before you find it."

"Find what?" I ask.

"Yourself."

She kisses my forehead and walks away, and I easily find myself back in pages wanting to know what happens next and wondering how everything will end.

In the silence of our hotel room, away from the scorching sun and the loud crowds by the pool, the story comes to an end. I read the words and realize the unexpected dramatic ending to this incredible story I've been reading.

The conclusion is unexpected, and for a moment, I don't believe it. I need to reread the last few sentences to try and fully understand them.

Potential.

That's a word I've always loved.

So much of art and entertainment is about potential.

So much of life is about potential.

When you walk onto a field ready to play ball, it's all about the potential. What's the next big play, the next score, the next decision.

Life is all about potential.

And *In Your Memory* drips with it. It's not publishable. But it's trying to do something that for half the book I couldn't see. I couldn't understand. The opening third is not only problematic, but boring. But I see what Vivian was attempting.

God bless her soul. She hasn't lost it. She just wandered down the wrong path.

I can't wait until Jen comes back to the room. I know that Vivian's manuscript has the *potential* to be brilliant and to be a home run with my help, and I want to tell Jen that. This manuscript might be the thing to help me find the direction I need to jump-start a career that needs CPR.

So I sit on the bed and wait for her to come back. I drift off for the moment, hearing Jen's words whisper to me and comfort me in the silence of the room.

I can't wait to see her again.

Our future is set. We don't have to worry anymore. Not about anything.

I'm officially drunk.

I've been drinking Coronas all afternoon and through dinner, and after bringing Jen onto the dance floor for a slow waltz to the music, she tells me this.

"I'm just celebrating."

"Why?"

"Because Vivian's manuscript has a shot. It's actually got potential."

"So did it end happily?" Jen asks.

I laugh. "Yes. But no. It's complicated."

"Life always is."

"Yeah. I didn't see it coming though."

"What?"

"You'll have to wait to read the book when it comes out."

"That's not fair."

"I don't get to see your movies till they come out," I tell her.

"True."

"You know when you see a really awesome movie, and afterwards you just sit there listening to the music as the credits roll? How your skin still has goose bumps and you're amazed and exhausted and contemplating everything?"

"Uh-huh. Well, except for the goose bumps part."

"That's what a great book does."

"Vivian will like hearing that."

"Yeah, well, she won't like most of what I say. But that's okay. She wants the truth, and I'm going to give her the truth."

"It's the first time in a long time that I've seen you this excited," Jen says.

"You just said I'm drunk."

"Well, yeah, that too."

We leave the hotel restaurant and walk the lit grounds of the hotel. The rain is gone and it's a clear, humid night.

I decide to tell Jen my decision. Why I'm thrilled and elated.

We're on a walkway that goes down to the ocean. I stop her and look at her, the wind blowing her long tresses.

"I made a decision," I start out.

"What's that?"

"If I sell *In Your Memory*, I'm quitting."

"Quitting Roth?"

"Quitting. Period. Leaving the industry."

"What are you going to do?"

I hold her in my arms. "I'm going to be with you. I'm going to try and find myself and find you and find us."

"You're crazy. You're intoxicated and crazy."

"I love you, Jen. And I know—I've been working so hard—I know this sounds lame, but I've been doing this for us. And I don't want to lose you. I don't want to lose us."

She looks up at me and smiles. Before she can say anything, I kiss her. For a very long time.

It's morning, and we're eating outside when Jen points out to the sky above the trees and high above the ocean. "See that?"

I look and then let out a grunt.

"What?" she asks.

"There's no way you're getting me on one of those."

"They have them for two people to go on," Jen says.

I see the chute gliding far above the water and know I'd pass out if I were the person strapped into the parasail.

"Uh-uh."

"Come on," Jen teases.

"No way."

"Okay, if you won't, you have to at least let me."

"I'll take pictures of you parasailing," I tell her.

"Deal."

The day is calm and the sky is blue and the weather is hot but not too stifling. We'll be going home tomorrow.

I think again of the manuscript and can't help thinking about the ending.

A wave of goose bumps bristles on my skin.

She stands on the edge of the beach with bare feet planted and buried in sand. Her two-piece black suit is covered with a vest. Her long dark hair falls over the blue and yellow vest as the dark-skinned man buckles her up and links and locks her onto the chute.

Another man stands there, waiting, holding a large chute, ready to go.

The boat begins to gurgle in anticipation.

"Ready?" the man asks.

"Yeah!" Jen says.

She looks at me.

I suddenly feel a slight ache.

Then she smiles, giving me one of those *Everything's going to be all right* sort of glances.

"You're next," she says with a laugh.

"In your dreams."

"Take some pictures."

"Okay, ready!" the man holding on to Jen says.

She holds both hands on the harness. The chute opens up and the wind expands it, and suddenly Jen is up and begins to glide away.

She's an angel hovering above the ocean, fluttering away.

Her long legs dangle from her sitting position. She looks back and waves with one hand that's still holding on to a holster.

The man next to me smiles and obviously sees my apprehension. "She okay," he says in a heavy accent.

And the boat guzzles away and I see her grow smaller, hover higher.

Wind picks up and whips my hair.

The parachute diminishes in size as it moves away from me.

Don't let anything happen to her please don't let anything happen to her.

What if you lose her, a voice asks me.

What if something happens, another voice says.

She's far out above the ocean and against the horizon, and the wind continues to blow hard. I can't believe the last few days were so rainy, and all of a sudden the clouds opened up and the sun came through.

Jen is a floating dot on the horizon.

I watch her and see the chute go up slightly.

The sun burns against my forehead. The skies are a majestic, tranquil blue. This is what life should be like. Serene and surreal and amazingly colorful and picturesque.

I see the dot on the horizon, a hovering moving snapshot gliding along.

A dot that suddenly falls.

The picture blurs and shakes.

God no God please oh God no

I stand there and watch and it doesn't feel real, it doesn't seem right.

It's too beautiful out here. It's too perfect.

Yet my wife is against the horizon and the chute behind her tosses and then tangles and then suddenly deflates—can they do this—and I see the image get smaller, the line to the boat suddenly plummet.

And I open my mouth to scream but the words are gone.

The man next to me runs toward the shoreline and shouts foreign words but those are gone.

The dot disappears.

The line falls.

The image is gone.

And I know this is Jen my Jen my sweet precious Jen my wife the dot the image that now I can't see that is far out there on the ocean in the ocean

dear God no God no please no

And the sun shines and the sky is a perfect serene blue and life suddenly comes to a drastic, awful halt.

how to disappear completely

Heart of Darkness

The days and weeks following Cancun feel distant, removed, as though I read about them instead of living through them. They are both a blur of activity and a blanket of silence. It's almost three weeks to the day I stood on the beach and watched Jen drop down to the ocean below. I sit in a nice office overlooking the Chicago street. The woman across from me talks as if this is normal, as if every man knows what it's like to lose his wife, as if I'm part of a to-do list she needs to check off.

"Tell me about the funeral."

I shift in my leather armchair and wonder if I should be startled by the question.

"So—third session, and we dive into the details of the funeral?" I ask.

Dr. Fuller is probably younger than she looks and acts. The tough, square jaw and short, neat blonde hair frame a face that doesn't back down, that gazes in an intense and unrelenting way. Even the forced smile she gives me feels more condescending than nurturing.

"You have talked a lot about Jen and you, about the memories between the two of you, about how you're trying to cope with the fact that she is gone. But you haven't said a word about the funeral."

"It's hard to talk about, much less think about."

"I understand," Dr. Fuller says.

"It was small, private. We just didn't want—well, I told you, Jen had hardly any family to contact. A couple of cousins. She only has a mother, and they don't speak anymore. I didn't even know how to contact her. I tried. Everything felt so—rushed. It's weird. Life stops, and yet you find yourself in this tornado of duties, actions."

"Did you have family in?"

"Yes. For a while. It took my mind off it. I've been trying to work through everything."

"What have you been doing?"

I laugh, a nervous sort of laugh. "I organized my home office and cleaned our apartment three or four times. I've been working on a manuscript, extensively going through it. Probably going through it too many times. I don't know. I sleep a lot, and when I wake up, I try desperately to do something, anything, to keep my mind off Jen."

"Have you decided when you're going back to work?"

"I took an extended leave of absence, but I told my boss I'm working on this manuscript. They understand. I'm not sure when I'll be going back."

As I talk, I realize that in a weird way, this is what I am to the authors I represent. I listen to them and ask questions. That's all. They tell me their problems, and for the most part, I don't fix them, I just listen.

Maybe I should be a therapist.

"When you slow down and think about your wife, what comes to mind?" Dr. Fuller says.

"I still feel that she's just—that I can just open the door and see her, touch her. That none of this is real."

"That's denial."

"Yeah, maybe. But it's a pretty good place to be." I curse, feeling my body sweating and tight. "I should've never let—"

I can't finish my words.

I'm not crying. I refuse to.

It still doesn't make sense.

Jennifer is dead. It doesn't feel real, or right, and that is exactly why I'm telling this to a stranger.

Maybe it will help.

Memories are like streaks of contrail in the open sky. You never know when you're going to look up and find them. How long they will last. When they will dissipate.

For some reason, one morning in Chicago after everything, I find myself remembering a private moment between Jen and me after our wedding.

In the middle of the large banquet room, a closed-off set of winding stairs led up to a small loft. It was shrouded in darkness, so no one could see me lead Jen up the carpeted steps.

"What are you doing?" she asked.

"Shh—don't say anything," I said. "And be careful. Don't trip on your dress."

"Don't let go of me. This train is pretty long."

We reached the top of the stairs and saw the shadowed area full of a few tables and chairs stacked on each other. I brought Jen over to one side of the loft, where we peeked over to see the mass of people below. The DJ was blasting a Beach Boys song that had everybody moving on the dance floor.

I still held Jen's hand and looked at her. "Have I told you how beautiful you look?"

"About a hundred times," she said, as stunning in her wedding gown as when she first stepped through the doorway to walk down the aisle.

I kissed her gently. We kissed for a few minutes, then Jen moved away.

"Someone's going to miss us," she said with a smile.

"I know. I just wanted to get away and make out with my wife."

She put her arms around me and kissed me again. We embraced in the darkness, by ourselves finally, away from everyone else.

"I don't want this day to end," Jen whispered.

"I do," I told her. "I want to get away from everyone and have you all to myself."

"Should I be frightened?"

I laughed at her.

She pulled me to her again and kissed me. "I love you, Colin Scott."

"I love you, Mrs. Colin Scott."

"Thank you."

"For what?" I asked.

"For being patient with me these last few months."

"Thank you for marrying me," I said.

We embraced for a few more minutes, knowing that there would be plenty of time for that and more later.

We had all the time in the world.

Or so we thought.

It's all a dream and I'm going to wake up and find her there by my side holding my hand and smiling.

But every time I open my eyes, there is no Jen.

Day after day, morning or night, there is no Jen.

And that's the worst thing about it all.

She will never be coming back.

I never even had a chance to say good-bye.

The knock on the door sounds like someone pounding to get in. It's ten o'clock in the morning and I'm wearing nasty pajama pants and a T-shirt.

I open up the door and stare at the lanky figure in front of me.

"So this is the great agent in action?"

This can't be real. But then again, nothing that's happened in the past thirty-three days feels real. Why not add this to the rest of the madness?

"Elephant got your tongue?" Donald Hardbein says.

"Shouldn't that be cat?" I ask, checking to see if he has something in his hand. Like a weapon.

"I thought you would appreciate creativity."

I nod. "How can I help you?"

He looks me over and laughs. "Looking the way you do, I'm not sure you can help anybody."

"Thank you."

"Ever hear of a razor?" he asks.

"Ever hear of privacy?"

Again, his laugh. It's a hysterical sort of laugh, frightening more than amusing.

"I thought, since you have been a wee bit negligent in returning e-mails and voice mails, I would come find you."

"Donald—"

"Please, no excuses."

"Look—you don't understand. There's been—" And I honestly don't know what to say. How do you just lay it on the table? I can't utter the words. I can't tell him. "What do you want to talk about?"

He beams a smile that looks scary. "Literature and art and the great American novel."

"Which you wrote, right?"

"All write. I do too."

"What?" I ask. He's not making any sense.

"Thirty minutes. That's all I ask."

"May I change? Or would you like me to go out like this?"

"I can come in."

"And I can change," I tell him. "Not to be rude, but my place is a little—just wait out here for a moment."

I look at the man with the large, intense bug eyes. "How did you find me anyway?"

"You can find anyone these days," Donald says. "You just have to open your eyes and look."

I shut the door behind me and get dressed. I don't have the energy to tell Donald to leave me alone. I'll sit down across from him and listen to his idea and then just be honest.

I search the war-torn apartment for my keys. I realize I haven't left since seeing Dr. Fuller a few days ago. I find them next to a picture of Jen and me. It's one of the most recent shots we had taken, this one during an afternoon stroll in Millennium Park. I pick the picture up and stare at it for a long moment, then put it facedown on the shelf so I don't have to look at it again.

"So—are you on vacation these days?"

If only he knew. The poor guy.

"Yeah, you can say that."

"Reading any good manuscripts?"

"Sure."

"I just read this amazing book by—"

"Don—what do you want to talk to me about?"

"Can't we just sit and chat?"

Donald Hardbein is probably in his late fifties. I don't see a wedding ring on his finger. I'm still wearing mine.

"You have a book you want me to read."

"It's all business with you, huh?"

"Where do you live?"

"I get around."

"Where do you get around from?"

"Vermont," Donald says.

"Okay. So what if I showed up on your doorstep in Vermont, smiling and asking how you are?"

"I'd welcome you in. Have a coffee. Or a drink. Depending on the time, of course."

He smiles and winks. Nice.

"Did you bring your book?"

"Oh, no no. You don't think I'd do something that crazy, do you?"

I just look across the table at him. We're in a diner a few blocks away from my apartment. I'm on my third cup of coffee.

"Did you ever hear about Hemingway's lost manuscript?"

I nod. "That's why you have backup. Discs. Hard drives."

"It's all here." He points to his head.

"What do you mean?"

"It's all up here."

"The book?"

"Yes."

"Don."

"Yes?"

"What are you smoking?" I ask.

"It's all up here. Every word."

"Is it anywhere else?"

He shakes his head, then continues eating the BLT he ordered. One might think his mouth is not capable of opening large enough to take a bite of the megasized sandwich, but that would be wrong.

"So this book—this—"

"It's a novel. Two hundred and forty thousand words."

"In your head?"

"Yes."

I nod. Nice. This guy comes to my door and pulls me out of my home and my exile to tell me his manuscript is finished.

In his head.

"What do you want me to do with it? This 240,000-word manuscript? You want me to read it?"

"That would be easy," Don says.

"Reading your mind?"

"Reading the book."

"Then—what do you want me to do?"

Donald is sensing my irritation. He says *Okay okay* a few dozen times like Joe Pesci and then he holds out his hands in a "Hallelujah" sort of gesture.

"I just want you to be open to the possibilities."

"The possibilities," I repeat. "The possibilities for what?"

"For anything. For life, for love, for an everlasting legacy."

"What are you talking about?"

"I'm talking about our future, Mr. Colin."

"That's plural."

"Oh yes. This story—it's going to be a journey."

"I don't need to take any more journeys anytime soon."

"You're going to want to take this one. Trust me."

He continues to finish up his sandwich, and I wonder why, of all the people in the world, this quack had to come knocking at my door.

In Your Memory is a strange novel.

It took about fifty pages before I even understood where Vivian was going with it. It took another hundred before the action really got moving. Midway through there's an event that changes everything. Then, and only then, does the manuscript approach what it could be. At the end, it reveals its full potential. The problem is that she will probably lose most of her readers midway through the book. And even those patient and persistent enough to endure will ultimately be confused by the ending.

In my office at home, I have the novel divided by chapters and spread across the carpeted floor. I never would have guessed that a woman who wrote a brilliantly popular fantasy series would go on to write a dark, almost gothic tale with chapter titles all coming from Simon & Garfunkel songs. At first, I didn't even realize that she was doing this, with chapters like "Somewhere They Can't Find Me" and "The Sun Is Burning." But around the fourth or fifth chapter, entitled "The Sound of Silence," I caught on.

It fits in its own unique way. The main character is a man about Vivian's age, and he loves Simon & Garfunkel. When his life begins to spiral downward, he seeks solace, and this is one area he finds it in.

In a movie, this would be fine, but sometimes it's difficult communicating the soundtrack to a novel to the reader. What about all those out there who have never even listened to Simon & Garfunkel, all the younger readers who were raised on Harry Potter and who probably don't even know about *The Graduate*? This is one of many problems, and in my office, with my own soundtrack playing in the background off my iMac, I ponder *In Your Memory* and dissect each bit I can.

It takes my mind off other things, off the reality of life, off the brutal cold certainty that sits outside this office.

Like a scientist in a lab, I make notes, tweaking and experimenting.

Vivian is going to love this. I know she will.

I hate nighttime. Not what television refers to as prime time, which I spend a great deal of time being a couch potato in front of, but the deep heart of night. When the masses outside my apartment are sleeping, when life is moving on.

I have a hard time sleeping. And when sleep does come, it's unbearable. I dream of the funeral. Muted, dim images, like an old black-and-white film, run through my mind. I go to bed thinking of something else, but the moment sleep arrives, so do the dreams. Or the nightmares.

I see Jen's cousins coming up to me, hugging and embracing me. Talking about her and me as if we're dear acquaintances, as if this isn't the first time I'm actually meeting them. There's my mother, controlled and stern and glamorous throughout. My sister, who isn't showing yet or at least hides it well.

The funeral is small and the few faces pass by and I just stand there or sit or move around, but throughout the entire process, I'm unmoved. I'm jaded and immovable at my wife's funeral.

This cannot be. This is the true horror of reliving it all, again and again.

Everyone is dressed in black and they force fake smiles and I feel like this is just an extension of the profession and the existence I've built around me and I bide my time knowing everyone will eventually leave.

And they all do. My mother is the last to leave and I hug her and lie and tell her I'll be fine. She makes me promise to come down to Florida but I know there's no way I'm going to. And when they close the door behind them, I feel like it's finally real, that this is real and final.

And that's when, for the first time, I sit on my couch in silence in complete darkness and breathe in and out, thinking, hurting, aching, wondering, and yes, finally crying.

And then I wake up. And her picture is in my heart, in my soul, and I know it will be there all day long, until I am somehow able to drift back off again to a place where memories are real and sadness can be outrun.

The Grapes of Wrath

Something clicks. It's the middle of the night and I can't sleep and all I'm thinking about is the story, Vivian's *In Your Memory.* And I suddenly realize what it's missing.

The secret ingredient.

It's small. Most of them are. But it drastically changes the story.

It will require Vivian to do more work. But it will be worth it. I know it will.

I wake up and scrawl a note on paper. I set it on the dresser, and notice the electronic thermometer.

I should get rid of it. It's no longer needed.

"How are you?" Pearce asks me over breakfast at a family restaurant on the Fox River.

"Good."

"No, you're not."

"Yeah, I know. What's going on with you?"

"What's going on with *you*?"

"I've got some new ideas for tweaking the house."

"What now?" he asks. "Don't tell me you've designed a whole new wing for the mansion."

I unveil my latest designs for the basement, and we spend half an hour talking about the possibilities. So far, only the frame of the house has been erected. Pearce has been occupied on other projects.

As we talk, I find it easy to shift away from the subject of how I'm coping. I'm surprised how easy it is for people to accept the reality. Jen is gone, you have to move on, that's just life. But I'm glad; I don't want to unpack a suitcase full of anguish every time I talk with somebody.

Pearce says they should have all the drywall up by the end of August, which is a month away, and all the major appliances in.

"The master bath is taking a little longer than I thought it would. . . ."

He keeps talking, but all I can think is *yeah, sure, whatever.* I was going to take Jen with me and show her everything that had been done. Maybe she would have said, "We should move in here," and maybe we would have actually done the unthinkable. Move to the suburbs into a dream house.

A part of me hoped, and actually believed, that the longer I spent working on that house, designing it and specifying everything from the crown molding to the ornate chandelier in the dining room, the more inclined I would be not to sell it. To make it our own.

Our own.

Pearce sees me drifting off.

"I'm sorry," he tells me. "You surviving?"

"Yeah."

"What else have you been up to? Besides changing the design for the hundredth time."

"Reading a lot. Spending time in the library. Going to see movies."

"Have you gone back to work?"

"No. I've been working a lot from home. The thought of going back in—it's still a little too—I don't know. Still a little too much."

"Why don't you ever give me a call?"

Last time I saw Pearce was—yeah, right afterwards. During the hazy time when everyone in my life showed up to give me one big giant group hug that lasted a week, and then they all left at once. I'm sure he was there, wasn't he? I just don't remember seeing him.

What's wrong with my memory?

"That'd be fine," I say, lying.

"Kristy would love to have you over." A pause, then Pearce clears his throat. "Colin, I believe things happen for a reason."

I look over at him. I can't believe he actually said that.

People say things they don't mean and things they don't understand when someone else is grieving. I know this. I've probably made my share of ridiculous comments over the years. But still, this is surprising, coming from Pearce.

"The situation with Jen—I know it's bad. I can't imagine what you're going through. I just want you to know—Kristy and I would like you to know that we're praying for you. I don't want to sound all religious and that, but that's the only thing I know to do during tough times."

"Pray," I say, looking him in the eyes.

"Come on, don't give me that look."

"What look am I giving you?"

"Like you want to take that waffle and shove it where the sun doesn't shine."

I breathe in and then laugh. It feels good to laugh.

"Anybody else, I probably would," I tell him. "Look—I just . . . It'll take awhile for me to get back to—"

I want to say *normal*. But what exactly is normal? Waiting and wondering where your wife is? Putting in eighteen-hour days and wondering what city you're sleeping in?

"I'm just not big into the whole faith thing."

"Can I ask why?"

"Sure. It probably has something to do with the fact that my father got real sick when I was twelve. We prayed a lot for him. The church we went to prayed for him. Everybody prayed for him. And he always told us that God would take care of us, of him. God and his plan. His mighty plan. Guess that plan included Dad dying after all those heartfelt prayers."

Pearce looks at me and says nothing. What can he say? This is my trump card when talking to anybody trying to sell religion.

"And I guess that also includes Jen, right?"

"Colin—"

"You asked."

"God doesn't do these things to hurt us."

"Yeah, but if he's up there, he allows them to happen, doesn't he? Someone like that doesn't get my vote, sorry. I can handle things now, I'm an adult. But a twelve-year-old kid. What does he know about life? How is he equipped to take care of his mother and sister?"

"We live in a fallen world."

"No," I tell Pearce without any hesitation. "We live in a crippled world where people use God and church as crutches. I might have a broken leg. I might even have to amputate it. But no way am I using that crutch. No way."

Pearce keeps eating. "Kristy and I would still like you to come over."

"Is she going to preach at me?"

He laughs, seeing the look in my eyes. "She's probably going to preach at both of us. But she's a fabulous cook. And it looks like you need to eat more, since you barely touched your plate this morning."

I can handle things now. I'm an adult.

I hear my words as I scroll through photos on my laptop, looking at digital images of Jennifer that exist solely on this machine. I know I need to print out copies. If something happens to this computer, then they'll be gone, just like her.

I see shots from our recent walk in Millennium Park. There is a picture of Jennifer on the walkway over one of the Chicago avenues. She's looking casually away from the camera, accustomed to having her photo taken. It's a shot that could be featured in a magazine ad—it's that good. I showed it to Jen, and she could only point out the flaws.

"Beauty is about what's on the inside, not the outside," she told me over and over.

I always agreed. Then added that I couldn't help seeing her outside beauty as well.

Sometimes I marveled at her insecurities. They were probably the result of a selfish mother and a weak father, a couple who never encouraged or motivated her. Jen had to encourage and motivate herself. She kept a hard shell around her that protected her from the uncaring parents of the world. I was one of the few people who broke through.

I think of that walk we took and our conversation about our lives and our future. We didn't argue, but we ended up disagreeing about something. About our lives together and about where we were headed.

Why am I thinking of it now?

I see Jen smiling and see those vibrant eyes looking at me and boring a hole through my crumbling heart.

I don't know what I'm going to do without her.

Maybe kids are better equipped to handle grief than adults.

We don't know what we're losing when we're young. The world is still big and bright, and we stare at it wide-eyed.

But our eyes grow more and more narrow as we get older.

Mine are almost shut.

I sit in my office surrounded by stacks of papers, each one a chapter with several pages of notes on top of it. I'm trying to figure out the best way to communicate all of this to Vivian without writing a book myself when my cell phone rings.

The Roth Agency. I answer it and hear Darcy's friendly voice on the other line.

"Am I catching you at a bad time?"

"No. Just working in my office here. What's up?"

"I just wanted to—to let you know something. I didn't want to e-mail you. It's about Vivian's manuscript."

"What about it?"

"I just thought you should know—Ted's gotten involved."

"What do you mean? How?"

"I just think—" She stops for a moment, then starts to whisper. "I can't really talk. I think it would be a good idea if you came in. I know you're taking time off—it's just, it might be best."

I want more information. "I'll try to make it in this afternoon."

"Okay, that sounds good," Darcy says. "And Colin. Hang in there."

Hang in there.

A lot of people have told me to hang in there. But what exactly am I supposed to hang on to?

I'm out on the street on the hot summer day when I fall to my knees and try to breathe. The air has gone. The sounds around me have muted. All I can think is about my bursting heart.

I can't go to work. I can't fake this. I can't talk and communicate as though I care about anything else.

Vivian Brown's manuscript suddenly seems pointless. The world around me fades away and I'm a man on a sidewalk holding his chest and trying to breathe.

I eventually get to my feet. I know I can't go to work. Not like this. I have nothing to say, nothing to give.

Sometimes I dream of Cancun. Sometimes I dream of making love to Jen. And sometimes I dream that she calls me to wake me up from these fantasies.

"Hello?" I answer in my dream.

"It's me," says her voice, calm and quiet.

And I can't say anything, surprised and bewildered.

"How are you doing?" she asks.

"Okay," I tell her, lying.

Can the dead see you? If they can call back home, wouldn't they be able to see you?

In dreams, anything can happen.

"These past weeks . . ." she says, her voice trailing off.

"Yeah, I know," I tell her.

Unbearable, excruciating, painful, dark. I know it all too well.

"I just—it's just—where can we go from here?" she asks.

"It's not your fault," I tell her.

"It was my choice."

I should have gone on the parasail first.

"I let you go."

"I just want to help you," she says.

"You can't. Not anymore."

And the next morning the conversation seems so real, so true. But I know it's as real as Vivian Brown's stories.

A day passes. I don't answer Darcy's calls. I don't answer her e-mails. I just leave messages saying I will be coming in soon.

There is a heaping mass of unopened mail on the kitchen counter, growing each day. I don't bother chucking the credit card applications or unsolicited junk. I decide to hold off on the bills. I read papers—some parts, anyway. But they remain strewn about the apartment. Jen would kill me if she saw the mess I'm making. But—yeah. She can't exactly do that, can she?

One day, as I'm flicking new mail onto the mighty mountain, I notice an envelope. It has my name scrawled in blue handwriting, familiar blue handwriting.

Jen's handwriting.

I feel like vomiting.

I stare at the letter in my hand and wonder if I can open it.

Jen would routinely send me postcards and letters from location shoots, so what now?

Postcards from beyond?

Sounds like a novel one of my authors should write.

Maybe she wrote it before the Cancun trip. Maybe she was just trying to be fun. Maybe she wrote a special memory down so that she would surprise me with a letter a week later.

Little did she know that a week would be a month and a half. And that she would not be able to see my reaction.

I breathe out and can feel my body shaking.

I can't do this. Not now. Everything still seems so fresh and raw, and I'm trying, really sincerely trying to move on.

The letter goes in the bedroom on the dresser.

I will open it later, when I am able to handle the words written down.

The last words I will ever hear from Jen.

I feel something wet against my cheek. It's a kiss, but nothing gentle or romantic. It's slobbering and continuous. I open my eyes and see it's a little dog. It's a terrier. And it keeps licking my face, wanting to play. I start to get up, then realize that this is a dream, that I'm reliving part of Vivian Brown's book. It's surreal. Sometimes I wake up and sometimes I'm actually walking before I realize that I'm zoning out and sleepwalking.

I can't help it. Every day I add to my Good, Bad, and Ugly list. I reread sections of *In Your Memory* and continue to make notes and suggestions on the ways Vivian can improve it. There are a lot of good things to write about, which is always an encouraging thing when you're planning on auctioning it off and making it one of the biggest contracts in publishing history. But I'm going to make an audacious suggestion that we wait. Vivian wants honesty, and my honest answer is that the book needs more work, especially the beginning.

It's good to feel like I'm doing something, even if I'm lounging at home drinking coffee and scouring through a manuscript. Yet as immersed as I am in the book, and in Vivian Brown's future, I feel I'm still ultimately doing something for nothing. What's the point? It's my life now, my career, *my* journey. Everything is solely mine.

It sometimes doesn't feel as though Jen is truly gone. I can't think the word, can't utter it. Yet even in passing, her disappearance, her leaving, her . . . death, there, I've said it, her death, the death that I can't get over and get around, that pervades every bit of my being, still doesn't seem real. It feels like all I need to do is dial the right number to hear her voice, or see the right image and see her live smile. Jennifer can't possibly be gone. She has to be somewhere, even if she isn't nearby, even if she isn't ever going to come back to me.

You can run, but you can't hide.

A voice whispers this over and over. And it comes from the grinning mouth of grief.

Listening is hard work. If you don't believe this, try to truly listen to someone you loathe.

"It's just—there are other authors who make it all the time and I just can't seem to make it ever and Meg says to give it time but I don't know how much longer I have to wait . . ."

And I don't know how much longer I can take this.

Meet Gretta Tornburg, who will never ever be satisfied. She doesn't need another three-book contract. She doesn't need a bestseller. She doesn't need to land on the bestseller list, which she brings up every single time we talk. She needs serious, big-time help. She needs a shrink. A three-shrink contract.

I've got one I can recommend. One I'm going to see after work.

"I've been writing for a long time, and I used to get respect. . . ."

And I used to care, too.

My first day back, and amazingly enough, the publishing world has not changed a bit.

"Gretta, please shut up and stop feeling sorry for yourself."

This is what I want to say, but instead I just listen. I listen and say very little. What an amazing conversation.

"I'm sorry for venting," Gretta says again.

I'm sorry for listening.

There is nothing to say, nothing to offer. Gretta refuses to understand reality. Most of her audience consists of seventy-year-old women who don't have e-mail and don't buy books from Amazon.com. She's got an audience, but come on. She wants an ad? What for? She wants a newer Web site? Who's going to browse it? Blogging is something she thinks plumbers do. She wants to land on the bestseller list? That's not going to help her psychotic personality and her fundamental emotional needs.

Publishing success is not going to fill a void, Gretta.

I know.

I'm twenty minutes away from my lunch meeting with Roth and I can't stop moving, can't stop clicking the keys on my computer. I have so many e-mails I need a staff of five just to get through them. I don't recognize the name on this one at first.

Ian Pollock.

Ian-Ian-Ian-Ian-oh yeah. The young man. Something to do with a street or a road.

Passover Lane.

Dear Mr. Scott:

I'm sorry to be bugging you again, but I never heard back from you regarding the pages of *Passover Lane*. I have been reworking some of it and feel very good about it.

I quickly skim the note. If he knew everything going on with my life, he probably wouldn't be writing me. But he doesn't know. It's okay. Most of the authors don't know, and that's how I want it to be.

The fact is I have no clue where I placed the folder he gave me.

I quickly type an e-mail back.

Ian: Sorry not to have gotten back to you until now. Could you send me the section again—I have misplaced the chapters you gave me. I'll try to look it over sometime soon and give you input.

Thanks. Colin

Notice I say sometime soon and then add that I'll give him input. Input means help on making it better. I'm not going to start representing him. I already know that. I don't need to read anything more to know he has a long ways to go. But I can have a nice diversion. Any diversion is welcome.

I keep clicking away.

"Sometimes all a man has is his work," Roth says to me in the back of the limo.

It's the first time I've seen him in over a month. He didn't make it to the funeral, and he never really explained why. I figured when he didn't show up that this was too heavy and that death scares a lot of people, especially those a little too close to it. I don't hold it against him—everybody has to deal with it their own way. I'm still trying to figure out how to deal with it myself.

I'm wearing a coat and tie, trying to look the part for this lunch meeting. Roth talks about his health and his new outlook on life. Then he brings up Jen.

"When my first wife left me, it took me awhile to let it go. Oh, I know, it's different, but in the end, it's the same thing. You're alone. And you can start getting a little batty in the head, if you know what I mean."

I nod. *Yeah, I know.*

"How are you doing? How are you really doing?"

"I get out of bed. Take one step after another."

"You know what you need? A night on the town with the guys. Go to the Admirals Club. You know—some of the ladies there will take care of you. So I've heard. They'll stay with you, for a price. You can have an escort for a day. A week."

I look over at him and see he's being earnest.

What a pig.

I expect something like this from Ted, but not Roth.

"Get Ted to show you the ropes. I think he's quite familiar."

This is my buck-up-kid speech. Try to forget about your dead wife by going to a strip club downtown. That's nice.

The things I'd love to say if he weren't the boss. The things I'd love to share if I had my name on the letterhead.

The Lincoln rumbles through the beautiful August day. Every time I look outside, I see smiling faces and laughter and energetic conversations. Am I the only person in this city who is sad? I think back to the night at Roth's place, looking out at the ocean and feeling alone. This loneliness hasn't left. It's filled every inch and pore of me.

Strangers look our way, and I can't help but wonder. Can Jennifer see me? Can she read my thoughts? Is she omniscient like a ghost, or is there some massive, big-screen television set up in heaven for her to watch whatever channel she wants? Channel 35: The Colin Scott Channel. See how your husband unravels and wanders around aimlessly weeks after your untimely death.

Where are you, Jen?

It's nice to ponder. Just like Pearce's words. They're supposed to comfort. Like the words of the preacher who said great things about Jennifer. They're all supposed to do that. They're supposed to pray and talk about heaven as if it really, truly is a place people are destined to go to.

I can't fault Roth for his comments. In fact, I should applaud him. At least he has the nerve, the guts, to speak the truth.

Pearce has his words of comfort, Roth has his.

Neither helps.

Memories, like this one, play in my mind as easily as I breathe.

I'm sitting to the left of Jen. I hold her hand as the waiter pours wine.

"What's this about?"

I only smile. The waiter leaves us in our little nook in the restaurant. It's a booth skirted off by a curtain. I hold up the glass and make a toast.

"To the future," I say. "To our future."

We clink our glasses and sip the sweet, cold Riesling.

I take the envelope out of my coat pocket.

She rips it open and takes out a key. A look of surprise covers her face. Her mouth opens to say something, but I only nod.

"There's no pressure. But there's a place for you here in Chicago. And it will always be open."

I know she won't say a yes or a no right away. We've known each other for five months, and this is a big step, a huge step.

I left it up to her.

I always left everything up to Jen.

"I want to talk about Vivian." The voice calls me back to reality.

We're halfway finished with our salads and with the overview of my authors. I see Roth is still staying true to form with his bourbon. I feel like tossing a few back myself after discussing my list of failures: Lisa Beck, Kelly Moyet, Kurt Dobbs. There are more to add to the list, names I don't even want to think about. One author angry that I haven't responded to him in four weeks. Another worried about the status of her manuscript. Like parents of kindergartners anxious and eager to hear about their little darlings.

At this point it's meaningless. All of it. Even Lisa Beck and Kurt Dobbs. They're all meaningless except one name.

Vivian Brown.

I've been working and waiting for this moment, this moment where I show Roth "why I earn the big bucks." Or why I should.

I'm thinking of how to begin with my overview of *In Your Memory*, with all the work I want her to do, with how I feel we should approach her.

"I finished her book," Roth says.

This doesn't surprise me. For something this big, Roth is going to read all of it.

"And?"

"Loved it. So did Ted."

I watch him pick up the glass of bourbon and finish it. I stare at him for a second, then at the glass.

"Colin, I wanted to let you know—Ted and I visited Vivian."

"Excuse me?" I say.

"A week ago," Roth says, his eyes unwavering, his beard glistening in the restaurant's lights.

I move in my chair and start to say something when Roth beats me.

"It was just to touch base about the manuscript. To talk about strategies."

I breathe in. Breathe out. I recall a drunken man's words one late night in Laguna Beach.

You're a good kid and a good agent, Colin. She's yours. You negotiate the next contract, you keep the monies, you get the recognition. She's all yours.

"What—" I stop and breathe again. "What'd you guys tell her?"

"What do you think? It's a home run."

I laugh. "A home run?"

"Absolutely."

"Mr. Roth, you've gotta be kidding me."

"I knew you wouldn't like hearing we went to visit her, but we couldn't stand still—"

"The story has some issues," I say.

"Issues?"

"Yeah, some major issues. It needs a lot of work."

"Oh, I know. That sort of thing will get done in the editorial process."

"No—I mean, some big-picture stuff. It's not ready to go."

"Ted and I think it is."

"Ted?" I curse. "Since when is Ted involved with this?"

"We're not taking anything away from you."

"We?"

"Ted is a good guy. I know what I told you. I still want you working with Vivian, with us on this."

"With *us*?" I feel the sweat beads on my forehead. "You guys go see Vivian to do what? Pop open the champagne and celebrate the manuscript?"

"I don't drink champagne," Roth says.

"Yeah, and I don't lie. The novel is not complete."

"I beg to differ."

"Since when have you . . ."

I stop and look at him. Five weeks. My life swirls down the toilet in five weeks, but publishing, publishing, my friends, moves on. It always moves on, and if you snooze, you lose.

"It needs work," I tell Roth again. "I've made notes—"

"What notes?"

"I'm working on them. I've been working on them for the last few weeks. It's complicated. It's not an easy fix."

Roth chuckles in a condescending way that makes me want to take a pepper shaker and bat it over his head. "We've had the manuscript for a month and a half. I think you can understand where we're coming from."

I run a hand through my hair and curse again.

Where do you think I'm *coming from?*

"This is Ted's doing, right?"

"No."

"Bernard, don't lie to me."

I never call him Bernard. He knows I'm serious. We both know I'm treading on dangerous territory.

Roth gives me a wry smile and puts his hand over mine. "It's fine. Nobody's lying to you. We have not yet negotiated for it."

"When are you planning to?"

"We're putting proposals together."

"Now?"

"Yes, now," Roth says. "This book can be published next year."

I slip my hand out of his and shake my head. "*In Your Memory* needs more work. It's fine—it's great. I mean, it's better than anything we've got from other authors. But this is Vivian Brown we're talking about. Vivian Brown."

"I know her name."

"Yeah? Do you know how rabid her fans are? You know how they were with book three? How do you think they'll be, reading an entirely new book from her?"

"Pleasantly surprised."

"Pleasantly surprised? Come on."

"Where do you see problems?"

I want to start talking about it, but I hold back.

"No. Not now. Not here. I've spent a long time working on my report."

"Too long."

how dare he

"What did Vivian say?"

"About what?"

"When you gave her the green light on the book?"

"She asked about you, of course."

"And?"

"And we told her you gave it a thumbs-up."

I curse and throw down my fork. "You're kidding."

"Ted told me you gave it the go-ahead."

"And you trusted him?" I'm standing now, ready to walk out.

"I hired him." Roth is still cool and composed. He's used to this, usually with publishers.

"So I'm out, and this is what happens?"

"Sit back down, Colin. Come on."

"No."

"Colin—"

"I need some air."

"Colin, please."

"Enjoy your lunch."

This is the way the world works.

I pause and someone else plays.

I stall and someone else stalks.

I fall apart and someone sews up the seams.

The city streets of Chicago seem shadowed and cheerless as I walk them and hail a cab to take me back to the condo. To an empty home.

I ball up a fist.

Ten years. Ten years of hard work. Of the proverbial blood, sweat, and tears. A decade of putting up with big personalities and big mouths and big wallets and big pains. A decade of all of that, for what?

nothing

To slow down and get a flat on the edge of the freeway and see the car pool pass you by. Fly by, as a matter of fact.

No way this ends.

No way they're going to take this away from me. Not after everything . . .

stop it stop it right now

I think of Vivian and *In Your Memory.* Of the eighteen-page report I've written. I begin to plan. How to get back in the game. How to be the hero again.

I'm furious.

She was my ticket out of here. She was my get-out-of-jail-free card. Think of some trite cliché on escape and she was it, she was the one.

They're not going to win.

I arrive in front of my building and step out onto the city street and look up toward the window of the condo and realize that I've already lost.

more than I'll probably ever know

I wonder again if Jen can see me.

If so, she is probably shaking her head right now in disappointment.

Is it that easy to move on?

I don't know. But I'm going to hope and see.

The Catcher in the Rye

Chicago sounds restless tonight. It's Thursday night, and I still can't shake my anger over today's lunch with Roth. I haven't been able to stop moving, from coming back to the condo and working more on my report on *In Your Memory*, to checking e-mail and surfing the Web. I'm sitting on the deck overlooking the city streets and I drift off and think of Jen.

There are always moments in life that take you by surprise, that come like a crashing wave and send you hurtling upside down gasping for air and sucking in a mouthful of sandy water. Times like that were when Jennifer demonstrated why I loved her so much.

Once early in our marriage, I landed a big author deal that resulted in a first book that bombed as far as sales went. The publisher wanted to cancel the remaining two books on Sam Templeton's contract, and the author was contemplating never writing again. I stood in the middle of a hailstorm that could have seriously derailed my budding agenting career.

Jen took action. "We're going out," she said, not meaning to dinner but for some drinks.

We went to a local tavern. Jen wasn't a big drinker and only nursed her appletini. But after I'd had a few beers, she started in.

"You're too hard on yourself."

I shook my head. "I made this deal happen. I made a lot of promises, both to the publisher and the author."

"And it was your fault the book failed? That's ludicrous."

She reminded me of all the things I already knew. Sometimes good books fail to connect. Sometimes talented authors don't reap the rewards of their efforts. Sometimes publishers don't succeed in positioning or marketing and selling their titles. Sometimes good books bomb.

"I know that," I kept saying over and over.

"Then why can't you stop feeling sorry for yourself?" she asked, but not unkindly. "Colin, you're a great agent. You see the potential in authors you work with and you try to tap this potential. And with Sam Templeton, I think you did. The reviews on the book were great, right? You did everything possible to make the book succeed. But in the end, you weren't the reason it did poorly."

"Tell that to Sam. Or to Scribner."

"My last movie ended up doing fifteen million at the box office. It cost fifty million to make. You think people aren't looking to blame someone? But some things just happen. We can only do our job—and try to do our very best—and then be content with the outcome."

I nodded, but she knew I was still unconvinced.

"I want to take you somewhere after this," she told me.

We ended up at the large Borders in the center of the city. It was a multilevel store, with probably half a million titles shelved throughout its walls. She led me down a dozen aisles of books, from fiction to business books to biographies to art books to parenting to children's books.

"You think out of the hundreds of thousands of books in this store that it's *your* fault if one of them doesn't sell well?"

I couldn't help laughing. "I don't know."

"Yes, you do," she said. "You are the reason a book happens, not the reason it succeeds or fails. Some things are out of your hands, Colin. You can't get bogged down when things don't work out. That's not who you are."

I stood looking at my wife in the middle of the bookstore. She wasn't just my spouse, she was my closest friend, my advocate, my champion.

I embraced her and let go of the worry that was growing like a cancer inside me.

You can't get bogged down when things don't work out. That's not who you are.

I knew that once. But Jen was always around to remind me.

I can't go to her on this one.

Looking down at the city below, I realize how scared I am.

Time has somehow ceased to exist for me. Three o'clock can be A.M. or P.M., to me they feel the same.

It's Friday afternoon at the office, and I'm here because Roth and Ted aren't. I'm killing time and decide to check out a Web site called MovieNewsandNotes. For some reason I'm curious. For some reason my fingers find their way to Google and to type in the words *Immersion* and *movie*. I get a bunch of sites including the official Web site belonging to novelist Stephen Conroy, but one link goes to the movie information site. It has information about the production in process.

Casting news on the Gore Verbinski project, *Immersion*. Julia Roberts is set to play the lead role in this tale. . . .

I keep looking, scrolling through the online gossip. The movie is set to begin filming in the fall and will take place in the Smoky Mountains of North Carolina. I type *costume designer* and *immersion*, but nothing comes up. No mention of Jennifer Scott. No mention of the loss to the Hollywood industry.

Why are you doing this?

I don't know. I can't help it. I get out of the Web site and sip my Diet Coke as I look around an office that has been mostly abandoned the last couple of months.

Reminders of Jennifer remain. I don't have a big desk here. On top of it sit a monitor and keyboard, an in-box always annoyingly full, several manuscripts, and several framed photographs. Our wedding day where we embraced and look unbeatable. A shot of us on Christmas Day years ago. The two of us smiling in front of the Eiffel Tower. And a photo of us in Cancun. I know I shouldn't have even developed the photos we took there; I shouldn't have put Jen's photo out in full view like a football trophy belonging to a paraplegic who can never walk onto the field again. But it reminds me of another time. That I once had something, that it was good, and that—

That I will move on? That I will find love and hope again? I can't say I believe any of that. Jen's photo simply confirms a life I once lived.

Darcy has come into my office and asked a question.

"I'm sorry—what?"

"John Berrin's manager called. They want to set up a meeting."

"We always get calls like this on a Friday," I complain. "Authors should know never to call their publishers or their agents on a Friday afternoon."

Darcy nods. She looks cute in her jeans and a black top with short sleeves.

The thought of taking a trip to visit Berrin provokes a sigh out of me. "I'll call them and see what they want."

"Colin?"

"Yeah."

"Could we—I know it's a Friday, but could we get on the same page with some of our authors?"

I glance at her. "Yeah, sure."

George Orwell once said this: "All writers are vain, selfish, and lazy, and at the very bottom of their motives lies a mystery. Writing a book is a long, exhausting struggle, like a long bout of some painful illness. One would never undertake such a thing if one were not driven by some demon whom one can neither resist nor understand."

I think maybe I'd have liked working with Mr. Orwell. I think that he and I could relate. We'd share stories and our fundamental belief that, yes, every writer is selfish, vain, and demon-possessed.

This is what I'm thinking as Darcy goes through a list of these haunted souls. The names depress me.

The Roth Agency has over a hundred authors. Of those, thirty-some are "mine." I work with them, talk to them over the phone and e-mail them, negotiate with publishers for them, read and critique their manuscripts. Or specifically, as Roth likes to stress over and over, champion them. I am their champion.

Sometimes I think of this and laugh. I champion them. People I mostly don't know on a personal level, insecure characters that I don't *want* to know personally, people whose worlds revolve around themselves and who mostly don't know or care what just happened in my personal life a couple months ago. People who I sometimes think might truly be insane, or mentally imbalanced, or in need of a long vacation where they never come back.

Or possessed.

The 80-20 principle rules the Roth Agency as it does every publishing house out there. Eighty percent of your business and revenue comes from 20 percent of your authors. In our case, it is probably like the 90-10 principle.

Or maybe the 99-1 principle.

"I'm almost done with Zucker's manuscript," Darcy says.

Does the world really need another business book? we wonder. *Do we need to know who moved our cheese?* Well, we sure hope so. They don't need just another, but one by Stan Zucker. A former CEO of some company that got lucky and made it big who now gives financial advice on talk shows and CNN. His first book was called *Cents and Sensibility.* And even though it is basically the same dreck that every publisher kills poor, defenseless trees for every year, we're supposed to act as though Zucker is unique.

But the masses don't concern themselves over the literary quality of fiction or the deep, profound moral and theological arguments of nonfiction. They want what Stephen King once referred to himself as: the literary equivalent of a Big Mac and large fries. King was just being his humble, ordinary-guy self. I'd represent King even if he weren't a mega-ridiculous-selling author. Because he's a passionate writer who also gives readers what they want.

So give them what they want. We won't stand in the way.

"Are you okay?" Darcy asks.

"What do you mean?"

"Just—with everything."

I meet her unflinching gaze.

"Yeah, I'm fine."

She hesitates for a moment, then asks, "Would you maybe want to —I don't know. Maybe go somewhere—have a drink after work?"

Is she asking me out on a date?

Back up. That'd be a negative. Darcy's not interested in those things —not with someone like me.

Not with everything that's happened.

It's six in the evening, and everyone has already left the office. The only plans I have are to walk home, grab some Chinese takeout, watch some dismal movie on cable, and try to finish reading Stan Zucker's book.

I don't think Darcy's asking me out, not in that *out* sort of way. But I don't think she wants to talk business. She's the type who hates taking work home.

Her eyes see my surprise but simply wait for my answer.

"Sure," I finally say. "Where'd you like to go?"

I look at the rows of liquor across from me and wonder what would happen if the world came to an end and we got stuck here with nothing but thousands of gallons of booze to consume. I look at Darcy and think of a lot worse people to be stuck with. Like Donald Hardbein, the insane author I keep worrying is going to show up at the front door again.

"What was she like?"

We're sitting in a neighborhood joint called the Star Lounge. It has a decent-sized bar and tables in one room, sofas and lounge chairs in another. Darcy said she comes here sometimes with friends. I'm seeing a different side to her tonight. Not so serious and studious. She looks a little different, too. I notice she's not wearing her glasses. And she's wearing more makeup than usual.

I drain the beer in front of me and place the empty bottle on the torn napkin underneath it. "Good question."

The bartender asks if I want another, and I nod. I glance at Darcy, who seems more relaxed than I've ever seen her. She's drinking some fancy martini I've never heard of.

I ask her if she ever met Jen, and she says no.

"Jennifer was beautiful. I mean really, truly beautiful. She always hated me telling people that she used to be a model. Like she was afraid they'd think she was stuck up or mindless or slutty or whatever. I don't know."

"How'd you guys meet?"

"At a movie premiere."

"Really?"

"Sounds real romantic, huh? We chatted and got to know each other in a room full of strangers. Then I proceeded to try to win her over for the next few months. She resisted at first. You don't think of finding The One in the random way we did. But it can happen."

"Maybe that will give me hope," Darcy says.

I zone out for a couple minutes as Darcy opens up about her love life. Or lack of love life. I can't help thinking back, a DVD of a hundred thousand hours playing all at once, so many memories and images to choose from. The first time we ever sat down to talk, where every word coming from Jen seemed electric and hypnotic. When I couldn't stop thinking of her and didn't want to spend any second away from her.

That fire and passion—where did it go? How could I have lived with her and loved her and yet spent so little time with her?

Everything I should have said and should have done plays in my mind in a millisecond.

"Colin?"

"Yeah."

"I'm sorry to bring her up."

I shake my head and smile. "No, it's okay."

"Really?"

"Yeah. I have to move on."

"It's that easy?"

I don't answer her. I don't want to lie. Nor do I want her to know the truth.

She sips her second or third martini and glances at me. The look is startling—it's vulnerable and intense and it's a look I've never seen on her face before.

"I think that my problem is I'm looking for a certain type of person," Darcy says.

"It's good to know what you're looking for."

"Not when he's someone you've worked with the last few years."

For a second I can't say anything.

"Colin, you don't know how many times I've dreamt of this. Of sitting here, being able to just tell you . . ."

"Tell me . . . what?"

"Tell you how much I adore you."

What?

"Darcy—"

"Please, don't say anything," she says, putting her hand on mine. "I know that it's still early—I know that maybe this is crossing the line. Maybe I'm just a little tipsy and a little impatient, but I can't help myself. I just want you to know that if you want to confide in anyone—open your heart up—I'm here."

This can't be happening.

I look and still see her hand on mine. It's a small hand, much smaller than Jen's long and slender touch.

"I can't imagine the pain you're going through, Colin. But I want you to know I'm here for you. I've always been here. Waiting."

Waiting.

Yikes.

I nod and take a sip of my beer and can't for the life of me think of the right thing to say.

I've spent the whole weekend perfecting my report on *In Your Memory.* I am still debating whether to show it to Roth or just go ahead and send it to Vivian.

Do it, a voice tells me.

The keyboard is calling my name as I open an envelope from Knopf and check out their new catalog. Two of our authors are inside.

Go ahead, do it.

It's Sunday evening. Next week will be another week to deal with Roth and Ted and all of that nonsense. But tonight it's just me, and I can still hear Vivian's voice telling me to be honest, to tell her the truth.

Do it.

I turn to my computer and open up my e-mail. I type in three letters. VIV. It gives me the rest of her name. Vivian Brown.

I start to type. I know this is long overdue, and the longer I wait, the less meaning it will have.

I know I shouldn't send it. Roth—what's he going to say or do?

I'm hoping that Vivian will read the report and be astounded by my brilliance and be open to the suggestions. They're suggestions, after all. Only suggestions.

But they're coming on the heels of Roth and Ted good ole idiotic Ted giving it their blessing.

So many of the big-name authors no longer get edited. They might as well have people on staff at publishers with the title of Official Spell Checker, because sometimes that's all it seems they do. Yes, copyedit and proofread. But for a manuscript to be good, to really sing, you have to edit it. It has to be cut and trimmed and moved around and tweaked and toned.

I believe Vivian knows this. And that the temporary green light given to *In Your Memory* will be overruled by common sense and courteous suggestions.

Yeah, eighteen pages' worth.

Dear Vivian:

I hope all is well with you. I'm back in the office, trying to sort through the mess that has accumulated on my desk. I wanted to send this e-mail to you before any more time passes.

I was surprised, to say the least, to hear about Roth's trip to see you and about the green light given to *In Your Memory*. It's a wonderful work, Vivian. Truly brilliant. And as I read it, I was excited about the ways you could improve it—as you improved the Marover books and made them into international bestsellers. *In Your Memory* is a deeper work, if I dare say that. It's more complicated, less plot-driven, and thus susceptible to nagging little problems that won't be hard to fix.

More than the nagging little problems, there were a few big picture issues that I think would make sense to correct. I know I'm going out on a limb here. Roth said he approved it. I decided to at least send you my report. You can decide whether it has any merit and if you want to work on some of the issues mentioned here.

As usual, I don't simply point out problem areas, but I give reasons why they might be challenging for the book and for the reader. I'm long-winded in my report (as usual), so please bear with it. I spend the

first three pages saying why I love it, and I want you to know that I do love this book. The story is amazing. It moved me to tears more than once, and it made me reflect on my own life. In some ways I felt like I was Jack. At times I truly felt like I was living his life.

Please let me know your reaction to this report. Again, this is coming from me, not from Roth. I feel that once you see the report, you'll understand how *In Your Memory* can be a better book. I look forward to working together with you to make it an absolute home run.

All the best,

Colin

I attach the report that is titled *IYM Overview.*

For a second, I just sit and look at the e-mail. Then I hit my mouse button and click on Send.

It's one thing to avoid someone in a fifty-story corporate building, but another in the confined offices of the agency. So far, Darcy's managed to dodge me at the coffeemaker, has stepped away from her desk twice when she heard me coming, and has avoided coming into my office for any reason. I usually get a "Good morning" at least.

I make sure she's at her desk and silently make my way toward it, then knock on the wall to make sure I don't spook her.

"Hey," I say as her head jerks up.

"Oh, hi, Colin," she forces out.

I look around and make sure no one is around. "Can we talk?"

"Sure."

"The other night—"

"Please," Darcy blurts out, her eyes unable to meet mine. "I was a little—I sort of lost my way."

"Darcy, I just wanted to—"

"I didn't mean to kiss you—or try to—by the car. I know that was . . ."

"Awkward?" I ask.

"Yes."

"I didn't see it coming. And that's why I moved—it's just—"

"No, it's fine. I understand."

"It's not you. You have to understand—everything with Jen. Moving on is harder than it looks."

"I'm sorry." She looks like she wants to fold up her body and put it in a suitcase and ship it to Guam.

"Please, don't be. I just—we have to work together, and I don't want things to be awkward."

"I made an idiot of myself. How can they not be?"

"You were very kind to someone and opened up your heart. Very few people do that nowadays. I just—you have to understand, it's not you. It's all me."

Darcy looks down at her desk and nods.

"But, Darcy? Thank you."

I'm at O'Hare and feel the vibrating phone in my pocket.

"Hello?"

"Traveling these days?" the caller asks.

Not again.

"As a matter of fact, Don, I am."

"Have you had a chance to read my e-mails?"

"No. And I told you, I probably won't be able to get to them right away."

"What does it take to get respect around here? Huh?"

"It's not respect. It's time."

"This little trip of yours—"

"Donald, look—"

"No no no. You look. I go out of my way and make small talk and chitchat and all I get is the major runaround. I deserve so much more than—"

I click off the phone before he can finish that deep thought.

Maybe I need to change my number. Or call the police.

Donald is not a bad guy. He won't hurt me.

Sure about that?

He just needs validation. At least he writes and cares about that writing and is honest.

Something's wrong when I actually admire my stalker.

It's the first business trip I've taken since coming back to the office. I'm hoping that moving will keep me from the abyss that's hovering just below. Maybe, sooner or later, the pain will lessen and that heavy sole stomping my heart will subside. Meanwhile, all I can do is keep working, keep typing, keep planning.

Plans. Plans have a point, don't they? A purpose.

What is mine?

I get to the fancy hotel in southern California and check in. Out of habit I set up my laptop and plug it in. I boot it up, hoping for something from Vivian.

It's been five days. Five days and not a peep.

That's not like her.

Something's up. I know it. I wonder if I went too far.

I'm here for an afternoon meeting with Jon Berrin. Rock star and prospective author.

I dial in and retrieve my e-mails.

Sure enough, Vivian's name shows up in the in-box.

I take a breath and open it.

I read it quickly, nervously, and with each word, with each paragraph, I realize that I made an awful mistake. Perhaps my mind was clouded over by recent events. Of course it was. My whole life is draped over in a black womb and there's no way to be logical. But I missed the boat big-time here.

The e-mail doesn't even sound like Vivian.

Colin:

I'm disappointed and surprised by your e-mail. And I was thoroughly crushed by your report on *In Your Memory.* When I heard you say it was long-winded, this of course made me nervous. But after reading it, and reading all the suggestions and work you want me to do, I cannot believe you sent it. Especially without Roth and Ted reading it.

When you say I'll understand how "*In Your Memory* can be a better book," don't you realize I did everything I could to make it the best book I thought it could be? I understand that I told you that I wanted you to be honest. And I will agree it needs tweaks and changes. But you make it sound as though I handed in a first draft. If you only knew how hard I had worked on this book, Colin—if you only knew the sleepless nights and agony I put into it—you might not have been so quick to type up your nice little notes.

The work you want me to do would take months. And I have to say frankly that I agree with the other guys. I think it's ready to go. It needs an editor, of course. But the revisions you're wanting me to do . . . you're wanting a whole other book, Colin. I can only give you the best *I* can offer. That's all I'll ever do as an author.

I'm sorry you feel this way about *In Your Memory.* I know there are other agencies who will see the vision for this project and support it 100

percent. I'm sorry to hear you didn't feel I lived up to my potential on this book. I feel otherwise.

I would politely like to ask that all correspondence from here on come from Mr. Roth.

Vivian

Uh.

Oh.

I know things are bad. But then I see the **CC: Bernard Roth; Ted Varrick**.

Jon Berrin sits across from me at a six-person, oval-shaped wood table. Next to him sits his balding, chubby manager who introduces himself to me but whose name I instantly forget. Liam or Lee or something like that. On the other side sits his lawyer, Jacquelyn Avery, a petite curly-haired brunette with a smattering of red lipstick on her full lips that I can't help noticing as they move. And they move a lot. In front of Jacquelyn are folders and papers. I listen to what she says, but I can't help glancing back at Berrin.

Every other second, I ask myself what I'm doing here.

Picture some infamous member of a popular and outrageous rock group, the kind you hear about in the news. Lead singer overdoses and comes back to life. Drummer convicted of assaulting a member of the crowd. Guitarist too wrecked to play sold-out Miami show.

Berrin was the lead singer of a big-hair band of the eighties called Toxin that was known more for its offstage antics than the actual music they performed. If music is what you called it. Berrin has come to me, with his manager and with Jacquelyn, to try to find a home for his tell-all autobiography.

Before leaving, Roth told me to land this deal, that it's a big no-brainer. That means he doesn't really care what the end result will be. The front side will bring in a nice advance. This will help me "get things back in order."

That was before Vivian's nice little e-mail.

Berrin and his gang are talking big, big stuff. They act like this is Mother Teresa's autobiography. Or Harper Lee announcing she's written another novel.

I try to lower expectations.

Even as I talk, I'm thinking about Vivian. The Vivian debacle.

"Publishers have some reservations after a few lackluster performances with other celebrity bios," I tell them.

"Yeah, but you have to understand, this is different. I'm really going to write this book. *I'm* telling the stories, not some ghostwriter or something like that."

Holy momma, not that. This scares me even more. I study Jon in his black shirt with the gray-and-black tie and short hair. This guy doesn't look anything like the headbanger he was in the eighties. The thing I can't just tell him is that Jon Berrin, regardless of how many albums Toxin sold and how many women he slept with and how many times he destroyed a hotel room, might be a classic "has-been."

"The offer from Warner is a good one," I say. "They haven't gone up since we last talked."

"Tommy Lee got twice that," Jon states with frustration.

"So did others. And there's a reason they're in the closeout bins as we speak."

"So you're saying this is the best offer?" Lee or Lenny asks, his forehead dotted with sweat.

I nod. I could try to coax this conversation, but I don't care.

"Here's the thing I'm worried about," the manager continues.

"Look, we're aware of some of the things that have happened to you in the last year—"

"That isn't relevant," I state.

"—but we really feel you haven't pursued all of the opportunities that might be out there."

"The agency has tried all the major publishers," I say.

"Yeah, but—I mean, have you *really* talked to them? Have you really sold them on Berrin's story? Have you really talked to *all* of them?"

I nod and look at Berrin. "I'm not trying to do a con job here, Jon. I'm telling you the truth. Our firm has landed more *New York Times* bestsellers than any other agency over the last five years—"

"And that is why we came to you," Lee/Lonny says. "And I know you can't help personal issues affecting your life."

The audacity of this guy surprises even me. A death is considered a "personal issue." The death of my wife, an issue.

Rage rolls up my throat like bile.

"This has nothing to do with that," I say. "We can hold out for bigger offers, but I really doubt any will come our way."

"I need an agent who doesn't have doubts," Berrin says, his green eyes cutting through mine.

"It's not about doubting."

"Then what's it about?"

"This is reality. Publishers are careful about throwing millions of dollars away."

"So you're saying they'd be throwing money away?" Berrin asks.

Enough already.

"Look, we're done here," the former rock star says. He stands up.

"You gotta be joking," I utter.

"No. You've been sitting on this for the last six months. Man, I got half the book already written." He curses.

"I've met with five publishers on this personally. Do you know how rare that is?"

"We feel this is a rare book," Leon says.

"Come on."

They all stare at me, at my response.

"You're wanting a major publisher to give you what? Three million dollars or something for *your* life story? You really think that's going to happen?"

"Of course I do," Berrin says, still standing.

"Picture some businesswoman living in New York City. Or a farmer in Idaho. Or a college student in Texas. Or any number of people in small towns throughout the states. You expect these people to buy your book? A book about a rock-'n'-roll guy who wrecks his life and now wants to brag about it?"

"Mr. Scott, that's really not appropriate."

"Cut the b.s. We left being appropriate behind ten minutes ago."

I stand and collect my leather portfolio. "We're done, right?"

"Oh, yeah," Berrin says. "You bet."

"I've wasted half a year trying to sell this rubbish you call a book."

"I'm sure someone else will gladly work with us," Lee says.

"Even if they do, nobody really cares. Jon Berrin. You know, when this came across my desk, I had to ask who you were."

"Mr. Scott—" Leon tries to say.

"A washed-up rocker from a hair band from the eighties. Yeah, that has bestseller written all over it. Man, let me buy a caseload."

They gawk at me, and I realize I'm shouting.

"The thing about people like you, the thing you'll never understand, is that the world out there doesn't revolve around you. That the short amount of time in the world's history when a lot of idiots actually paid money for your moaning and wailing on a record—it doesn't matter. For a time your pathetic music made people enjoy their parties. But that was two decades ago, and the world moved on. Now your name and your music is pointless. All the money you made and lost and all your pitiful stories about all of it—it-just-doesn't-matter."

Berrin feigns an unconcerned laugh, but his face is flushed with embarrassment. Leon stares at me with a mouth that might as well be wide open and an expression that says *I wish I had the guts to say that.*

I don't wait to hear their responses. I leave the room and walk down a hallway and step on an elevator and then walk out of the office building to find a taxi.

A personal issue.

This isn't personal. It's all about business.

And I've closed shop for the day.

"Why don't you marry me?"

She looked at me and smiled. Sometimes her eyes looked so luscious, so ethereal, so otherworldly. Contrasted with the way they almost appeared sad. This combination made Jennifer such an enigma. What rested beneath those eyes, that slight smile on full lips I loved to kiss?

"You're crazy," she replied.

"I know."

"Are you proposing?" she asked. "I don't see a ring."

"You really need a ring?"

"You bet. And a big mansion. And some glorious huge spectacle of a wedding."

"You got it," I said. "Then what?"

We stopped walking and she slid her arm around my back and tugged me close to her. She kissed me. The crowd passing by on the lake's shore, the joggers and walkers and bikers and roller bladers, all disappeared. None of them mattered. Some probably watched us lock in an embrace. But Jennifer didn't care about the rest of the world. And that was one reason why I loved her so.

Oh to have a moment like that back.

I stand on the moving walkway and listen to the sounds of new age music and voices saying the walkway is about to end. Glittering lights of orange and blue and red illuminate the walls I pass. I can almost close my eyes and fall back to sleep. Almost.

I take a train to the remote parking lot. It's close to two in the morning. What a wretched trip. Flying out to Anaheim on last minute's notice, all to have the deal blow up in my face. I don't even wonder if I could have saved the meeting, the client. I don't want him. Does Roth? I don't care. I just want to get back home.

First Lisa "it's all about my fans" Beck. Then the Kurt Dobbs fiasco. Then Vivian Brown to make it a trifecta.

Well, folks, let's just add Jon Berrin to the carnage.

And, oh yeah, I forgot about Kelly Moyet.

The names and numbers are adding up so that I can't keep track of them. I'm a laundry list of disasters.

I walk off the train and downstairs and through cars to find my BMW. I stride down one row, then another. It's cool for the August night. There is a slight breeze.

"What's up, man?" says a voice behind me.

I turn around to see a tall kid, scrawny, wearing a black jacket, one hand in his pocket.

I continue walking and hear his steps rumble up behind me.

"Hey, you, stop."

I halt as he orders, my heart racing. He has short hair, buzzed like a Marine's. A pimply face, narrow, with distant eyes.

"Give me your wallet, man."

He produces what looks like a flat object, possibly a knife, possibly a short piece of metal, maybe a gun, though I really doubt it. As he produces the object, I drop my briefcase and ram him in a full tackle. My arms are positioned like a defensive tackle's, readying to take on some big guard. I slam into his hundred and fifty pounds and propel him into an SUV. His head and back pound against the metal and the wind is knocked out of him and whatever object he is holding drops to the pavement and he utters a choking "ugh."

Man it feels good pummeling someone.

As he stands clutching his chest, I wail a fist against his head. I imagine landing some incredible blow, some awesome and inspiring boxerlike punch that sends him across the parking lot. Instead, I hit him between his temple and ear. He simply screams out a wimpy "Oww" and shields his face.

"Get out of here." I wonder if my voice sounds as loud as I think it does.

The kid scampers away. I find my briefcase and pick it up and turn to keep looking for my car.

Then I pause, glancing at the black pavement to find the mugger's weapon of choice.

A shiny, stubby handgun rests on the ground. Heavy enough to be real. Probably loaded.

I slip the revolver into my briefcase and keep looking for my car.

This will be the last business trip I take for quite some time.

2:47 A.M. I arrive home.

If that's what I can call it.

I don't turn lights on, but set down my briefcase near the door and my keys on the glass dining table and walk across the wood floor toward the uncurtained windows.

The night, even at this late hour, glimmers.

On one side, the windows offer a view of downtown Chicago. I see the bright skyline in the distance. On the other side, the dark secrets of Lake Michigan.

Sometimes Jennifer and I would come in and not turn on the lights and find our way toward the family room couch between both views. We would behave like a couple of teenagers, all over each other, immersed in passion. Sometimes we'd even sleep on the oversized white couch that is probably just as comfortable as our bed. Waking up with the morning light too bright to look at right away.

This place feels hollow without her. Nearly everything that occupies this apartment belongs to both of us. Or belonged. Every piece of furniture, every piece of art, voted on and decided by an overwhelming majority of two to zero.

I look out toward the city and wonder how I can go on. I've been trying. But it's been more like running. Running away. Running from her. From this place.

Is this what grieving's all about?

Of course.

So how am I doing? What sort of a grade do I get for this grief? C-plus? A-minus? I don't know. All I know is I'm trying to move on, but it's not working.

Being here suddenly feels scary. As if someone's going to step out of the shadows and start talking to me at any moment. Sometimes I wait for her to.

I know this is pathetic. What do I want? A voice from the grave?

I go to the fridge and find a bottled water. Something reeks of old age, but I ignore it and close the door. I gulp down the water as I sit back on the couch that sucks me in.

Can the dead see you? Can they read your thoughts and hear your words?

I love you Jennifer. I'll always love you. I will always and only love you and I know you might not believe that but I will. Always. Only. You.

Can she possibly ever hear me again? Does she echo these words?

Somewhere between telling Jennifer I love her, that I still need her, that I still want her—somewhere between saying all of this out loud and thinking it and acting like a nutcase talking to the dead—I fall asleep.

As I Lay Dying

Open your eyes.

"Jen . . ." I start to say.

But that's always when I wake up. Really wake up. Wake up to reality. To the sound of my voice talking to myself, to a body sleeping next to himself, to a life living with itself.

I want more.

After the California trip, I need time to regroup. Like maybe a year or so.

I take a few days off. Both phones ring, with voice mails from Darcy and Ted and Roth. I delete all without hearing them. I get e-mail I delete. More e-mail. I need space and time and I need life.

I wander my condo in sweatpants and a T-shirt. I feel so out of shape. My diet consists of food I can have delivered. My beard is starting to get creepy.

I look at photos. Some are missing. Did I put them away already? Why is it that I feel like my life is in one random déjà vu? Like I've been here before but I'm missing something? Why do I feel like this is a movie and the end credits are going to roll and I'm going to walk out of the apartment and find her, find them, find the life that has suddenly escaped?

This is ugly, and I know it. But I'm scared.

I might not have a job when I leave the condo. But that doesn't scare me.

It's the fact that I don't care.

The things I want to say to Roth and things I want to do to Ted—that's what scares me.

Everything is unraveling.

Everything is falling apart.

I'm trying to disappear and I believe that I've discovered how to disappear completely.

Why'd you do this, God?

Are you up there? Are you? I want a sign. I want something. I feel like I deserve it.

I didn't say much when you took my father. I didn't because I figured that was life.

I didn't say anything when you decided to make us wait. Wait for a child we wanted.

They say you can see everything, that you're all knowing and all powerful. If so, then you knew what was in our hearts. Why couldn't you be so powerful as to give us our hearts' desires?

I didn't say anything, but I'm saying something now. I don't care how and why and when and what. I'm saying something, and I want an answer.

Maybe an answer can't come because I'm talking to an empty room in an empty condo.

Maybe an answer can't come because you're not there.

Adam and Eve and Noah and Moses and King David are all characters in a fairy tale. Made up by some author with imagination like Vivian Brown. All those stories are just part of the lore, part of the way of making schmucks like me cling to something when there's nothing to cling to.

Maybe there was a man named Jesus at one point in history, but he was just a good man with crazy strange powers. He didn't die to save anybody. He didn't rise from the dead.

If he did those things, then why can't you raise Jen?

You can't because you're not there and you've never been there.

I don't need a Bible full of a bunch of clichés.

I don't need a lecture on how to live my life.

I don't have a life anymore. I'm empty and angry and if you're up there, if you're really truly up there, help me. I'm lying here dying and you know it and you can see this pain. It's a plain and an ocean and a universe of pain and you know that nothing will ever get rid of it nothing and I will do anything say anything be anything if you just help me help me God help me.

Please God help me.

I will believe but I need help.

God I need help.

You have to live, Colin.

Yes, I guess I do.

But what I'm doing now isn't living.

I don't go outside. Don't call in to work sick. I occasionally order in food. But I don't care anymore. Grief is a twenty-four-hour job.

It's an amazing thing, the way grief sucks you in and holds you down like an ocean's undertow. The surface is right above you, just an arm's length away perhaps, yet you can't swim to the top. You're unable to do anything except watch the light dim as you sink lower and lower.

Perhaps that is exactly what happened to Jen.

It's late at night so late and so dark and the cell phone near the sanctuary of my bed rings. It goes until it gets voice mail. A minute later, it rings again.

I fumble for it in the black and pick it up.

Colin?

The voice seems so close, so real, so soft.

Colin?

And I answer with a yes.

Are you okay?

And I answer with a no.

I can't come back. Not now. Not like this.

And I don't answer.

Colin—I'm worried about you.

And I say you should be.

Just hold on. Just be careful.

And I ask how.

Morning smiles like the face of a newborn child.

And then the conversation fades away and I look and see that it's early morning.

Under the Volcano

MovieNewsandNotes.com says that *Immersion* has still not started shooting. There are rumored rewrites on the script. Julia Roberts is having to juggle her schedule to fit the movie in. Thomas Newman, noted movie composer of works such as *The Horse Whisperer* and *American Beauty*, will be writing the score.

It's two in the morning and I'm surfing the Internet. I Google Jennifer Scott and see a listing of the movies she's worked on. I type in Vivian-Brown.com and see a note to her readers, how she's currently writing a new novel that she's excited to finally unveil. She says writing, not rewriting.

I'm bored and should be sleeping and should get up tomorrow and go to work but I don't want to. Ever since the trip to see Jon Berrin, I haven't set foot back at the agency.

The writing is on the wall.

I should be browsing FindANewJob.com. Or GetALife.com.

"Colin, I know you're there. Pick up the phone."

I can hear Roth's voice yelling into the phone, adding profanities as he orders me to answer.

"Colin, it's been two weeks."

Another curse, another order. But I just sit there on my couch.

Go back in? For what? They're already moving ahead with Vivian. They don't need me.

But you need them, a voice tells me.

Yes, I know. The mail keeps bombarding me with bills. Endless bills. Pearce keeps leaving me messages about the standstill on the house in St. Charles. The bank has called. My mortgage company has called. My rent check is late. I know how much I have in my account. I've got money saved, but not enough to cover me if I lose my job.

Maybe I should be worried.

Maybe I just don't care.

I'm looking for a copy of the report I sent Vivian when I find the partial manuscript in my briefcase. Ian Pollock's story. I forgot all about it.

It's probably average at best.

Then again, everything is subjective. Everything is based on opinion. And upbringing. And bias. And mood.

You can show a group of editors the same idea. One might have just had a lousy batch of Chinese food and not be interested. Another might be going through bad times with his wife and may not be interested in a book about failed relationships and how to repair them. It might be a guy who is sick and tired of warm and fuzzy stories. It may be a young woman recently promoted who doesn't like the dark and edgy violence of your material. If you're new, it's all skewed. It's regarded with thin eyes and narrow views.

If you're big, then everything is a free-for-all. Then you can sign a contract for *whatever* on a napkin. You can come up with a series on soil growth and make it into a three-book deal.

I pick up Ian Pollock's book. I stopped on page two the first time I started to read it. Why should I continue when I have a hundred other pressing things to read? Why should I give this kid my time and energy? Well, now it's because I have nothing better to do. My authors—what authors do I have? I have nobody. Vivian Brown. Vivian who? They're all gone.

Ian's still out there.

So I start reading again. Page three. Egad.

Page four. Hmm.

Page five. He really needs a copy editor.

Page six. Whatever.

But suddenly I begin to see something. Someone. I hear, amidst the myriad of adverbs he can't resist using and a penchant for description that borders the ridiculous, a voice. Full of angst. Naïve, but somehow unique.

And on page seven, I am actually drawn in.

They tell you that if the first paragraph doesn't hook you, try again. And definitely if the first page doesn't hook you, do over. And I've tried at least twice reading this, this story, and have not yet been hooked. Until page seven, when the character stops moaning and finds a dead body and thus gets the inciting incident and begins the story.

Page seven is where the novel should begin.

It's where I finally hear Ian Pollock's voice.

And it's actually pretty good.

He writes with a passion and intensity that remind me of someone else.

I'm not thinking Vivian Brown, either.

He reminds me of myself. Ten years ago. Full of spunk, ambition, drive, passion. Ready to take on the world.

I don't care how many times I'm rejected I'm going to keep at it over and over and over again.

I don't care what they say. I'll keep trying again.

If this one doesn't work, I'll simply start another.

I have a story to tell and I keep telling it, in various forms and styles and genres.

It's my story and it's dying to come out.

And by page ten, I'm thinking I've found someone.

But the truth is this:

He found me.

"You look terrible," Roth tells me.

"Why, thank you."

"I'm serious."

"And I'm appreciative of your fashion advice."

Roth curses and looks toward the kitchen. "Got anything to drink?"

I nod and walk toward the cabinet where we stored whatever liquor we had. I see that I've polished off the gin and vodka, but there's a little rum. Roth allows me to fix him a rum and Coke.

We make space at the end of the glass-topped dining room table. Papers and unopened bills litter the rest. It's Wednesday afternoon and Roth decided to stop by my place. No way I could avoid letting my boss come into my condo when he's downstairs buzzing to get in.

"You need a secretary in here," Roth says as I clear some of the papers away.

"I need more than a secretary."

Roth takes a sip of his drink. "This is hard for me to do, Colin."

I nod. I'd be a moron not to know what's coming. When I heard the doorbell ring for the third time followed by Roth's barks to let me in, I knew the moment had arrived.

"I was going to send Ted," Roth says.

"Why didn't you?"

"Because I thought you might end up shooting him."

Roth doesn't realize he's not far from the truth. I still have a loaded gun in my bedroom. I think about the handgun more and more these days.

"Thanks for coming yourself."

"I don't know what happened, Colin."

"Want me to rehash?"

Roth shakes his head. "Eventually you gotta get up and get moving. A heart attack wouldn't stop me a few years ago. I was back—"

"This is different."

"Yeah, sure, it's different. But we're talking about your life. You still have yours, and you have to move on."

"Is this a pep talk?" I ask.

Roth gives me a hard look, one I know well. He's given it many times to many publishers. I always feared being on the other side of one of those.

"What on God's green earth were you thinking, sending Vivian that e-mail?" he bellows.

"I was giving her the truth."

"Without even *showing* it to me? After you knew we had approved that manuscript?"

"I like that."

"What?"

"*We.*"

Roth curses. "Who cares about Ted? All right, after *I* approved it."

"Behind my back."

"Behind your back? You were out. Dealing with—dealing with things."

"Things." I let go a harsh laugh.

"Yes. And I'm sorry about them. And I'm sorry that business needed to move on. But it did. And I made a call."

"So did I."

"Last time I checked, it's my name on the letterhead, Colin."

I should say something back, and normally I would. But I'm too tired. And I don't really care.

"I have to let you go."

"Yeah, okay."

Roth stares at me, perplexed. He waits for a moment, expecting more.

"That's it?" he finally asks.

"What?"

" 'Okay'? That's all you have to say?"

"What else should I say? You've made up your mind. I've seen that look on your face. I've heard that tone. I know you're not changing your mind."

"I could be persuaded, if you argued your case."

"There's nothing to argue," I say. "I'm too tired to argue."

"You'll move past this," Roth says, as if trying to win me back.

"I was tired before any of this happened. I was tired, but I still had a reason to care. Now, I feel nothing. Nothing but exhaustion."

Roth downs his glass. "Tell me something," he says.

"What?"

"Did I misjudge you?"

I shake my head.

"I mean, I know people. I *get* people. And somehow I'm thinking that this—that you—were a wasted cause."

"Maybe," is all I'm able to say.

Roth stands up, and I just stay seated, my eyes following him out. He looks back, and I see a look of regret on his face. I wonder what he's regretting. Jen's death? My career's death? My current sorry state of affairs? The fact that he invested so much time on a wasted cause?

I don't know.

I'm too tired to care.

We're standing in the kitchen drinking iced tea. I've just gone over different drawings and torn-out sheets from magazines like *American Dream Houses.* Pearce laughs at me as I describe the proposed ideas for the crown molding in each of the rooms.

"What?" I ask.

"No, this is good. I like this."

"You like what?"

"Obviously you've been doing your homework," he tells me.

"I know I've been MIA for a while."

"It's understandable."

"There's something else I should probably tell you."

"Yeah?"

"This is my job now."

"*This* being . . . ?"

"*This* being right here, helping get this house up, helping to make it a dream house that will sell for a lot of money."

Pearce just stares at me for a minute, not quite comprehending my words.

"I got canned yesterday. Not that I blame them, since I've basically been missing there too."

"Man—I'm sorry, Colin."

"Yeah, me too. This house—this is all I have now."

He looks around the kitchen, then back at me.

"You don't have to say anything meaningful," I tell him. "I just thought you needed to know."

"Yeah, okay."

"And don't worry—you're going to be paid. I've got enough to be able to—"

"It's fine," Pearce interrupts.

"How are we looking overall with the house?"

"Things have been on hold for a while. I can only do so much without being able to get a crew—"

"I'll help. I don't know how—I mean, you know how much of a builder I am. But I'll help in any way I can."

"Having an extra pair of hands is everything," Pearce says, always the optimist.

He proceeds to tell me the things that need work. Ladders and several open toolboxes and uncarpeted floors and wood blocks and cans of paint surround us.

All I can think is how much work it's going to take to finish this place.

What was I thinking, buying this thing?

But that was when the dream was still attainable. The great American dream everybody wants to have and every author wants to write about.

I didn't know it would turn into a Stephen King novel.

Rain sprinkles the glass, the lights from the oncoming traffic shimmering in the liquid covering. I drive down Interstate 88 and stay in the left lane of three headed east into the city. The afternoon's snuck up on me, and now I'm paying for it by driving home in rush hour. At least the traffic heading west looks worse. My hands grip the steering wheel and ache from the work on the house.

There is something invigorating about physical labor, something you can never get out of typing e-mails and sitting on your can drinking diet sodas and yapping on the phone and pursuing contracts. The dried blood on torn knuckles, the blisters, the effort of a long day of hard work, with physical exhaustion but no emotional overload. I'm doing something again. As though the last few months, the last few years, have been nothing but circling smoke rings in the sky that always fade away.

As I merge onto the Eisenhower heading downtown, and the Interstate becomes stop-and-go, my eyes feel heavier. I am thankful I don't have to make this commute every day, that I've been free from this for most of my career. Taking the morning walk, grabbing a cup of coffee, getting to work fifteen minutes early—that's been my life. Having the nice apartment along Lake Michigan certainly helps.

Better not get used to it, pal. Not in your current sorry state of financial affairs.

I often used to wonder where I'd live if I ever made it big. Huge. If I ever managed to make a Colin Scott Agency or Associates or whatever it might be called. Would I head back to the suburbs and settle down? Or would I, or I should say would we, stay in the city? The question doesn't matter anymore. I don't care where I end up. It looks like the Colin Scott solo project has been launched a little prematurely. Its founder and owner is temporarily overloaded. The last thing he needs is the angst of several authors ringing around his neck. He needs time and space. He needs to find himself.

And he needs to stop referring to himself in the third person.

I stop the BMW and watch the rain continue to fall. My eyes drift off for a second and then open again. I shake my head and inhale to try to wake myself up. The physical labor is good for something—I'll probably get a good night's rest for the first time in a while. Maybe I'll even take a snooze right there on the Eisenhower.

Traffic continues at this snail's pace, and one stop lasts a few seconds. I nod off and then my head jerks itself awake. I stare ahead and the bumper in front of me is no longer there, so I speed up.

Then I notice the empty lane in front of me. And next to me. And a third lane over.

I glance into my rearview mirror and no longer see lights.

Nothing's there.

I turn my head around and glance out the back window. Nothing but darkness.

Absolute emptiness.

It's like some elaborate prank where all of a sudden the vehicles behind me turned off their headlights at the exact same time.

I see miles of empty highway behind me. And in front of me.

Okay.

I decelerate and keep looking around me. First in front, to the side, then over past the Metra tracks to the other lanes. Nothing there either.

I curse out loud and stop the car.

Shake my head.

Then look out again. Same thing.

Breathe in, breathe out.

What's going on?

I can feel my heart beating against my chest. I do the thing to my head again, as if to jostle my temporarily paused brain, closing my eyes, then opening them again. Same thing. Nobody around me. Not a car in sight. Nor a headlight, nor a train, nor a person, nothing.

You've reached the end now son.

The lights lining the highway are still on, as are the distant signs for the nearby exit. Rain continues to fall.

Is this what they call the rapture? I've read a few novels about all that. But for some weird reason God decided to take automobiles back to heaven too?

I put my car in park and open the door. This isn't a dream. It can't be. The cold air outside would have woken me up. The rain that will probably start freezing later glazes over me as I breathe in the sharp tinge of cold. I scan all around and still can't spot one single car.

My BMW still rests, waiting, its lights jutting through the rain and the dim light. I walk in front of those lights and see an open stretch of highway waiting for me, beckoning me. Nothing around.

I keep walking. A hundred yards, more.

This is real. This is not a hallucination. The rain dampens my hair, dripping down my face. My palms feel the droplets. My lips taste the rain.

I am alone.

I begin to run like a madman.

Have you ever been chased in a forest, knowing that if you turn around you'll trip and fall and be caught? Like in some slasher flick? This is how I feel. And the harder I run and the farther my legs take me, the more panicked I become. Fear and adrenaline and confusion rocket through my body and my mind. And as I manage to get further and further away from the headlights, the more furiously the rain begins to pound.

Just me and you God and I'm not losing.

Not this time.

Drenched, sweaty, out of breath, out of mind, I stop.

"You want me up there?" I scream out loud. "Come get me!"

I turn around and I realize that I am in the middle of the busy Interstate and cars are racing at me and there is no way to get out of their enraged path.

I shut my eyes and cringe and then find myself with one arm over my face as the lights begin to merge into one, all focusing on me, piercing into my eyes, banging against my head, calling my name . . .

"You okay?"

I look at the open window and then squint at the spider glass windshield in front of me. Some pieces of glass lie in my lap. An airbag has been ripped open, and I'm just sitting there, wondering what's going on. My headlights look embedded in the concrete edge of the freeway.

"We got someone coming to get you," the man with the light says.

Now I know I must be dreaming. The guy talking to me looks like Mr. Roth dressed in a cop's outfit.

A question Jen asked me in Cancun suddenly scrolls through my mind.

"Is it worth it?" she asked.

"What?"

"All of it."

"I don't know. Ask me in a few years."

We were lounging poolside, me reading the manuscript and Jennifer reading *Vogue*. We had been in Cancun for several days and the rain had finally stopped.

I should've made her stay there, by my side. But I couldn't.

Jen was always independent, even in her death.

I wake up thinking of this conversation, and I say something out loud and realize I'm in a bed at the hospital. The only person I can think for them to call is Pearce. His business card is in my wallet, so they call him.

All I got out of the crash on the Interstate was a concussion. They checked me for drugs and alcohol, then wanted to know if everything was okay. They even sent in a shrink after I told them my wife had died and I have "not been myself" lately. Now I'm just waiting for a few more tests before being let go.

Not myself. Yeah. I guess I can say that.

I must have swerved into the guardrail on the Eisenhower, and though I hadn't killed myself or anyone else, I created a nightmare of a traffic mess for the evening commuters and banged up my BMW pretty bad. At least I was okay.

Are you okay?

Jennifer asked me that by the pool.

I close my eyes and I'm back there.

"I'm just tired," I told Jen. And I was.

You seem unusually so.

Pearce is driving me home. He asks again if I want to stay with his family.

"Thanks, really. But no."

I think of having to hold one of his three kids or make small talk with Kristy. She's pleasant and the kids are great, but I'm not in the mood to be around a family.

"How are you feeling?"

"Hungover," I say. "I don't know what happened out there."

"You should be taking it easy," Pearce says. "No more nail guns for you."

"I haven't been getting a lot of sleep lately. The kind I have hasn't been the best."

"I'm not going to hear about you doing something goofy, like swallowing a bottle of aspirin or something?"

"No, not me."

"Good," Pearce says.

"I've never liked aspirin. Maybe extra-strength Tylenol." I laugh at my own joke.

"That's not funny."

"Thanks for picking me up," I tell him.

"Call me tomorrow."

"Okay, Mom."

I say *yeah* a lot these days.

"You've gone two months without paying a rent check, Mr. Scott, and I need to see something in the next week. . . ."

Yeah.

"Do you want me to pick up your things from the office, or do you want to swing by when Roth and Ted are out. . . ."

Yeah.

"Do you want to come down and stay with us awhile, because we can always make up the extra bedroom. . . ."

Yeah.

"We're thinking about naming the boy Colin after you, what do you think, huh . . ."

Yeah.

Everything can go on hold so easily. A world can become so busy, so overwhelming, so consuming, but when you have no one there to be busy and overwhelmed and consumed for, why bother?

So I don't. I let the days keep slipping by.

Yeah.

I'm picking up lemons when I see him. Donald doesn't even try to hide—his tall figure with the long head and wide eyes is pretty hard to miss. I just stand there and wait as he strolls up to me.

"Little shopping today?"

"What is this?"

"Excuse me?" Donald says, as if he has no idea why my tone and glance reek of disdain.

"Do I have to wonder if you're following me every time I walk out my door?"

"Not every time."

"What do you want?"

"What do I want? Hmm. Let me see."

"You want me to read your book."

Donald feigns shock and amazement. "Hallelujah, it's a miracle!"

"Look—I don't think you want me to—"

"Oh, I know."

"You know what?"

"Your—shall we say, *separation* of sorts from the Roth Agency."

"I got fired."

"You could protest."

I shake my head and throw the lemons into the bag.

"I assume you'll be bringing some of your authors with you?"

"And where would that be?" I ask him.

"To your new agency."

I laugh. The guy just doesn't get it.

"I'm out. It's done. I've been in the publishing game long enough."

Donald narrows his eyes and gives me a suspicious look.

"That's impossible."

"*Nothing* is impossible."

"Oh no?"

"No."

"Not even getting your life back on track? Having a family and a home in the suburbs and a nice beautiful wife and 2.5 kids?"

I just stand there, utterly in shock at his audacity, at his error in judgment. An open, gaping wound, and he's not just pouring salt on it, he's dousing lye all over it.

"You said anything is possible," Donald says, with a mocking grin on his face. "Tell me, Colin. Do you truly believe that?"

With the plastic bag holding five lemons in my right hand, I rush past the shopping cart and bash the lemons against Donald's smug face. I pummel him into the display of fruit. Donald falls backward onto the table and launches five hundred lemons everywhere.

When a manager finally gets to me and grabs my collar and orders me off Donald, I'm hovering over him with both hands wrapped around his neck, squeezing as hard as I can.

And all throughout, Donald taunts me, asking me the same question over and over.

"Do you believe? Do you believe?"

The reality sometimes is not that bleak, not that dark. Sometimes when it comes down to those last few seconds, a heart is not full of emptiness or darkness. I'm holding some stranger's gun in my hand

and I put it in my mouth and I wonder why not and go ahead and all those things but it's not despondency I feel but an ironic fullness. I feel bloated with memories of everything that once was. And everything that could have been.

All that could have been . . .

I remember voice mails and answering machines and messages.

"Jen, it's Colin" and "Hey, what's up?" and "Where are you?" and "I'm going to be late" and "I love you" and "Can't wait to see you." Spoken in some other town, or uttered on a hotel answering machine or on a cell phone. Said miles away. Always miles away. Just like it feels now.

I remember the love, the passion, the kisses. But I can't remember much else. Except being away.

Movies seen. Rented and in theaters. And dining out and in crowds and shopping and traveling and going on vacaction but not a lot of still, living time. The sort of time I long for, the sort I always dreamed about. Build a fortune and retire early and then spend quality, quiet time together. Sitting next to each other reading. Holding hands walking down the street. Sipping coffee across from one another on a city bench. Seeing art and museums and animals and the world together.

I want it back.

I want her back. I want a chance to do it over again and a chance to say more than "love you" or "see you" and "can't wait to be back home." Home. What a concept anyway.

Everything you should have said.

Yes, I know, and yet I can't do anything anymore. I can't leave any more voice mails. I can't receive any more e-mails. I can't take any more photos of her even though so many are strewn about the bed I'm sitting on. I see her again. She looks beautiful. But beyond that, what is there? Beyond the physical beauty, what was there?

Did I really know?

I lick the barrel and know this is wrong but I feel so weighted down and unable to move. I'm sad, but it's so much more than that. Nobody can ever understand unless they're in the same boat. Messages left and regrets offered and sympathies said and all of them mean nothing anymore. It's just Jennifer and the memory of her.

Where are you and will I see you if I press this trigger?

I don't know.

I doubt there's another place to go.

That would mean there would need to be faith.

Did I even have faith when Jen existed? What about those moments of doubt and question that would always and only abate when I took her in my arms?

Another place?

I don't believe there's any other place than here. And in the vaults of memory.

You said anything is possible. Tell me, Colin. Do you truly believe that?

I can still hear the madman author's voice, can still feel the muscles in his neck as I tried to squeeze the life out of them, can still see his delirious and insane look as he told the cop he wasn't going to press charges, that I'm one of his friends.

Do you believe?

And the answer is no, I don't believe, I never believed and will never believe in anything again. I begged and pleaded with the idea of a God above and got nothing but silence.

The phone next to the bed rings. I take the gun out of my mouth and listen to it ring. Twice. Three times. Then I hear the answering machine.

It's probably Ted calling to rub it in. Or maybe Roth wanting me back. Or Pearce calling to talk about the house. Or Donald asking about the manuscript he gave me before I left the grocery store.

And then

"Colin?"

I look at the answering machine.

"I don't know what to say," the voice says.

There's noise in the background. What time is it anyway? Late. That's all I know.

"I just wanted—I'm thinking about you."

And you know there's no voice because it's her voice.

Colin I just wish I could see you. I've been up and thinking—I miss you so much. I miss you but know I can't be with you.

It's all in your mind.

A voice mail from heaven. From that other place. How sweet.

I just—maybe we should talk. Maybe just—if you—I don't—I'm sorry.

And then nothing more. The answering machine stops.

I look at it and in this dream the light throbs and I stare back at the gun and wonder what I'm doing.

This must be a dream. Another dream.

I press the delete button on the machine without listening to it again.

In the morning when I wake, there will be no message.

But the gun will be resting at my side, still there, still waiting.

Invisible Man

It's amazing how two months can disappear.

October and November are blurs, smudges, forgotten fingerprints. I try to recall how a day became a week and a week became two months.

I lose myself in Vonnegut and the Beatles. I cocoon myself in my condo. I try not to think of the business or the business of suffering. I try to separate my mind and my body from the present, from the now.

Sometimes it's easy to do.

Sometimes I find myself waking up out of a dream. Sometimes I find myself falling asleep into a nightmare.

It's scary that sometimes I don't know the difference.

"Hello darkness my old friend, I've come to talk with you again. . . ."

The words and music of Simon & Garfunkel echo in my mind. As do the words and voice of Vivian Brown and her novel *In Your Memory.*

I'm almost packed up, if packed up is what I can call it. There are so many things I'm leaving behind at this condo, so few items I'm taking with me. It's okay. They say you can't take anything with you when you die and I feel like I'm already dead, so it doesn't matter that much.

I have a box of all my notes and scribbles on the manuscript. It doesn't grieve me to think of the lost deal or the lost job. It really truly grieves me to think that this book may be published and live up to a quarter of its potential.

That's what kills me. What I long for is something more. Something above average. Something that can transcend the genre and the story and can last.

I hold a photo of Jen and me in my hands.

Something that could last.

What lasts anymore these days? Does anything?

In Your Memory had potential. It *has* potential, but my time with it is over.

It will do well, I'm sure of it. A handful of book reviewers might even give it starred reviews. And readers will enjoy it. But I don't believe it will have the impact it could have had, or last the way it could have lasted.

Some authors are content to have their books be beach reads. But Vivian—she has always been about more than that.

I close the box on her manuscript and know that it's a thing of my past. Like all the things in my past, I need to let it go.

I'm walking to get my car when my phone vibrates. I take it out of my pocket and look at the screen.

It says I have a new message.

I flip open the phone and see that I have a text message. I don't text many people, so I wonder who it might be.

I can't help but think of Donald Hardbein.

Leaving so soon?

I stand there in the muted light of the overcast day, making sure I read the text right.

I look around.

I keep walking to my car, but a minute later the phone buzzes again. I look back at the screen.

Where are you?

Again, I can't help but look around. There is a slight breeze, and the temperature is cool for this late fall day. A woman is walking her dog. There is a couple walking. Nobody else is around.

It says the text is from Unknown. That helps.

I decide to answer. I type my message quickly.

Who is this?

I wait for a minute, than another.

Hello? I type.

The message comes back quickly.

You know who this is.

Donald? I reply.

There is nothing for another minute. This is why I hate texting. It's like having a conversation with someone from opposite sides of the Grand Canyon.

Who is Donald?

I quickly type back **who is this?**

Please . . .

Please what? I ask.

Don't be that way.

I stare at the message and wonder what it's talking about.

What way?

Again, I wait for a minute. Then another. I can see why when the message comes up. It's long.

You need to take things easy. Take them slow. Don't rush. Things will fall into place.

Again I type **Who is this?**

I'm worried about you, the message says.

Is this God? I ask.

Yes, and I'm worried about your soul. ☺

This text scares me.

I don't have one.

Then I try to shut my phone off, but then wonder if it's been off this entire time.

One Flew Over the Cuckoo's Nest

The house echoes when I walk. I feel like a mouse in a circus tent before the show's come to town. Silent and still, it's a 10,000-square-foot tomb. Thankfully the heat works. The December night is cold.

I've been here for two weeks. The apartment is long gone.

Amazing how easy it is to get rid of something along Lake Michigan when you really want to. Or make that really *have* to.

Merry Christmas and Hallelujah. Some couple will be spending a nice Christmas in the apartment I basically handed over.

I didn't have a choice. And with Jen gone, I didn't really care.

I left most of our stuff there. Part of the package deal. Move into your very own fully furnished apartment complete with the haunting memories of the deceased woman who bought it all. The couch Jen and I would sometimes sleep on or make love on. Gone. Our bedroom set. Gone. The dining room table we both selected. Gone. Most everything gone.

Now I've got a mattress I bought at a thrift store. Several suitcases and boxes. Some other items are packed and stored in a corner of the family room. The space is massive, and I'm sitting on a beanbag chair in the middle of the room when my cell phone rings.

It's 11:34 P.M. I can't sleep. But why is my phone ringing?

The centerpiece of the living room is the magnificent fireplace that is topped by an ornate mantelpiece. On an adjacent wall, underneath tall windows filling half the wall from the ceiling down, I have hung a plasma television I brought from the apartment. It looks oddly out of place in the bare-bones room. I mute it as I walk to the kitchen counter and pick up the phone, wondering who might be calling at this hour.

Perhaps it is Mr. Roth telling me he made a big mistake and he wants me back.

He reconsidered after reviewing my well-thought-out overview of *In Your Memory.* Not only does he want me back, but he's going to triple my salary just because he behaved like a moron.

The number on the phone is an unrecognizable area code.

Most of the authors I worked with don't have my cell number, and the names of the few that do would pop up on the caller ID screen. *Unknown* is what it says.

On the fifth ring, I press the Talk button.

"Hello?"

Colin.

I inhale suddenly and jerk my head to glance behind me, as though the voice is coming from one of the many empty rooms in the house. As I move to the middle of the spacious living room, I look up at the second-floor balcony staring down at me.

I don't respond. I know I'm imagining it.

Colin. Are you there?

I swallow and feel my whole body shudder, and I grip the phone. A chill washes over me. It's one thing to dream this, but I'm not sleeping. I know it. You don't feel and see goose bumps on your skin in your dreams.

"Who is this?" I ask, though I already know.

Colin, it's me.

I want to look back at the caller ID on the face of the phone, but I don't, in fear of losing the voice. A soft voice, airy and gentle and incredibly familiar.

I want to cry. It's been so long since I've heard it, since I've heard her.

You are dreaming this, I realize.

"Why are you calling?" is all I can think to say.

I was worried about you.

"Why?"

I know what happened.

I look around the dimly lit room again and can't shake the feeling that I am being watched. Or that I am fast asleep on the beanbag in front of the plasma screen on the wall, zoning out after watching *ESPN SportsCenter*.

Yet the beanbag remains empty. I kick it with my foot, and white stuffing falls out on the maple wood floor. I'm not dreaming I know I'm not dreaming.

Colin, are you there?

"Who is this?"

You know who this is.

"What's going on?"

What do you mean?

"I mean, why—how can you be calling? You're not really there. I know you're not. You can't be."

You're making me worry.

"This is not happening."

Col, please.

My whole body quivers.

I have not been called Col in a long time.

Perhaps somebody else might embrace this call, this second chance, this dreamlike séance. But I don't want to speak to the dead. I shouldn't be able to speak to the dead, and this is just one more thing I am losing. How does it go? Does it go like this? You lose your wife, then your motivation, then your job and your home, and finally your sanity.

Uh-uh, I think. *No way.*

I might be losing everything else, but not that.

"Whoever you are, I'm not buying."

And I shut off the phone before I can hear Jennifer's voice say another word. But I know she won't. Because I know it's not Jennifer and it will never be Jennifer and real or imagined it doesn't matter because she is gone.

The phone rings again. I stare at it on the kitchen island, a dark marble countertop that so far has only been used to hold boxes of pizza or bags of fast food.

It rings. Twice. Three times. Four. Five.

Pick it up and talk to her.

Six. Seven.

What about my voice mail, I wonder.

But it keeps ringing. And ringing. Until I finally open up the receiver and press the Off button and silence it.

The dreams, the demons, whatever they might be, are gone.

For now.

I hear creaks at night. As if Jen's ghost wanders around the black, empty rooms upstairs. I avoid them after sunset, the carpeted floors that are bare and spacious. The stairs that turn three corners, making a square as they twist upwards, seem to be a doorway to another dimension, a gateway to a darker place. Alone, I try not to think about the noises in the settling house, because I know that's all they are. Grunts and groans of a newly built house settling. That's all they can be.

Until the night I hear the knocking. It is several knocks, as if somebody is tapping on a door. Except this door is upstairs. Perhaps a closet or a bedroom door. Most of them are closed.

I shrug it off and continue reading my book. This is what I do when I'm not tweaking the house plans or studying a magazine on house renovation. I brought most of my favorite books with me from the apartment and office, but it's amazing how many I left behind. Books that are no good, books that I stopped reading halfway through. I recently purchased a few other books at Barnes & Noble, including Stephen Conroy's latest, *Before You*. I'm a hundred pages into the story when I first hear the knocks. About five in a row, not an occasional crack, but five deliberate taps. My eyes shoot to the ceiling, and I stop breathing to listen. Nothing. Nothing for several minutes except the pulsing of my heart beating faster.

I keep reading until ten minutes later. Another set of knocks. All in a row, all deliberate.

This time I shut the book and stand up. I listen for a moment, then walk to the kitchen to find a flashlight. It's a small one, a gift from a publisher years ago. I hope it still works. I turn its head slightly to get light, and the small beam lands on the wall. For the next few seconds, I listen again but don't hear the knocking. This doesn't stop me from walking toward the stairs and heading up them.

What really happens when you die?

I wonder this as I take that first step. This has been one of those thoughts lingering around my head since I lost Jen. What really happens to that part of you inside that makes you who you are? I don't want to say *soul* because that implies things I don't believe. A soul refers to something that sticks around, that continues, that might have faith and can last an eternity. I don't even want to say *heart*, because that's the term used for Valentine's Day and in every possible way to talk about love. Spirit, perhaps? Life force? Ghost. Essence. Whatever I call it in my own mind, I'm curious where it goes. If it goes anywhere. Did any single part of Jennifer pass on to somewhere else?

And can that same part be haunting me now as I walk up the stairs toward the empty second story?

You need to get some lightbulbs up here, I remind myself. No more of this boogeyman-in-the-dark routine with the flashlight. I'm not scared or freaked out. I just want to check and see if there is some animal up here—some animal that has a talent for tapping on doors just like somebody would standing outside your home.

Before I reach the top of the stairs, I hear it again. This time longer. Another set of knocks coming from my right. A noise that sounds like someone's waiting for me to open up a door and let them in. There are two bedrooms to my right, one right off the stairs and the other down a hallway at the southwest corner of the house.

The light jerks and moves across the walls and the closed door to the bedroom closest to me. I open the door and wait, the narrow beam of my flashlight spilling into the room and cutting the dark like a moving lighthouse. I search the room and the small closet and find nothing. The one window in the room lets me see the moon, full and cold in its color.

Someone might be up here. Waiting. With an axe in his hand.

I walk toward the back room and shut out my ignorant thoughts. The knocking comes again. This time I continue walking, continue toward the tapping, continue toward the noise that doesn't stop until I reach the closed door.

Did I close this, I wonder. *Did Pearce?*

And then, silence.

I can hear my breathing. It feels much colder up here for some reason. I wear socks and flannel pajama pants and a sweatshirt, my typical home attire. I wonder what I will do if I see someone, or if someone sees me. My scraggly beard that looks more messy than full, my crumpled attire, the bags under my eyes, the pouch around my stomach. Maybe I'll scare the ghost.

I push the door open and wait and listen. My flashlight moves around the room, and I can't keep my hand from shaking.

Silence. Nothing but utter silence.

I clear my throat to hear something, anything more. Then I enter the room.

No knocks. No voice. Nothing.

"Hello?" I ask, more just to hear something, anything.

The closets are empty. The room is empty.

I rub one of my eyes with my palm and shake my head. Is this cabin fever? Or am I still downstairs, zoning out in my beanbag with the Stephen Conroy novel resting against my chest, dreaming this?

I turn off my light and find the darkness thick and claustrophobic. I listen for the knocks again, for any remote sound.

But I just keep waiting.

"Jennifer?" I ask.

No reply. Just stillness and black. I move toward a window, the moon still hovering above in the crystal clear winter night. I touch the window and feel the chill and know I am not dreaming. I can smell my sweat and fear. You don't do that in dreams.

"Jen," I say again. "What am I supposed to do now?"

Again, nothing. I move toward the middle of the room, in complete darkness, waiting. Waiting for a tap, for a knock, for another voice.

I let out a curse and kneel to the floor.

"How can I go on?"

I just wait for an answer. I've been waiting for an answer for weeks now, for months, ever since I let her strap herself to the cords of a parasail and be taken away. From me, from us, from our life together.

"I just . . ."

And the voice that speaks sounds so different, so confused, so weak. Can it really be my own?

"I just want you back. . . ."

But no one answers. And, if my heart really wants to admit the truth, no one hears either.

"You believe in ghosts?" I ask.

Pearce looks down at me from the hole in the ceiling. We are putting up canned lights in selected places in the kitchen and family room. Does the house really, truly need canned lights? No. But it's something else to make it more appealing, to give it a higher value. We plan to put them in the basement as well.

"No," Pearce says.

"What—you think people just make them up?"

Pearce laughs. "You seeing things in the house?"

"No. I'm just wondering."

He studies me and then resumes screwing in the fixture.

"I don't see people wanting to come back and haunt people after they die," he eventually says as he climbs down the ladder. He wipes sweat off his forehead and looks at me. "You doing okay?"

I nod and tell him "Sure."

"You're not going to go Jack Nicholson in *The Shining* on me, staying out here alone?"

"No," I say with a laugh. "I'm not an author, remember. I'm an agent."

"Well, I'm keeping the axes away from you, anyway."

Odd how I just thought of that last night.

We keep working for a while, and Pearce asks me about my ghost inquiry.

"Sometimes I wonder," I tell him. "That's all."

"You know—we should go out tonight. I can tell Kristy I'll be late."

"And do what?"

"I don't know—first thing, get you out of this house. See some other people. To see the living. Get you to shave and look halfway decent."

"I'm not shaving," I say.

"Whatever. Come on—it'll be good for you. We can pick you up a girl."

"I don't want to 'pick up' a girl."

"Sorry," Pearce says. "I mean, maybe you can meet a fine young lady. Maybe not too young, but you know."

I shake my head. "Why don't you save me the embarrassment and just call up an escort service."

"Colin, seriously, man, you need to get out. This whole thing—I mean, what's the deal here? It's been five months, and I just think—"

"You just think what?" I smart back.

"I just think it's time. What are you going to do about your work?"

"I haven't gotten that far."

"You might want to get that far. This isn't good for you. Working on this house. Living in this house. Being all alone. Crashing your car on the freeway. Asking me about ghosts."

"It was just a simple question."

"The Colin I know doesn't ask simple questions," Pearce says. "The Colin I know has the answers. Right?"

"Possibly."

"Possibly? You gotta be kidding me. You're the only one I've ever had an argument with about placement of a staircase—a staircase, mind you—even when you knew I was right."

"I still think I was right," I say. "It could have worked where I suggested."

"Please don't ever go into construction."

"Bet you anything I will sell this place for a boatload of money."

Pearce laughs. "Now that's more like it."

"What?"

"The Colin I know and love. Seriously, let's go out tonight. Just hang out. Have some beers. Relax."

"Okay," I say, even though I don't really want to.

We're at Sweeney's Pub, located on the main street in St. Charles just a stone's throw from the Fox River. It fits in the corner of a hundred-year-old building. It's little more than a large bar with a smiling, busy bartender and a wooden floor with tables scattered around. Tonight a crowd packs it and makes it standing room only. Pearce looks at me as we enter the doors and asks if I want to stay.

To my own surprise I tell him yes, I do. There's no good reason why I should want to actually go inside Sweeney's and wait ten minutes to get a beer and then stand next to strangers brushing up against me as we listen to conversation and Irish music and breathe in cigarette smoke and somehow try to carry on a conversation.

Maybe being surrounded by living, breathing, talking people makes me feel alive again.

Maybe.

On our second round, Pearce begins talking about a project he once worked on not too far from here, where the owner of the house wanted to put on an addition and then went bankrupt midway through. I laugh at Pearce's expressions and the story, about how the wife came over in the middle of the night and told him he had to stop working on their home, how the husband suddenly thought Pearce and his wife were having an affair, how the situation continued to escalate —until I see Jennifer standing across the crowd talking with someone.

What?

My moving gaze catches the back of her long hair and stops. Jennifer. Sweet Jen. Then I see her face and know it's her.

It can't be her.

"—and this guy, he was telling me that he owned a gun," Pearce continues talking with a voice that's getting hoarse from shouting. "Pretty subtle. I told him several times nothing was going on, but he stopped paying me and basically wanted me out—"

But I'm not listening. I'm looking somewhere else.

She laughs, and it almost brings me to tears.

I know I'm not drunk. So what's going on here? It can't be there's no way it can be.

How do I tell Pearce I'm cracking up?

"—so then he threatened a lawsuit! His wife was like, seven years older, and not too attractive anyway—"

"Pearce—want another one?"

"What? No. I'm good."

"I'm going to get another."

He looks at my glass, three-fourths full.

"Sure you need one?"

I haven't pounded a beer since college, but it only takes me a second. "I'll get in line and get a couple more."

Pearce seems a little amused. I move away from him, shifting through the crowd, moving sideways past shoulders and clusters of people laughing and drinking and talking. What a wonderful life all of these happy, buzzed people must have. I move toward the bar and toward her, toward the image I see, toward the ghost of the woman I loved and still love and would give my soul to bring back, if I had one. She talks with people and they listen and I can't understand how she can be so close and yet so far away.

She stands at the corner of the bar, about a dozen people between us. Heads and faces that separate us. I reach the bar and find an opening and wait and watch her and notice how beautiful she looks.

You're beautiful and will always be beautiful and you can't be gone you just can't be gone.

"What do you want?" I hear someone shout as I just stand there, unmoving, watching my former wife talk to people I don't recognize.

"Hey—you ordering something?"

The bartender looks at me, a young woman impatient in her tasks. I order two more beers and then wait. And watch.

She wears a dark blue shirt, collared and button-down, with black pants. That's all I can see. The long hair falling down to below her shoulders, the long hair I used to stroke my hands through, long straight hair I can picture hovering above me and falling down and covering my face just before I close my eyes.

Jennifer glances my way and then looks away. She must have seen me. I know she had to. And yet, she just looked the other way.

What is this?

I breathe in and pay for my beers and wait and drink a beer quickly and forget about Pearce and continue watching her. Her glance creeps my way again, but the look on her face is curiosity, not love or loss or desire. I finish the beer, perhaps to give me courage or perhaps to settle my nerves or perhaps simply out of anxiety. My eyes water from pounding the heavy beer and I begin working on the other draft, Pearce's beer. Pearce, the guy who brought me here and who waits for me across the room.

But someone else waits for me. And I go to her.

Colin, man, come on, don't do it.

But I ignore the little annoying voice inside as I walk through the crowd and finally manage to get next to her. And I know that this is no ghost, that she is here, that she is real, that she has come back to me.

So I open my arms and embrace her, the dark-haired angel who belongs to me and will always belong to me, the woman I love and adore and have finally found again, who I smile at as I declare out loud

"I love you."

For a second, there's a strange recognition on her face. Something passes between us.

And then, instead of an "I love you" back, I'm struck with the fiercest and most intense pain I can ever remember feeling when the back of my head suddenly gets pummeled by what feels like a cement block.

A blinding hot flash of light and then it all goes out.

Voices, a man and a woman, so quiet, so subdued, so tired, whisper in my darkness.

"This can't be happening."

"It is. It's got to. I don't know what else to say."

"I don't believe it."

"You might not now. One day you will."

"No."

I look up and see a figure coming toward me, moving his hands toward me, grabbing me to squeeze the life out of me—

"Colin, man, whoa, hold it. It's just me."

"Huh?"

"It's me, Pearce."

I look and can see faint wisps of snow falling. It's really cold and all around is pitch black.

"Where am I?"

"You're at my house."

"Huh?"

"Hanging out with you is a real treat," he says. "You almost got us both killed, you know that?"

"What happened?"

My head is groggy and I can't remember anything after—

Jen.

"Where is she?"

"What?" Pearce asks as he helps me to my feet.

The world is more unstable than I thought it would be. Pearce grabs me, and I notice his rock-solid arm.

"I got you. Come on."

"Did you see her?"

"Her? You mean the woman you groped? The girlfriend belonging to the bruiser who split a beer over your head?"

"Huh?"

"Yeah, let's go."

We walk for a few minutes.

"And be quiet. I don't want the kids to wake up."

"I want—take me back to the house."

"Easy, killer. You're staying here tonight. No more ghosts or visions for you."

We walk into the house, and Pearce leads me to a small room with a sofa.

"Relax. Sit. Come on."

"Pearce—"

"What is it?"

He's standing and I look at him, my head killing and dizzy.

"I'm not—" I let out a sigh. "I'm not losing my mind. At least, I don't think I am."

"Look—I'm going to make some coffee. I don't trust you sleeping—this might be the second concussion you got in a month. We're putting you on injured reserve."

He walks away, and I think back to the woman in the bar. I know it was Jen. She was there. It had to be her.

Is this what going insane feels like? Rational, controlled, deliberate delusions?

Insane people don't know they're insane, do they?

I just sit and close my eyes, but when I do the world spins around, so I open them again.

I keep them open for a long time.

There was a time when I had more friends than I do now. When life wasn't as busy, when Jen and I were starting out and were still a young couple. But our married friends all started having babies, and suddenly we found that we could no longer keep up with the Joneses. It's one thing if the Joneses have a big house or a nice car or a little, fluffy dog or a favorite vacation spot. But the Joneses, all of them, with their little multiplying families, suddenly took the fun out of hanging out. One by one, the friendships deteriorated to an occasional phone call to ask about doing something, maybe a simple card at Christmas-time showing their growing, happy little family.

The growing Joneses out there used to depress Jen, but they made me angry.

I think of this as Pearce's wife, Kristy, talks with me in their kitchen and makes scrambled eggs. They have three children: Emily, Sara, and Joshua. A cute, fun-loving little family. But as I spend the morning with them, my pounding head slowly becoming more steady, sipping coffee and eating a hearty breakfast, I realize that I don't feel jealous or angry at what Pearce and Kristy have.

They have a great, normal family.

I'm not jealous. I'm only sad.

All the money and success in the world can't buy everything. I knew that long ago, of course, but I know it more now.

What Pearce has . . . I'd give anything—anything—to be in his shoes.

"Can I show Mr. Scott my hamster?" Sara asks.

I'm amazed at this kindergartner's polite manners, and how she holds my hand as I go to see the cage in the laundry room.

"—and we named her Cornflake because she looks so little and brown. I thought of that name—"

And as I look down at the sapphire eyes gazing up at me and feel Sara's hand in mine, I have to do everything in my power not to break down and cry.

My laptop sits on a black ceramic top in the kitchen. The kitchen is immense, with a huge island in the middle and three sides, so I've got plenty of room to put the computer on an edge. I called the cable service to come out and install all the lines necessary to get high speed Internet. I'm suddenly plugged back into the mainframe of life, hooked back up to the Matrix.

I don't have my work e-mail anymore, of course. I wonder who's taking care of those messages. Maybe Darcy. I wonder how she's doing. But I'm afraid to call and find out. I log into my personal e-mail account and wade through my in-box, deleting everything I can.

Now I'm standing, looking at the message I spent half the morning typing. I sip a third cup of coffee and just stare at it, reading it over again. I probably won't get any response, but I know it won't hurt to try. I'm not trying to change anything. It's just me saying a few final words to Vivian.

Most of the authors I worked with are distant memories. They're like photos in a scrapbook that I can go and look at if I want to, but I choose to ignore them. I might never think about them again. You build these close, tight relationships that really end up being all about business, and that's it. They're drenched with insincerity and undeserved praise, but when they're done all you have is a name on a piece of paper. A signature on a contract. A contract that says Roth's name on it, not mine. And just because I'm gone doesn't mean the literary world stops. Relationships continue on without me. It's that simple. Because they weren't really relationships to begin with. They were business dealings. Not partnerships or part of the family, but simple business acquaintances.

But Vivian Brown was always more than that.

I used to believe this. I guess in some ways I still do.

Hi, Vivian,

I hope you don't mind my e-mailing you. With Christmas and the New Year approaching, I wanted to jot you off a quick note.

As you probably know, I'm no longer working with the Roth Agency. This was unexpected, but a part of business. A part of life, I guess. I wanted you to know that I don't harbor any bad feelings toward you. I know that my e-mail and my report on *In Your Memory* were only part of the reason why I was let go. My personal life has been the main reason. I left Roth with a lot of regret, especially in regard to you.

I want you to know that I sincerely appreciated working with you. I wish you the best with your novel and the rest of your writing future. You're an incredible talent. Just please remember this: Even the best can be better. Don't cocoon yourself from getting input from those you trust.

And be wary with that trust.

I look forward to great things to come in your writing career.

Your fan, always,

Colin

I wonder if it sounds too melodramatic, too schmaltzy, too gushy. I don't know. My perspective was lost awhile ago. Perhaps somewhere down the road I will be able to find it again, to be able to uncover that cocky and aggressive guy who always landed the deal, always had the answers, always knew what came next.

There are no more deals. I know that as I send the e-mail. There are no simple answers. And there is no way, absolutely no way, of knowing what comes next.

That afternoon, I check my e-mails. I can't help it. After so many years of staying glued to the computer, it's a natural reaction.

I can't help but wonder if Vivian's going to reply. She probably won't, or maybe it will be short and sweet. But a part of me has to check.

There is one lone unopened message. Probably my chance to get Viagra.

But I see the name, and it's from Ian. I forgot that I wrote the guy weeks ago, when I was still living in my apartment.

Dear Mr. Scott:

It was exciting to hear that you enjoyed the section of *Passover Lane* and wanted more of it. I'm sorry not to have sent this to you before now. I've been working and tweaking the remaining novel. I wanted to get it as strong and clean as possible before sending it to you.

It's still rough, of course. I took your advice and shortened the beginning—cutting the first six pages or so. I've tried tightening up the rest of the story, but the word count is still around 130,000. But I figure it's easier to cut than it is to add.

Please let me know what you think—whenever you get a chance to read this. I know you must be busy now that you're on your own. I called Roth and they said you no longer worked with them. So I'm hoping that I can be added to your client list. That would certainly be an honor.

Thanks again, and have a wonderful Christmas holiday with your family.

Sincerely,
Ian Pollock

I can't help but laugh.

What amuses me more? The fact that he wants to be "added to my client list"? Yeah. That's a mighty big list. I'd be starving on that client list. If I were still shelling out all that cash for the apartment every month.

Or the remark about having a wonderful holiday with my family?

Ah, yes, the poor kid doesn't know. He doesn't have a clue I'll be eating a turkey dinner with ghosts of the past, present, and future all rolled into one.

Maybe I'll swing back by the pub and see Jen again. Or see a woman named Daria something or other who Pearce says looks nothing like Jen except for having long black hair, and who has an offensive lineman for a boyfriend.

Yeah, Merry Christmas to you too, Ian.

I open up the document entitled *Passover Lane* to make sure it came through. It's there, all 130,000 glorious and surely stuffed words.

Note to self. I need to get a printer.

For all my clients, you know.

Sometimes I answer the cell phone out of simple routine. You do something enough times in your life, you'll have a hard time stopping.

"Hello?"

This time it turns out to be Donald Hardbein.

"I've written fifty pages."

"That's good."

"I just e-mailed them to you."

"That's great."

"They're better than the ones in my head."

"Fabulous."

"I trust you will have some time over the holidays to read them."

"Yeah, sure I will," I say, noticing a hole in my sock. "My schedule is going to be dying down a little, so, yes, I'll make sure I get right on that."

"Good. Good man."

"All right, then."

"Oh, and Colin? Please tell your wife I say hello."

And then he hangs up before I'm able to catch my breath.

Snow's been falling since yesterday. It's getting close to being a foot, the news says. And it's just going to keep coming all Christmas Eve and tomorrow on Christmas Day.

It's around seven o'clock and, thankfully, Starbucks is still open.

I could have taken Pearce's invitation to spend Christmas with his family, but his little wife thinks I'm demented. Heck, Pearce thinks I'm a fruit loop, with all my visions and craziness of the last month or so. He's got his family. They're planning on going to church anyway, which thank you very much doesn't interest me. The calls I get from Mom and her husband—yeah, sure, I could have gone to Florida, but they'd just baby me and make me feel more insane than I'm already feeling. I've gotten a few calls from my sister, but I don't want any of that either. I still need time and space and distance.

But since it's Christmas Eve, I decide to hang out at a Starbucks just to be around some people and see some life. I'm almost done with the long book I've been reading, *Before You.* And I'm planning on finishing it before the coffee shop closes.

I remember reading a novel years ago by Stephen Conroy. When you work in the book industry and an author suddenly starts getting "buzz," you check him out. The book was *The Long and Winding Road,* about two childhood friends who grow up and go different ways. It was a long and dark book, but I enjoyed it very much. I saw him interviewed on the *Today* show a couple years ago, but I hadn't read anything else of his until now.

Before You is a book I might not have been very interested in before—well, before everything happened with Jen. Before Cancun. It's the story of a man who gives up his current life when he is allowed to go back to the past and change the course of his life. It's got elements of *A Christmas Carol* and even *It's a Wonderful Life*. But Stephen Conroy's voice is fabulous—witty and humorous and poignant at the same time. It's not a huge book—probably 80,000 words or so. But to me, it's magnificent.

I think of the movie in production for his book *Immersion*, and remind myself to check the Web site to see how it's coming along.

It's been so long since I've just been able to sit down and enjoy a book. To read without wondering how much of an advance the author got, or how bad of a writer the author really is, or how this author ended up going to that publisher.

The book is dedicated to his wife. *For Isabel. All roads have always led to you. Thank you for being there for me.* In the acknowledgments he mentions Alan Dierge, his long-term agent, whom I've met before.

Yes, I can't help noticing those things.

But all I really care about is the story. About a guy named Patrick who is able to go back in the past and change his life—the decisions he makes, the people he surrounds himself with. Patrick thinks he deserves a better life. But in the end, he still ends up coming across Ashley's path and falling in love with her. Ashley is his wife and the woman he ends up starting a family with. The circumstances of how they meet in this "second life" are obviously intriguing. She's married, but then loses her husband and Patrick comes to her side and can't help but fall in love. Patrick doesn't know he's living another life, another life "before you," the *you* being his wife.

I sound like a fan because I am, and it feels great because I haven't been a fan in a long time. When you work on material and see the ugly mud pies coming in to the office, the first draft dreck that crosses your desk, it's hard to enjoy the final result when it finally gets printed with a beautifully embossed cover.

"Is dreck a word?"

Ah, the past. How random bits and pieces come out of nowhere to wreak havoc on your sanity and your soul.

The end of the novel approaches, and I rush toward it, turning the pages just as every author would want his ideal reader to do.

Patrick is forced to make a decision. Is his life any better now than it was? And even though he falls in love with Ashley again, obviously knowing they're meant to be together, what is the cost to her?

And the minutes pass and I forget everything until I read the wonderful, surprising final paragraph.

And final line.

It makes me smile, and I close the book and exhale.

This is what I've missed for so long.

Being moved.

I'm driving a rental car while my BMW undergoes a makeover. It's a small car, a Ford something, and I'm so used to being reminded by my German car when the tank is low that I am amazed when the rental stalls on the side of the road. It takes me a few minutes to realize it's out of gas.

Christmas Eve in a snowstorm with a belly full of coffee and I'm stranded.

I try to restart it. I've run out of gas before. A car I drove in college used to do it a lot—I'd be literally driving on fumes, but I could always make it to a gas station. But not this car. It's down for the count.

I get out and look around. I'm not that far from the house. Miles, yes, but I can walk it. I've wearing a winter overcoat, a peacoat that's warm, but I don't have a hat or gloves. I start walking down the side street.

The still in the air is refreshing.

My boots keep me from slipping as I walk down the unplowed street with an occasional streetlamp guiding my way. I'm not sure exactly how far I am from the nearest gas station, or from downtown St. Charles for that matter. I just know that there probably won't be many people up and around on this night.

I look at my watch. Ten-thirty. Starbucks closed half an hour ago. Only an hour and a half before Christmas officially arrives. This will be the first one I am spending alone. And in fitting matter, I am definitely alone.

The temperature is warmer than I assumed it would be. Massive flakes fall, and some melt on my face, but it feels almost soothing, invigorating. I look back and see my steps in the powder trailing me.

I can see light from probably two hundred yards away. Cars turning into a lot. Illumination from a building. I jog a bit before I realize what I am running toward. It's a church on the corner of an intersection. A small church seemingly in the middle of nowhere. I reach the parking lot and see people filing into the building. I brush myself off and enter the doorway to find people milling around the lobby. The sanctuary is darker than I expected.

What's the name of this church? I wonder, then I have an awful thought. What if it's some Mormon gathering or a Jehovah's Witness service? They don't meet on Christmas Eve, do they?

Does it really matter? another voice asks. *It's basically the same mumbo jumbo.*

"Welcome," says a friendly woman in her fifties as she points to the coatrack.

At this point I feel like I need to stay. I can't say "oops" and leave.

Plus, I am colder than I realize and want to stay warm. And chances are high that people going to an eleven o'clock church service on Christmas Eve will be charitable enough to give a guy a ride home afterward.

Soft organ music plays as I near the entrance to the sanctuary. It's not a large church. There are three aisles running down to the altar. I'm surprised at how full the place is already. As I begin to walk in, somebody gives me a candle.

I stand there, wondering what in the world I'm supposed to do with it.

"We light them at the end of the service," says the man who gave it to me.

I nod and head toward a half-full pew near the back of the church. If things get too weird, I can escape and head back out to the snow. Or simply wait in the lobby until the service is over.

A family sits to my right, an elderly couple to my left. This confirms my thoughts on church. It's for older people, for families, and for people needing to fill their lives with something. I have never harbored any ill feelings toward church or God or any of that. I believe some people need those things in their lives. Some people refer to them as a crutch, but I think of church as more like a placebo—something you take that's harmless and actually meaningless but causes you to believe in its worth. Something that convinces you that it's helping. And who knows? Maybe church does help. Maybe it makes those who attend better people.

What is your placebo? a voice asks me.

I think of Jennifer, of hearing her, of imagining that I had seen her. Perhaps she is my placebo. Perhaps I am deliberately believing in her to be able to move on.

We sing a hymn and the pastor begins to talk and I wonder when I last visited a church. My thoughts drift away easily. I don't remember.

My wedding, of course. But before then? Surely sometime in my youth, perhaps when I was nine or ten.

A twinge of guilt simmers in me as I sit in the pew, listening to the parts of the non–Santa Claus Christmas story about the baby in a manger. I don't understand why I feel guilty. Is it because I don't belong here? This is why I dislike churches and services and preaching and all of that. Because they claim to be right and everyone else is wrong. And if you are in the wrong, you are in trouble.

"Christ came into the world to save us all."

Yeah, thanks. That's a touching thought. But how about this one? Did he come to save Jennifer? Did you save her, God? Christ? Whatever you want to be called? You took her from me on a summer day when she was drifting high over the ocean. She fell because what? It was her time? What about saving her? Why couldn't you use your so-called powers to save her?

I know why, I think as the pastor continues to talk about the joys of Christmas and the hope we all have.

I know why you didn't save her. Because you couldn't.

I don't feel anger. Yet I know I don't feel hope. I feel numb. Even though I've warmed up, I still feel chilled inside. I listen to the pastor and know that he believes in the words he utters. He talks about things like faith, hope, joy, love, all those nice things. But faith—what is faith? Believing in something without needing certain proof.

I once had faith in Jennifer and me. I believed that we would grow old together and love each other forever. But that didn't happen. She left me, and the only proof I have now of our love is the memories locked inside. Unable to ever be let go. Ever.

Where are you?

If all these people can believe in a savior and a messiah, why can't I? My own personal Jesus, as the song goes.

Near the end of the service, we sing more hymns, carols that even I am familiar with. "We Three Kings" and songs like that. And then a prayer, which I don't close my eyes for, but listen to like a college student enduring a boring professor discussing theories and hypotheses. And then, as midnight arrives, we light our candles and sing "Silent Night, Holy Night."

I don't know the verses by heart like the others around me, so I just listen.

"Silent night, holy night, all is calm, all is bright. . . ."

And in the flickering glow of hundreds of candles, the moving mouths of a congregation, the second verse of a song I've heard thousands of times before, I see her.

My savior.

I know this is my imagination, and yet I see her in full view. Just two seats in front of me, to the right, sitting in a blue-and-white turtleneck sweater, Jennifer sings. Her face glimmers from the candle, but of course, that's just my imagination. Just like seeing her in the pub. Or hearing her at home.

And they begin to sing the third verse.

"Silent night, holy night, Son of God, love's pure light . . ."

And Jennifer turns toward me, knowing I am there, smiling at me with a heartfelt, compassionate, loving smile.

"Radiant beams from Thy holy face, with the dawn of redeeming grace. Jesus, Lord, at Thy birth, Jesus, Lord, at Thy birth."

I want to climb up out of the pew and across people's shoulders and backs and past their legs and arms and laps and get to Jennifer and touch her and simply know I am not imagining any of this but that she is here and that it really is a miracle for Christmas.

If God can raise his son from the dead, he can certainly raise my wife.

She wipes a tear from one eye and I look at her in confusion, wondering what is wrong, why she is upset. Is it because she's not really there? Because she can't communicate with me? Or is it because—because I am sitting here in a church going mad and making all of this up?

I want to believe she's really there.

But I don't know.

The pastor finishes talking and everyone blows out their candles and the church is bathed in the shadow of midnight. There is a final prayer, and then the lights come back on and the organ plays in glorious triumph. I look toward Jennifer and see people standing and talking but I can't find her. I walk toward where she sat but don't see anyone. I look all around and even sprint past people but can't find her anymore.

Whoever I saw—whatever I saw—is gone.

I wish she could take me with her.

"Hello?"

Colin?

"What do you want?"

Don't hang up again.

"This isn't happening."

Please.

"Talk."

I can only hear silence.

"Hello?"

I don't understand—

"No—I don't understand. What am I supposed to do?"

I just wanted to talk, to tell you—

"What?"

I don't hear anything.

"Tell me what?"

I want to see you.

"That's funny. I want to stop seeing you."

Why do you say that?

"'Cause everywhere I go, I keep seeing you."

I saw you too.

"Where?"

Last night. At church.

"Really? What about the pub? What about in my dreams?"

Are you okay?

"No. I'm not okay. I don't even know if I'm having this conversation. I might as well be talking to myself."

You're not making sense.

"Am I dreaming this?"

No.

"I don't even—my cell phone has been off."

Col, please.

"No."

Please. I just—I won't be here for long—

"Here? What's here?"

There's not much time—

"Yeah, tell me."

Please.

I let out a sigh. This is too much.

"If this is some divine intervention, or communication, or whatever, tell the boss I'm not particularly amused."

She gives me the name of a place and a time. And that's all.

Perhaps she knows I'm about to hang up.

But how can you hang up on someone you're not really talking to?

The Naked and the Dead

Every relationship has a starting point, and I remember ours. That moment at the fancy banquet hall in Chicago. And the next day in the hotel lobby. The moments that started everything. So seemingly trivial, simple, easy. A girl I'd be introduced to as Jennifer Corella, an acquaintance I'd have no idea would alter my life in so many ways.

And then years later, with so much in between, it happens again.

I'm hoping to see her, hoping to run into her, hoping she will be where she said she would be. But she can't be, of course. I imagined the conversation. I imagined it the way I've imagined so many things.

I walk the same steps I've walked before, looking in mall shop windows where lifeless mannequins smile back at me, wearing the latest fashions. I walk not so much to shop or even to browse but to get out and be around people. Living, breathing people whom I can touch and who don't haunt me into the wee hours of the morning. I see the teenage couple holding hands, or the young mother with the baby stroller, or the older woman with a bag in hand probably returning something from Christmas. I see people, human beings, and I feel a little more normal. I stop and buy a pretzel and sit and eat it and eventually continue walking as I sip on a soda. This is normal living in normal town, USA, the day after Christmas, and I force myself to believe that I'm normal, too. I round a corner, where the escalators shoot down to the bottom level, and I suddenly see her.

It can't be her.

I stand on the edge of the opening peering down at the ground level of the mall below. There is an open area for sitting just below. I first glimpse a long black coat that I recognize, with a turtleneck popping out of it. Her hair blends into the coat. She carries a bag and is looking in windows herself.

This can't be happening.

But already so much has happened that has not been real. Why should this be any different?

She said she would be there.

I watch for a moment. She doesn't whirl by like a fading image in a dream. Instead, she simply ambles over the tile floor, glancing in a window, coming closer to the clear area below me.

I step onto the escalator. I don't rush down it, I don't even walk. I simply let the steps slide down and make sure I keep her in full view. She lingers at the doorway of Express, a store facing the bottom of this escalator, then she turns and heads toward me.

And then, once again, she's there.

She stops. Her face is angelic, as it always was, those blue eyes so cutting and powerful. I reach the bottom and step off, closer to her now, only thirty yards away.

The eyes soften. And she moves closer to me.

I stand in the center of the mall walkway as strangers move past. This is not my house and not a closet or a church or a bar and I'm not imagining this and I know I can't be. This is real and her smile is real and that simple soft first greeting is real, too.

Hi.

And with everything that needs to be said and everything that could be said I simply utter the same thing back to her, back to Jennifer, back to the woman whom I loved and lost and now found again.

Shopping?

"Not really," I say.

A smile.

You always hated shopping.

"Still do."

I simply stand there, Jen so close now, close enough to touch. I want to and feel like I might but know that if I do she might vanish in a sprinkle of fairy dust. So I simply stay within arm's length.

How are you?

"Confused."

She studies me, nods, then looks down.

"How are you doing?"

I'm here. That should say something.

I want to ask her what it really says. What is the meaning behind her being here? Do ghosts shop at the Gap? Or is this whole conversation made up?

"How long are you going to be—around?"

A little while longer. That's all the time I've been given.

I study her, the lines of the lips I kissed so many times, the long nose and the ample forehead. Again, I want more information, but I don't dare push it.

"Will I be able to see you again?"

When would you like to?

"Tonight," I say without thinking, purely from the heart.

Okay.

"That easy?"

Yes.

"I don't get this."

I have so much to tell you. I just—I just don't know exactly how.

"Me too."

I didn't want to simply show up and shock you.

"I've been getting used to being shocked. Now I'm simply—stunned."

She studies my eyes and gives away a sad smile. *You look so tired.*

"Sleep has been difficult."

I'm sorry.

"I don't think it's your fault."

I left you.

"How could you have known? You didn't make yourself—"

Colin.

A wave of goose bumps flows through me. Just the very whisper of my name across her lips makes me believe this is impossibly real.

"Yes."

I will come over tonight.

"Okay."

Can I ask you one thing?

"Yes."

Don't complicate things. Don't overthink. Just let things—let them happen.

I want to say more, but I can't. I look at the bag she is carrying and notice the light blue logo of a clothing store I don't recognize. I nod at her and she tells me good-bye and I watch her walk away. My legs feel unable to move, my mind heavy and aching. I wonder if I'll see her again, and what will happen, and when this—whatever "this" refers to—will end.

Shortly before seven, the power goes out.

I find a flashlight and check the main generator to switch it off and on. Nothing happens. It's snowing again, and I wonder if it has something to do with the storm. I curse in anger, wondering if Jennifer will make it. I make sure my cell is on to catch her call. Dinner will be wasted. I planned on fixing spaghetti. The meat sauce still needs to cook for twenty minutes. I was going to wait to put the pasta on after she arrived. Jennifer always loved my pasta, one of the few things I prepared for her.

Who am I kidding? I hardly ever prepared anything for her.

And ghosts don't need to eat anyway.

I look in the cabinets and find a pack of candles, the thick kind that don't need holders. There are six of them and I light them all, placing them in various points in the family room and the kitchen. Shadows wave all around me as I try to conjure up

spirits

some light and warmth, but really, what's the sense in this? She won't make it, not tonight, not in this storm, not in her—

But the doorbell rings and I feel a rush of fear and adrenaline and curiosity.

The glow of the candles flickers as I rush to get the door.

It can't be I don't believe it's really going to be her—

I open the door, and there she stands. No glowing aura or floating feet or hanging halo can be seen. She stands in the long black coat with a matching hat serving as the landing ground for dozens of snowflakes. The storm blows into the house, and I simply stand there, staring at her.

She steps up to me and brings her gloved hand behind my head and pulls me closer to her lips and then she kisses me with those lips, hungry and wet and inviting in their touch. The kiss lasts until I pull back, out of breath, bewildered.

"Jen . . ."

It's okay.

"I'm not exactly—"

Don't.

"What?"

Don't shake your head like that.

She pulls me to her and locks arms behind my back.

You're trembling.

"It's cold."

You could let me in.

I nod and realize I'm blocking the doorway, so I move and let her pass. I close the door.

I'm sorry.

"For what?"

For that. I just—I couldn't help it.

"It's fine with me."

I know this is a surprise.

"That's quite an understatement."

You don't want me here?

"Of course I do. Except, what is here?"

She takes off her coat and drapes it over one arm.

St. Charles, I believe. In a house that's quite empty. And dark.

"Oh, yeah. The power went out."

She wears a form-fitting dark turtleneck sweater that reveals her long, lithe figure. The waterfall of hair blends into the sweater. For a moment she blends into the room and I lose sight of her. I blink several times, afraid her image is simply a mirage. But I see her smile and her outline in front of a candle.

You look like you've seen a ghost.

"Is that what you are?"

She laughs and takes my hand.

Remember what I said.

I nod, thinking of her earlier request. How can I possibly complicate things any more than this? This is beyond complicated. This is impossible. Her hand in mine again, so natural, as she leads me to the kitchen.

"Dinner is ruined."

That's okay.

"You sure?"

I'm not exactly hungry.

"I have wine."

Hmm. I might pass on that.

"On wine?" I ask her.

I don't want to get sleepy. Who knows—you might try and take advantage of me.

I wrinkle my eyes, again not understanding, not knowing what to say. This feels stranger than a misty-colored dream, yet more real than any sleepy reverie might be. As she walks to the middle of the family room, she turns back to see me.

What are you thinking?

"I honestly don't know, Jen."

Hmm. That sounds good.

"What?"

My name. Hearing you say it again.

"Jen."

Yes.

"Are you really here? Is this all in my mind?"

Feels like it, doesn't it?

The moving candlelight shows the slight smile on her lips.

"I don't know what this feels like."

I am really here.

"You are?"

For now.

"And tomorrow? And the next day?"

Shouldn't we get through tonight?

"What is tonight? What is this all about?"

She walks up closer to me and looks up slightly, those eyes once taken for granted, then branded on my soul, now so close and yet still so utterly far away.

It's about me finding you again.

"You finding me again? I've been here."

She touches my lips. *Not here.* Then she moves her soft hand and presses it against my heart. *It's here.*

"Don't leave me again."

It's not that easy.

"Why not?"

What did I leave?

"I never want you to leave me. Ever."

That won't be up to me.

"Jen, I'll do anything—"

Shhh. A finger interrupts my mouth.

"Jen—"

Tell me about your last few months.

"What about them?"

About Roth. About the job. The house. Everything.

"There's no time."

There is now.

She sits down on a beanbag, then beams as she glances up at me.

I get the chair. Sorry.

"It's fine."

Come here. Talk to me.

I sit down beside her.

Tell me what happened at Roth.

So I tell her. Without a thought of the ruined dinner or the downed power or the chilled wine. It doesn't matter. I'm communicating with Jennifer, talking with her, knowing she is listening to me, knowing she is there and not on the other end of a phone on a ten-minute break one of us has. We are in the same room and the same house and the same state for once, and she is listening to me and we have nowhere else to go.

So I talk. And tell her about the last few months.

Picture a guy in a dark and empty house lit only by candlelight, talking and blabbing on to himself with no one to answer his comments and no one to hear them.

Maybe this is me. I don't know.

At the moment, I don't care.

"I've talked more with you in the last couple hours than in the last couple months. Maybe the last couple of years."

That's good.

"Maybe it's the wine."

Or it could be me.

"And what about you? You haven't said a thing about yourself."

What do you want me to tell you?

"Tell me what it's all about. Why we're here. What happens. Where you—where you went."

To look for my heart. And my soul.

"Did you find them?"

I've started to. So much has changed. There's a freedom that I can't begin to tell you about—

"Try."

I can't. It just—I realized sitting by a pool—

"What pool?"

Listen—I realized what we had—what I'd lost. What I left behind. I thought that maybe—maybe—there could be a chance, a way . . .

I look at half of Jen's outlined face and wait to hear more. Anything more. But she doesn't finish her statement. Her hesitation only makes me fear prying even more.

"Jen—"

Maybe I should go.

Wind purrs outside, and midnight left a half hour ago. We see flakes light up the darkness outside the windows in front of us. Her vehicle is surely covered over with snow, and the roads are probably awful. And of course, I want her to stay and can think of a hundred reasons why she should, so I ask her to.

Well, typically I would say no, you know, if this was a first date. She grins. *But since I'm still wearing a certain ring on my finger that you once gave me, I think it might be okay.*

"I'm not wearing mine."

That's understandable.

"No. I took it off—I didn't want something happening to it with the construction."

It's okay.

"Where are we with everything?"

What do you mean?

"With us. I feel like—I just don't want to ruin anything if we—"

She lies next to me on the carpet, the fireplace going thanks to some logs Pearce had left in the garage for me. We stretch out on a blanket and I feel her touch my shoulder.

It's okay.

I shudder.

"What if I—I mean—I just don't want to try and touch you and suddenly not feel—"

Feel what?

"Nothing makes sense."

Does this make sense? Come here. It's okay.

I can't help trembling. My hand feels unsteady, like a drunk reaching to pick up a bottle. I place two fingers over generous lips and see them curl into a smile. They are soft, moist, but most of all, real. I know my fingers feel something.

I move to kiss Jennifer.

And it is gentle, slow, deliberate, dreamlike.

As we kiss, we move closer to one another. I feel her body press up against mine, feel her arms lock behind my back, her lips touching my own.

This can't be a dream, I think. *I can't be imagining this.*

Colin.

"Yes?"

I'm so sorry for the way things ended up.

"It wasn't your fault."

Yes, it was. It was all my fault. It was my decision.

"It was an accident."

And before she can say anything further, I kiss her again.

She pulls away for a moment.

Can I ask something?

"Yes. Anything."

Can you just—hold me tonight?

I look down at sad eyes, so heavy and so full of untold feelings.

"Of course. If you don't go anywhere."

So we just hold one another as the fire burns and the candles go out and the snow outside continues to fall and as Jennifer's breathing slows to a steady quiet in my arms. I try to keep awake as long as I can, keeping my eyes open, watching the shadow of her next to me, listening to her to make sure she is still there, feeling her to make sure she hasn't left me. But eventually my eyes drop. A heavy, satisfying sleep drapes over me.

In the morning, I awake in the same position in the family room, curled up with the blanket wrapped around me a couple times. The fire still maintains a few slow-burning embers and the morning light saturates the room around me. As I open my eyes and adjust them to waking reality, I see that I am alone.

"Jen?" I call out, the first of many times.

But she is gone.

Snow continues to fall. I look out the front window to the driveway and see no car, no tracks, no sign of the woman who visited me last night.

Nothing.

As I walk into the middle of the family room and pick up the blanket, the soft perfumed scent of Jennifer still lingers in the room.

She was here and I know she was here and I'm not losing my mind.

I scan the room again.

"Jen?"

But nothing. The day is new and I am still on my own with no new answers and only the memory of yesterday to give me comfort.

Or haunt me.

Light leaks in through the white cocoon outside. I am finally picking through the contents of the hastily packed boxes that litter the dining room like a child's play fort. Most of the boxes are full of books. And each one contains a journey, and a memory.

The assortment is as random as my being in this house, and my experience last night. I pick each book up and study them one by one.

How long has it been since I saw these as anything other than adornments to a crowded office and a crowded life? Other than wallpaper to an agent's heart and existence?

The titles and the names are so familiar. And an hour slips into three as I open and skim and organize and read.

You'd think an agent would love reading. But I had grown incapable of separating the words from the author. I had grown jaded by knowledge and uninterested in another journey. Familiarity had bred much contempt.

But not anymore. I never drank beers with Hemingway or had dinner with Michener or negotiated for Wouk. I've met King and Crichton but don't know the men they really are, and that's fine by me. Let there be a little mystique, because mystique is good. It allows me to think the author might be a good person. It lets me take the journey they're about to take me on.

The phone rings. I go to find it thinking, believing, knowing who it might be.

But it's Darcy.

"How are you?" she asks.

"Fine."

"Have you been with family?"

"Uh, yeah, you could say that."

"I hear you're living in the house in the suburbs."

"It's a little empty, but it's fine. Power went off last night for some reason, but it came back on today. I've been going through my books—I found my first edition of *All the President's Men*. It's in pretty good shape too."

"Colin?"

"Yeah."

"Are you—do you need anything?"

A shrink, maybe? Wait, I already bailed on that after a few sessions.

"No, I'm fine."

"Are you sure?"

"Yeah. How are you doing?"

She talks a little about her Christmas and about work, but just a little. It's sorta like the family member of the deceased asking a guest at the funeral how they're doing. You don't launch into a conversation about the Bears or something trivial. For some reason, Darcy feels the need to say little.

"I just want you to know—I'm still here for you."

Someone else is, too. I think.

"Thanks," I tell her, then hear her wish me a Happy New Year and wonder how it can be any worse than the one I've just had.

Filming to start on *Immersion* in January in Asheville, North Carolina, and surrounding areas. Sequences include winter scenes where the main character (played by Julia Roberts) travels to North Carolina for retreat after discovering her husband's secret life. Filming will last through the spring and will be helmed by Gore Verbinski, noted director of *Pirates of the Caribbean* and *The Ring*.

I Google Jennifer Scott and *Immersion* together, but the connections are all fruitless. There is no connection between Jennifer and the movie.

Because there is no Jennifer.

I'm sitting in the café at Barnes & Noble reading the opening chapter of one of those gritty, tell-all contemporary memoirs. We had a chance to represent this guy but passed. He certainly has a talent with words and visuals. But he might as well be writing fiction. Nobody remembers entire conversations they heard when they were two. It's accepted nowadays, and the word *memoir* is almost as meaningless as the term *author*.

"Mind if I have a seat?"

I can see the tall shape out of the corner of my eye and just know who it is, even before I look up.

"Yes, I do mind."

"Now, Mr. Colin. Are we going to have another awkward altercation? If you remember the last time, you were quite nasty to the head of that produce department."

I just look up and stare, waiting to hear what Donald says next. He pulls up a chair and examines the book I'm reading.

"Boring. Why would you waste twenty-five dollars on rubbish like that?"

"That's why I'm reading it first. To make up my mind."

He produces a book for me. I recognize it immediately.

"Now this—this is something you need to read."

I smile. I can't help it, even sitting across from this creep. "*Every Light Ever Known*. Where'd you find this?"

"Tucked away."

"Seriously? I haven't seen this in years."

"Really?"

I take the hardcover that's in mint condition and study it.

"Nick Souter. Man, I haven't even spoken that name in—"

"Let me guess," Donald interrupts. "Years?"

I ignore him and enjoy the moment.

"Have you read it?"

"Have I read it?" I laugh. "You want to know something? This was the first book I ever agented. The first contract I ever negotiated. Look—"

I open to the back and show him the acknowledgments page. *To a friend and colleague who made this happen. I'll always owe you, Colin.*

"That's me he's talking about."

"And how'd the book do?" Donald asks, with a look that says he already knows.

"Went out of print in the first year. Major tankeroo. Yeah—I don't know if Nick ever published again. I tried to get him to write, and I stayed in touch with him—but nothing ever happened."

"And you moved on to bigger and better things."

"No," I say. "No—he really gave up. Publishing's a hard business. You know that."

"Yes, I do."

"It sucks the life out of strong men. I wouldn't be able to pour my life into a project only to see it get washed down the drain all because of poor buy-in and position and marketing and all this useless, meaningless stuff that has nothing to do with the book itself."

"But as an agent, you don't pour your life into a project?"

I shake my head. "I do the necessary work to make sure that project *has* a shelf life. But no—I don't have to do that kind of work."

"So these past ten years have been what?"

"How do you know that?"

"Know what?" Donald asks.

"Know how long I've been doing this."

"It's not secret. The information is out there."

"So this is what being stalked feels like."

"I'm not stalking you, nor your lovely wife."

I stare at him and feel the anger inside me again.

"Would you mind leaving?"

"Of course not. But please—keep the book. It's my gift to you."

"I don't take bribes."

"It's not a bribe, Mr. Colin. It's a reminder."

"Really? And what would it be reminding me of?"

Donald stands and gives me a clownlike grin.

"Of the man you used to be. Of the man you're still capable of finding again."

And then he's gone, drifting off by the magazine section and out the door.

When I ask the customer service department to look up Nick Souter, they can't find anything on their system. No name, no *Every Light Ever Known,* nothing.

I feel guilty walking out of the store carrying the book without paying for it.

The new year approaches, and I wonder if I'll see Jen again.

I wonder if I ever saw her in the first place.

There's so much to do. I start writing out a to-do list for the coming year:

Finish house

Sell house

Then I stop. This is pathetic. Isn't the house basically finished already? Isn't a part of me scared to go ahead and try and sell it? Why can't I just go ahead and do it? I start thinking of everything I should do, of everything I want to do, but nothing else comes to mind.

Find a job

That'd be nice.

Find my sanity

That'd sure be swell, too.

The phone rings, and I assume it's Pearce.

You're there, her voice says with surprise.

"I am."

I suddenly forget the new year only two days away. I forget the snow outside and the fact that I need to add to my to-do list:

Shovel the mile-long driveway

I've been thinking about you, about the other night.

"Me too."

Should I apologize?

"For leaving?"

For staying.

"You're still my wife. Always will be."

Will I?

"Of course," I say.

All the things meant to happen—this wasn't one of them.

"I would have taken your place."

Colin.

"What?"

Don't.

"I'm being honest."

There isn't a place to take. It's not that easy.

"None of this is."

Her voice sounds like it's next to me, whispering in bed, resting on pillows, a breath away from her sweet touch and soft kiss.

Was the other night real?

Is this real?

"You know, one thing I've thought about these last few days while you've been—well, actually, the last few months—"

What?

"I remember all the times we used to spend on the phone. How we talked on the phone all the time, but we never really talked about anything. It was always about travel plans and schedules and what was on my wonderful little PDA and what your next movie would be and all of that. I just thought—what if that was all there was to talk about? What if I never got the chance to talk with you again?"

You're talking with me now.

"Am I? I mean, am I really? Really, truly? Is that what this is?"

Of course it is.

"I just—I don't know."

It's okay. Talk.

"We always used to talk about the future. About waiting to do this and that. We never got around to doing any of it."

Some things weren't in our control.

"And some were. A lot of things."

I know. I regret that.

"I regret every moment of it."

That's why I came back.

"Back from where?"

Does the where really matter?

"Then why did you come back?"

To try and—to try for something—

"What?" I ask after she trails off.

There are things—ways I've changed. Things I now believe.

"Are you talking—things you've seen?"

Yes.

"I'm curious."

There's so much. I can't just dump them on you. I know how you're skeptical.

"I am?"

Of course you are, her sweet voice says. I can see the smile attached to the words. *But that's okay.*

"I'm talking with you, right? How's that for skepticism?"

You have no choice about talking with me.

"I don't? I could disagree."

It's what I might say while talking with you.

"Dump it on me, as you said."

Baby steps.

"Why? None of this—all of it. I mean, look at everything that's happened."

You never had much faith, Colin.

"I had faith in us."

We both bought into a fantasy of love and happily-ever-afters.

"Isn't that the whole myth?"

It's not a myth. It doesn't have to be.

"I believed in you. I always have."

And I know you loved me.

"Then what?"

Could you believe in an us *if you had absolutely no way of knowing that it could be real, that it could be true?*

I think for a moment. "That sounds like too deep a question for me to answer."

Maybe.

"I believe in us."

But what else do you believe in? What if everything suddenly ended now? What if—

"Everything did suddenly end for me. A few months ago. In Cancun."

No, I mean really—

"And I mean really, too. Don't you understand, Jen?"

Don't you?

There is silence. This feels like I'm having a philosophy discussion with one of my professors from school.

Col?

"I'm here."

It's too hard to talk about—too hard to explain.

"I just want to see you again."

I have to go soon.

"Please—"

One more time.

"If that's all I get."

Do you ever wonder if things would be different—or how they would be—if I'd been able to get pregnant?

"I try not to."

I can't help but think of it.

"It wasn't meant to be."

Maybe not. But—

"But what?"

I stopped being me. I realized I couldn't control everything even though I tried, Col. God knows I tried.

There's a pause, then Jennifer tells me she'll see me tomorrow. And like a spirit, the call and the voice both vanish.

I hear one of our last conversations, one of our last real conversations, a conversation between two people intertwined, not between the alive and the dead.

"I just don't think it's ever going to happen."

"Don't cry," I said.

"Why? Why us? Why?"

"It's okay. I'm here. It's okay."

"I just want it all to be over—all I do is worry—"

"It's going to be okay. I promise you."

But all the promises and plans in the world can't change destiny.

A great love comes once in a lifetime, if that.

When it's there, recognize it. Hold on to it. Don't let it go.

Don't take it for granted and then look on the horizon and watch it slip away.

Jennifer rings the doorbell, and I open the door and surprise her with one red rose. It matches her long dress, and as she walks in I touch her and forget this time that embracing her might mean embracing a puff of smoke and might ultimately send her away. This time I put an arm around flesh and blood and pull her close and smell her citrus-smelling perfume and kiss her warm neck. Then her cheek. Then her red lips. Lips that invite me to kiss them, a kiss that lingers for a moment.

As I move away, she wipes my lips.

Sorry. You have—there, no more.

I don't know if ghosts wear lipstick, but this dream or fantasy seems so attuned to details that anything is possible. Absolutely anything.

"You look—breathtaking."

Thank you. It's New Year's Eve.

"I hope you know that it's okay if you want—if you want to—"

To stay here?

"Yeah, I mean, that's what I was thinking."

Me too.

I smile, and it feels like she can't be gone, that she couldn't have left me, that this is so real and what happens tomorrow?

Tomorrow is a universe away. Tonight is ours.

The fire has been going at least an hour by the time I open the card table and place the tablecloth over it. We sit next to each other in folding chairs. I stop apologizing after Jen tells me to. I take the boxes out of the bag one by one, knowing I've gotten way too much.

"I got beef broccoli, sweet-and-sour shrimp, here are some spring rolls, fried rice—you like cashew chicken, right?"

Is someone else coming? Jen asks.

I shake my head. "I just didn't know—I wasn't sure what you would have wanted."

You know me.

"Do I?"

She grins and leans over, her long arm bare under the straps of her dress. She takes my hand, then pulls me close to kiss me.

I'll have a little of each, she finally says.

I take the large spoon and scoop out her dinner. I do the same for myself, suddenly hungrier than I've been in years. I pile helpings onto my plate. I go to pour her a glass of wine, but she says thanks but no. I give her a Diet Coke instead.

Dinner is wonderful, magical. I remember many nights sitting beside her eating the same kind of food, watching television and talking during commercials. If only you knew. If only you knew that those moments couldn't be brought back, that they could never be redone. Now, we take our time.

Jennifer brushes back the hair from her face and smiles as she takes her first bite.

Conversation flows smoothly. Unlike my pitiful to-do list, there are too many things I want to talk with Jen about. I ask her questions and eagerly await her answers. Once again it's like a dream. A soft, color-coated dream.

"Can I ask something?" I ask after the boxes are closed again and our plates are stacked on top of one another on the edge of the carpet in the family room.

Of course.

"Where'd you go?"

When?

"These last few months. You know—after Cancun."

Home.

I study her, and her answer is as natural as breathing. Is that what she calls heaven? Or is there no such thing as heaven, and *this is* truly what happens when we're gone?

"What was it like?" I ask her, moving a little closer, sipping my second Styrofoam cup of wine from the bottle I opened an hour earlier.

It was—it was quiet.

"Will you—will you have to leave again?"

Yes.

"What am I going to do when you're gone?"

I want you to find yourself. Don't give up.

"And then what, after I find myself?"

Then find me.

I just look at her, sad, confused, frustrated.

She reaches out and holds my hand and her touch feels warm and I move closer to kiss her. I rest my head on one of her legs and look up at her, this picture of a heavenly angel.

"What are you thinking about?"

Miracles.

"You coming back—that's a miracle."

I have to believe they can happen.

"How come?"

That's all I have left, Colin. Faith.

Her hair feels real. It's silken against my fingertips, against the palms of my hands. I stroke it and breathe in its citrus scent and know that this must be real and that she must be real. Yet I tremble and feel unsure. I quiver and she asks what's wrong and I say nothing and kiss her again. Her lips brush against mine, her hands and arms surround me. I can sense her against me, her touch so light, her form the same. Nothing is different, and yet I know that everything is different. Perhaps this is all imagined and I'm imagining the best parts, the tiny and most meaningful moments. But her embrace, her touch, it is real, she is real, and I believe that for the moment, she is truly there.

What's going on in that mind of yours?

I tell her that I wonder if she's there. If this is all a dream.

I keep telling you—of course I'm here.

She takes my hand and puts it against her heart. *Feel that?*

My hand shivers and she kisses me and says that she'll always be there not so far away and that eventually if it's destined that I'll come find her. I ask her where but a kiss answers my question and I finally let myself go, lost in this insulated hold, lost in this four-color vivid dream.

I love you.

And I whisper the same words into her ear.

I'll still love you, even when I'm not here.

But she's here now, and for the moment that is all I care about.

a glance

hair skims my cheek

open palms

the glistening of her ring

a short breath

the room circles twirls tumbles turns

her eyes tender soft sad

Everything is now forgotten.

Nothing matters anymore not the job nor the pages nor the royalty figures nor the bestseller lists nor the smiles and the clients and the authors nor the sun and the moon and the stars that leak into the lovely living room.

Is it real?

Everything, life itself, has been put on pause.

I give you everything and my all and there will never be another no not ever another like you.

Time and loneliness and longing and heartache culminate in this. This heaven.

And in the background in a glowing gold, numbers let me know it's a new year.

no surprises

A Portrait of the Artist as a Young Man

It's a cold, dim January afternoon. The kind where you bundle up in a blanket in front of the fire and listen to the wind against the windows. The kind where you drift off gazing into the crackling flames and the shifting shadows. The kind where you are silent and still enough to have some sort of idea how you ended up here. And why.

A hundred names and titles and songs and images cover you in this sweet solitude. You've finished reading another novel today, journaled for about half an hour (a habit you stopped years ago), downloaded from iTunes onto your laptop a few classic albums you've been wanting. You're tired from your mind working overtime, spinning and turning, ideas flowing and inspiration abounding.

You're trying to do what Jen asked, trying to find yourself, trying to find the essence of what made you *you*.

You're in third grade and your father gives you a comic book called *Tintin and the Crab with the Golden Claws*. This isn't just a comic book. It's a passport to adventure and imagination—a whole series of books written by a Belgian man called Herge back in the thirties and forties.

Tintin is a boy with his dog and they have incredible adventures around the world.

You haven't thought about Tintin in a long time. You wonder how you can get your hands on a copy.

You remember sitting in a theater with your father in the summer of 1981. You are ten years old and you only have two more years left to be with him, but you don't know that. All you know is that there is a really cool guy named Indiana Jones who hates snakes and always seems on the run from someone. And *Raiders of the Lost Ark* changes your life forever. You go see it half a dozen times in the theater, and it makes you want to direct and write screenplays and act and be Harrison Ford.

You remember listening to your father's records. The cover of *Abbey Road* in your office at the condo belonged to him. It's now in a box, one of the few you took with you. You remember that album well. "Come Together" and "Something" and your favorite, "Here Comes the Sun." You assumed that every rock group made albums like this. To you the Beatles were just some group from a long time ago, but they made cool music. Your father loved them, and he had a massive collection of records even while you were starting your own tape collection.

He particularly loved Elton John. Who doesn't? There was a time when Elton John came on the scene and blew everybody away with his talent and his voice. A kid who kept putting out album after album. The seventies Elton John is who your father loved and adored. And he would play you albums like *Madman Across the Water* that featured songs like "Tiny Dancer" and "Levon."

There is so much to try to recall. Listening to somebody's copy of The Smiths' "The Queen Is Dead" and wondering what you were missing. Reading *The Prince of Tides* one spring break and wanting to move to South Carolina. Watching the movie *Seven* and being creeped out by its intensity.

So many songs, so many sentences, so many scenes.

They are all a part of who you are, the fabric of your life, the spine and the skin of your soul.

When did you stop enjoying these things? The art in them. The craft and the creation. The act of enjoying them.

You're not sure. You just know that sometime, over the years, as you learned more about the business side of the arts, selling, making money, you lost something.

But now it's still, and you're alone.

I want you to find yourself.

And you're going to try. A part of finding your way is to slow down and pull over and stop and take out the map.

It took all of this to make you slow down. And it took Jen to make you take out your map.

Don't give up.

You don't plan to. You don't know what your next move is. But you're not going to give up. You're going to find yourself, whatever that looks like.

Then find me.

And yes, then find her, wherever she might be.

Animal Farm

It's January 21 and the snow has come and gone and the sunshine wakes me from this dream.

I think of New Year's and can still feel her lips against mine, her sweet and soft good-bye.

I'm almost convinced that it happened.

Almost.

But she's been gone ever since.

I enter the familiar office and find things to be the same. Darcy looks up from her desk and does a double take and tries to get out my name before I pass by.

"Just getting a few things," I tell her.

In my old office, behind my old desk, I find Ted on the phone, schmoozing and sucking up to some no-talent moneymaker. He finishes his train of thought but watches me as I open a filing cabinet and begin to pick out files.

He's fumbling over his words now. "Excuse me, I, uh, there's something I have to take care of immediately. Can I call you back?"

He hangs up the phone and curses as he gets up and lurks behind me. "What do you think you're doing?"

"I never did have a chance to clean out my things."

"Roth brought you whatever personal items you had. Those are not yours."

I show him a blue file. "See this? This is my handwriting. These pages of info—they're mine. All this is mine."

Ted takes a step forward, and I look up at him.

"I swear, Ted, don't. I'm the fired one, the one who lost his wife, the one with nothing to lose. I swear—back off, or I'll bury that big head of yours so far in this filing cabinet you'll forget where you are."

He pauses for a brief second, then moves back. Ted's a big guy, but he's gotta see the complete disconnect and carelessness in my eyes. He knows something behind them is probably not altogether sane.

"That's illegal, you know," Ted says, a few steps away from me.

"These are all my files. They're notes. You probably didn't bother looking at them, did you?"

"You can't steal Roth authors."

"Authors are free to do what they want."

"Not when they've signed contracts."

I laugh. "You and I both know just how meaningless those contracts are. Authors and publishers get out of binding terms every day."

"And you stealing our authors is, what? Legitimate?"

"I'm just wanting to give some an option. A chance to have more attention, more freedom, more behind them than a braggart trying to land them a multimillion dollar deal."

"Still the idealist, huh?"

I put the files in my leather briefcase. I walk up to Ted and look at him without blinking.

"You know something?" I ask. "You're way too smug and self-absorbed to be a truly great agent. You'll never make it to the big leagues."

"At least I'm in a league," he says back.

But I'm already heading out the door, past a standing Darcy who calls out after me.

I've got everything I need. Road maps to try to find my way.

I'm trying, Jen. God knows I'm trying.

I'm in Charleston staying at a Fairfield Inn north of the city. Times have certainly changed. Author meeting #1 yesterday ended disastrously with Oren Phillips. It would have really been nice of him to have saved me the time and money and just said no over the phone. I just ate my complimentary continental breakfast where I spilled half of the carton of Rice Krispies over the carpeted floor. Now I'm checking e-mail on my laptop, which is perched on a small table. The heater next to me blows in my left ear.

Amidst the typical junk, I see a message from something called CobaltDesign. I open it just to see what offer I have today.

Colin:

It was hard to leave you. And hard not to pick up the phone and call these last few weeks.

How are you?

Jen

First she comes to my house to haunt me and make love to me. Now she e-mails and taunts me.

How am I?

Without even thinking, I quickly type back.

Bewildered.

I press Send and then wait. Of course, nothing comes back. I have to wait.

And so the fun begins.

I hear Bono singing "Like a desert needs rain, like a town needs a name, I need your love. . . ."

It's midnight. I hear the sound of a new e-mail come on my laptop.

You there?

I smile. Of course I'm here. I'm always here, on the other end, on the other line, waiting, wondering.

Yes.

I wait.

I miss you.

And that's it. Short, sweet, simple.

And strangely satisfying.

"Like sweet soul music, like sunlight, I need your love. . . ."

"Colin, you know I love you," Miriam Moore says to me. "And I always have."

This is Tucson, Arizona, and I've forgotten what time it is or what month. Back home it's snowing, but here I'm wearing a shortsleeve shirt dining out and listening to a former client whom I helped build whom I helped *make* tell me delicately and politely *no thanks.*

"It's just that I can't leave Roth, not now, not after everything—"

And she goes on and on and I smile and I nod and I listen.

"Like coming home and you don't know where you've been. . . ."

I want to hear your voice, her e-mail says.

I want to smell your skin, my e-mail replies.

I want you to smell my skin, her e-mail says.

Then let me.

Where are you? she asks.

Denver.

You've been traveling a lot.

I know, I write.

I miss you.

You don't have to miss me, I say. I can be there.

No, you can't. You know that.

I want to say something deep, profound.

Yeah.

"As the room spins around . . ."

In Miami after three hours of brainstorming and hearing an author utter, "I'll think about it," I get another e-mail from Jen.

Where are you?

I type back: Miami, where are you?

A day later: Not far away. What's in Miami?

Back home, I write: Nothing was in Miami. A lost cause.

She e-mails me that night: Don't give up.

I leave the computer on so I can try and e-mail her and get an ongoing conversation. It's late when her e-mail comes in.

I quickly reply. When can I see you again?

A few minutes later: I don't know. I'm still waiting. Believing. Hoping.

I type back I'm hoping all of this is real.

I wait for a response. It finally comes.

Just don't wait for me.

"Like faith needs a doubt, like a freeway out, I need your love."

And that's it for e-mails, at least for a while.

I have some time to kill before my flight leaves San Francisco, so I stop by a bookstore. I should just leave the book business altogether. But I doubt I'll ever stop browsing, ever stop reading. I end up buying one of the bestsellers, eager not for a good story but to see how the hype compares to the actual product.

I can't help thinking of the tally. Twenty-three authors solicited, twenty-three offers rejected. I thought that maybe someone would see the work and time and energy I put into their writing career and decide to go with me. But it's not that simple. Half of them think I've cracked up, and the other half are simply too scared or secure to move away from Roth. I can understand, of course.

It's just not the response I was expecting.

I'm sitting by the gate reading when I see him. I'm too tired to put up a fight. I wave him over.

"Are you following me?"

"Yes," Donald says.

"Look—"

"I'm staring, and I don't like what I see."

"Meaning?"

"That's exactly what I'm looking for. Meaning. What are you doing anyway, Colin?"

"It's not your business."

"Is this what you're looking for?" He points to the book I'm holding.

"It'd help pay some bills, that's for sure," I tell him.

"But you haven't found what you're looking for, have you?"

"Says who?"

"Says I. This—all of this—these trips, the authors, the business. This is the reason you lost yourself in the first place."

Who is this guy?

"How much of my life have you been spying on?"

"Enough to know what a sad sack you are."

"If you knew it all, you'd know I deserve sympathy."

"For?"

"I'm too tired to get into it. Got that?"

"That's a nice tall cup of coffee you've got next to you."

I nod as if to say I don't give a rip.

"It's not going to wake you up, Colin."

"Excuse me?"

"You've got to do it on your own."

"Donald—please. *Please*. I beg of you. I implore you. I don't have any energy left and I can't and won't and *don't want to* deal with you. Don't you get it? Can't you ever get it? Please—leave me alone."

He smiles, nods, then stands up and walks away.

The young man storms into the restaurant with half his shirt untucked, his coat open and snowflakes covering it, his hair tousled and several days' worth of beard still on his face. He scans the booths, then lights up when he sees me. He scurries over to the table and produces his free hand to shake mine. It's cold and feels like sandpaper.

"Oh, I'm sorry I'm late," he says in an exasperated gasp. "I got stuck in traffic on the expressway—it was really bad—"

"It's fine."

"No, really, I'm so sorry, Mr. Scott."

He's still standing. I can't help smiling. "It's okay."

Ian Pollock is half an hour late. For a while I was wondering if we got the right place to meet. Rock Bottom Brewery is between St. Charles and Ian's home city, Palos Heights. It's 6:30 P.M. and I'm not bothered at all. The Tuesday night crowd is light.

The guy takes off his coat and sits in the booth across from me. A waitress spots him and comes up right away.

"Oh, I'll have—whatever he's having."

"An Amber Wheat?"

"Sure," Ian says, clearly clueless.

"Do you have an ID I can see?"

Ian nods nervously, takes a minute to find his wallet in his coat pocket, then shows the waitress his license. She thanks him and leaves.

"Still get carded—even though I'm twenty-seven."

"Enjoy it while it lasts," I tell him. "They didn't card me."

"You look young."

I laugh. "Yeah, but I feel real old."

"Do you?"

"When guys like you get carded. And don't call me Mr. Scott."

He laughs and apologizes again for being late.

"It's fine, really."

"I couldn't believe you wanted to meet. I got your e-mail and read it maybe a hundred times."

"I liked *Passover Lane*," I tell him right away.

Of course he knows this. If I hadn't I wouldn't have agreed to meet.

He, of course, doesn't know that I have no one else *to* meet. But that's okay.

Maybe the name of this place is truly appropriate.

Ian waits for me to say more. I can see that eager, hungry, desperate look. The kind that begs for input, direction, guidance, and most of all, praise.

Every author wants praise. If they ever tell you they don't, they're lying.

"I really like your voice," I tell him. "It's fresh. Kinda hip. Sort of in the vein of a Nick Hornby."

"He's one of my favorite writers."

"I can tell. Sometimes it works. It's a bit rough. But that's okay."

Ian's beer comes and the conversation stops for a moment.

"So, Ian. Tell me about yourself."

He gulps down his first sip, and I can tell he's nervous. It's like a job interview.

"Well, I've been writing all my life. As I've mentioned before, I've written eight other novels before *Passover Lane*. Trying to get them published on my own. Trying to find an agent."

"You've sent me a few."

"Yeah, I know. They were pretty bad. I graduated from U of I with a communications degree and have been working in video since college. I work with a company that helps produce trailers for movies. I do a lot of editing, stuff like that."

"You like movies?"

"Yeah, love them."

"Ever written a screenplay?" I ask.

"I've tried. But I think I love books. I'd rather write a book and have them base a movie off it. It's hard breaking into the film business."

"It's hard breaking into the publishing world too."

"Yeah, I've discovered that."

"You like what you do?"

Ian looks at me, a few freckles giving away his boyish nice-guy appearance.

"No, not really. It's money."

"And family?"

"I've been married for four years. To Lauren. No kids."

I nod and quickly ask another question. "So is *Passover Lane* the best thing you've written?"

"Yes, I think so. I mean, when I wrote it I started trying to do different things. I initially made it third person, then I changed it to first. And some of the characters changed into—oh, man!"

As Ian spoke he waved his hands in an energetic, nervous fashion, and ended up accidentally waving one hand into his half-full beer. The glass fell into his lap.

Ian stands and grabs a cloth napkin and curses. "I'm sorry. Ah, man."

His khaki cargos look as though he's had a major accident down there. The waitress comes and brings him more napkins. She tells him she'll bring him another beer.

The guy shakes his head, angry at himself, wondering what he was talking about.

"Ian? Just relax."

"I know—I'm sorry. I was driving like a madman on the highway thinking—"

"It's fine. I'm here. You made it. There's no rush."

"You don't have to be anywhere anytime soon?"

I shake my head. "No."

Nobody's home. Nobody's back at the house.

Nobody's coming back either.

"So, what are your dreams? Where do you aspire to go with your writing?"

"I just—the thought of being published—I mean, it's something I've always wanted—"

"No," I interrupt. "I mean—if you could have anything you want. If everything could work itself out, what would be ideal?"

Ian rubs his nose and then squints his eyebrows, thinking. "I'd be able to write full-time. That's all I've ever wanted to do. Be able to support Lauren. And a family, maybe, too. We're at that point—sort of, at least—trying—thinking about it. Now's not a time to quit my job and try and follow dreams. Not if we were to have a child. But my dream is to write every day."

"You wouldn't get bored?"

He shakes his head. "No. I've got a list of ten, fifteen maybe, ideas I'm dying to write. It's so hard—finding time. Making the story I work on halfway decent. If I could write full-time—I'd do just that."

"And those eight novels you wrote. Did you finish each of them?"

Ian nods. "Want to hear something crazy?"

"Sure."

"In my mind, I've got a shelf of books that are mine, and I'm trying to sort through what I want them to be. I haven't even gotten one published—don't know if I ever will. But I'm already thinking about my bibliography, what it looks like, what my legacy will be."

"That's great."

"It's probably foolish. Crazy."

"I know crazy," I say with a smile. "And I kinda like it."

I find myself energized talking to this guy. He's talented; I could see that from his manuscript. He's not brilliant or masterful, but then again, who is? Especially at twenty-seven? He's not F. Scott Fitzgerald, but that's probably a good thing.

Asked point-blank what he longs for, it's not a multibook contract with a load of advance money.

It's not bestseller lists and starred *PW* reviews.

It's to write full-time.

To do what he loves doing, all the time.

And support his family.

A future family.

I like this guy.

After hearing Ian talk awhile about *Passover Lane*, and after sharing comments on how he can improve it, all comments I've written down in a document I'll give to him tonight, I tell him what I'm thinking.

"I think this would fit in well with Triten House Publishers. Ever heard of them?"

He nods. "I've sent them some manuscripts before."

"They're just over in Carol Stream. I have a few contacts there. I'm thinking about maybe giving this to one of the editors, meeting with them."

"Really?" Ian says, stunned.

"I've given you five pages on how you can improve the story. You do this, and do it well, I'll be able to sell it."

"Just like that?"

I laugh. "Hopefully. But then again, nothing works out as easily as that. Well, few things do."

"Vivian Brown does, right?"

I think of *In Your Memory.*

"Even Vivian needs to work on her books."

"Are you still working with her?"

I shake my head. "I'm no longer working at Roth. And she's one of their authors."

"Can I ask—what happened?"

"Personal stuff," I say, and leave it at that.

"So you're starting up your own agency?"

"You can say that."

Ian nods and smiles. He clears his throat.

"Is there—would I be able to be a client?"

"You already are."

On my way home, I do the math.

If, and that's a mighty big if, I landed a contract with Triten or anyone for Ian's novel, we'd probably be looking at something in the $10,000 range. Fifteen percent of that is $1,500. Double that is still only $3,000. A three-book deal for twenty a pop would still only get me $9,000, and that would be staggered, as contracts always are.

I go from a financial overspill to a drop in the bank bucket.

If I even sell Ian Pollock.

It's something, a voice tells me. Something.

It's the middle of February and I'm driving home and feeling excited.

It's not Vivian Brown, but it's something.

This guy's got potential. He's got a future. He's hungry and he's personable and he can tell a decent story and he's willing to learn and *that* is what I'm looking for.

That was what I used to look for before it came down to landing the big book deal and dealing with the celebrities and big names. Before it became all about numbers and nothing else.

The Colin Scott Agency? Is that what I'm going for?

Is that how I'm going to find myself?

I don't know. I'm taking it day by day. Just like the house. Just like life after Jen.

She left with a kiss and a "love you" the morning of January 1. I still get an occasional e-mail from her, as if she knows I still need something, anything, to keep going.

I miss you, I tell her.

I think she can hear me. I think she came down from heaven or wherever to give me a jump start. In everything. And she's still monitoring my progress.

The year is still new, and I'm still trying to start over again.

The Sun Also Rises

I'm starting to read Hemingway's classic *The Sun Also Rises* again. I can't remember the last time I read it. I'm enjoying it more than I thought I would.

One evening, I Google the title to get more information. I didn't realize it came from a phrase from the Bible. I find a Web site with Bible verses in it.

Good to know they have the Bible online. They have every kind of imaginable porn in a thousand varieties, might as well have some Bible verses too.

The passage is from Ecclesiastes.

"Everything is meaningless," says the Teacher, "completely meaningless."

Wow. Finally a Bible verse that I really, truly get.

Yes, everything is meaningless, Mr. Ecclesiastes. Pointless drivel. You must know the publishing industry, because that's utterly meaningless too.

"What do people get for all their hard work under the sun?"

Amen to that. Wow, I like this guy. It's good stuff.

"The sun rises and the sun sets," so the passage goes.

Who knew Mr. Hemingway read the Bible?

"Everything is wearisome beyond description. No matter how much we see, we are never satisfied. No matter how much we hear, we are not content."

I'm beginning to wonder if this is really the Bible. This is heavy stuff. Sounds like Albert Camus, not the Holy Word of God.

"Nothing under the sun is truly new."

Again, I gotta agree.

"Of making many books there is no end; and much study is a weariness of the flesh."

I decide I'm going to make a T-shirt with this quote on it and start selling it. It's perfect.

I am actually absorbed in reading this. I'm wanting to see if there is a happy outcome, some, "It's this bad, but . . ." So I keep reading.

I get to the end, looking for some sort of conclusion, some sort of hope. "Don't let the excitement of youth cause you to forget your Creator."

But that's not what happened to me, is it?

I don't want to think about this anymore, I don't want to keep going.

"Remember him before the door to life's opportunities is closed and the sound of work fades."

Is it too late? Has the door closed and the sound faded?

"Yes, remember your Creator now while you are young, before the silver cord of life snaps."

But it already snapped years ago, didn't it? Didn't it, Colin?

For the first time in a long time, in a very long time, I remember something else about my father. Not listening to Elton John albums or hearing him read from the Chronicles of Narnia.

I remember him reading Scripture to my sister and me. Bible passages.

Yeah, and where did it get him? Where did that faith in mumbo jumbo get him?

He read old stories about Noah and Joseph and Moses. And he read about Jesus' birth and Jesus' death.

But all that knowledge and all that faith . . . it got him nowhere. Twelve years old, and there was no one left to read to me, to play me music, to take me to movies. Mom wasn't into that sort of stuff.

"Fear God and obey his commands," is the final suggestion from Ecclesiastes.

But I don't want to. Because my father did exactly that, and it got him nowhere.

Nowhere.

Everything is meaningless. Everything.

"Every man's life ends the same way," Hemingway once said. "It is only the details of how he lived and how he died that distinguish one man from another."

Do I believe that?

What *do* I believe?

How did Charles Scott live, and how did he die?

A late-night bout of Web patrol produces the following blurb on AintItCool.com, a popular movie info site.

Julia Roberts is sidelined for a few weeks while shooting the film *Immersion* in the Smoky Mountains of North Carolina. Reports say the actress was filming a scene running up a hill and twisted her ankle. The Gore Verbinski project will be delayed for a few weeks, but the projected

Christmas release is still planned.

"You're looking better," Pearce tells me.

"You're not," I say, joking.

"Thank you very much."

He's standing in the kitchen, holding a cup of Dunkin' Donuts coffee. I've got one too, along with a box of Munchkins.

"I wanted to talk about the financial situation," I say, stressing the last word. "You know I'm waist deep in debt."

Before Jen died, security was always a paycheck away, a deal away. I handled the finances, and didn't handle them very well. Jen got paid on and off, depending on her project. Sometimes we'd find ourselves with over $100,000 in our checking account, the result of several recent checks coming in. Other times I'd find $2,500 or less, and would wonder how in the world I was going to pay next month's rent, along with the other bills.

The BMW was bought outright, with Jen deciding against a car since she was on the road so much. The apartment sucked up a lot of our earnings. It was out of our price range, but I had hoped a little too much. I thought I saw writing on the wall with Vivian Brown. Maybe more like dollars on the wall. So I sank most of our savings into the house.

Who knew that everything would go up in smoke and blow away? Who knew—who knew anything like this would happen?

I still had the BMW. It had been repaired, and insurance covered most of the costs. Maybe I should sell it for a little extra cash, but I couldn't force myself to do it. Not just yet.

The house in St. Charles was bought for $725,000, due to the large amount of land and the condition of the landscaping, including the beautiful trees surrounding it and the long lawn behind. Initially, when Pearce told me how much everything would cost, from leveling the initial house and putting up the new one, the cost for everything additional was going to be $500,000. Now we were approaching a million, with more work needed.

I'm no accountant, but I can see that I'm getting dangerously close to going bankrupt. I need to sell it and sell it fast for enough capital to start a business again. And maybe, just maybe start a life again too.

So I run all of this by Pearce. All the numbers, figures, and I ask him how quickly he can finish and sell the house.

"Tell me something," he says. "Do you want this looking average, or do you want it remarkable?"

"Everything's about money, my man. What's the price difference?"

"It just needs a little more time, some more cash, and it's going to be beautiful. And you're going to sell it for a boatload."

"I need a boatload. If I decide to start a business."

"Are you?"

"I think I already have."

Pearce nods and finishes another Munchkin. "Good for you."

"Look. This last year—everything that's happened—you've put a lot of your own time into this project."

"You're paying me."

"But you've done a lot more than you needed to do. And I still owe you. A lot."

He looks around the kitchen. "It'll be a shame, selling this place. You attached to it?"

"In a weird way, yes. But it'd look a lot better with some furniture, among other things."

"A large family would fit in well."

I nod. Pearce realizes what he said and apologizes.

"I miss her," I say, looking out at the back lawn.

"Yeah."

"Do you believe—when people die—they go somewhere?"

"Sure."

I sip my coffee. "Heaven and all that?"

"Uh-huh. But first you got to live your life down here."

"I guess we do."

"She's not coming back, Colin."

I look at Pearce. I wish I could tell him the truth. At least the truth as my mind knows it. The truth of what I saw last month. The truth of what I believe I saw.

"What if— What if she did?" I ask.

He doesn't say anything for a moment. This is entering hard territory. The territory where no answer fits, no answer is right.

"I wouldn't wait," Pearce says.

And I know he's right.

"How do you keep such a positive attitude?" I ask him.

"It's the meds," he says with a laugh.

"Seriously."

Pearce thinks for a minute, as if he's debating telling me something. "Do you know that Kristy's father is dying of cancer?"

I shake my head. He hasn't mentioned a word about this.

"Yeah. He's got a few weeks—days—left. And it's—well, it's been tough. Real tough. And I know it might sound either corny or clichéd—man, I don't ever want to sound like one of those hypocritical pastors that steal money from the church or have sex with their secretaries. It's just that our faith is the only thing that's made us get through this. It's the only hope we have. Kristy has been extraordinary. Unbelievable. She's lifted my spirits, and it's *her* father."

"But your faith—faith in God, in heaven, in harps and hymns?"

Pearce laughs. "Yes, definitely in harps and hymns." He shakes his head. "Come on."

"What?"

"It's faith that her father is going to be better off when he takes his dying breath."

I stare at him for a minute. Studying him. Waiting and watching.

"And you really believe this?" I ask.

"Yes, I do. I don't try to cram it down people's throats. Colin—you're a friend. A client, sure. But a friend too. And it would be wrong of me if I never shared this with you. I just—I'm not that good at it. All I know is that I believe that there is a God and that his Son died on the cross for all of us and there is a heaven. I believe all of those things because sometimes, some days, it's the only thing that gets me through."

"I just don't think that's the sort of thing for me," I say.

"Sure, yeah, maybe not. But be open. This might be the way God is talking to you."

We change the subject and talk about the plans ahead, and I decide with Pearce's urgings not to skimp on the rest of the house. A couple months, three or four at the most, and it will be finished, in time for the summer selling season. In time to reap the benefits of hard labor and money invested.

That's faith, right? Believing in selling this. Believing in the big payoff. That's my faith.

It's not exactly what I thought when I first purchased it. Not exactly what we thought.

But plans change. They always change.

"I just want out," I once said to her.

Out of what?

"Out of the business."

You spent a third of your life in that business.

"So?"

That doesn't mean anything?

"Not anymore."

What about all those grand plans? Those plans you had when I first met you?

"Plans change. They always change."

It's March 18, a Thursday night, and I hear my e-mail signal incoming mail. I go to the computer and see a message from Triten House.

Dear Mr. Scott:

My name is Shelby Andrews, and I work as an acquisitions editor for fiction at Triten House. Thank for you sending us the proposal for *Passover Lane* by Ian Pollock. I will be reading it in the next few weeks and will get back to you as soon as possible. It looks like it might have some potential—I've read a few pages and the story synopsis you sent in.

I met you briefly at a book signing with Vivian Brown years ago. It's a pleasure to hear from you, and to know that you think this might be a project for Triten House.

I'll be in touch.

Shelby

It's a quick response. I thought for sure it would be another month before I heard anything. Granted, it'll take awhile for Shelby to read the manuscript. She surely has many more waiting in her office or cubicle, in piles surrounding her.

It's something. But I know the business well enough to not get my hopes up.

I just sit at my computer, zoning out, staring and thinking, when another e-mail comes.

The words CobaltDesign pop up on the screen and sink my stomach. It's been weeks since I've heard from her, maybe even a month. I don't breathe as I read.

Dear Colin:

I am sorry for taking so long to e-mail you. A part of me says to stop this, to stop writing. But another part reminds me that I can't. I wake up with that reminder. With that hope.

Do you remember when we first started dating? When we would rush to see each other in some dive I'd picked out for us in Chicago? When you'd keep me up until two? Sometimes just talking, sometimes more. ☺

I miss those innocent, far-off days. When our careers were a simple dream—a simple notion. When we longed to have responsibilities, but didn't have them just yet. Because we had time to enjoy what truly matters—each other.

I just wish we had started trying to have children earlier. Then maybe things would have been different.

Life isn't what is given to you. Life is what you make out of it. I feel we were given a chance once, twice, maybe several times.

I pray that there is another chance. I'm not sure how.

I'm sorry for pouring out like this, not knowing how you are doing and how these words come across. If you want to know the honest truth, I just really miss you. I feel very alone tonight.

"I love you" can be such a trite and overused phrase, and I dare not utter it anymore because I don't know the ramifications of saying it. But in my heart, I believe I do, Colin.

Take care. And don't stop believing.

Jen

I don't reply. I'm not sure what to say.

I believe that I'm losing my mind and that I lost it some time ago but that pales in comparison to losing you Jen.

That night, I dream of her, in my arms, as she was on New Year's Eve.

I'm staining an antique dresser I picked up at a garage sale when the phone rings. I pick up my cell phone and say hello and someone spews out a stream of verbal abuse.

"Who is this?" I yell.

"You know exactly who this is," a voice from yesteryear says, adding a few juicy curses.

Ted Varrick.

"What do you want?"

"Good try," he says, a burst of anger lacing his words.

I don't say a word. I don't know what this is about, but I don't care either.

"You're messing with the wrong guys, Colin."

"Okay."

He curses. "Don't give me that nonchalant 'okay.' Was this your plan all along?"

"What?"

He curses again and tells me I know what he's talking about.

"Ted. If you don't say something that makes sense, I'm hanging up on you. I don't work with you anymore, and don't give a rip about anything that goes on with Roth."

"Roth is disappointed."

"The guy who *fired me* is disappointed? Yeah, that mood seems to be catchy."

"Stealing authors is illegal."

Ian Pollock? How in the world do they know about him?

"Nobody's stolen anybody."

Ted laughs, and says I'm full of something not very nice.

"That's touching, to hear you say that."

And I wonder again why in the world they'd care about Ian.

"You're getting a little something in the mail—the problem is, I don't know where to send it," Ted says.

"I know *exactly* where you can send it."

"Amusing," he says dryly. "It's a little letter from our lawyer."

"About what? I don't know what you're talking about."

"Really? I think you're lying."

I hang up. I don't need this and don't need him and know I'm not doing anything wrong. Ian Pollock never signed an agreement to work with the Roth Agency.

Did he?

But who cares? The kid's unknown. It's not like he's John Grisham and I'm taking him with me.

Ted's an idiot.

I write a note on a yellow Post-it.

Call Darcy.

Then I think about it and crinkle up the note and toss it in the garbage. I go back to my project in the living room.

April is already here, and the longer I'm away from it all, the less I miss it.

I haven't worn a tie in months. And I think I've lost a little weight, because my shirt doesn't feel as tight as it used to.

I drive up past a brick wall that says Triten House and park in front of the three-story brick building. There's a pond and a longer parking lot that's full of several hundred cars.

It's amazing how life sometimes can circle itself around and plop you back down to the start of it all.

I remember sitting in my car in this parking lot during a rainstorm and listening to Peter Gabriel's "Solsbury Hill" as I was about to go in for my first business meeting as an agent. *My heart going boom boom boom* was too appropriate. I was twenty-four years old.

Now I'm thirty-five, and I feel as though I'm starting over. I'm at a crossroads, inspired and motivated and on fire.

I'm no longer some kid who feels like he can change the world. The world has changed for that kid, and he has seen what it looks like. It's like a glistening, glowing rock that you turn over to find rotting, black muck underneath. The world out there was once fresh, the publishing industry idealistic and visionary. But the underbelly of it reeks, and he knows this, and has helped contribute to this, and wants almost nothing else to do with it.

Almost.

A voice whispers

I want you to find yourself.

The door is open just a crack, Colin. Are you brave enough to push it with all your might?

Is this finding yourself?

And if I find myself, then what?

Find me.

I open the door. Sunlight cracks through the spring sky.

Peter Gabriel's voice still sings in my head. "I'll tell them what the smile on my face meant."

With my heart going *boom boom boom*, I know I'm starting over.

And it feels good.

Shelby Andrews is youthful and blonde and cute in her black suit and red shirt. She greets me with a firm handshake and leads me up to her office.

Triten House. I wonder if she knows I did my first official contract with them.

We talk about books and several of Triten's authors that I know about. Shelby leads me to a sparse meeting room with a table for eight and asks if I'd like anything to drink. Vodka tonic perhaps, I think with humor. But I shake my head and politely decline. She sits across from me and opens up a file.

And the weird thing is, I'm nervous.

The lower part of my back is sweating. My jaw is heavy, and the words coming out aren't as sure as they usually are. Shelby does most of the talking.

"I had the chance to finish Ian's novel a couple days ago," she starts telling me in a tone that I already can read through. "It was very, uh, raw and open in some areas."

Her words aren't negative, but the way her eyes aren't looking directly into mine, the way her voice sounds a little hesitant, the way her body language is already putting up a slight wall—all these things tell me what she's about to say in a lot more words.

"I thought a lot about having Ian rewrite *Passover Lane.* The voice is compelling at first. It sort of wears on the reader after a while."

I don't agree, but that's okay.

"The fundamental problem is the scope of the novel, and the various subplots."

And for the next ten minutes Shelby talks about the manuscript and suggests ways to rework it. I listen, nod my head, occasionally agree. Everything about this is wrong. I'm saying nothing. She's saying everything. This is not negotiating. This is listening to a critic. This is getting one woman's opinion.

The old Colin Scott would have ended Shelby's pontificating nine minutes ago. He wouldn't even be here, sitting down with an editor. He'd be wanting to talk to the publisher about a five-book deal for some big name, not sludging around in the trenches with Dimples here and listening to her tell me *no* in a hundred different ways.

But not now. I don't have any legs to stand on.

"So," I finally say. "You really don't want to buy *Passover Lane*, do you?"

"Well, no, I'm not saying that."

She's basically wearing a sign that says *Heck no*, but she's really "not saying that"? Come on.

"What are you saying? You want him to rewrite this?"

"I think he definitely should rewrite this. But I'm not sure if that will get it a green light. Lately the executives at Triten have been saying no to unknown authors. We've been hurt by the economy, just like the rest of the industry. And publishing a new author is certainly a risk."

"Yes, it is."

She keeps talking. "With someone like Ian, there is obviously talent."

Even though she has said nothing positive and given me a hundred ways his writing could improve.

". . . and if he works hard, he might be able to sell this book."

"Just not to you, right?" I ask, unable to hide my smile.

"I never want to say no."

"You don't, huh?"

"Well, no. I mean, there's always a chance—"

"That he could go on to be a big name and then remember the acquisitions editor who hated his novel."

"I never said I hated his novel, Mr. Scott."

I chuckle. "Please, it's Colin. Okay, hate is a strong word. How about we say strongly dislike."

"I just think, for the timing and the amount of risk—"

"Yeah, yeah, I know," I say. "Did you write those suggestions down?"

"Yes, I did."

"A few of them might be helpful."

I think Shelby is a little surprised when I say this. She takes out a document from her file and gives it to me.

"All right," I say. "So why did you have me come here? All to hear how Ian needs to improve his novel and how you're really not interested in publishing it? Couldn't you have just sent me an e-mail?"

"Of course. It's just—well, I thought, since you're starting an agency, we could talk about some of your other clients."

I look at the young blonde as though she's just said something in Chinese.

"What?"

"Well, I know a few other authors you represent, and I just wanted to see if there was a possibility of talking about projects with them."

Is this young lady on crack?

I let out a laugh.

Shelby clears her throat and utters, "I know it might be premature, that there will be the appropriate time—"

"Shelby?"

"Yes?"

"What are you talking about?"

"Your—other authors. Triten would certainly be interested in working with them."

Has Donald Hardbein been talking to her?

"In particular, what other authors?"

"I'm sorry," Shelby says. "I wanted possibly to talk about Vivian Brown."

Hello?

"Really? Vivian Brown."

"Yes," Shelby says, her face earnest and nervous.

She must not have gotten the memo.

"A lot of other publishers are interested in Vivian," I say.

"Of course."

Maybe Roth hasn't sold Vivian's book yet. Or maybe they have and Triten doesn't know about it. Or this poor young woman got her cue cards messed up and is trying to read the wrong guy.

"There is a bidding war."

"I just wanted to share why Triten might be the place for Vivian."

I nod. If she only knew. She'll be embarrassed when she discovers the real agent, the Roth Agency, sold Vivian's book to Random or Warner.

The privately-held Triten House, even though it's had its share of growth and success since I left its doors, is still small potatoes. Could they handle a book with a five-million print run? With movie tie-ins and a possible series to follow?

Shelby actually begins to tell me reasons why they could handle a book like *In Your Memory* and an author like Vivian Brown.

For a few minutes, I feel like the old Colin Scott. Holding the cards and watching and waiting. But this is a fleeting moment. I hold no cards. Just a heart card, a five of hearts, let's say. Someone with a big heart and that's it. Ian's not going to get me far.

"This is all fine and wonderful," I tell Shelby. "Tell me this. If I consider the things you've said about Triten and Vivian, will you consider Ian's book?"

"I've already considered his—"

"No, no, no. I mean really consider it. I mean take it and help him become somebody. Don't wait for another publisher to have to grow him. *Be* that publisher. You know it's a decent story."

"Of course. It's just—"

Shelby considers this supposedly pivotal moment.

"Please tell Ian to look at these suggestions and rework his book and then give it to me."

I nod. "I will tell him that."

I stand, even though Shelby is not finished.

"We really believe Vivian Brown would find not just a publishing relationship, but a home."

I nod. Yeah, uh-huh.

The young woman actually seems to believe her own words.

Families don't pay other members to come join them. They don't cancel contracts and make stipulations and set deadlines and sell subsidiary rights. They don't print five million books and then shred five hundred thousand after returns come in. This is not about a family.

"Look. I will pass along Triten's heavy interest to Vivian."

But she's not mine to offer.

If that big day comes, will that be it?

"When you say *it*, what does that mean?"

It. Over with. Done and finished.

"That'd have to be a big day."

See—it'll never be enough. For you it's about the journey. The destination is an afterthought.

"And what about you?"

My journey can change. You and I both hope it does. I'm after the destination there.

"So am I."

I just never see things changing, Col. I always see you running and dealing and spinning. I never see you slowing down.

"I will."

It'll take a miracle.

It didn't take a miracle, Jen.

I sit in an empty booth and watch the basketball game up on the monitor and wonder what Jen would think of me now.

It used to be about the journey. And years ago, when Jen and I had that conversation in the silence and still of our apartment, in another world and another life, I knew that she was right. But the journey wore me down. The passengers alongside of me for the ride got tiresome and annoying. I ended up forgetting the destination. I just ran and ran and ran, on to something, somewhere.

It would have taken a miracle to slow me down. But instead, it took Jen dying.

What I wouldn't give to have it be the opposite. To have a miracle instead.

Everyone needs a miracle once in their life.

I guess mine happened when I first met Jen. And when I discovered she loved me as much as I loved her.

Everyone probably only gets one miracle.

"Give me another," I say out loud, to anybody who can hear me. Maybe even to God above who just hasn't yet been able to hear and act on my prayers.

Instead of a miracle, I'm given the guest appearance of Donald Hardbein.

"Mr. Colin," he says, holding a beer in his hand.

"Do I even need to—"

But before I can finish, he sits. Nice.

"Things are going along well, right?"

"I'm sure you know they are," I tell him.

He smiles and looks like a specter.

"How did your young client take to the news about Triten?"

I would ask him how he knows this, but I've given up trying to find that out. It used to creep me out, now it just tires me.

"Excited, as any author would be."

"Yes. I remember the feeling. The biggest hurdle is that first contract. That beautiful, glorious first contract."

"That it is," I say.

"So what I want to know is when you'll give me a shot."

I stare at him. "You have a manuscript ready to give me?"

Donald nods.

"All right then. Send it to me."

"Just like that?" he asks.

"Sure."

"The Colin Scott I spoke to almost a year ago didn't want anything to do with me. Even a couple months ago."

I laugh. "I don't know if I have any choice. I could call the police, but I'd rather not go to the trouble."

"So you'll take a look at my book?"

"I just said I would. If—if—you stop following me."

"Maybe I'm doing this for your own good."

I laugh again and take a sip of my drink. "There's an element of professionalism that you're sorta missing here, Donald."

"I could be your big break."

I nod. "That's true."

"But you doubt it."

"Honestly? Yes."

"Ah. Honesty. I love it."

"E-mail the manuscript to me, and I'll give you my two cents' worth."

I know he has my e-mail address. Along with every other address I have.

"Well, I don't mean to take up any more of your time." He stands and drains his drink, then looks down at me.

"Your time is worth considerably more than two cents, Mr. Colin."

"Sure."

"You'll realize that soon enough."

He grins like a madman and then takes off.

I turn on my phone and find two voice mails. One is Pearce saying he'll swing by around ten to continue working on the basement with me. He says he'll bring the coffee, a tradition that I'm liking.

The other is from Mr. Roth. Hearing his voice startles me.

"Colin, it's Roth. You know the numbers, so give me a call. Tell Darcy or Ted to put you through. I'm around all day today. We've got to talk, and I don't want to do it over the phone and don't want to even think about tossing e-mails back and forth. We gotta meet and gotta meet now, so call me."

Maybe he has seen the error of his ways and wants to fire Ted and rehire me.

Maybe Vivian is begging for me to come back, after working with Ted and Roth on her manuscript.

Maybe the authors are in an uproar about me being gone and decided to go on strike until Roth begged for me to come back.

And maybe flying pigs can sing the Hallelujah Chorus.

I think for a minute and decide, why not?

I dial the number and get Darcy's voice right away.

"They didn't fire you yet?" I ask her.

"Colin."

"The artist formerly known as Colin. Yes, it's me."

"How are you?"

"Things are really hopping."

"I bet," she says, and I laugh, then realize she's being serious.

"Calling for Mr. Roth?"

"Yes. He actually left me a message not long ago."

"I'll put you through."

"Whoa—hold on. Darcy?"

"Yes?"

I can picture her at her desk, the deliberate and diligent young woman I always tried to make laugh.

"Do you know what this is about?"

"I think we both know what it's about," she says in a distant tone.

"What's that mean?" I ask.

But she's already put me through to his line.

I remember meeting with Mr. Roth for that first job interview. I knew everything there was to know about him—everything that had been said or written down. I knew many of the authors he represented, where he lived, the history of how he built this company up, and why I thought I fit with him. I was nervous, a sort of nervousness that never seemed to abate over the years. I grew more comfortable opening up and speaking my mind to him, but I never fully felt relaxed.

Now I'm meeting him downtown. So many years later, a lifetime of change in between, I'm no longer nervous. I owe him many things, and because of that, I agree to this meeting. In the two minutes I spoke to him earlier, he said it was imperative. His tone, his wording, everything meant something was up. He's got that edge, that annoyed testy fighting-gloves-are-on attitude.

So I agree to meet him in a lounge a block away from the office, one where we sometimes went for cognac and cigars. I'm fifteen minutes late because of the traffic. An attendant leads me over to two plush armchairs sitting across from one another and separated by a small table. Roth is there, halfway through with a cigar, eyeing me calmly as I arrive and shake his hand.

"I thought you might be having second thoughts."

"Traffic," I say.

I sit, and a waiter asks what I'd like. I order sparkling water.

Roth looks at me for a moment. "How have you been?"

I wish I could come back with a line they'd utter in the movies, something like *I've been spectacular, you miserable son of a—* "Fine," I say.

"So what are we going to do about this quandary?"

"What sort of quandary are you talking about?"

"Colin, please."

"I don't know what you're talking about."

Roth puts the cigar down and takes a sip of his drink. It's in one of those oversized glasses, and it's almost empty.

"So how's she doing these days?"

I'm still are in the dark. "She?"

"Vivian."

He's reeling me in. I've seen him do this before. He's friendly, calm, leading, but soon enough the anger and authority will course through everything he says and the recipient will have the love of God scared into him.

"I haven't heard from Vivian in months."

Roth laughs.

"I'm telling you the truth."

"Colin, we know. There's no need to lie. We know she's working with you."

I shake my head. "I don't know what you're talking about."

"And the thing is this—technically, she can do that. She never officially signed anything with us. So you wanna know what *I* think? I think you were planning this all along."

I can't help the laugh that escapes out of my mouth. "There are lots of things I didn't plan. The whole last year wasn't my plan."

"Really?"

"You're the one who fired me, remember?"

"Maybe you knew I would."

"Maybe you're as crazy as I am."

"Now, now. Easy there."

I'm about to erupt. How dare he suggest that all of this was planned? My wife died, and he forgets that so soon?

"Colin, we want you back."

"What?"

"I understand Vivian's reasons. I can see them now. And in light of everything going on, I can understand where you're coming from."

I still don't have a clue what he's talking about.

"What about Ted—"

"This isn't about Ted," Roth tells me. "This is about you and me. And Vivian, of course."

"What did Vivian tell you?"

"She copied us on the e-mail she sent you."

I think about my e-mail that has been untouched for days. I wonder why I haven't checked it—then think about Jen's last e-mail and know I didn't want to read another from her.

"So you—you read that?" I ask Roth.

"Of course we did."

"And?"

"And?" Roth chuckles. A waiter brings him another glass of the dark liquid he is drinking.

"So, all this . . . ?"

"Publishing is about relationships, Colin. How many times have I told you that? You know this, and I have to give you credit. You certainly pulled this one over on me."

"Pulled what?"

"The proverbial wool. Maybe you want a raise. Maybe you really want to branch out on your own. I know what I promised you. I know I said Vivian was yours, and she is, but you still need this agency as a backbone. As clout. You can't do it without us."

"So you want to rehire me. That's what this is about?"

"I'm willing to play nice."

"Since, of course, Vivian wants to work with me."

Roth smiles, as if I'm finally laying down the cards I've been hiding and bluffing with.

I feel warm and fuzzy and wanting to slip my skin and run out of here.

"I don't want to play hardball," Roth says.

"The Roth Agency has no authority over Vivian. You and I have talked about that a hundred times."

"My lawyer says otherwise."

"That's 'cause you pay him to," I tell Roth. "Look. You fired me once. I tried to make—"

"I made a mistake," Roth says.

"Yeah. We all do."

"So we both made mistakes, right?"

"I made mine a long time ago."

"What was that?"

"Selling out," I say. "Selling my heart and soul for something I discovered I don't believe in anymore."

"Please, Colin. Sit down."

"No."

"So it's your 'heart and soul' that's driving you? That's nice to know, especially considering Vivian's worth."

I shake my head. If only this idiot knew I had no idea five minutes ago about Vivian and her e-mail and her change of mind and heart.

But I haven't changed my mind. My heart is in the right place again.

"I'm done playing games," I say.

"And why is that?"

"Because I vowed I wasn't going to end up like you," I tell him.

And with that, for the second time and probably the last, I leave my former boss sitting by himself.

I know I'll be hearing from him again.

From his people.

I rush out of the building. I've got an e-mail I need to read.

There are actually two messages from Vivian.

One is dated about a week ago—April 12. The header is simply Me Again.

Dear Colin:

The last few months have been hard on me as a writer. I was wounded when I first read your comments on *In Your Memory*, and I wrote you hastily, in anger and frustration.

But with the holidays over and a few months to let those words sit and stew, I know that you were justified in sending that e-mail. The e-mail that I know got you fired. You shared your thoughts not because of a chip on your shoulder, but because you wanted to help me out. Wanted to make my book as good as it could possibly be. Wanted to do exactly what *I* asked you to do—be honest.

So first off, please accept my apology for being so offended. I've read your comments on *In Your Memory* almost a hundred times. And each time I've come to understand and agree with them more.

It's hard sometimes for an author to hear that her baby isn't beautiful. But the difference between an author and a mother is that the former can work on her baby and make him more beautiful. The mother has to live with the end result and hope that perhaps with time, the child will outgrow his ugliness and grow into a full, respectable, attractive adult.

You know that everyone at the Roth Agency has treated me with an abundance of respect due to the phenomenal success of the Marover

Trilogy. But sometimes I feel that this respect is undeserved. I'm the same housewife who penned *Sliding into Forever* and who needed others' input, *your* input, to make it a bestseller. I forgot something vitally important along this journey: that input was not merely helpful to my writing, it was critical. I *needed* it.

You put yourself out on a limb when you sent me your comments about *In Your Memory*. You've always been honest, Colin. And as authors, we treasure the truth. For that's what we seek. Your editorial comments challenged me, then your last kind "farewell" e-mail convicted me.

So permit me to go out on a limb too. I want to work with you on *In Your Memory*. You and you alone. I've already been working hard on making changes on the novel—changes you suggested. I don't know if you are considering agenting on your own, but I want to be represented by you. I want you to work with me on the novel, and I want you to sell it. I trust you and always have, Colin, and publishing is all about trust. It's about trusting your instincts as a writer and putting them down on paper. It's about trusting those around you to make that story better. It's about trusting an agent to find you a publishing home. And it's about trusting that publisher to do the most with it.

There are a lot of sharks out there, Colin. I feel I'm wading in deep waters. And I believe this, even if it sounds a bit corny—I believe you're my life raft. I've just been too stupid lately to realize it.

Please let me know what you think about working with me (again!).

I hope you are doing well.

Vivian

It's too much. Way too much. I can't believe I just read this, can't believe Vivian wrote this. But she's not done. I see there's another e-mail sent right after this one, with the title **P. S.**

Colin—By the way, I just wanted to let you know that I've taken your suggestion (one of many I've finally taken!) and have changed the title of *In Your Memory*. I agree that it's not a bad title, it just doesn't have that breakout zing to it.

Let me know what you think of the new title: *Sky Blue*.

I think it has a real ring to it.

Viv

In the almighty words of the old Chicago Cubs baseball announcer, Harry Carey: "Holy cow."

He's back and he's better than ever before.

The sun's rising and ain't it beautiful yessirr it certainly is.

Today is the first day of the rest of your life.

Today is the day it all begins again.

He was down but not down for the count.

I sip coffee and cannot help feeling invigorated. I burn with life. I want to go outside and run around and do something, anything. I don't really care what. I just have to do something.

Is this a dream?

I've stopped asking that. It doesn't matter.

The Colin Scott Agency is starting.

It's already got a client list.

Vivian Brown.

And, oh yeah. Don't forget Ian Pollock.

Two authors.

A phenomenal bestselling writer coming back with her newest book.

And an unknown kid bearing his soul and bleeding over a novel and hoping it will sell.

The Colin Scott Agency.

Two clients.

Less is more.

Less is better.

Today is the first day of the rest of my life.

And today, it starts again.

Look Homeward, Angel

In my dream I touch my child.

I sit on the edge of a king-sized bed, watching her in the muted light. My hand reaches into the white bassinette onto the swaddled creature that sleeps silently, without movement. I touch her to see if she is still breathing. This feels so real, this touch. Her little body jerks, then wiggles, then is still again.

Something is different. I'm a different man. The things that used to matter don't matter to me anymore. It's about this, this creature, this place, this home.

I want to believe there is a reality like this, that it isn't merely something conjured in my dreams. I'm good at imagination and dreams.

God give me that hope. Please God.

I go to hold the baby and then she is gone, the room is gone, everything is gone. I awake with a jolt and find myself on the carpeted floor of an empty room on the second floor.

This was the room I had picked to be the nursery. If Jen and I had been able to . . .

If.

The carpet is soft but cold and I stare up at the ceiling.

This is my home now.

It's time to stop dreaming.

As much as I should be thinking about the future, I still find myself wading in the past.

I remember Jen coming to my side as I was lost in a manuscript. Her look said it all.

"What's wrong?" I asked.

"Everything," she said. She looked down at me, a sky full of storm clouds behind her.

"What's that supposed to mean?"

"This life. It isn't working."

"What isn't working?"

"You and me."

"Jen—"

"Tell me something. Is it worth it?"

"I hope so. Ask me in a few years."

Jen knelt beside me and took my hand. "I don't think I can wait that long."

And for another ten minutes we talked, and I mostly listened, and nothing seemed right. Jen just needed encouragement, needed to be by my side and in my arms. I believed I—I believed *we*—could get through it just as we always had.

"I don't know what I'd do if I ever lost you," I said.

"There's nothing else to say."

"I don't believe this. This isn't happening."

"You might not now. But you will one day."

And even now, I still don't fully believe she's gone.

I receive an e-mail from Jen the first week of May.

I was checking out a movie Web site that let me know that filming for *Immersion* had finished and that they were in post-production on the film. Why this movie has fascinated me so much, almost to the point of obsession, I don't know. Part of me wonders what Jen would be doing now, when she would finally be finished had she been there.

Would it have been her last movie?

As if on cue, an e-mail pops up on my screen.

The subject is Thinking of You.

Dear Colin:

How are you doing? I never heard back from you.

There's a lot I need to tell you.

I just don't know how to start. And I can't do it like this.

Jen

I read it over and again and suddenly, unexpectedly, start crying.

For a while now, I've believed that I was moving on, getting better. There were no visits or calls or e-mails from my deceased wife. The craziness of the past winter could finally be left behind. I was moving away from my delusions and madness and hysteria. If that was the way I grieved, so be it.

But now this.

I think of waking up in the room that was supposed to be the nursery, about my promise to move on and stop with this madness.

I wipe my eyes and breathe in.

I type a quick response.

Jen:

I know you're not out there for me to talk to, for me to see. I need to let you go, once and for all, as much as I love you and will forever love you. I need to move on with my life, and I can't with reminders of the pain and loss I carry around every day.

The fifth stage of grief is acceptance, so I've read. I'm trying to accept it. I'm trying to move on.

Please just let me be.

Colin

I send the e-mail into whatever weird cyberspace zone it goes to.

Perhaps this is only an e-mail for my misguided mind. But with a busy month ahead, I can't get sidetracked.

Jen is gone, and I have to accept that fact and move on.

"So is this the moment when I crack this bottle against the side of the house?"

"That's for boats," Pearce says.

"Oh, right. Okay."

I open the bottle of champagne even though it's only one in the afternoon. Pearce has just finished giving me a full inspection of the house. It's finished. All ten thousand square feet. And a full basement. Done.

It's the middle of May, and we're standing on the second-story deck that overlooks the lawn. We give each other a knowing look, men who have gone through battle together and survived. I raise my coffee mug, the only glass I had in the house.

"To one beautiful house, and to the patient man who didn't abandon me throughout this project."

Pearce smiles. "And to the new owner, who's going to plop down a hefty sum on it."

"Cheers," I say, and drink.

"Next project is doing something with that yard," Pearce says.

I glance at the massive backyard. The lawn slopes downward toward an upside-down horseshoe-shaped forest in the back. The previous owners never kept things up. I know it would cost a good chunk of money just to deal with the overgrowth and the landscaping.

"So you sold the book yet?" he asks.

Pearce was the first person I'd called to share the good news about Vivian. He hadn't sounded at all surprised.

I stop looking at the lawn and glance back at him. "Not yet. Book Expo."

"Book what?"

"That's the name of the convention—remember, I went last year? In LA?"

"Oh yeah. So you'll have a big bidding war."

"That's the plan. And this year it's in Chicago."

Sometimes I think about it—how will it happen and who will it be and what will transpire. Then I stop and realize I'm getting ahead of myself. I've signed no agreement with Vivian. It's all verbal. She might change her mind, though she's not a spontaneous and trivial person. She's working on the rewrite for *In Your Memory*, otherwise known now as *Sky Blue*.

I like the title. I think it's got potential.

"I better get going before I start enjoying this stuff," Pearce says. He shakes my hand and cups my shoulder in a friendly embrace. "You make sure you get those publishers to fork it over."

"I'll try. I'm an agent. That's my job."

"Glad you still remember that," Pearce says as he heads down the stairs of the deck.

I stay here and enjoy the serenity. It'll be hard leaving this big house, even though I've never felt moved in and comfortable. It's easy to grow accustomed to your surroundings and your situation, regardless of what they may be.

I think I'm almost ready to move on.

But Jen still seems just a breath away.

I open an e-mail from Ian Pollock. So far, five publishers have turned down *Passover Lane*, including Triten. Rejection is a harsh word, and I don't use it when communicating with Ian. I use phrases like "decided against" and "not a right fit" and "saw potential" and all of those euphemisms. Not that it makes Ian feel any better. Rejection is rejection, however you slice it.

Colin:

Thanks for your e-mail, though it was very disheartening to hear the news. I'm beginning to wonder if this is going to be the case with every publisher, if being new and unknown is too big a hurdle to get over.

I think waiting is the hardest part. Waiting and wondering if all this hard work will amount to anything. I hate waiting. But that's all I can do.

I've started another novel, different from *Passover Lane*, not as big and ambitious. It's a story I've been wanting to write for a while. I figure I have time, right? Maybe it could be a follow-up to *Passover*, who knows?

I want to do whatever it takes to make it as a writer. And I know

that all I can continue to do is write—write better, learn more about the market and the craft, and hope that something will break through.

But thank you for taking a chance on me, and for your hard work on my behalf. I know you're probably investing more than you'll get out of this. I want to reward that chance in a hit. I know, of course, that you want this too.

Please keep in touch. I'll do the same.

Happy rest of May to you!

Ian

I think of Ian and can't help liking him.

Writing a book is an act of faith. You venture forth not knowing the destination. Not knowing the outcome. A hundred things, perhaps a thousand things, nip and harass you, hoping to deter you from the goal. Whether you're just starting out or are a *NY Times* bestselling author writing book five in a seven-book contract, it's the same. It's about believing in something you can't see and don't know will happen, but continuing to push along toward the final result.

That's faith.

Someone else once spoke to you about faith, didn't she?

I quickly type Ian an e-mail.

Ian—Hang in there. You've got a great attitude and dogged perseverance. That's what any writer needs, especially one starting out. I hate waiting too. It's always surprising when something does sell, or doesn't. But we'll find a home for *Passover Lane*. Trust me on this.

I think it's a good thing to start writing something else. You don't want to wait and let a whole year pass and realize you could have been doing so much more.

Continue to have faith, Ian. Don't stop believing. You'll get there. Hopefully sooner rather than later. But you'll get there.

Your friend (and agent too)—Colin

I reread the e-mail before sending it.

Continue to have faith, Ian. Don't stop believing.

Maybe I should tell myself the same thing.

Did I ever have faith? Did I ever believe in something?

What about Jen? What about believing in her? In us?

Her last words were about faith. But for her—it's different. It doesn't count. It's a fantasy, something caused by my downward spiral and my grief and my delusion. I created an image and a memory of her. It can be nothing more than this.

I send the e-mail to Ian.

It's one thing to have faith in yourself. This I can preach.

But having faith in someone else. I don't know.

I still have a ways to go before that happens.

It's pitch black and deep in the middle of late night or early morning when my cell phone rings. I thought I turned it off. I almost always do. It rings several times, then stops, then rings again.

I finally get up and go toward the sound.

Colin?

"Yes."

Are you there?

"Yes."

I wonder if this is a dream. If so, don't let me wake up. Let me talk to her. Just for a few minutes.

How are you?

"Fine," I say.

I just wanted—I needed to hear from you.

"Are you—okay?"

Yes.

"Where—" I begin to say, then stop.

I'm not sure if I want to know her answer.

I think about you every day, her sweet, soft voice says.

"I think about you too."

I miss you.

"You sound . . . have you been crying?" I ask.

She sniffs and clears her voice.

"Jen?"

After your last e-mail . . .

"I just—I don't know how—"

I still think there's a chance.

"What?"

For us. I just need to know—things have to be different.

"What? How?"

There's silence. I don't understand any of this. "Can I see you?" I ask her.

It's up to you.

"You keep saying that. Nothing's up to me."

It's not that difficult.

"I don't understand."

You will, she says to me. *I'm just not—it's too soon, and I—*

"Jen—"

I love you, Colin.

"Please don't go. Again."

I'll be here. Just take your time.

There is a click, then silence.

I wonder where Jen is. Is she in the same dream I'm wading around in? Is she on a cloud in the skies looking down at me?

I miss her so much and I can't do a thing about it.

It's up to you, she said.

What'd she mean by that?

It's not that difficult.

Getting up and moving and going on without you is difficult, Jen. How can it not be difficult? Every waking moment without you has been hard and continues to be hard.

You can't be out there haunting me for the rest of my life.

Sleep doesn't come for a long time. Unless I'm already deep in it.

I drive my BMW away from Chicago onto the Interstate and toward the western suburbs. I have just signed off to lease an office downtown where any respectable agent would and should be. I've had dinner with Darcy, suggesting the possibility of her working for me in the future if everything turns out as expected. Now, close to nine, I'm driving home and wondering what I've gotten myself into.

James Michener once said, "As a younger man I wrote for eight years without ever earning a nickel. It was a long apprenticeship, but in that time I learned a lot about my trade."

I soar through the night with the window down and the sunroof open and wonder if *my* apprenticeship is over. If the last ten years of my life will result in this big break, this golden opportunity. Can I take that big step, that huge leap of faith? I'm starting over, starting new. Can I really do it?

I know enough.

But do I? Will I be as tough as Roth and willing to negotiate and make the hard calls? Can I have a staff and make sure I provide for them? Is this the moment where I finally step up and put all my training and experience to work for itself?

I'm ready.

But I'm also terrified.

What if Vivian wakes up deciding she's made a big mistake? What if the deal doesn't get done? What if the publishers yawn at the proposal?

What if I screw it up?

These voices torment me as I speed home. To a house I wonder if I can sell.

I'm looking through boxes again, sorting through old mail and photos. Thinking of Jen. Thinking of the call from the other night and wondering where she is and why my mind is cracking like a nut. And that's when I find it.

I remember receiving it and putting it away for safekeeping until a better time when I'd be ready to open it. It's an envelope addressed to me with no postmark. The letterhead of Hotel Aquasoul is on the parcel. I get a knife and carefully open it, then take a second before looking inside, afraid of what I'll find.

I produce two sheets of paper. One is letterhead from the hotel in Cancun. The letter is unmistakably in Jennifer's handwriting, a page of carefully composed blue words.

My dearest Colin:

I write this high above the clouds knowing that you will see it eventually. I'm sending you something I found tucked away in a book not long after we got married. I've kept this with me for a long time now and know it needs to go back to you.

I hope this will encourage you and allow you to find your place in this world.

When I first met you, I was inspired not only by your drive but by your belief in yourself and where you were headed. I have always admired your confidence, Colin. But that confidence has faded and turned into cynicism. And that cynicism is bleeding over into every area of your life, including our relationship.

You have to find your way again, Colin.

I love you. I love the man I fell in love with years ago, the dreamer who never stopped dreaming, who never stopped believing.

I hope and pray you'll start again.

Sincerely,

Jen

I wipe away tears from my eyes and open the other piece of paper, this one in my own handwriting.

It's dated in April over ten years ago, when I first started working at Roth.

A young punk of twenty-five who thought he knew where he was headed and what he would offer the world.

It's more like, what would the world offer him?

A young kid who wrote a note to himself. Probably inspired, full of vigor and vision and drive and ambition. Probably full of caffeine, too.

At the top it says WHY I DO WHAT I DO

And then underneath, a list I recognize.

The Heart of the Matter by Graham Greene
On the Road by Jack Kerouac
Beloved by Toni Morrison
The Call of the Wild by Jack London

The Stranger by Albert Camus
Catch-22 by Joseph Heller
Tender Is the Night by F. Scott Fitzgerald
To Kill a Mockingbird by Harper Lee
Heart of Darkness by Joseph Conrad
The Grapes of Wrath by John Steinbeck
The Catcher in the Rye by J. D. Salinger
As I Lay Dying by William Faulkner
Under the Volcano by Malcolm Lowry
Invisible Man by Ralph Ellison
One Flew Over the Cuckoo's Nest by Ken Kesey
The Naked and the Dead by Norman Mailer
A Portrait of the Artist as a Young Man by James Joyce
Animal Farm by George Orwell
The Sun Also Rises by Ernest Hemingway
Look Homeward, Angel by Thomas Wolfe
Great Expectations by Charles Dickens
From Here to Eternity by James Jones
Deliverance by James Dickey

Yes, I remember this list. The last two lines especially move me.

Sometimes, great writing lasts.
And the work I do might last too.

I can remember writing this list down to motivate me, to keep me on track. To show me that you can love the work you do and can strive for something larger than you or the writer could ever dream of.

A decade later, I'm reading idealistic words from an optimistic guy entering the publishing arena. Ready to make a difference. To really, truly *matter.*

People assume that when you're older, you're wiser. I don't buy that. Sometimes I think I know less than I once knew. That I am less confident than I used to be. With life. With love. With work and basically with everything.

Just because you have more miles on you doesn't mean you're wiser.

And the work I do might last too.

I once believed that. But somewhere along the way I got disillusioned. Jaded. Perhaps it came from success, from money, from routine, from experience. I think in some ways it was a little of each.

The harder I worked, the more I got sidetracked. Until I slid off the tracks once and for all.

But I'm back on.

Does that mean I'm headed the right way?

What would Jennifer do?

And how did she know to send this to me?

Some things never last. A life, a love, a legacy—some things pass away just like that.

But some things remain.

It's all about knowing what those things are.

I'm starting to dream, Jen. I'm starting to believe again.

Great Expectations

I remember Jen's words. "When does the future ever become now? When will all the work pay off?"

June has arrived, and with it, my future.

The Book Expo convention is in Chicago, so thankfully I don't have to fly. My creditors are beginning to stop extending my limits and giving me additional cards. I don't need to spend anymore; I need to deposit a check. And after today, I'm thinking I'll know approximately how much that check might be.

I set up shop at the downtown Marriott. It's only five minutes from McCormick Place, where the convention is being held. I'm doing what I was taught at Roth—getting a suite, setting up meetings every hour, ordering in food and beverages, acting as though I know what's going on and I'm a professional. I am a professional. Without a staff. Or a monthly income.

It's early in the morning, and I'm going over documents that I'll be giving to the publishers. A synopsis of Vivian Brown's completed novel, *Sky Blue.* The synopsis is six pages long. And even that seems too short, not worthy of the incredible novel she's written. But it will have to do. I have sales figures and other details on her other books, just in case they need to be verified. The other publishers know this, know who Vivian is, and won't really care what *Sky Blue* is about. They'll want to know how many books, how much of an advance per book, and so on.

It's eight in the morning, and I call Vivian, though it's six o'clock her time. She said in an e-mail it would be okay. I told her she could be out here—the Colin Scott Agency would fly her out with money it doesn't have—but she declined. She's going to let me do the necessary work. All she asked was to be told who the interested publishers were and what they brought to the table. Then she would let me know her thoughts.

The phone rings twice before Vivian greets me.

"How are you doing?" I ask.

"How are *you* doing?"

"I'm ready to go."

"That's good."

"You know the one thing I'm going to be asked today? Well—one of the two things I'll be asked all day?"

"What?"

"Why I'm no longer with the Roth Agency," I say.

"Just tell the truth."

"That I was fired?"

"You were."

"Yeah, I know. But a lot of these guys know Roth personally. They like him."

"This is just business, right?"

"Of course."

"You got fired, and I followed after you. That's the story."

"Works for me," I tell her.

"What's the second thing?"

"You've already told me what you think. But—they're going to ask about a potential series."

"How can this possibly be a series?"

I laugh. "I know. The characters find each other. Nothing else can happen. Nobody wants to read book two if there's no drama in it. But you never thought the Marover books would be a trilogy."

"You have my word—there will be no follow-up book to this one."

"And multiple book contracts?"

"You know what I think of those," Vivian tells me.

Vivian has always wanted to sign as few documents and contracts as possible. She would always rather take a one-book deal over a three- or five- or ten-book deal. That's just Vivian. She always says, "What if I die having only written two of the necessary ten books? Will I have to come back from the dead to finish up my contract?"

Most authors don't care about the risk a publisher takes. But Vivian does. She sometimes cares too much. But that's her decision, and I respect it.

"Okay," I say, repeating it again so I'm sure we're on the same page. "No series. No multiple-book contract. Should I tell them about the next book?"

"Don't you dare."

"Not even a hint?"

"No," she says firmly.

Vivian is one of those superstitious authors who believes if she talks too much about a project, it might possibly doom it. But she's alluded to another epic series that she's always wanted to do. She got a stand-alone love story out of her system. Now she can do something bigger, something larger in scope than the Marover books.

An agent, and a publisher, can only dream of working on a series of books like that.

"I won't say a word," I tell her in all honesty.

We talk for a few minutes, and I tell her I'll call again in the middle of the day to let her know how things are going.

"I trust you, Colin. Have fun."

A year ago, I would have been inclined to tell her not to trust me. And fun? Nothing about what I did was fun. But I know Vivian's trust is justified. And I do plan on having fun. Lots of fun.

"It's so good to see you," begins the day of pleasantries and crockery talk when Jack Ward strides in and shakes my hand.

A part of me wants to ask where he was when I lost my wife, when I got canned, when my life was going down the toilet. But that's okay. None of the people here care about me. And the more honest they tend to be, the better.

Eight meetings.

Eight chances.

Jack Ward, publisher and head honcho, is the first one.

So we talk.

While each meeting is different in a way—sometimes, as with Jack, there's only one person, while other times there's a caravan of people who tag along; sometimes we get right to the project at hand, while other times someone asks me some random question that has nothing to do with anything, making me wonder why they're stalling. Every single publisher asks about my situation with Roth, and I give them the honest truth. We talk about Vivian, her big name and big following and impressive numbers and yada yada and then we talk about *Sky Blue*. I tell them the same story, even if they ask four more times about it. One book, one contract, no series, no multi-book deal.

Every one is the same until the final meeting.

But back up.

Coffee and pastries are served in the morning, then soda and nuts and cheese and crackers in the afternoon.

Each publisher gets a folder. It has the synopsis for *Sky Blue* in it, then the date we'll hold the bidding war. I don't actually call it a "bidding war," but we know that's what it'll be.

All of the big publishers are represented. Random House is represented by two groups: Bantam (Vivian's former publisher) and Doubleday. Simon & Schuster. HarperCollins. Penguin Putnam. Time Warner. St. Martin's Press. And there's Triten House. The lone little guy of the bunch.

Part of me wants to see Triten House land the deal. But I know—we both know, I and the guys from Triten—that they've got a minuscule chance. Even they would agree that they would be unsure how to deal with the volume of a title by Vivian Brown. But I let them come.

The final group of the day is one of the big guns, and they come with two men. Both of them incredibly intelligent, incredibly smug and arrogant. I've met one before—a stocky man named Stan Block who always seems high on glue, with a plastered smile over his chunky face. Stan's the publisher for one of the big houses and has a great reputation for—well, let's just say he's got a great reputation.

They don't even have time to sit before Stan looks at me and without blinking an eye says: "We're prepared to offer Vivian whatever she wants for *Sky Blue*. Blank check. And we'll do it today."

Hamma mama.

"Excuse me?"

"You heard me the first time. Whatever she wants. I know you're handing out these—" Stan looks at the folder with a slight disdain. "But we're ready to sign something here and now. Today."

Holy Toledo.

The bus has pulled up to the corner. Get on fast and get on now.

"Don't you want—"

"You might want to call up that little author friend of yours," Stan says, that smile still there, his chunky cheeks intimidating.

I don't like the guy, but I don't have to like the guy.

Blank checks. I like those. Lately, I've come to like *any* checks with my name on them.

We talk for a few more minutes, him all smug and me all stunned. Then I excuse myself to call Vivian.

She's there—I've talked with her twice today. This is the last meeting, and I tell her Stan's exact words.

"They've done that before," Vivian says.

"What do you mean?"

"With the third Marover book. They contacted me and said the same thing."

"Through Roth?" I ask her, not remembering this.

"Oh, no. They called me up. It might have been Stan himself. Said the same thing. What would it take to go with them. Blank check—all of that."

"What'd you say?"

"I told them to talk to my agent. I'm not sure if they ever spoke to Roth."

"Maybe they did."

"Did they even ask what the book is about?" Vivian wonders.

"No," I say.

I can see where this is going.

Most authors—you pull the blank-check approach on them, and they'll crumble. Who wouldn't?

Vivian Brown. That's who.

"Tell them thanks, but no."

Wow.

"Are you sure?"

"Yes, I'm sure."

I'm too stunned to say anything.

For the love of all that's holy don't do it Vivian don't please don't!

"What if they buy my book and hate it?" she asks.

"I doubt that's going to happen."

"I love Tom Hanks, but I still have to read the reviews of his next movies before I go see them."

I chuckle. "You've got a good point."

"It's the same sort of thinking that made me question if going with Bantam is necessarily a good thing. Just because they've had success with my last set of books doesn't mean they should want *Sky Blue.*"

"They want it," I tell her. "They feel they deserve to publish it."

"And in some ways, they do. But I want someone to come alongside me. I want to know that the publisher believes in it. So I'll say no thanks to the blank check, but come back with an offer after reading the synopsis. Right?"

"Sure."

You're killing me, Vivian.

It's sorta nice telling Stan where he can put that blank check of his. I do it as professionally as possible. One thing in this business. You burn a bridge, you might find yourself one day in the future running for cover and needing to cross that bridge. Stan tries to argue, but you tell him that's what Vivian told you. He says he wants to talk to her himself, but you tell him that's a bad idea.

"Why is that a bad idea?" he asks.

He has yet to sit down at the table.

"I think you guys tried that once before."

Stan just looks at me.

"Get back to me on the date inside. And give Vivian some reasons why you want to publish her."

"Why? To sell millions of copies of her books. Why else?"

"Let me give you a bit of advice. Don't let that be the reason. Not with Vivian."

Stan laughs and curses for no reason in particular. "You're an agent. You know the deal."

"Sometimes it's not about the money."

Stan just laughs and shakes his head, as though he's saying *Yeah, right, whatever.* And I don't blame his ignorance, his cockiness, his firm belief.

He just doesn't know whom he's dealing with.

An author who cares more about the product than the price tag associated with it.

And an agent who's just gone through one hellish year, and has forty-five dollars in his checking account and a thousand reasons to slug the first jerk he comes across.

"You'll hear from us, Mr. Scott."

Stan and the man accompanying him, who has not said or done a thing, leave the suite.

It's done.

At least this part is done.

In a week, the whole thing should be finished.

We will have ourselves a winner.

The sort of money that's being tossed around—not even counting Stan's ridiculous blank check—boggles my mind. It's bigger and better than I once hoped and dreamed for.

But hopes and dreams—they don't always come in the packaging you want them to come in. They have strange ways of arriving when you least expect them, or when you don't care about them anymore.

I sit here and wonder how everything happened so quickly, so easily, so swiftly.

I wonder how I got here in the first place.

I wander the rain-soaked city streets.

Alone.

Ready to spend my fortune and pay off my debts and start a new life and a new career.

All alone.

And every single dollar and every single digit that will go into every different account will try and mean something, but I have this awful feeling it's going to mean nothing at all. Not without someone by my side.

Not without Jen.

I mapped out a course long ago. Everything in life pointed to this goal. This destination.

Yet it feels empty and hollow. I've won the heavyweight title match, but I don't have an Adrian in the audience to yell out to. And I know there is only one person who can satisfy this longing and need in my life.

Where are you and how can you come back?

I pass the building where I first met her.

I miss you so much and when will I ever stop?

"Can you hear me?" I call out, but not to Jen. "You hear my thoughts? I don't deserve this and never deserved this and I don't believe in you."

Such flattering words probably don't help the situation.

"I'm talking to you, and if you can hear me, if you've ever *thought* about hearing me, now's the time."

Maybe he's up there with Jen. Who knows?

Rain falls as I walk along in my trench coat, and it makes me feel real, alive. My hair drips, but it's too dark outside for anyone to notice what a wet dog I am.

"I don't care about anything anymore. I need Jen. I'd give anything to have her back. You hear me? So much has happened that I'll believe in anything, *anything*. Or nothing. I just—I want to get rid of this ache inside. This empty hole. Nothing I can do will fill it."

I keep walking, and maybe strangers passing me by hear me uttering words out loud, pointed upwards, looking at the sky and getting drenched.

"I'd give it all up. Everything. Just to have another chance."

I know this is praying, but there's nothing left for me to do. I've tried it on my own for a long time. I've been hoarding chips my whole life and am ready to cash them in. But I'd give them all up for another chance. For life again. For redemption.

"I gotta believe she's out there." I pause for a long time. "I have to believe you're up there and that you can hear me and that you can save me."

And rain falls. Harder now. I speak louder in case he doesn't hear me. In case he's ignoring me like I've ignored him.

"Show me a way to her."

And I hear nothing but the rumbling of thunder and I see nothing more than empty wet streets lit by lightning.

"God, forgive me for every mistake I've made."

I keep walking, keep talking, keep praying.

It's the only thing left to do.

I want to wait for an answer. But I'm afraid an answer will never come.

I wake up before sunrise and am halfway done with a large Dunkin' Donuts coffee before I see sunlight.

One might think that Vivian would want to be here on a day like today. But she's got tweaking to do. And a life to live. She expects an offer, a hefty one at that, and she wants to know about it. But she doesn't need to be at my side in an empty office in Chicago to give me the okay.

For her, this is part of the process. She's lucky, Vivian says time and time again. But she doesn't want to get overly involved in this part of the business. She'll let me do my job.

I've been in this office approximately three weeks. I've paid for a month's rent. There are no windows. It's on the third floor of a nondescript low-rise ten minutes from Michigan Avenue.

There is a metal desk with rusty drawers on each side. I sit on a hard, black metal chair with padding that's falling out—the sort of chair you might find in a diner at a local restaurant. Except for a fax machine in the corner, there's nothing else in the room—nothing on the walls, on the floor, on the ceiling. It's just the desk and the chair, and a new phone I bought at Best Buy that has two lines coming into it and can put several people on hold.

I've got a pen and a yellow notepad.

But I'm hoping, after today, I'll be able to set up a nicer office. The kind the publishers will think they're dialing into when they call my number.

Maybe something looking out at the lake.

In a former life, I had something like that.

Yeah.

The phone rings. It's the first of the day.

By now, everybody has seen the story synopsis for *Sky Blue*. They have read the first twenty pages. They know what they're asking for, what they'll be bidding for.

I pick up the receiver, wondering which publisher it will be and whether it will be The Call.

"Big day, huh?" an animated voice asks.

"Donald, come on—I don't have time."

"I know. But just hear me out. One minute."

I think of the last time he called. I decide to listen to him, unsure of what he might decide to tell me next.

"So before you become rich and famous and all that good stuff, I want your promise on something."

"Donald, look—I just can't."

"You can't what?"

"I can't read your book. Whatever book you're claiming to write. Whatever book you keep telling me you're going to send. Don't send it to me. Send it to someone else."

"And why would I do that?"

"Because—just because. Because they'll be able to give you more attention. Because they're

sane

probably more focused."

"Come on. I thought you were back in the game. That's what Ted told me."

"I'm not sure where I'm at. And I can't really—what'd you say?"

"I don't think your former colleague really likes you," Donald says.

"You talked to Ted? What did he say?"

"Oh, he says a lot. Where you're heading, what you're up to. At first I thought he did it just to get rid of me. But recently I've realized the truth."

"Donald—"

"It's been far too easy to get information from Ted. I ask him about you, and he always, always, tells me."

"And why are you asking about me?"

Donald laughs. "Because I believed that you'd finally give in, that you'd finally see past the first ten pages, that you'd see the perfection in the prose."

"I don't have time for this. Not today."

For a moment there is nothing but silence, and I wonder if he's still there.

"There is one thing I know, Colin."

"What's that?"

"You will read my book, one way or the other."

"I've told you, what you need to—"

I stop in midsentence because the line is dead.

And that's okay, because I've got a job to do.

One publisher has already said no. They basically wanted the Marover Trilogy Part Two. It's like a studio wanting George Lucas to do another Star Wars. Vivian has made it clear there are no more Marover books and this is a stand-alone book that's different in many ways. That can be better. But this particular publisher, knowing the high stakes, said thanks but no.

The first publisher to call offers ten million dollars. We talk terms for a few minutes. Staggered royalty rates, movie rights (which Vivian is keeping and I'm going to try and sell), and on and on. It's a decent advance. Almost any author would be in heaven getting this much money. But Vivian Brown is an exception.

"Her last book sold *forty* million. Not four million. You know that, right?"

"But this is no Marover Trilogy," the publisher is saying.

And I have to agree. But nobody knew the Marover Trilogy was going to do what it did. They bought it for what—ten thousand?

That's the beauty of publishing. The remarkable, awesome, beautiful thing. A publisher can pay an author five dollars for a book and still end up making fifty million off it.

Of course, the author and the agent will benefit too.

The second publisher offers a one-book deal, with an option on the next book or series, for twenty-five.

Million.

Hello, Jupiter, we've reached your orbit.

For one book.

Some small publishers make twenty-five million in revenue in an entire year.

Some actors make it on one movie.

Vivian is a Tom Cruise of the literary world.

But twenty-five million?

I want to choke, but I tell him that's very fair.

Yeah, very fair.

I was thinking fifteen at the most.

My mind is whirling like a ride at an amusement park when I hear him say, "I think the thing that impressed me the most about the story is when his wife dies . . ."

PAUSE.

"Excuse me?"

"Well—I mean, I didn't see it coming," the publisher says. "To me it's a great, epic love story of sorts, and then all of a sudden Vivian pulls the rug from under my feet and kills off the heroine. That surprised me."

"Uh-huh." I'm thinking, feeling a bit strange, but unable to stop thinking of the offer.

We talk for a few minutes, and I tell him that I'm going to put him on hold, that I've got a few other phone calls to take.

On a sheet of paper, I have the publisher's name and **25** written in big bold print and circled. Ah, the professionalism.

Jack Ward gets on the phone and makes a small offer, not even worth my time. I give him a good old Rothism: "Well, Jack, you're in a ballpark. But it certainly isn't ours."

And he keeps fishing, keeps trying to see what the other offers are.

"The thing I'm wondering," Jack begins to ask, "is when the character's wife comes back from the dead and starts haunting him—"

MUTE.

I don't hear anything else he says.

"What are you talking about?"

"What?" Jack asks.

"That's not amusing."

"What do you mean?"

"If you think that's going to help in negotiating—"

"What?"

"Bringing up—how dare you—"

"Colin, what are *you* talking about?"

"What you just said."

"Yeah? So what? It's the story."

"What story?"

Jack Ward laughs. "Look, you feeling okay? Is this negotiating getting to you?"

"I'm fine."

"I'm talking about *Sky Blue* here. You sure *you* read it?"

I laugh. Have I *read* it? I've helped shape and craft it! I wrote the synopsis and carefully worded it and made sure that Vivian approved it. Have I read it?

I tell him thanks for playing but please come back when you're ready to be in the major league.

And then I get Stan.

Blank-check Stan.

Slimy Stan whom I know Vivian will say no to.

"How much is on the table?" he asks me.

comes back from the dead and starts haunting him

"Colin? You there?"

"Yeah."

"How much?"

"What do you think of the story?"

"It's fine."

"That's really high praise," I say in full sarcasm.

"I did like the twist when the woman fell in the ocean and drowned. Very surprising."

STOP.

This is not happening and you're not hearing this.

I curse and can't help it.

"Excuse me?" Stan says.

"What—why . . ."

But I can't say anything more. I'm choked up and stunned.

"You there, man?"

"Why did you—what are you talking about?"

"What do mean? The sailing accident. The last chapter in the synopsis?"

"Stan, hold on just a . . ."

And then I simply put the receiver back on the desk and see the lights blinking waiting hoping praying and yet all I can do is grab the proposal for the manuscript entitled *Sky Blue* by Vivian Brown and I open the folder and start reading as though I've never read it before.

It's several pages, but various lines stand out.

burned-out salesman

sick of his profession and life

disconnected

struggling marriage

loses love of his life

sailing accident

tropical location

falls into depression

suicidal

visits wife in alternate world

finds hope

finds redemption

a haunted love story

I read the words over and over again.

sailing accident

sailing accident

sailing accident

Shouldn't it be *para*sailing?

What is happening what is going on what is this all about?

And the more I read, the more the words blur.

The more my life distorts.

The more everything seems unreal.

No.

But this is real.

"Hello? Colin?" a voice from the phone on the desk belts out.

And the lines wait. The deals hold. And the men and women hang on for my word.

But a word isn't going to come. Not today.

I get up and run out of my office. And I run down the hallway and run for my life.

They remain on hold.

The sky is open and clear. And, dare I say it, blue.

I look up once I'm out of the building.

"What is happening to me?"

But nobody answers.

Nobody ever answers.

He's only twelve and even though he's gone through it all everything the whole ordeal of family and friends and dressing up and saying good-bye and seeing the body of his father and seeing it all he still doesn't believe still doesn't want to believe so he takes off his tie and closes the bedroom door and opens up his comic book and shuts out the world and loses himself in another world and feels better or at least tries to feel better and believes that it will all be okay everything will be okay.

That twelve-year-old is still very much here. I did this after my father's death, and I did this after Cancun, after she left me there, all alone.

Jennifer left me in Mexico, but . . . but what if she didn't die?

I gasp for air but it doesn't come.

I see Lake Michigan rush past in the distance. The water reminds me.

It reminds me of another place.

No.

Her eyes those tears rain and drops falling together outside underneath clouds and air gusts and a waiting taxi and a waiting

no it can't be

good-bye.

And it comes. Her parting words, the disappointed expression, the sad strain, the break we'll be taking, her leaving me in Cancun.

NO.

And everything afterward happened to be made up.

In your memory.

Sky blue.

I think again of the pitch sheet and the synopsis. One I helped write. I think about it again. And again. And again.

No.

But yes, Colin. Yes. Believe it. It's true.

It's made up.

Life is made up. Everything is made up. You don't believe anything anyway, do you, do you, Colin, do you, Colin Scott?

Belief is only for the faithful.

"That's all I have left, Colin. Faith."

Everything. Every big and little thing. It's all

In

Your

Memory.

But what if that memory is unreliable?

Like its narrator?

No this can't be happening.

Pieces fall into place. And then I remember two things.

The movie. The one I've been obsessed with for months. The Gore

Verbinski project Jen was going to do, the one we argued about.

Could she . . . Is there any chance . . .

And then I think of the letter Jen left and her words:

> . . . you have to find yourself and your way, Colin. . . .

When I read it, I assumed it was fantasy, that I was deluded, that it was insanity.

But I'm believing now. And the only thing—the absolute only thing that matters now—is finding Jen.

I think of the call.

I still think there's a chance.

And maybe there really is one.

It's up to you.

I'm running to my car, planning to head home.

I'll be here. Just take your time.

But I've taken my time, I've had all the time in the world to find myself.

And it's no longer the chase or the contract that I'm looking for. It's Jen.

In the car, racing home, I scroll through the last twenty calls I've received. And there is the last one from Jen.

I call the number, and a stranger's voice greets me.

"What—where am I calling?" I ask the man.

"Excuse me?"

"Where are you?"

"Right here," the twangy accent says, "at the Heart Oaks Bed and Breakfast. Just outside of Bald Creek, North Carolina, about an hour north of Asheville."

That's all I need to know.

The sun is brighter brighter than I've ever seen it be and I feel like a new man under a new sky with blues I've never seen and a warmth I've never felt. I want to run around naked run around with a smile on my face but instead I just run. I'm running. I'm running and it's all a blur.

The sidewalks and the stores and the stares and the sensations filling my shoes. Everything is electric and I can't help myself I can't help but float but glide but fade away. Past strangers past storefronts past stopped cars past everyone and everything.

To get to her.

I waited for her.

I've been waiting for a long time such a long time such a very long time and this morning the sky opened and the sun shone down and the sky so blue so utterly blue whispered against my ear and kissed my cheek and reminded me of the life I have the life I own the life I need.

I no longer wait for her.

I run to her.

Through men and women and boys and girls. Through security and waiting guards. Through life.

"Where are you headed?" someone asks me.

"What about the contract?" another voice asks.

"What do you want to do?" another asks.

Voices I don't care about.

My future broke apart in a hotel room in Cancun when I was too busy to notice.

The grief took hold and threatened to kill me.

But what doesn't kill you only makes you stronger.

And that cliché applies because I'm not dead and she's not dead and I'm only stronger.

This morning I'm stronger. I have faith. I have faith in miracles. If God could create the heavens and the stars and the earth and the sun, he could surely do anything. And he could bring Jen back to me. I didn't need to understand how.

Nervous breakdown?

Okay.

Fiction and fact blurring together?

Okay.

Changing the course of time and fate and destiny?

I don't care.

All of it works.

Through a terminal, to a gate, down a passageway to a seat on a plane, all I can do is think of all the things left to do. Left to say. Left to show. Left to hear. Everything in my life has always and only revolved around me and I never knew that there were others so many others and especially there was one who I had somehow let slip away. Perhaps I will never see Jennifer again but I am going to try once and for all.

"Would you like a drink?" the flight attendant asks.

I'm so excited I can barely keep from shaking, from moving.

I want to get out of the plane, want to float down to her.

I want to fall into her.

She's real and she's there and she's waiting.

I'm no longer waiting. I'm living.

And I'm coming to her.

I need to tell you things, Jen. I need to show you true love. And I want to believe. I want to believe the things you said you believed in. Not just in myself but in something more. In a God above who can hear prayers.

He heard I know he heard me I believe *that he heard*

I want to believe without feeling, to know without truly knowing. I want to know you're there and yet not have to see or feel you.

I am coming back to you.

I've been searching, but I think I've found my way.

I've found my way back to you.

I recall the accident. It was real. It was real, and I can still see the boat coming back to shore carrying her. I remember going to the hospital. And I remember waiting and wondering if she would be okay.

Jen was okay. But it changed her life, falling, in a way I wouldn't understand. In a way I couldn't understand.

I remember the conversation, one I didn't want to hear, one I eventually forgot about.

"I'm scared, Colin," she told me.

"Scared of what?"

She teared up, and I went to hold her but she didn't want to be held.

"What if I had died?"

"But you didn't," I told her.

"I'm scared. I'm scared of dying. I'm scared of what's on the other end."

"Jen—"

"I believe there's more. There's more than just this, this, this body and this room and this life. I've always felt that way. I'm just—I'm scared."

"I'm here."

"But you can't always be there, Colin. You can't prevent me from getting cancer the same way you couldn't prevent me falling into the ocean. Why was I allowed to live? Why?"

I wanted to say something, but I couldn't.

"I believe God protected me. I don't know how or why, but I believe this in my heart."

"Jen—"

"No. I need to understand. I need to get things in order."

"We can do that."

"I need to do that. On my own."

"You need more space."

"It's not about more space. It's another life."

And I didn't want to talk anymore. I wanted her to feel better and recover and then let this all be some distant memory. But she wouldn't change her mind.

It's a cool evening, with the sun slowly sinking away behind the stitchwork of clouds and surrounding hills. My rental car pulls alongside the curb and I get out. There's a café just up the hill. Half a dozen tables are outside, and I see waiters moving back and forth.

And from thirty yards away, I see the back of Jennifer's head with her long, dark hair spilling out below her shoulders.

This is real. It's not a dream. It's not a fantasy in the pages of a book. It's real.

The man at Heart Oaks B & B had told me that Jennifer was probably here, in Asheville at this quaint Italian restaurant. She usually comes here Friday nights. A part of me wonders if she goes by herself, but from where I'm walking all I see is a table set for one. She's reading a magazine and sitting, facing the opposite way.

I don't know what my opening line should be. There are so many things I want to tell her.

Love is not something you wait to come to your door. Sometimes you have to go out and find it and fight for it and even fear losing it. I once believed that, and I believe it again.

As I'm slowly walking up to her on a sidewalk, I see her head turn and glance at me for a second, then turn back. As if she knew I was there.

And then she turns a second time, this time recognizing me, this time seeing me.

She looks startled at first, then sad.

"Jen . . ." I say, as if somehow none of this is really happening.

"I'm here," says this beautiful woman.

And I walk up to her and kneel at her side and embrace her. And I'm about to say something when I suddenly and unexpectedly begin weeping.

"I'm so sorry, Jen," are the only words I can think of saying.

And she puts a hand on my head and tells me in a soft, sweet, gloriously angelic voice

"I love you, Colin."

And then I notice and feel her belly. And a rush of joy and surprise pulses through my body as I look up at her, one hand on her bulging tummy, the other holding her arm.

"Jen—?" I ask, hysterical, afraid, unsure, breathless.

"Yes."

And it's June almost exactly six months since the year turned over and I held Jen in my arms before she left and she told me that she longed for and prayed for a miracle and told me this was one last chance and one last hope.

I still think there's a chance.

Those were her words to me. And now I know what they meant.

"Jen—" I say again.

"God answered our prayers," Jen says, tears of her own falling down her cheeks.

And somehow, I know she's right.

God answered my prayer. The only one ever offered and never deserved.

He sent you back. He gave you back to me.

But he did more.

I place my head gently against the beautiful baby growing inside of my wife and my love and I know that it will never ever get better than this because this is where our entire journey has been meant to end.

Here, in Jen's arms, in the embrace of our family.

Everything is about to change.

And all I can do is cry tears of joy and kiss her belly.

Everything else is going to be okay. Even if it doesn't make sense all at once, even though I'm trying to figure it out and rethink my steps and wonder how I got here, I know that everything is going to be okay.

From Here to Eternity

In my dream I touch my wife, touch the outline of the child inside her. She feels real, they feel real. The slight chill in our room at the bed-and-breakfast feels real. The glowing remainders of the fire appear real.

"Jen?" I whisper.

She cuddles up and asks *what* without opening her eyes.

"Are you real?"

"Yes," a half-asleep voice murmurs.

"Are you really here?"

"Yes."

"I saw you fall—I saw you drop into the ocean."

She opens her eyes and looks at me.

"I saw you die," I say.

Jen looks confused. "You were there at the hospital with me right afterward. I was fine."

"But I—"

For a second, I conjure up pictures. A funeral, a casket, a procession in black.

Did I imagine all of this?

But I know I didn't. Because it was imagined for me. All in Vivian's novel.

The one I was still reading when Jen left me. The one I was reading when Jen actually told me good-bye.

I put my hand back on her belly and remember.

"Do you believe in answered prayers?" I ask.

"You're touching one."

Stephen King once said, "Fiction is the truth inside the lie."

The story was made up, imagined, but there was truth inside it. I believe it.

Grief doesn't always have to accompany death. Loss doesn't always have to equate a life.

I grieved the loss of Jen.

The world of literature pushes for tragic endings while the public wants happily-ever-afters. The world of art strives for open interpretation when the masses want to be spoon-fed the message, if there is one.

All I know is that Jen left me on a cloudy day almost a year ago. She said she was leaving Cancun, leaving me, leaving us. She said she wanted to give each of us time to find ourselves again, to find our way, and then maybe we could find a way back to each other. For her it was questions about life and death. The accident had brought things to a head, and she needed to reevaluate everything. As for me—my cynicism, my jaded outlook on life—it had become too much for her. I had put our future on a pedestal, making it the thing I focused on. In doing so I put Jen and us—our present—in the background. She wanted me to find my place, to find where I belonged.

So after the accident, after it was all done, she said we were over. And even as I watched her climb into the taxi and ride off, my mind still didn't fully believe she was gone. I always assumed she would be back. Too absorbed in a world of my making and too focused on the future, I couldn't see the obvious. The best and brightest thing in my life and my future said good-bye to me and left. And every assumption ever imagined and every dream ever planned couldn't bring her back.

And somewhere in the process, fantasy became reality. And vice versa. And the world I'd spent so much time and energy building came crumbling apart. And my creative mind took hold and created a new reality—a dark, hopeless reality I allowed myself to wallow in.

It's that easy.

Maybe.

A year later, and an entire lifetime apart, I follow Jen up a gravel road toward a lodge on a hill. Behind us stretches out a mountain with a bald top. Cords and chairs cut several lines into the open grass of the ski resort.

"So where are we going again?" I ask her.

"You have to trust me on this."

"I do."

The road flattens off and we walk toward the empty building.

"I've spent a lot of time this spring working around this area, so I thought this would be the best place to show off Bald Creek."

Jen smiles, and I picture last night again, looking down on her as she fell asleep against me. Even though we didn't need it, we had lit the fireplace in her cozy room. And as the flames flickered and illuminated against her closing eyelids, I kept mine wide open for most of the night. Scared she would be gone in the morning. Scared this was another dream I had concocted. But early in the morning, as I woke unable to feel my arm that had fallen asleep under Jen's light weight, I shifted and felt her still there. So I moved to a more comfortable position but held a hand softly against her arm to make sure she was still there and wasn't going to leave me.

Somehow, my life is different now. I made my way to her, and she isn't going to leave me again.

"Come on. I told Rodney to meet us here."

"And Rodney is . . . ?"

"He runs the lift. He's going to let us take a little ride."

"You know—I'm not the biggest fan of heights."

"Last night you said you would."

"Last night I would have said anything."

"You just wanted to sleep with me, didn't you?" she teases with a grin.

"Well, yeah," I say. "I guess I wanted to six months ago, too."

Jen pauses for a moment and grows serious. It's amazing and awkward the way our conversation flows just as naturally as it did a year ago. Neither of us want to dredge up the past, even though it's unavoidable.

"I've tried figuring out ways to tell you," Jen says.

We're standing on the side of the lodge, in between a rustic log cabin and a rising forest.

"I understand."

"No." She picks up my hands and looks directly in my eyes. "I just wanted to be sure, Colin. The first few months—I found out I was pregnant, and then waited, and waited. I prayed to God that it was real and that everything would be okay. And then three months passed, and that's when I contacted you—I just didn't know exactly how to come right out—"

"It's fine."

"I gave up on us. You didn't."

"You were the first to be honest," I tell her. "That's all."

"I didn't know—I wanted it to be up to you—I knew if I told you about the baby, then of course you would come back."

"I would have."

"But I—"

Now tears come to her eyes, and this is exactly why we didn't want to go here. It's unavoidable.

"Jen, please—"

"But you came anyway."

She embraces me and kisses me first on my ear, then on my cheek, then my lips.

"Thank you for coming back to me."

"Thank you for taking me," I tell her.

Moments later, after wiping her eyes and composing herself, Jen introduces me to Rodney. He's got long white hair and an acne-scarred face and is probably in his late sixties. He's smoking, but when he sees us coming, he flicks out the cigarette and smiles.

"There she is," he says.

Jen introduces me and then tells me why Rodney is doing us this favor. "I got him to meet Julia Roberts."

"I loved *Pretty Woman*," he says in his Southern drawl.

"She knows some famous people," I say.

"So you wanna go to the top, right?"

"Just give us maybe half an hour, okay?" Jen asks.

The ski lift starts up, and the chairs fly by faster than I'd expected. Rodney tells us to just stand in the designated spot and sit down when the chair arrives. I've never skied, so this is a new experience. All I'm thinking about is the height of the mountaintop above.

"You okay?"

I nod and stand next to Jen. The three-person chair scoops us up, and we sit in its center, side by side. The chair slowly rocks as we take off. I can feel my heart beating.

"Look at me," Jen says, so I do.

And I know that it's just the moment. But I've never seen her look more vibrant and beautiful than right this very instant. Her face looks alive and content. And there is something behind her eyes, something I can't fully describe, something that gives me such an overwhelming feeling of

"Hope."

"Excuse me?" I ask her.

"I hoped you'd let me take you to the top."

"You know I get sorta queasy—"

"I know."

She takes my hand as we get farther away from the treetops below.

"Jen?" I need to say this. "I truly believed you died in Cancun."

Jen looks at me not with surprise or bewilderment but with a calm, peaceful look. And I wonder.

"That's not the point," she tells me. "The point is whether I'm living now."

I look over and see Jen's hair whip across her face. She brushes it back to reveal a smile. The chair jerks, and I shudder and look down. Then I feel her hand in mine. She gently squeezes me.

"It's going to be okay. I'm right here."

Two days later, I'm at a bookstore in Asheville, and I feel the vibration from my cell phone.

"You mind?" I ask Jen, who's strolling the aisle of baby books with me.

"No."

"I'm about to make somebody's day."

"This is your favorite part of the job," Jen said.

"You know, I think it is. I used to think it was getting a check."

"The check is the necessary part."

"Not anymore."

She smiles, knowing what that means.

I've been in touch with Darcy, who is already working for me even though it's not official yet. Perhaps she knows more than I do. A lot of people have known more than me for quite some time.

I recognize the number from the one Darcy gave me yesterday.

"Is this Ian Pollock, the up-and-coming novelist?" I ask.

"Mr. Scott?"

"Haven't I told you it's Colin?"

"How are you?"

"The question is, how are you doing?"

"I'm well, thanks."

"How's the writing?"

"It's okay. I haven't written much lately—work's been busy and—I've sorta been stuck. But it's going good, I mean—"

"What if I told you I finally stepped it up as your agent and landed you a contract?"

"Excuse me?"

"What do you think about a three-book deal? With your first coming out next year?"

"*Passover Lane*?" the startled voice asks.

"Yes. A much-improved version of *Passover Lane*, mind you, but yes. *Passover Lane*."

I don't hear anything on the other end.

"Ian?"

"Yes. I'm here."

"You okay?"

"No, yes, I'm fine, I'm great. I'm just—I'm driving home. It's all sorta, too much. I'd really—to be honest, I'd given up."

You're not the only person who'd given up, Ian.

He clears his throat. "So, should I start working on it again? I mean, will they call—will you talk to them—how does this all work? I've got a lot of ideas on how to make it better."

Hallelujah. His first question isn't how much. Or who the publisher is. Or if it's going to be a hardcover or what his royalty rate will be.

Ian isn't worried about figures or fame or fortune. He's worried, in the end, about the product. The creative work.

He doesn't need to know that it's the same publisher who inked the Vivian Brown deal. There were some cards I could play, being the agent in control. And there isn't anything unethical about asking a favor of the winning publisher. All I did was ask, and they saw the potential I see.

"It's going to take me awhile to get all the details to you, Ian. But just trust me. You're going to like the terms. This is bigger than I thought it could be."

"Three books?"

"Yes. Think of it as three chances. You've made it, man. You're crossing that first hurdle."

He is silent for a minute. And I can picture him driving, his eyes tearing up, his gut feeling full and outrageous, ready to take on the world. He finally just says, "Thank you, Mr. Scott."

"No, Ian. Listen, and listen to me good. *Thank you.*"

And what about Vivian? What about the publishers left on hold, waiting? What about the fact that I called her to say it would take a little more time?

The details and the drafts don't matter now. Nothing matters except that I'm by Jen's side. That both of us are taking some time for ourselves. That I'm getting to know the woman I almost lost, that I did lose.

But conclusions aren't as fulfilling with nagging little story lines that go nowhere.

The one remaining question is answered in an e-mail from Darcy. I've told her I'm taking time off and to simply try and do one favor while I'm still in North Carolina.

I read my e-mail on Jen's laptop, while she begins working on a pecan waffle with whipped cream. That's a first for me—seeing Jen eat something like that for breakfast.

Colin:

First off, let me say again that I'm thrilled to be working with you. I heard the news about Vivian—*Publishers Weekly* actually called Mr. Roth for a quote! Congratulations. I officially put in my two weeks and plan on getting out of here soon. (I'm e-mailing this at night from home so I don't feel so guilty.)

As you requested, here is a copy of the suggested contracts for Vivian. I've taken a look at these and have made marks (my little copy-editing marks, as you call them). Everything looks great. But take a look at it. It's not every day I look over a contract this big.

As you requested, I e-mailed Vivian to let her know we're tweaking the contract, but that everything looks good. She e-mailed back to say to take our time. So don't worry about her—she's doing well.

I'm glad to hear you're taking some R & R—after the Vivian deal, you can take a permanent vacation. Though I'd like to have an employer, so I guess you really shouldn't do that.

I'll talk with you soon. Take care.

Darcy

I open the attachment. The contract is around twenty pages long. It's just for one book, as Vivian wants, but most authors and agents could work their whole careers without seeing figures like this.

I look at them and can't believe them.

But, then again, of course I can believe it. Anything is possible. Anything.

I close the computer and put my hand on Jen's shoulder, checking again to make sure she's really there. That's the one thing I know for sure now. Jen is there.

"I don't want to spend another second without you," I say.

I kiss her forehead as she continues to polish off the waffle. I want to tell her about the contract, but I'm going to wait. The figures don't matter.

What does is the woman sitting before me now, a princess and a queen and the love of my life.

These are the things I know now.

Love is not what you hold on to, but what you give away.

It's not about what's in front of you. It's what you leave behind.

It's not about feeling. It's about faith.

And to believe in Jen is easier than believing in myself. I don't have to touch her to know she's real.

Is it so hard to believe someone died and came back to life to save me?

It's a wonderful story. That's what it is.

And with so little out there to believe in, and so many made-up stories rolling around, I like this one.

The publishers on hold—the ones who waited for me even as I chased down my wife to another state—they got on line again. They always do. And we reached a conclusion.

A very, very good conclusion.

But in the end, it's not about the money. It's not about a contract. It's about the project. And about the journey. And for me, for my life, my career, my family, I'm still on a journey. An incredible journey. One that finally has a destination.

Someone to finally believe in.

The jaded, cynical Colin used to discourage aspiring authors from getting into the publishing world. Because in my mind, it was all a game. A big fat farce there was no escape from. But it's amazing how a perspective can change so quickly.

I no longer want to dissuade aspiring authors or talk about the improbabilities of fame and fortune in the publishing arena.

What keeps coming to my mind is another author quote.

Stephen King, one of my favorite novelists and truly one of the great storytellers of our time, said that "writing isn't about making money, getting famous, getting dates, or making friends. In the end, it's about enriching the lives of those who will read your work, and enriching your own life, as well."

Amen.

And as for Jen and I. We've found faith in something more. In something else. In something bigger and greater than either of us could ever fathom.

That's what matters. That's what counts.

DELIVERANCE

It's sometime after midnight, and I find myself checking e-mail for the first time today. It's early November, and heavy rain is hitting the side of our house. It's one of those nights when you're thankful for a roof above you and a warm home around you.

I open the e-mail newsletter from *Publisher's Weekly*. The headline startles me.

Doubleday to launch the "next great voice in fiction." Donald Hardbein brings his ambitious novel out of hiding.

I can't believe it, but of course it's true. Doubleday is going to publish Donald's novel. Some agent I've never heard of has inked a deal of over a million. That's why this is news. Because of the money. An editor is quoted saying she hasn't been this excited about a novel since the publication of *Cold Mountain*.

I shake my head. Unbelievable.

Sometimes that's all you *can* do—shake your head and laugh.

The laughter feels good.

I'm working my way through the e-mails when I hear a noise from our bedroom down the hall. I feel the chill of the floor on my bare feet. I go to the wailing cries to try and quiet it, to soothe our child.

With the baby secure in my arms, I leave our bedroom, trying to give Jen some peace. Outside the rain is turning to snow. The wind is picking up.

Not long ago, I strolled these empty halls alone. An incomplete man in an incomplete home. But not now. Not anymore.

True love waits in haunted attics.

And so many other places. So many other places.

I go to my office and sit in the armchair and rock back and forth.

In the corner near my office is a pack-and-play and the diaper bag next to it and a blanket on the floor. I look at the struggling face, searching for something, striving to find sleep. The pediatrician asked a question at the hospital: what do babies dream about? Because we dream about our own experiences, but when you don't have any experiences yet to conjure up, where does the mind go?

The mind is a delicate, deep, and ultimately unexplainable thing. That's what I know.

There is a dim light on, enough to let me see the big desk. The slight cry combats the noise outside. I rock and shush and look at the clearest and most obvious sign that there is a God. This little face, so soft and precious and helpless, confirms what I was beginning to believe. That there is a God. There is nothing or nobody else that could create a being, a life, a gift, like the one I'm holding in my arms.

My little baby girl.

I look across at a large desk full of projects. Full of a life. A life that suddenly doesn't seem that important, about a path that suddenly doesn't seem that destined.

But there are glimmers of hope on this desk. I know that this desk holds glimmers of faith on it.

The confidence of a writer branching out and trying something different. And believing—trusting—in her agent.

The determination of a young novelist who won't give up, who won't be dissuaded, who won't back down.

The audacity of a stubborn fool to dream and dream huge, to know deep down he's got something that can be a masterpiece.

These are all examples of faith. Faith. The substance of things unseen.

But there is a deeper kind of a faith. There is believing in a love even though you don't see it or hear it. There is accepting that miracles can happen, that you can lose the love of your life and find her again. That's deeper faith.

And then there is the kind that you can't describe, the kind you can't make sense of.

The kind that says there has to be something more in this life, something bigger and better than just us humans. A faith that says there has to be a God, because nobody else could create a being as precious as a baby, could manufacture the miracle of life and birth.

I can't make sense of this love, this hope, this faith, this sacrifice. God is a father as I am a father, and I see more now but I can't imagine giving up my child, loving someone so much and then letting them go. This is the faith and the love that I don't understand, no matter how much I talk with Jen or Pearce or others who share this same hope and faith.

I know now there is a God above, and that he controls everything, from the little hairs on my baby's head that I stroke my chin against to the giant conglomerates that run the publishing industry. Everything is under his control.

I believe this because of the woman in our bed, in our house, who took me back and who gave us another shot. A woman who changed because of her faith and beliefs. Ones I'm still trying to get used to, still trying to understand.

There are some things in life that can't be fully understood, that can't be fully explained. Jen is one of those things. Our love. Our hope. I can't explain it.

But in my arms I hold my child. She is precious and she is a miracle. She is everything I hoped for and she is more. She is fragile and she is freeing and she embodies every single living and breathing thing I know about faith. She gives me the will to try and to change and ultimately to believe in this God who sacrificed his own child.

The publishing world won't change, but I will. I want to find the next Ian Pollock, the next Vivian Brown, and share these hopes with them. And I may or may not be so fortunate, I don't know. I don't need to know. All I know is that I'm a husband and a father, and these are the things that matter now, the things that drive me. And I'm hoping, trusting that I'll understand more about my place. But for now it's here, holding her, gazing into the sweet precious face of our daughter.

Grace.

AUTHOR NOTE

When you carry a story like this around in your pocket for so many years, it's tempting to want to gush and thank the whole world in the acknowledgments. But let's face it. No amount of words can express the appreciation I have for those in my life who put up with an artsy, angst-filled, idealistic, and moody author. So many people motivate and inspire me in so many ways. Here are some of the people who I'm very lucky to have in my life:

Sharon—you've heard so much about this story for so long, and you've lived a little of it too. I love you and love seeing what a great mother you are to Kylie.

Mom and Dad—thanks for being fans and sounding boards.

Claudia Cross, my agent, who helped shape and hone this story about her profession.

Andy McGuire, who acquired this book and continues to believe in my writing. You're my ambassador of quan.

LB Norton, who once again took another unique journey with me, and made it so much better.

Carole Johnson, who invited me into the circus; Ron Beers, who taught me how to trapeze; and Carla Mayer, who helps me deal with the clowns.

Linda Gooch, my favorite Texan.

Keri Tryba, my favorite Italian (and diva!).

To all my publishing colleagues who have shared much of Colin's angst at some point in their career—thank you for making my job so much fun.

To all the authors I've known and befriended over the years—thank you for encouraging me and helping me see the variety of artists working out there.

When I was a teenager living on top of a mountain in North Carolina, I never knew that publishing would become such a huge part of my life. It's an industry that sometimes frustrates and boggles the mind. But I still love it and always will.

Until next time.

Travis

March 2007